Advance Praise for

Beneath a Southern Sky

"Forget the movie of the week. *Beneath a Southern Sky* reads like a dramatic film, but has substance of eternal importance. Six months after reading it, I'm still digesting what it means to me. Everyone will be talking about this book!"

—LISA TAWN BERGREN
best-selling author of the Full Circle series and *Midnight Sun*

"There aren't many novels that keep me awake reading into the wee hours of the night, but *Beneath a Southern Sky* did. Nathan, Daria, and Cole slipped from the pages of this book and into my heart. I experienced all their heart-wrenching emotions, agonized over every decision they had to make, and rejoiced as they triumphed by God's grace in the midst of an impossible, hopeless situation. Bravo, Ms. Raney!"

—ROBIN LEE HATCHER
best-selling author of *The Forgiving Hour* and *Whispers from Yesterday*

"*Beneath a Southern Sky* has magnetic qualities! I just couldn't seem to put it down! In her normal, five-tissue fashion, Deborah Raney has created an impossible situation for her heroine, Daria Camfield. As I read, I thought I imagined all the ways Raney could tie her book into a neat little bow. Not so! The poignant ending of this thought-provoking novel took me unaware and lingered in my mind for days afterwards. You *definitely* won't be disappointed."

—LISA E. SAMSON
best-selling author of *The Church Ladies*

BENEATH A
Southern Sky

A NOVEL

DEBORAH RANEY

WATERBROOK
PRESS

BENEATH A SOUTHERN SKY
PUBLISHED BY WATERBROOK PRESS
12265 Oracle Boulevard, Suite 200
Colorado Springs, Colorado 80921

Scripture quotations are taken from the Holy Bible, New Living Translation, copyright
© 1996. Used by permission of Tyndale House Publishers Inc., Wheaton, Illinois 60189.
All rights reserved. Scripture also taken from the King James Version.

The characters and events in this book are fictional, and any resemblance to actual persons
or events is coincidental.

ISBN 978-0-307-45876-6
ISBN 978-0-307-45938-1 (electronic)

Published in the United States by WaterBrook Multnomah, an imprint of the Crown
Publishing Group, a division of Random House Inc., New York.

WATERBROOK and its deer colophon are registered trademarks of Random House Inc.

Library of Congress Cataloging-in-Publication Data
Raney, Deborah.
    Beneath a southern sky / Deborah Raney.—1st ed.
        p. cm.
1. Remarriage—Fiction. 2. Absence and presumption of death—Fiction. I. Title.
    PS3568.A562 B4 2001
    813'.54—dc21

Printed in the United States of America
2010

10 9 8 7 6 5 4 3 2

For my mother,
Winifred Ann Teeter,
who taught me to love books and
who, by her example, taught me—teaches me still—
how to be a Christian wife and mother.

and

For my mother-in-law,
Shirley Ann Raney,
whose love and friendship I cherish
and who raised the wonderful son who became my husband.

I love you both with all my heart.

chill spring rain washed the Kansas Turnpike, and the angry grey skies overhead offered no hope for an end to the downpour. It seemed to Daria that hers was the only car on this lonely stretch of highway. The deserted road seemed a fitting metaphor for what her life had become. She passed the Emporia exit and shifted in her seat, settling in for the long haul. She'd been on the road for well over an hour, and her destination was still more than two hours away. Was two hours long enough to decide what she would do when she got there? Was a lifetime long enough?

She took her hands off the wheel and rubbed away the beginnings of a headache. As she turned her head from side to side, trying to ease the taut muscles in her neck, her eyes fell on the yellow piece of paper that lay on the passenger seat beside her. In this world of fax machines and e-mail, she hadn't realized that people still sent telegrams. And yet it seemed appropriate somehow. She couldn't imagine news such as this 8 $1/2$-by-11-inch sheet of paper held coming any other way. Daria turned her eyes back to the road. She didn't need to read the telegram again. She had it memorized. But committing the tersely worded message to memory didn't answer the heartrending question it begged.

Barely forty-eight hours ago she had thought she was the happiest woman alive. But nineteen words on one thin yellow sheet of paper had changed everything, and now the reality of her dilemma nearly took her breath away. How did a woman choose between two men she had always loved with all her heart?

The relentless drumming of the rain on her windshield and the incessant rhythm of the wipers carried her back to another time, to another rain, and bid her to walk the paths of memory one more time. And like the silver ribbon of highway that curled ahead, the past three years of Daria's life spooled out before her.

Columba: The Dove

*T*he fingers of the jungle breeze swept across the village, playing the palm fronds like so many harps. Under the conductorship of the wind, the symphony of the rain forest rose to a crescendo. Over the *plip, plip, plip* of the raindrops' chorus, thunder struck its clashing cymbals before the clouds moved in, lowering a curtain on the sun.

Daria Camfield looked up from the skirt she was mending, and her eyes scanned the village for her husband's tall frame. Though the rains weren't usually severe this time of year, she always breathed easier when Nathan was nearby.

As though her thoughts had summoned him, she spotted Nate loping down the pathway, holding a large banana leaf over his head. She knew his makeshift umbrella was not meant to protect him as much as to shield the book he was carrying close to his chest.

"Hey," she hollered in greeting as he jumped the narrow stream that separated their hut from the village proper. The wind had begun to blow the rain underneath the thatched roof of the stoop where she sat, so she wove her needle safely into the thin cotton fabric of the skirt and rose to greet him.

Nathan leapt gracefully onto the stoop of their stilted hut, flashing Daria a wide smile. "Hey, babe. What are you up to?"

"Oh, I'm trying to fix this stupid skirt I tore yesterday," she huffed. "What I wouldn't give for a sewing machine."

He gave her a long-suffering look. Nate had never been sympathetic to her complaints about the lack of modern amenities in this remote South American village. She let it go and tilted her head to receive the kiss he offered.

He tossed the soggy banana leaf over the side of the stoop and took his precious book inside the hut. Daria followed him in, leaving the door open behind them.

"I'm hungry," he said, glancing around the small room as though food might materialize at his declaration.

She threw him a smirk. "What else is new?"

"Hey, I'm a growing boy!" he said with mock indignation.

She reached up and tousled his damp hair affectionately as if he were a little boy, but when he reached for her, it was a man who took her in his arms.

"I love you, Dr. Camfield," she whispered huskily. They had been married for three blissful years when they arrived in Timoné, but during their two years as missionaries here, she and Nathan had found new meaning to a scripture they'd only thought they understood: *And the two shall become one.* What had grown between them made their earlier romance seem like an adolescent crush. Nathan Camfield was her life, and she loved him with a love so fierce it sometimes frightened her.

Extricating herself from his arms, she went to the narrow shelf that served as their pantry. She sliced a banana in half, then reached for the thermos. Without electricity or an indoor stove, she'd gotten in the habit of making extra coffee over the fire each morning so they could share a hot drink during the afternoon rains. She poured a mug for Nate and one for herself, then took them to the table where Nate had opened his book. It seemed her husband always had his nose in one science text or another. She wondered what he'd do when he'd finished reading everything they'd brought with them.

The rain on this day proved unrelenting, reminding her of the rainy season they'd recently endured. She finally took up her mending again and they sat together, listening to the drops on the roof, enjoying this excuse for a rare respite from the hard work that life in Timoné demanded.

She put her needle and thread aside and watched her husband

now. His head was bowed over the book, and his forehead was furrowed in concentration. But any minute, she knew, he would look up with the light of discovery in his eyes, and read a passage aloud to her.

As though he'd read her mind, his voice broke into her thoughts. "Listen to this, Daria."

She started laughing.

"What?"

"You are just so predictable, Dr. Camfield," she chuckled.

He rolled his eyes, then, ignoring her laughter, he began to read to her from his book, his voice deep and authoritative. He hadn't finished one paragraph when a shout rose from below their hut. "Dr. Nate! Dr. Nate!"

Nathan and Daria jumped from their chairs and ran out onto the stoop. Quimico, one of the young men from the village, was hurrying toward them. Next to him was a native man Daria had never seen before.

Nate ran out into the rain to speak with the two men. Daria stood watching from the shelter of the doorway. The stranger gestured widely and spoke in a dialect that Daria didn't understand. The man waited then, while Quimico translated. She could make out a few of his words through the rain, and when Nate replied through Quimico, her heart began to pound. It sounded as though Nate was agreeing to go to another village with the man. Since their arrival, news had traveled that Timoné had a "medicine doctor," and Nate had been summoned to outlying villages on several occasions. Daria hated it when he left, abandoning the safe sanctuary of Timoné and her.

The men finished their conversation, and while Quimico and the stranger headed back into the village, Nathan came to the hut, his head bowed against the rain.

"What was that all about?"

He refused to look her in the eye and instead went to his side of their sleeping mat, lifted a corner and pulled an empty knapsack from underneath it.

"Nathan, what's going on?"

He answered with his back to her, stuffing provisions into the bag as he knelt on the floor. "There's an outbreak of fev—of illness in a village upriver."

He had stopped himself midsyllable, and Daria knew exactly why.

"Is it dengue, Nate?" she asked, her voice tight.

"I'm not sure," he hedged. "I couldn't get much of what he said, but whatever it is it's devastated the village. They've lost twenty lives already—mostly children."

Anger rose in her. She knew his words were calculated for her sake, that she'd feel guilty if she selfishly asked him to remain when little children were dying upriver.

"Nathan, where is this village?"

"Upstream a ways," he said, still busily arranging items in his knapsack.

"How far?"

"It's a distance, Daria. Quimico thinks it's a couple of days up the Guaviare."

"Two days! Nathan, it takes one whole day just to *get* to the river!"

"You're exaggerating."

"You'll be gone a week."

"I might be, Daria." He yanked on a zipper and began adjusting the straps.

His steady, measured answers made her furious.

"When are you leaving?"

"First thing in the morning."

She started pacing the short distance of the room, desperate to come up with the words that would keep him home. "Nathan, what if it is dengue?"

Still kneeling on the floor, he turned to look up at her. "I honestly don't think it's dengue, Daria. It sounds more like some sort of influenza."

"But you don't know that."

"No, I don't."

"Nathan, you almost died the first time." She was pleading with him now, her hand on his shoulder, forcing him to look at her. "You're a doctor. You know dengue is worse if you get it again."

"It can be, Daria. But I don't think this is dengue." He looked down, ostensibly to check his watch.

"How could you possibly know?" she growled. "You're just telling me that because you've already made up your mind to go."

He stood now and put his hands on her shoulders. "Daria, stop it. You know I have to go. It's why we came here. You know that, Daria. God did not bring us this far to refuse help to those who need it."

She bit her tongue to keep from asking him what this "we" business was, and yet felt as guilty as if she'd let the words fly.

"Don't worry, babe." He softened a bit. "I'll be fine."

"Then let me go with you," she begged.

"Absolutely not. You'd just slow us down…and what would you do when you got there?"

"I could help, Nate. I could—"

"No. You're staying here."

She reached out and gripped his arm. "Nate, please…just listen to me."

"There's nothing to discuss, Daria." He set his lips in a tight line.

Why was he being so pigheaded? Couldn't he see that she was just worried about him? She hated him just a little at that moment. But she knew her husband well enough to know that nothing she could say now would change his mind, so she stood there watching him, silent.

The rains had stopped. Nate put the knapsack beside the door and stepped onto the stoop. "I'm going to go help get the boat ready."

Trembling inside, she followed him.

Nathan descended the steps, but when he got to the bottom he turned to look back up at her. "If it makes you feel any better, I'm going to ask Quimico and Tados to go with me."

She turned on her heel and slammed the door.

When Nathan returned to the hut that evening they ate together in chilled silence, the only sound that of spoons *thunking* against pottery bowls.

Daria refused to make eye contact.

"Is there any more of that great salsa you made?" Nate asked.

Daria rose and retrieved a Mason jar from the shelf, setting it in front of him a bit too forcefully.

"Thanks." Nate cleared his throat.

When they finished, he motioned to her with his finger. "Come here."

Daria put her hands on her hips, studying him.

"Hey, come here," he repeated, his voice coaxing and gentle.

She hated when he did that, because she knew he would melt her defenses. But she walked over to him, and he pulled her onto his lap.

"You know that I love you," he said, tracing her cheek with a slender finger.

The tears came then, and he held her close, stroking her hair.

Finally he told her, "Daria, I'm sorry. I know you don't want me to go, but I think you understand why I must."

She nodded, resigned, now desperate to make things right between them before he left.

He put a hand on her cheek. "We need to talk before I leave, okay?"

She sniffed and nodded.

"You heard me speaking to Bob earlier?"

She nodded again. Bob Warrington was their radio contact at the mission in Bogotá.

"He's going to check in with you almost every day while I'm gone. But you know he can't always get through, so don't worry if a couple of days go by and you don't hear from him. And don't be afraid to try to contact him. I told him where I'm going, and he felt things were stable enough that it would be safe."

Nate didn't say the words, but Daria knew he was referring to the drug runners and the paramilitary who often posed a threat to outsiders. She tried not to think about it.

"I could be gone awhile," he said gently. "It'll probably take us three days or so to get there, and I have no idea what we'll be facing when we arrive. I promise I won't stay a minute longer than I need to. It'll seem like a long time. I just don't want you to panic if it takes longer than you expect."

She nodded.

"If anything happens and you need to…to get out…of Timoné, you go to Anazu. His nephews know the river well, and they can get you to the airstrip in San José. But you be sure Bob knows you're coming so he can meet you. I don't want you there alone."

She nodded solemnly, hating to have to listen. Why was he talking this way? Fear crept up her spine.

He tipped her chin, forcing her to look at him. "You okay?"

"I'll be okay, Nate. I'm sorry I acted like such a baby. I know that just makes it harder for you."

"Hey, I can understand how you feel. I *am* a pretty fun guy to have around."

She giggled in spite of herself, loving the way he could always make her laugh. But he turned serious and drew her into the tight circle of his arms. "I'll miss you like crazy, babe. Every single minute."

"Oh, Nate, I'll miss you so much."

As soon as it was dark, Daria dressed for bed and plopped down on their mat. Nathan sat on the bench at the table, reading, his white-blond hair catching glints of lantern light. Watching him, a heavy melancholy draped itself over her. Sleep eluded her, and she tossed and turned fitfully, wishing Nathan would come to bed.

He read until late, then he blew out the lantern and came to her side. Lifting the mosquito net, he crawled underneath, kneeling beside her. "Hey," he whispered, "are you still awake?"

"I'm awake."

He took her by the hand, lifted the net, and pulled her up beside him.

"Come on," he whispered, leading her outside.

"Nate! I'm not even dressed," she protested, stretching the over-size T-shirt she slept in over her knees, and trying not to lose the flip-flop sandals she'd slipped on just outside their door.

He pulled her down the steps and toward the crude path that ran parallel to the river behind their hut. The moon was full so they didn't have need of a light, though Nate lit a small torch and carried it in front of them to ward off the jungle's wild nocturnal creatures.

"Shh! Come on!" He had that gleam in his eye—the one he always got when he'd planned something special just for her.

She followed him in silence up a rise to a small clearing. The jungle's wild denizens made it dangerous to venture too far from the village at this time of night, and yet she felt perfectly safe with Nathan at her side.

When they came to the center of the clearing, he planted the torch in the soft earth. He came to stand behind Daria and wrapped his arms around her, cradling her head on his shoulder. He cupped her chin in one strong, rough hand and tilted it toward the heavens.

The sight above her left her breathless. "Oh, Nate! It's so beautiful."

In the village, their view of the sky was filtered through a mesh-work of vines and palm leaves, but here the vista was unobstructed. The sky above them was a flawless canopy of navy-colored velvet sewn with a million glittering sequins. Daria felt as though she floated in a realm that was both sea and sky, fathomless and eternal.

But she wasn't frightened because Nathan was her anchor. They stood together in silent awe, matching the rhythm of their breaths each to the other. Nate had been studying the constellations of the Southern Hemisphere, and he began to point them out to her. His voice was soft in her ear, the bristle of his day-old beard sweetly familiar against her cheek.

"Look there, Dar," he whispered hoarsely, pointing, his arm brushing her cheek as he sighted a star pattern for her. "That's Virgo." He tipped her chin slightly to the left. "And see that star right there…the brightest one? That's Spica."

She nodded, standing on tiptoe to nuzzle her cheek against his. The star seemed to wink at her, as though it were in on Nate's little surprise.

"When you look at the sky every night I'm gone, find that star," he told her. "I'll be looking at it and thinking how much I love you."

Her throat was too full to reply. She wanted only to stand there forever, safe in his arms.

Morning came too quickly, and Nathan Camfield rolled out of bed with far more trepidation about the journey ahead than he had allowed his wife to see. He was hesitant to leave her here alone. He had asked Anazu and his wife, Paita, the only Christian converts in the village, to keep an eye on Daria. He knew they would take the charge seriously. The Timoné were a peaceable people, and he and Daria had always felt safe within the village. But still he worried.

He worried for himself as well. He wasn't sure what he would find when he arrived in the village to which he'd been called. *Chicoro*, the runner who'd come for him had called it. He only hoped the man had been right in judging the distance. For Daria's sake, Nate desperately wanted to return as quickly as possible. She seemed so fearful.

Daria was already outside making coffee over the fire when Nate came down the steps of their hut.

"Good morning," she said, as if it were any other day.

"Mornin', babe."

"I fixed some fruit." She held up a bowl of sliced bananas, guava fruit, pitaya, and a variety of the succulent berries that grew wild all over the rain forest.

He started to tell her he'd just have coffee, but then saw the pleading look in her eye. "Sure," he said, trying to force a cheerfulness he didn't feel into his voice.

They sat companionably on the stoop as they did every morning, swinging their legs over the side, sipping hot coffee from their treasured University of Kansas mugs. Nate ate Daria's fruit salad with his fingers, touched by her offering.

He turned to say something to her and saw that there were tears streaming down her face.

"Hey, hey," he whispered. "It's only a few days."

She tried to smile but failed miserably, her face crumpling as she wept.

He jumped down off the stoop and stood in front of her. Taking her chin in his hands, he planted kisses on her tear-stained cheeks, memorizing the feel of her lips on his.

Then he wrapped his arms protectively around her. "Father," he prayed, "Please be with this woman I love. Keep her safe while I'm gone and help the time to pass quickly for both of us. Father, give me wisdom to know how to help the people you've sent me to minister to—both in body and in spirit."

Through tears, but with a voice that seemed stronger, Daria prayed for him too, in her simple, straightforward way. "God, go with Nate. Keep him safe. Guide him in everything he does. And, Lord, please bring him back to me because—well, I've grown kind of fond of him and I think I'd like to keep him for a while."

Nate laughed and held her at arm's length, appreciating the way her dimpled smile reached her blue eyes. A strand of wavy blond hair had escaped her braid and, returning her smile, he brushed it from her high forehead. He was so proud of her for giving him this gift of laughter before he went. "Amen," he said, his heart full.

Together they washed the few breakfast dishes and then he went into the hut for his things.

They walked arm in arm through the village, and beyond to the place where the worn forest trail led to the navigable waters of the Rio Guaviare. Quimico and Tados and their families were already waiting when they got there, chattering excitedly among themselves. Nate loaded his things into the boat, and the two young natives lofted the craft onto their shoulders.

Nate pulled Daria into his arms and kissed her one last time. "Goodbye, sweetheart," he whispered, aware that the natives were watching and shaking their heads at this bold American display of affection. He released her and went to take his share of the boat's burden.

They started up the trail. The boat on his shoulders prevented him from turning and keeping Daria in his sight. But he didn't have to see her to know that her beautiful face was wet with tears and that her tender heart was praying for his safe return even now.

Two

The thin trail of smoke slithered toward the clouds like a cobra charmed by the music of the coming rain. Though it was hard to tell how distant the fire was, it worried Daria. It seemed more than a bonfire. And hours too early for that besides.

If there was trouble in another nearby village, they would come looking for Nate. He wouldn't be back for several days, and she would rather the neighboring villages not know that she was alone.

She turned back to the flatbread she was making, slapping the coarse dough hard with the heel of her hand, forming a thin disk that would fry crisp in a pan of grease over the coals. It was too late for lunch and too early for supper, but at least keeping busy helped soothe her worries. With Nate gone, she had kept an erratic schedule, eating and sleeping whenever the mood struck her. She hadn't realized how much stability his presence brought, even to the mundane things of life.

She looked again toward the grey wisp of smoke and noted that it was in the general direction of the village to which Nate had traveled. Perhaps he could see it from where he was and would go to help if it signaled trouble.

She missed him. Oh, how she missed him. The jungle was treacherous and unpredictable, but when Nathan was with her, it was truly a paradise. Once she had grown accustomed to the spiders, snakes, and amphibious creatures that teemed in their corner of Colombia, she had seldom felt afraid. The soft plunk of afternoon raindrops on massive palm leaves and the calls of the wild creatures that inhabited the rain forest had become sounds of security. They were as much the sounds of home for her now as the lowing cattle, distant train whistles, and song of the meadowlark had been on the Kansas prairie where she grew up.

Now, with Nathan away, Daria felt as though a part of her was missing. He had made trips without her before—to hunt with the Timoné men and, recently, to treat the ill in outlying villages. Usually he was gone overnight, two days at most. This time was different, and she wasn't prepared for the dull ache of loneliness that came over her on this fifth night of his absence.

She placed the circle of dough on a clean stone and brushed the coarse cornmeal from her hands. She climbed to the stoop and ducked inside the doorway to their hut. She took a frying pan from its hook on the wall and a can of grease from the narrow shelf over the window.

Though she had been a farm girl, she had never been a camper, and cooking over an open fire had been a hard-earned skill. She smiled to herself, thinking of the many meals of blackened bread and scorched meat they had endured while she learned, at Nate's insistence, to cook as the Timoné did. The small hut she and Nate had inherited from the missionary who had served before them was set apart from the rest of the village, but she knew the villagers had not missed the pitifully thick smoke that had rolled from her cast-iron skillet during those first weeks. Nor had they missed the reason for Nate's casual forays into the village proper just as their fires were emitting the enticing perfume of golden brown flatbread and tender roasted meat and vegetables. She knew she had been laughed at much in those early days, but she didn't care. They were a kind people and didn't intend to hurt her feelings. Besides, she knew how to laugh at herself—and she could lie in Nate's arms at night and delight in that sweetest bliss of shared laughter.

"That was an interesting recipe you made tonight," he'd told her one night after she'd ruined supper two evenings in a row. His tone was serious, but his smile blazed in the darkness. A long pause while she waited for his punch line. "Really, Daria," he said finally, "you should write a cookbook—except I hear blackened food is already passé back in the States."

She put an elbow hard to his ribs. "If you'd just let me have a stove you'd be surprised what a good cook I might be! Just think of the juicy pies and cookies and chocolate cakes and—"

Then he locked her in his arms and playfully rolled her over, his sweet tooth aching, she knew, at her torturous litany of his weaknesses. "Not fair!" he cried.

He deftly changed the subject with the kisses that were *her* weakness, wrestling her gently on the soft grass mat that was their bed. They shared their love in whispers and muffled giggles so their voices wouldn't be heard across the stream in the village.

She never had managed to wear him down about the stove—not even after one of the villagers acquired a propane cooker. Nate had come to be part of the Timoné culture, and to him buying a stove was like giving in to his spoiled American upbringing.

She shook off the poignant memory. Brushing a strand of sun-bleached hair from her face, she scooped grease into the skillet and carried it outside. The flames had died down, and the coals were just right for baking. Soon the corn bread sizzled, spattering drops of grease into the fire and filling the air with its fragrance. After a minute, she flipped the circle of dough expertly and put the pan back on the fire.

While the bread finished frying, she stretched her arms lazily over her head and panned her gaze to the darkening afternoon sky. In the hills to the north, the trail of smoke had grown darker, a swirling column now that was a deeper grey than the rain-heavy sky. It made her think of the funnel clouds that often ravaged the flatlands of Kansas. A chill went up her spine, and she wondered briefly if she should try to radio Bogotá and report the fire.

The wind came up as it did almost every afternoon, carrying swollen clouds, swaying the branches and palm fronds overhead, making a commotion as familiar as her own breath. As the first raindrops penetrated the forest umbrella, Daria took the skillet from the fire and hurriedly climbed to the doorway of the hut. She went in to sit at the crude bench near the window, her eyes avoiding the empty mat in the corner where she would sleep alone again tonight.

～～

Ten days had passed with no sign of Nathan or Quimico and Tados. For the first time in her life, Daria tasted terror.

Yesterday, after two days of silence, Bob Warrington, their contact in Bogotá, had gotten through to her on the radio. Daria attempted to sound unconcerned when she told Bob that Nathan had not yet returned. Now she regretted it.

She walked to the commons in the center of the village, her prayers for Nate's safety interrupted by thoughts of what she would do if he still wasn't back tomorrow—or the next day, or the next. She said a quick *amen* as she spotted the children gathering in the large, thatch-roofed shelter, which served as the village gathering place.

Little Jirelle came running to greet her, the light in her eyes twinkling from behind a curtain of shiny, jet-black bangs. "*Hollio,* Teacher!" she cried.

"*Hollio,* Jirelle. *Ceju na.* Come here." For her own sake as well as the children's, she deliberately repeated her Timoné words in English.

Jirelle shyly took Daria's hand and walked with her the rest of the way to the commons. Daria smiled, remembering how she had struggled with what her role as a missionary should be when they first arrived. Nate could offer his gift of healing—he had known since childhood that he wanted to be a doctor. She, however, had left college after her sophomore year, still not having declared a major.

She had found the first hint of her gift in her job as a teacher's aide when Nate was still in medical school. But what could she teach these Timoné children? She and Nate recognized something precious in the primitive simplicity of these people's lives. The Timoné had no need for the technologies that cluttered life. Nate was adamant that he and Daria had not come to Americanize or civilize the Timoné. They had come to offer healing—for the body and for the soul.

Finally unearthing the connection between her gift and their need, Daria had organized an informal Bible class. She had first begun meeting with the children outside the hut she and Nate shared, but her little group had soon grown so large that the village leaders suggested that she move to the commons. In spite of the language barrier, the twenty or so who were allowed to come for an hour each morning had learned much, and she had finally begun to feel that her presence here had meaning.

Daria let go of Jirelle's hand and went to greet the other children who were still straggling in from the crude pathways that wound through the village. Their high, nasal chattering filled the air.

"*Hollio,* Tommi. Hello, Gilberto. Gabrielle, is this for me?" She took a rather wilted hibiscus blossom the size of a dinner plate from a chubby little girl. "*Égracita,* Gabrielle. It is beautiful. *Mui béleu.*"

She greeted each child by name as they took their places along three rows of narrow benches that faced the west. The children quieted and she went to stand at the front of the shelter and opened the colorfully illustrated children's Bible. She walked up and down the rows, giving each child a chance to see the pictures of the brave and trusting young man named Daniel and the ferocious lions he faced.

"Who would like to play the lions?" she asked, pointing to the pictures in the book.

Ten grubby little-boy hands went into the air, and they all began auditioning for the role by baring their teeth and "claws" and yowling loudly. Their howling made them sound more like Colombian jaguars, and Daria earned their hysterical laughter when she demonstrated a deep roar. But they soon became fluent in "lionese" and went to stand in one corner of the shelter that she had designated to be the lions' den. She chose Gilberto to play Daniel. He was a bit of a ham and easier to manage when he had a starring role.

The impromptu production went splendidly, and Daria was grateful to have her mind taken off of Nathan for a while. But as she bade the children farewell and walked back to their hut, her thoughts turned again to her husband.

"Please, Father. Be with him, wherever he is. Bring him back safely," she whispered.

How long did Nate have to be missing before Bob Warrington would instigate a search? What if she couldn't get through on the radio? What if she needed to leave and Anazu refused to help her? She blocked the roiling questions from her mind and prayed that by tomorrow her worries would be needless because Nate would be home safe in her arms.

"Daria, I just want you to know that I'm doing everything possible to get a search party organized—in case we need it. We're not overly concerned yet. We knew it would take some time. But it has been a bit longer than we expected." She knew he meant to reassure her, but even though his words were chopped up on the airwaves, Bob Warrington's trepidation transmitted loud and clear.

Nate had been gone almost two weeks. It had been more than forty-eight hours since her last contact with Bogotá. Her panic had grown hourly as she stayed inside the hut, trying desperately to get through on the radio. She had wept with relief to hear the radio spring to life minutes ago.

"Bob, have you reported Nate missing yet? To our families, I mean?" She had to repeat the question twice over constant static before he got it.

"No, we haven't. Frankly, I was hoping you'd have good news when I got through this morning. Do you want me to let your families know what's going on?"

She hesitated. "No, not yet," she finally told him, shouting into the receiver. "Unless you think we should." Their parents had all been against their going. She couldn't bear to think of them worrying and wondering from afar when there was nothing they could do.

She waited for his reply, knowing that if he believed it was time to inform their families, he was more worried than he let on. But when he agreed with Daria that it would be premature to alert their families in the States just yet, she sighed in relief. "It's possible that everything is fine and that the trip is just taking longer than Nate anticipated," he told her. "But I do think it's time to start looking for him."

She knew his unspoken fear: Paramilitary units were thick in the coca growing regions on the Rio Guaviare. They were notorious for killing suspicious parties and asking questions later.

"We'll keep in close touch, Daria. We're all praying for you. I'm sure Nate is fine," Bob reassured her unconvincingly before signing off.

Knowing that it would be days before anyone could get to the village from Bogotá, Daria sought out Anazu in the village.

She found him crouching near the river's edge, cleaning a mess of fish. Kneeling beside him, she spoke in her halting Timoné. "Anazu, *kopaku*…please. It is time to search for Dr. Nate," she begged, trying desperately to strike the right balance of authority and deference in her voice. "Would you send Motsu and Javier to bring him back? *Kopaku?* Your nephews know the way on the river," she coaxed.

He looked up from his task, his dark eyes thoughtful and kind. "Dr. Nate is with men who know the jungle well. They will bring him home when the time is ripe."

His calm manner and kindness reassured her somewhat. "Yes," she told herself. "Quimico and Tados will bring him home." Yet her heart doubted. Even the families of the young men had begun to complain that Dr. Nate had not yet returned their sons and brothers to them as he'd promised.

She decided not to push Anazu on the matter and instead thanked him for considering her request. He nodded and flashed her a familiar smile, his white, even teeth almost glowing against the contrast of burnished copper skin. Deeply disheartened, she returned to the hut.

When the sun came up on the following day, Daria rose and went to stand at the small window over their bed.

"Please, Lord," she prayed. "Soften Anazu's heart. I need his help. Help me to know what to say to him, Father. Give me the words that will convince him that it's time to look for Nate. Give me strength."

She was just getting ready to walk to the commons for morning lessons when Bob Warrington's voice crackled over the radio. Her heart pounding, she jumped up and ran to the crude table where the radio sat.

"Daria?" Bob's voice broke up in an eruption of static, and Daria strained to hear his message. "I've spoken with Gospel Outreach, and they think it's time to send in a search party. They want you to try to get to San José del Guaviare. They'll fly over the area from there, but they want you with them if at all possible."

"I really don't know how much help I'd be, Bob," she said, her voice trembling. It terrified her to think of leaving Timoné without Nate. "I...I know the village, Chicoro, is on the river," she told Bob, "but even Nate wasn't sure how far upstream it was." Though she knew Nate had given Bob the information before he'd set out, she repeated all she could remember of what the runner from Chicoro had told them when he came for Nate.

"I still think you need to be in that plane," Bob insisted. "Is there someone there you trust to get you to San José?"

She told him of Anazu's refusal to go after Nate. "He might be more willing to take me to San José, familiar territory, but"—her voice rose an octave and grew thick with panic—"what if Nate comes back while I'm gone, Bob?"

"Leave a message for him, Daria. If that happens, he can radio me, and we'll get you back to Timoné." He spoke with measured words, as though he were speaking to a child. She willed confidence into her tone as they arranged for her to meet a contact at the airstrip in San José del Guaviare, two days down the river. Reluctantly she signed off and went to find Anazu again, her mind reeling.

Even before God, she didn't dare put into words what her leaving Timoné would mean, that something was terribly wrong, that Nathan was sick or wounded, or worse…in the Colombian jungle. But now that the plans were in motion, she was relieved. At least she was doing something. She couldn't continue to wait indefinitely, doing nothing at all. Perhaps she had already waited too long. Yet even if she could convince Anazu or his nephews to take her to San José, she worried that there was nothing she could do when she got there.

She castigated herself for not learning the Timoné language more fluently. During the year before they arrived, she and Nate had studied the Castilian Spanish spoken in most of Colombia, but they were not prepared for how different the Indian dialect of the Timoné was. She had depended too much on Nathan to communicate in the primitive tongue that was a peculiar mix of Spanish and Portuguese with a smattering of Swahili—from the African slaves brought to Colombia centuries before, they'd been told. Nate was beginning to speak the language quite passably and was teaching English to Tados and Quimico, his young protégés. But Daria still struggled. She had taught the children a few English words. They were quick and eager students. But now she knew she should have concentrated more on learning Timoné from them.

As she walked through the village, searching again for Anazu, such aimless ramblings filled her thoughts, veiling the growing knowledge that something terrible had happened to her husband.

Later that morning, Daria went through the motions of her Bible lessons. She tried not to think that this might be her last time with these children, perhaps forever. But when she found a round mahogany face and two brown beads of eyes staring up at her after class, her throat tightened. The young boy clutched something behind his back.

"*Hollio,* Tommi." It was a shortened version of his given name, which was, for her, unpronounceable. She had bestowed the nickname on him, and it had stuck. Even his mother now sometimes called him "Tommi."

She knelt down in the soft dirt beside him. "What have you got there?"

The broad grin he gave her made narrow slits of his dark eyes. "I give," he said in English, holding out a greenish banana. He thrust the sweet-smelling fruit at her. "Teacher," he said simply.

She held the banana to her nose and sniffed it appreciatively. "Thank you, Tommi. Just the way I like them. Green." Always the teacher, she pointed to the green stem and repeated her comments in her broken Timoné.

"Green," Tommi repeated, still grinning. Then he ran off to join the other children for a splash in the cool stream. Watching them, Daria fought back tears. These children had become such a part of her life, giving her so much more than she could offer them. Their sweet kindnesses, simple trust. Their love.

That afternoon Anazu began to ready the small boat that his nephews would carry on their heads through the rain forest until they reached the first entry into the Rio Guaviare.

"Thank you, Lord," Daria whispered as she watched the strong, sun-burnished backs of Anazu's nephews, Motsu and Javier, loading provisions into the boat.

She walked back through the village and climbed the stairs to sit on the stoop. The afternoon rains had ceased, and now the sun coaxed vapors of steam from the damp forest floor. Daria sat there, listening to the children playing across the stream, and yet a panic began to wrap its paralyzing tendrils around her. A small, still-sane part of her brain told her that she must go to San José del Guaviare exactly as she'd been instructed. If the search didn't turn up something right away, she knew they would probably offer to fly her out of Colombia and back to the States. But she couldn't bear to think of leaving Nathan behind.

The visceral part of her brain told her to get up and run. Run down the tangled path where she had seen her husband's broad back disappear almost three weeks ago. Run and search every green, wet inch of the godforsaken forest that had taken him away from her. Search until she found him and brought him home—home to Timoné.

But she stayed on the stoop late into the afternoon, watching Anazu's preparations from a distance.

As she sat there again that night, the fires in the village dying, Daria thanked God that Anazu had agreed to her request. Then for the thousandth time, she whispered a prayer for Nate's safety. She gazed into the star-crested sky and thought back to that last night she and Nathan had spent together before he left on his journey.

And now, aching for him, searching the sky for "their" star, she was consumed with fear that she might never have a chance to tell him that a starry sky would forever remind her of how much she loved him—and how much she was loved by him.

Early the next morning as she packed her belongings, the breakfast fires in the village reminded her that she hadn't eaten anything since Tommi's banana the afternoon before. Anazu had kept her well supplied with roasted meat, but she'd had no appetite. She fought back the nausea that had dogged her for a week; lack of sleep and food, and the tremendous stress of Nathan's absence had taken their toll. Finally she finished packing and went to find something her stomach wouldn't reject.

As she pulled her skillet from its hook on the wall, a shout from the forest pierced the air. The pan fell from her hands and clattered to the floor as she ran outside.

Quimico and Tados came into the clearing, striding breathlessly toward the center of the village. Her heart leapt into her throat and she ran to meet them, straining to see Nate's tall, lean figure.

The two men motioned wildly to her, shouting words she could not understand.

The villagers came running from all directions and gathered around the men.

Quimico spoke the same urgent words over and over again. *Fogo-rio. Defuerto.* Daria heard the syllables clearly, but her mind wouldn't allow them to make sense to her. It was as though she had never heard the Timoné tongue before.

But while his words seemed alien to her ears, the heartsick expression on Quimico's face spoke a language she understood only too clearly.

Three

*W*here is Nate?" She looked past the two guides, her eyes wild. "Nate? Where is Nathan?" She ran toward Quimico and Tados, screaming his name over and over again until it came out as a hoarse croak. Yet somewhere deep inside herself she knew the answer to her panicked question.

Quimico held up a hand as she came to stand before him. The stocky, brown-skinned native placed his arms across his chest and shook his head solemnly—a gesture that was startlingly like Nathan Camfield. Turning to Anazu, who had pushed his way through the other villagers, Quimico spoke rapidly in a low voice.

She separated two words from the jumble that poured from Quimico's lips. *Fogorio.* Fire. *Defuerto.* Dead.

And Nate's name. *Dr. Nate. Medicine Doctor.*

"No!" Daria sank to her knees, her heart in her throat, her head throbbing. "Oh, dear God, *no!* Not Nathan! Please, God! No..." she moaned.

She felt an arm go around her and glanced up to see Anazu's wife, Paita. The woman knelt beside her and began cooing soft words in Daria's ear, rocking her gently back and forth.

Daria was numb. She couldn't understand the words Quimico and Tados were spewing now to the gathered crowd, but she knew the only thing that had meaning for her. Nathan was dead.

The strength went from her, and she would have slumped in a heap on the ground if Paita had not held her against her strong, thick body. Paita held Daria upright until the men finished talking, then she beckoned for her daughter. Casmé came quickly to Daria's side, and the two women helped her to her feet and ushered her across the stream to her hut.

They helped her lie down on the grass mat in the corner. Paita poured a mug half-full of strong coffee from the thermos, and Casmé held it to Daria's lips while she sipped.

As the horror of the truth sank its teeth into her, Daria allowed the women to wash her body, submitting willingly to the Timoné ritual for widows in mourning.

As they silently sponged the cool water over her neck and limbs, she felt removed from her body, as though she watched herself from someplace above. They combed Daria's long, heavy, blond hair and fastened it, as she always wore it, into a braid that hung down her back. When they were finished with their ministrations, mother and daughter arranged the mosquito netting around her and then sat beside her, watching her closely. Several times Daria attempted to speak, but she could not make herself remember the Timoné words for what she wanted to ask. Finally she slept.

The sounds of the afternoon rains awoke her, and the hut was dark from the overcast sky, but she could see the silhouettes of Paita and Casmé through the gauzy film of the mosquito net. She reached underneath the netting for Paita's hand, and suddenly the words were there.

"*Que aconté?* What happened?" she asked.

She strained to hear the words as Paita began to answer. It was so important that she understand.

"Dr. Nate—the Medicine Doctor—put all those who were sick together in one hut outside the far village," Paita told her, speaking slowly in her own tongue. She used her expressive hands to illustrate her words, repeating the important phrases again for Daria's sake, waiting to see that she understood before continuing. "The medicine he brought was not enough for the many people, so they continued to die. The chief's young son died, and the chief grew angry with Dr.

Nate. The chief feared the sickness would destroy all the village, so he sent men to the sick hut to set a fire and destroy the evil spirits that lived in the people. Nathan was inside the hut. Quimico and Tados were in the village, but they saw the fire. They knew Dr. Nate was inside. They ran to save him, but the flames were too high. They called to Dr. Nate, but they could hear only the screams of the burning people. No one lived. All burned. All. They took their boat and ran away. They ran to the north. Away from Timoné. They hid in the forest for many days until it was safe for them to come back."

Paita finished the story and once more pushed back the net and wiped a cool damp cloth over Daria's forehead. "You sleep now," she said. "I will be here when you wake, and I will tell you the story once more."

It seemed to Daria that she slept for a week. When she opened her eyes again, the sun was climbing in the eastern sky and Casmé was gone. But true to her word, Paita was there, and she recounted the story again. This time Daria could not succumb to the drug of sleep to deaden the pain of the truth.

She sat up on the mat and took the cup Paita offered. She sipped carefully and stood on wobbly legs, fighting the nausea that swept over her. Walking stiffly to the corner, she sat down at the table and tried to coax the radio to life. Miraculously her call was answered within minutes, and she sobbed the news to Bob Warrington.

"You get to San José del Guaviare, Daria." Bob's voice filled the room. "Bring everything you can with you. Tell Anazu you must leave tomorrow."

"He'd already agreed, Bob, before… His nephews will take me. I trust them."

"Good. Someone will be waiting for you there. Daria…I am so sorry."

Numb, she copied down his instructions, signed off, and went to the doorway of the hut. She looked across the stream and saw that life was back to normal for the villagers. Children laughed and splashed at the water's edge, and the women worked outside their huts, talking quietly together.

Stepping outside, Daria sat down on the stoop and waited in silence while Paita fixed her something to eat.

She spotted Tados coming down the forest path with a basket of fresh fish, and the truth washed over her as though for the first time.

My husband is dead.

No! It can't be true! How was it possible that Nathan could have been dead so many days without her sensing it in her spirit? Without God letting her know?

Boldly she cried out to Tados. "*Ceju na.* Come here." It was a command, one the young man was not accustomed to heeding when it came from a woman. He remained where he was.

"*Kopaku,*" she pled, making her voice appropriately submissive.

Tados waded across the shallow stream and walked slowly toward her, stopping at a distance.

"Tados—" She swallowed hard, trying to think of the words. She wasn't sure she wanted the answer to the question she was about to ask, and yet an ember of hope ignited in her as she entertained the possibility that Tados and Quimico were mistaken.

Tados waited patiently.

"Did…did you see Dr. Nate? *Defuerto?* Dead? Did you see his…his body?" She stumbled clumsily over the alien words.

He slid the basket to the ground by his feet but did not reply.

She repeated the question, enunciating carefully, not sure if she had phrased it properly.

A shadow of emotion clouded his eyes. He nodded and surprised her by answering in English. He motioned wildly with his arms. "Everybody burn. Everybody die… All the hut," he said emphatically. "A big fire. Very big." Again his arms painted a wide arc. "I run to help Dr. Nate. I see only many body. Quimico see also. Nobody come out."

She was aware of Paita standing in the doorway behind her, but she needed no interpreter this time. Daria understood his halting words perfectly.

Now Tados held up a hand. "You wait," he commanded. Leaving his basket on the ground, he crossed over the stream and strode toward his own hut. A few minutes later he returned, holding something out to her in his upturned palm. "You take."

She descended the steps and took the object from his hand. Her breath caught as she recognized Nathan's watch—the expensive gold watch his parents had given him upon his graduation from medical school. Nathan never removed it except to bathe. She turned it over in her hand. Its face was black with soot, and though she tried to clean the crystal, rubbing it hard with her thumb, the Roman numerals on the face had been obliterated.

She looked up at the young native, a question in her eyes.

"You take," he repeated.

She thanked him. With a single, silent nod, he turned, retrieved his basket, and crossed back to the other side of the stream.

She heard Paita go inside. Climbing the steps, she sank down on the stoop again, and sat there staring at Nathan's watch, numb. She knew she must get word to Nate's parents and hers. Perhaps Bob Warrington had already taken care of that. She hadn't thought to ask him. There was a place in San José del Guaviare where they could sometimes get through by telephone or perhaps send e-mail—if the paramilitary groups hadn't commandeered it.

She could not see herself remaining here without Nathan, but neither could she imagine going anywhere else. Her life in the States seemed like a story she had read long ago, one she remembered fondly but that had no bearing on reality for her. She pressed her fingers to her temples and tried to stop the flow of thoughts.

For now she wanted only one thing—to weep. Nate was dead, and she needed to mourn him.

Daria merely went through the motions the rest of the day. She felt removed from her surroundings, as though she hovered in a different dimension. She folded the few items of clothing Nathan had not taken with him to the far village. They were heavy with his scent, and she held them longingly to her face before placing them in one of their small duffel bags. She packed her own belongings next to his, and she allowed herself to remember Nathan Camfield.

She thought of his hands. Skilled hands, strong and able and roughened because he wasn't afraid to work alongside the men in the village when he was needed there. Yet his hands were gentle when he examined a sick child, and sublimely tender when he loved her, when he caressed her face, her body. She saw his lanky figure. Nathan had run cross-country in high school and college, and he had a runner's body, full of energy, like a wire spring, never static. And his wit. He delighted in good-natured teasing. He loved to make her laugh. In her mind she heard his laughter now—a musical, contagious, uninhibited crow. Just conjuring it in her memory made her laugh out loud.

The sound of her own laughter shocked her. Reality struck—a spasm in the pit of her stomach—and her voice caught in her throat, suspending her breath in that strangling place between laughter and tears. She gasped for air, frightened at the depth and the conflict of her emotions. Near panic, a moan exploded from her. She wept then, her body racked with sobs for this loss of a very part of herself.

Her heart would never again thrill at the sight of Nate's lean, tan body hurrying across the stream, anxious to be with her after a day away from the village. He would never again make her laugh as he teased her about her cooking or babbled in her ear in his own silly made-up language, poking fun at her first feeble attempts at the Timoné dialect. She would never again lie in his arms, sleepy and wholly satisfied as his lover and his wife. Weak with grief, she fell upon the sweet-smelling mat—the bed where he had made sweet love to her.

She remembered how he had hauled the previous missionary

Evangeline Magrit's narrow single bed out of the hut the night they'd first arrived. He had proudly brought in the native-woven mat where she lay now. Nate's only concession to her comfort had been the extra padding their sleeping bags afforded and the thick mosquito netting that was knotted above her head now. She felt ashamed that she'd ever complained about this hard bed. It should have been enough that she shared it with him. Her sobs rose to strangle her, and the wails that issued from her throat now came out exactly as the keening cries of a grieving Timoné woman. In this nuance of the ancient language, she was fluent.

The weeping was cleansing, and, when the worst was past, a familiar peace began to fill the emptiness. A bittersweet realization flooded over her: Nathan was in heaven. This very minute, he was looking into the face of Jesus. It filled her with joy as she remembered how much he had longed for that moment.

She offered a prayer of thanksgiving for the years she had been allowed with her husband, for the precious love they had shared, and for the hope she had in Christ. And she remembered then that this was the reason she and Nathan had come to Colombia—to share that hope.

She must be strong and show these people how her God comforted her, how he made sense of the senseless. Yet how could she do that when she struggled for it to make sense to her?

Nightmares breached her sleep that night. In her dreams she saw Nate, badly burned. He staggered toward her from across the stream, but when he crossed over to their hut he metamorphosed into a skeletal body, only his smile remaining.

She started awake, and each time she fell back asleep, the dreams plagued her. Twice she actually thought she saw Nathan standing beside her mat, but when she reached out for him, the specter faded like a vapor, leaving her bereft and trembling with fear. She lay in the darkness, shivering in spite of the heat, unable to wipe away the terrifying visions.

She sat up in bed, trembling. Suddenly in her mind she saw clearly the column of smoke that had risen in the north sixteen days earlier. The blood rushed to her head, and she felt her heart beating violently in her chest as she realized for the first time that she had actually witnessed Nathan's funeral pyre. The thought chilled her, and then, strangely, it began to comfort her. In God's incomprehensible way, had he allowed her to be present at Nate's death? To see his entrance into eternity?

"Oh, God, give me your peace. Please, Father. Take these dreams away," she begged.

Finally she slept, and when the sun came up, she went into the forest where she cut thick bamboo stalks and tied them with vines, fashioning a crude cross. She didn't know where the idea had come from, but she planted the cross near a tree behind their hut. Then sitting cross-legged in the moss beneath the tree, she carefully etched Nathan's name and the dates of his short life into the trunk. Though it was an empty grave, it seemed important to mark Nathan's passing in this way. As she carved, she prayed, pouring her heart out to God. Finally she quoted the Twenty-third Psalm from memory. The ancient words and the ceremony of her actions comforted her. And though she still did not understand the why of Nate's death, God took away her need for understanding, and she felt the tiny ember of peace flicker.

As Daria tidied the hut, she set aside Nathan's books to give to Anazu, Tados, and Quimico. Her own books and other supplies she gave to the children. They seemed to understand that Daria was still in mourning. They did not come for morning lessons, did not follow her around the village as they had before. Instead, they waited, tentative, for her to approach them. She craved their chattering and their easy way with her. She wanted back the life she'd known here before.

But even as she craved her old life, she saw the boat that would take her away sitting ready at the water's edge.

As she returned from washing at the river, she came upon Tommi, hand fishing in a fast-running tributary beside the pathway.

"Catching any fish?" she asked him in Timoné.

With a fresh shyness in her presence, he held out a basket with five or six small trout in it.

She smiled at him and spread her hands wide. "You catch a big one for me, okay?"

"Okay," he grinned, using his favorite English word.

She walked on silently, bidding the little boy a final goodbye in her heart. She followed the path back to the village, committing the jungle to memory as she went. Several times along the way, she stopped and closed her eyes, listening to the soothing sounds of the rain forest, recording them in her mind. After today, she might never return, but she would hold this place in her heart, forever entwined with her memories of Nathan Camfield.

Anazu's boat sat ready at the trail's edge. It was time to go, and now she felt an urgency to carry the tragic news to Nate's family and to her own.

In an inspired moment, she made a gift of their hut to Anazu and his family. There was no Timoné word for *church,* but she explained as best she could that she would like them to use it as a place to pray and to seek God.

"It would make Dr. Nate very happy to know that you remember him here, and that you always pray to the one true God," she said in her halting attempt at the dialect.

Anazu thanked her for her gift. Paita embraced Daria, while Anazu's nephews loaded the small bundles that held her belongings into the boat. Then they hoisted the craft onto their shoulders and, without a word, turned toward the forest pathway that led to the river.

Daria followed, gulping back tears as she walked away from the cherished memories she had lived here with her husband. She remembered the day Nathan had disappeared down this same trail. It seemed like a lifetime ago.

Overhead the birds of the rain forest squawked and sang in a harsh cacophony. The sun burned down on her back, its scorching rays a comfort simply because it was something she could feel.

As she followed her guides along the trail, she turned several times and drank in the scene, trying to sear the picture in her memory.

Finally, as the village disappeared from sight behind a curtain of thick vegetation, Daria turned back to the trail. Forging ahead, she wrapped her hands protectively over the small mound of her stomach, cradling the only part of Nathan Camfield she had left—the child she was now certain grew within her womb.

Four

*T*he trees spread out beneath them as far as the eye could see—an ocean of emerald green broken only by an occasional glimpse of silver ribbon that was the Rio Guaviare. The Cessna 185 Skywagon swooped down into the swell of the jungle like a hungry gull, made a wide circle, and dipped left for another look.

"There!" the pilot shouted over the roar of the engine. "See how those trees are stripped—there on the east bank where the river curves?"

He flew lower, and Daria peered out the window over the left wing from her seat behind him. She saw the section of the forest he was talking about, the trees bare of leaves, their bark ashy and grey. Her heart lurched as she caught a brief glimpse of charred debris through the branches. A peculiar sense of reverence filled her. She was looking at the place where Nathan had died.

As they circled again, Bob Warrington put his binoculars down and turned to her from his seat beside the pilot. His face was pallid and drawn, as her own must have been. "Are you all right, Daria?" he shouted.

She could only nod and put her head against the window.

"There's nothing we can do here," Bob told the pilot, his voice grave.

The deafening drone of the plane's engine drowned out her sobs as it turned westward and gained altitude.

Coming through the doorway into the terminal waiting room of Kansas City International Airport, Daria felt as though she had stepped into another dimension. The bright lights and the throng of bustling, well-dressed travelers unsettled her. The mechanical jangle of computers and telephones and the public address system was strange to her ears, more surreal than the jungle sounds of Colombia had ever seemed, even in the beginning. Each breath she drew in carried a stranger, stronger scent than the last—detergents and soaps, colognes and lotions that all seemed to be garish imitations of the softly fragrant flowers and herbs of her rain forest. For a moment she ached for the familiar noises and smells of Colombia. She now felt more a foreigner here than she had felt at first among the Timoné.

"Daria! Daria!" She heard her mother before she actually saw her face. Margo Haydon's tremulous voice rose above the din. Then a gasp. "Oh, honey, you're so thin!"

She fell into her mother's embrace, grateful for someone to lean on. Her father wrapped his strong arms around the two of them, and for several minutes they stood there, holding one another, too emotional to speak.

Almost against her will, Daria, flanked by her parents, was swept into the crowd and carried along the concourse toward the baggage claim. As they walked, her father took her carry-on bags from her.

"Are you okay, honey?" he asked, putting an arm tightly around her shoulders.

Daria nodded, managing a small smile for her father. "I will be."

"You poor baby." Her mother patted her back. "I wish you'd never gone to that horrible place—"

Erroll Haydon shook his head, and Daria's mother clamped her lips shut. "Well, at least you're home now."

"Did…did Nathan's parents come?" Daria looked around the terminal but saw no familiar faces in the sea of people that flooded the airport.

"No, honey, they wanted to give you some time," her father told her. "They're pretty broken up over this whole thing."

Tears welled up in Daria's eyes.

"Let's go get your stuff and get you home," Margo Haydon said, setting her lips in a hard line.

In spite of her sorrow, it was undeniably good to be back with her family. The river trip to San José del Guaviare had taken its toll on her. And there she had waited for two agonizing days at an airstrip crawling with paramilitary before flight arrangements to Bogotá could be finalized through Gospel Outreach's headquarters.

And yet the farther her travels had carried her from Timoné, the farther she felt from Nate. As the plane had lifted from the tarmac at the airport in Bogotá, she had been overcome by panic, feeling as though she were betraying her husband by leaving him there. The mission had sent a search party into the region but had warned her that it was likely that, because so many had burned in the fire, they wouldn't be able to identify Nate's remains to bring them home. In a strange way it comforted Daria to know that Nate's body had burned, that she wasn't leaving flesh and blood and a grave behind. Only precious memories.

It seemed a lifetime ago that she had lost him, but in the presence of her parents, her grief was fresh.

Dead. It still seemed impossible. Nate had always embodied the word *life.* She pushed away the images of his lanky form, his pale blond hair whipping in the breeze, his crooked, winsome smile. She had to be strong in front of her parents, especially when she remembered how much they had been against her going away.

She recalled a late December day two years ago in this same airport. After all the years of planning and dreaming, she and Nate were finally going to Colombia.

Their parents had thought they were crazy. Both of their mothers cried for days when they realized that nothing they could say would make a difference. They didn't understand the faith that compelled her and Nate to go, the desire to see a world in love with Jesus.

"But there are so many right here who need help," they'd argued.

It was true. An hour from the Haydons, in Wichita, and only minutes from the Camfields in Kansas City, homeless people littered park benches and sidewalks with their foul-smelling bodies and battered grocery bags that carried the sum of their existence. Even in the small farming communities where she and Nate had been raised, there were those who had never truly heard the gospel message, had never understood the significance of Christ's sacrifice for them.

But that was not where God had led them. And to go anywhere else would have been to disobey the One they loved most.

After a bittersweet Christmas with their families, they drove to the airport in a four-vehicle caravan. They stood at the departure gate surrounded by their parents and Daria's brother, Nate's sister, and five young nieces and nephews.

She and Nathan boarded the plane on a river of tears. They carried three bags apiece, filled mostly with cooking utensils and medical supplies, along with a few books and writing materials. In their pockets they carried passports and their marriage certificate and photographs of their loved ones.

They had never looked back. But neither had they ever imagined that it would end like this, that Daria would return alone.

"Are you hungry, Daria?" Her mother's shrill voice jerked her from her reverie. "Should we stop and get something?"

"No, Mom. I ate on the plane." Never mind that it was half a bag of peanuts and a Diet Coke. It would satisfy her mother to know she had eaten something.

"Did Jason come?" Daria asked, anxious to change the subject. She was eager to see her brother, though she wasn't sure she could face his sympathy right now.

"No, sweetheart," her father said gently. "He thought it would be best to wait for you at the house."

"When…will the Camfields come?"

"They'll come to Bristol as soon as we let them know we're home."

They arrived at the baggage carousel, and Erroll Haydon motioned for his wife and daughter to sit down while he waited for her luggage to come around.

The rest of the day turned into a haze in Daria's mind. The long drive home, her mother helping her get settled in the room that had been hers as a child. Then a house full of visitors. Her brother and his family, and later the extended family and Nate's family, all came to see her. The outpouring of sympathy touched her, and yet it overwhelmed her so that when they'd all gone home she could scarcely remember one conversation.

On Saturday, one week after she arrived home, her parents' church—the old clapboard country church Daria had grown up in—held a memorial service for Nathan. It seemed as if the entire town had turned out. She stood beside her mother and father at the doorway in the vestibule and greeted those who came to pay their respects. After living in a uniform of cotton skirts and tennis shoes for two years, she felt ill at ease wearing stockings and heels and the simple black dress her mother had loaned her. But she smoothed her skirt and tried to smile and be gracious as friends and neighbors—most of whom she hadn't seen for years—filed by to cry with her and offer their support.

The wide doors to the vestibule opened once more, and a group of her high-school friends came in together. Her heart lightened just seeing them. "Nancy! Melinda!" Daria cried. "Oh, Cathy, it's been such a long time. Hi, Diane. Oh, thank you for coming, all of you." The smile she gave them was genuine.

Nancy leaned in close, her glossy red hair a long curtain. The sad smile on her face made Daria feel as if she truly shared her burden. She reached out and hugged her, taking warmth and healing from the embrace.

"How are you holding up, Haymaker?" Nancy asked gently.

"No one's called me that in almost ten years," Daria smiled.

Melinda, Cathy, and Diane moved close and formed a circle around her, and the knot of friends moved away from the door.

"Let's go talk outside," Daria said. She caught her dad's eye. "We're going to step outside for a minute," she mouthed, motioning toward the door.

Erroll excused himself from the conversation he was involved in and came over to greet Daria's friends. Then he turned to his daughter, putting a hand on her arm. "You go on," he reassured her. "We'll fill in for you here. You need to get reacquainted."

They found a shady spot away from the front door, and soon Daria was caught up in conversation, accepting their tender empathy, catching up on news of other friends who had moved away, even laughing as they remembered old times together. It felt wonderful to be with these childhood friends who knew her so well. Slowly Daria began to feel more like her old self.

As the conversation turned to high-school memories, Nancy reminded them, "Remember when you mixed up that little potion in sophomore chemistry, Daria?"

"Me? Well, okay," she laughingly conceded. "I might have done the actual 'cooking,' but you were the one who was supposed to be reading the 'recipe,' Nan!"

"Oh, man, I remember that!" Diane interjected, her blue eyes flashing. "There were those green fumes boiling out of the beaker and Zindler was waving his arms like a madman, trying to evacuate the room."

"That stunt just about got us expelled," Daria said, still smiling.

"Poor Mr. Zindler," Melinda chimed in. "I'm surprised he didn't retire that year."

"What do you mean?" Cathy chided. "He *did* retire that year."

"No!"

"That's right," Diane confirmed. "Remember, when we were juniors Dr. Unruh was the chemistry teacher."

"Oh, my goodness! You're right. I hadn't even thought about that," Daria said.

They dissolved into girlish giggles, all talking at once. She looked up with a wide smile on her face to see Nate's parents and his sister, Betsy, and her family coming up the walk to the church. She sobered immediately. What must they think of her that she would smile at her husband's funeral, let alone cut up with her friends, as they'd no doubt just seen her doing? She felt weighed down with guilt. And yet she was ashamed to realize that she resented the Camfields' interruption, for she lusted for more of the laughter, more sharing of happy memories.

Breaking away from her friends, she went to Nate's family. "Hello, Jack, Vera."

In spite of her flawless makeup and her impeccable designer suit, Vera Camfield had aged ten years seemingly overnight. She responded stiffly when Daria embraced her. Daria quickly turned to Nate's father. His hug was warmer, but he, too, seemed almost ill with grief. When Jack and Vera Camfield had come to the Haydons' house the day Daria arrived home, they had seemed so strong, speaking of Nate as though he were still alive, even managing to smile at memories of their son.

But the news had come yesterday that a search party had found the rubble of the burned hut on the river. It was a gruesome discovery: There were over two dozen bodies, many of them children, and those who hadn't been burned beyond recognition had been left to decay. Apparently the villagers refused to come near the place where the ill had died. The search team had buried the dead in a mass grave under the suspicious watch of a small party of Chicoro.

Though dreadful, the news had not surprised Daria, and in many ways it had put closure on Nate's death for her. But she reminded herself that Nate's parents had not had as much time to grieve as she had. The news of the search party's findings must have been devastating to them. Not only had the Camfields lost their only son, but they would not even have the comfort of a grave nearby to visit.

Daria turned to Nate's sister, Betsy, and her husband, Jim Franklin. Nate and his sister had always been close, and the heartsick expression etched on Betsy's face now broke Daria's heart all over again.

"Hi, honey," Betsy said, reaching for her. Daria returned her embrace, and they both broke down. Putting his arms awkwardly around them both, Jim muttered his condolences. On the sidewalk behind them, the Franklins' two preteenagers hung back, clearly uncomfortable to be there.

"Hi, Wendy. Hey, Zach." Daria forced a smile, wanting to put the children at ease.

Zachary gave her a self-conscious wave, and Wendy dipped her head and stared at her shoes.

"Thanks for coming, you guys," Daria told them.

Strains of organ music began to waft from the church, and through the open doors they could see people beginning to make their way toward the sanctuary. Daria directed Nate's family into the church where her mother and father were standing to receive mourners. They exchanged hushed greetings, and then they entered the dim sanctuary in silence.

Nate's family sat in the row in front of Daria and her parents, and Daria, overcome with emotion, watched them. As the memorial service finalized his son's life, Jack Camfield wept like a child, and his wife's face seemed to hold a shadow of bitterness. Daria knew it was irrational, yet she felt responsible for their grief, as though she should have prevented Nate's death. Witnessing their sorrow, waves of anguish and guilt rolled over her anew, and she wept until she finally felt drained of all emotion.

When the service ended and the mourners began filing from the church, Daria saw Betsy slip out the back door with her distraught mother leaning heavily against her. Daria started to go after them, but just then Nate's father came over to where she was standing with her parents.

Jack Camfield took Erroll Haydon's hand. "It was a beautiful service, Erroll," he said, a quaver in his deep voice that Daria had never heard before. "Thank you for all you did to arrange it." He cleared his throat and dipped his head slightly. "Well, I think we're going to head back home now."

Daria's father wrinkled his forehead and drew his thick brows together. "The women's circle fixed a dinner for the family, Jack. They've planned for all your family. Won't you stay and eat with us?"

The older man shook his head, then motioned in the direction of the parking lot. "Vera's pretty broken up. I think it's best if we go on home now. We have a long trip back to the city."

Daria stood by silently during this exchange, but at Jack's words she took a step toward the door that led to the back parking lot. "I'll go say goodbye—"

"No!" The word came out too forcefully, and several people turned to look their way. Softening his voice, Jack Camfield took Daria's hand. "No, dear, it's...best to leave her alone when she gets like this, but thank you. I'll tell her you were concerned for her."

Daria nodded numbly and thanked him for coming, then felt foolish for thanking a man for attending his own son's memorial service. As if he'd had a choice.

After an uncomfortable moment, Jack Camfield broke away. Muttering a stilted farewell, he disappeared through the door.

Daria's parents exchanged troubled glances, but her father took her gently by the arm and led her to the fellowship hall where the family was being seated.

When the dinner was over, her parents stayed behind to help clean up while Daria caught a ride back to the farm with her brother. Jason and his wife, Brenda, farmed with Erroll Haydon and lived just a few miles down the road.

"Do you want us to come in with you, Dar?" Jason asked as the car idled in the driveway in front of the Haydons' farmhouse.

"No, thanks anyway, Jas, but I-I'd kind of like to be alone for a while."

He nodded and swallowed hard, his eyes brimming with tears. Daria had rarely seen her older brother cry, and it touched her deeply.

Brenda leaned over the backseat and touched Daria's shoulder. "You call if you need anything, Daria. I mean that."

"I know you do, Brenda. Thanks. Thanks for everything, you guys. I don't know what I'd do without you." She climbed out of the car, waved them off, and hurried toward the house.

She went upstairs, changed into the one pair of jeans she owned, and pulled on a ratty T-shirt that had been Nate's. As she passed the mirror on the antique dresser in her room, the college insignia on the front of the shirt caught her eye. Unbidden, the memories came crashing back.

She flopped down on the quilt that covered the high, canopied bed, and a film began to play in her mind. There was a young Nate, smiling and carefree, standing in the hall outside the door to her dorm room at KU, ready to take her to a ball game. He walked toward her on a campus sidewalk, that trademark grin melting her heart. She could almost feel his arms around her, smell the briny, outdoorsy scent of his hair—pale, straight hair that was as fine and silky as a baby's. She had always teased him about that, secretly wishing she could trade him her own coarse, wavy hair.

Her throat filled with longing, and she gave in to the tears, railing at her loss, letting the sobs rack her body until there was nothing left to cry, crying out Nate's name over and over, though she understood fully that he would never answer her again.

She must have fallen asleep, for when she opened her eyes the sun was low in the sky and she heard her parents moving around in the kitchen downstairs. She climbed off the bed and went to the bathroom where she stepped into the shower and let the almost-scalding water run over her face, the sting of the hot water comforting.

She turned off the spray and dried herself methodically. In the full-length mirror, under the bright fluorescent light of the bathroom, she noticed for the first time how thin she had become. In spite of the slightly rounded stomach the growing baby had begun to give her, her ribs were starkly outlined under her flesh. She told herself she must keep herself healthy. This baby was all she had left of Nathan.

She pulled on the same jeans and T-shirt, swept her hair up into a careless ponytail, and went downstairs. The house was quiet again, and she found a note from her parents saying they had gone to her brother's for a few minutes. She scribbled a message for them on the bottom of their note and headed for the pasture behind the barn. The man-made terraces unfurled in waves across the prairie in front of her. This had been her favorite thinking place as a teenager, and she was drawn once again to the peace the spot offered.

The cattle in the neighbor's field started a plaintive bawling when they saw her, no doubt thinking it was time for their evening feed. She smiled at this everyday sound from her childhood and felt suddenly comforted, glad that something so far from Colombia finally felt familiar to her again, had the power to console her.

The Kansas sun was just beginning its slow descent, and the colors were spectacular. Watching the vibrant shades of purple and orange and pink against the deepening blue-grey sky, Daria felt a tentative hope swell within her, and a sense of home filled her anew. As she trudged through the prairie grasses, following the natural path of the pasture's rolling terrain, she prayed.

"Lord, I don't know what you want me to do now, but I know…you love me. I know you've been with me"—she tried to swallow the huge lump that rose in her throat—"oh, God, what will I ever do without him? I don't understand why you took him. I don't think I'll ever understand why you sent us to Colombia only to have it end this way. I know I shouldn't *have* to understand, God, but I want to."

In everything give thanks.

She heard the phrase exactly as Nate would have spoken it— when the mosquitoes threatened to eat them alive, when half his medical supplies were lost when the boat overturned, when the rainy season imprisoned them in the hut for days on end. *There's something to be thankful for in every situation,* Nate had always told her, even when she knew he wasn't sure he believed it himself. She took in a sharp breath. How many times had she and Nate admonished each other with those very words?

"Oh, thank you, God. Thank you for the years we had together." She stopped at the top of a rise and looked around her. "And thank you that I have this place to come home to, Father. Just tell me what I'm supposed to do next, God, because I truly don't know."

Immediately she was filled with thoughts of the child growing within her, and she knew it was her first answer. This child whom God had created of their love—hers and Nate's—would be her most precious and immediate assignment for the next few months.

She had not yet told anyone about the baby. She knew that she should see a doctor, make certain everything was coming along as it should. But something made her want to hang on to her secret. Her pregnancy was a blessing—a sweet remembrance of Nate and a tangible way for him to live on.

"Thank you, Lord," she whispered, laying one hand lightly over her abdomen. She stood on the hill, cradling Nate's unborn child that way until the sun disappeared behind a distant hedgerow. Almost instinctively she turned to the south and looked up at the evening's first stars. She remembered the night she and Nate had stood under a starry Timoné sky and said their goodbyes. They'd had no inkling that night that they were saying goodbye forever. The thought tore her heart in two. What might she have said to him had she known it would be their last night together?

She didn't know the constellations as Nathan had. She wasn't sure whether the star he had pointed out that night was visible in the Northern Hemisphere. What had he called it? *Spica.* She picked out a bright star that seemed to blink at her from the southernmost sky. For a moment, she pretended it was their star, and her heart was wrenched between two continents. She was happy to be home, yet engulfed by an intense longing to be back in Colombia. She was homesick to be in their little hut, caressed by the gentle tropical breezes, lulled by the myriad songs of the rain forest.

But even if she could go back, Nathan would not be there.

She wished he had known of her pregnancy before he'd gone off that day. What a comfort it would have been to have the memory of Nate's joy at learning the news. She knew he would have been ecstatic. It struck her that where he was now, he probably did know about his child, and the knowledge gave her peace.

Tearfully she spoke aloud, "Oh, Nate! I don't understand any of this. I miss you so much, babe. Oh, how I miss you. But I know you're happy. I know you're in God's hands now. And I…I'll take good care of our baby. I promise. He'll know how much you would have loved him."

The tears of grief that flowed were mingled with honest gratitude that God would give her this one last part of Nate. She turned toward the farmhouse and knew by the lights flickering in the windows that her parents were home again. They would be worried about her.

With the warm evening breeze in her hair, the heat of a Kansas August still lingering, she started back toward the house, toward a new life that was strange and unknown. A life that God had not abandoned.

Five

Daria blew a wayward strand of hair from her forehead, putting a hand to her aching back as she surveyed the kitchen. Chocolate jimmies, silver shot, and dollops of pink frosting sprinkled the countertops, and an array of fudge and heart-shaped cookies fit to dress the showcases of the finest bakery lined the oak table in the middle of the room.

With the corner of a checkered dishtowel, Margo Haydon reached up to wipe a smudge of flour from her daughter's face before slumping wearily into a nearby chair.

"You'd better get off your feet for a while, honey," she scolded. "I can finish up here. We don't have to take these to the church until five o'clock."

"I'm okay, Mom. I'll go lie down in a little bit, but I can at least wash up these dishes first."

Her mother started to protest, then waved a hand in resignation. "Do what you want. You will anyway. But don't blame me if your ankles swell up like balloons."

Daria was annoyed by her mother's remark, but she tried to ignore it, realizing that just about everything annoyed her these days. She filled one side of the sink with hot soapy water, and leaned her swollen belly against the counter's edge. The baby kicked hard in protest. Almost overnight she had gone from barely showing to look-ing every day of her eight months. The baby was resting low in her womb and her back was killing her, but she took comfort in know-ing that she had only a few weeks to go.

Daria had begun searching for a job her second week back in the States. She did not want to be a burden to her parents, nor did she wish to raise her child under their overly watchful eyes. But when her parents discovered her intentions to move out on her own, they begged her to at least wait until after the baby arrived. "Nobody would hire you in your condition anyway," Margo pointed out.

Daria had allowed herself to be persuaded, and now she was grateful for the reprieve. Staying with her parents had allowed her time to grieve her great loss, to plan for a future that didn't include Nate, and to enjoy her pregnancy.

As the baby's birth drew near, it was sinking in that, despite her mother's offer to baby-sit while she worked, her life was not going to be easy. There had been a small insurance check through Gospel Outreach, and Social Security provided a meager monthly check, but it was going to take a full-time job to make ends meet.

She rinsed the last mixing bowl and set it on the counter to dry. She stood on tiptoe, stretched, and kneaded her back with her fingertips.

"Daria, *please* go lie down." It was obvious that her mother had been studying her closely.

"Yes, Mother, whatever you say," she singsonged, failing in her attempt to make her mother laugh. She dried her hands and gave Margo a smile meant to appease. "Don't let me nap too long, or I'll never get to sleep tonight."

"A long nap wouldn't hurt you one bit. You seem to ignore the fact that you've got this baby to think of."

Daria put a hand on her bulging stomach. "This baby is kind of hard to ignore, Mom," she snapped. She left the room before Margo could respond. She knew she was behaving like an ill-tempered child, but she couldn't even bring herself to care.

She had tried so hard to get through this day—her first Valentine's Day without her sweetheart—without being maudlin. But her heart was breaking. Everything reminded her of Nate—the love songs on the radio, the frosted sugar cookies he'd loved so much, even the roses her father had bought for her. It was a sweet gesture, but it was also a painful reminder of the flowers she would never again receive from her husband.

She went to her room and lay down on top of the quilt on her bed. Her first week at home she had ended up sleeping on the floor beside this bed each night, unable to get used to the height of the four-poster and the softness of the mattress. How Nate would have laughed at that after all her complaining about sleeping on the floor in Timoné. She bit her lip and tried to think of something else. But thoughts of Nate intruded, and finally she allowed them free rein, wallowing in self-pity.

She rolled to her side, punching her pillow in anger and frustration. Before she could raise her fist again, an acute cramp sliced through her back. She took in a sharp breath and instinctively cradled her belly in her hands. She lay on her side, utterly still, listening to the rapid beating of her own heart, waiting for the pain to fade. It passed, but within minutes another spasm swept over her. Fear gripped her, and she temporarily forgot Nathan as she turned toward the clock on her nightstand and watched the second hand creep around the face—once, twice, seven times, and then another contraction began its crescendo.

"Mom!" The cry was scarcely out of her mouth when she felt a strange pop. A warm, damp spot spread on the quilt beneath her.

In spite of how quickly her contractions had progressed, her labor had been long and intense and shadowed by fear because it was several weeks too early. But now that Daria held the reward of her travail in her arms, all the agony quickly faded into nothing.

Natalie Joan Camfield looked up into her mother's eyes with a gaze that surprised Daria with its intelligence and awareness. The tiny infant had a full head of almost-black hair and navy blue eyes.

Daria couldn't help but laugh at her daughter's two grandmothers. As the older women stood by Daria's hospital bed, cooing over the granddaughter they shared, Margo Haydon declared, "You just watch, Daria. In a few weeks her eyes will lighten up and be as blue as yours."

"Oh, I don't know," Vera Camfield argued. "Her eyes are exactly the color Nathan's were when he was born. You can already see a bit of hazel in them." Vera's own eyes brimmed with tears, and Daria tried desperately to think of something to say that would bring her back to the present.

"Vera, do you remember how much Nate weighed when he was born?"

"How could I forget?" she said, smiling sadly. "He was nine pounds, fifteen ounces."

"Almost ten pounds!" Daria exclaimed. "Ouch! And I thought Natalie was big at six and a half pounds."

"Be thankful she came early," Margo said with a grimace. "She might have been ten pounds if you'd gone full term."

"Both my babies were big," Vera said with pride. "Betsy was almost as big as Nathan. Of course you'd never know it now."

The two grandmothers continued to compare stories and imagine family resemblances in their new grandchild until Daria was worn out with their banter.

But in spite of the commotion of the hospital and the constant stream of visitors, Daria felt as though she and her daughter were in a world of their own, held together by a bond that only they shared. In some ways, the baby's arrival had rekindled her grief for Nate, yet ironically it had provided healing for that grief as well. And though she couldn't look at Natalie without being reminded of Nate—in her eyes, in the tiny cleft of her chin—it was a comfort to know that in a small way, her husband lived on through his daughter.

She smiled through her tears and thanked God for this six-and-a-half-pound bundle—Nathan's final Valentine to her.

Daria sat in the well-worn recliner in the Haydon living room, wrestling with a fussy, hungry infant. Her mother hovered like a honeybee over a freshly opened peony.

"Are you sure you don't want to give her just a little formula? I've got it all ready." She held out a warm bottle filled with the strong-smelling brownish liquid.

"No, Mom," Daria said evenly, ignoring the proffered bottle and struggling to control her frustration. "Thanks anyway, but she just needs to nurse some more."

"Well, it doesn't seem like she's getting enough milk. Some women just don't produce enough, you know. There's no shame in supplementing with formula once in a while, honey. After all, you were raised on it."

"Mom, please!" The words came out more forcefully than she'd intended. She softened her tone. "Could you just leave us alone for a few minutes? I think she's a little distracted."

Margo set the warm bottle on an end table. "I'm just trying to help," she said, hands on hips.

"I know, Mom. I'm sorry I snapped at you."

"I don't mean to interfere. But after all, I did raise two babies myself."

Daria ignored her mother, and finally Margo sighed and took the bottle back to the kitchen.

For the first few weeks of motherhood, it had been wonderful to have her mother's expert help with the baby, to have all her meals prepared and served, and to have a free roof over her head. But now that Natalie was two months old and Daria was beginning to feel confident in her role, she was feeling desperate to have her own space.

Natalie finally fell asleep at her breast. Daria eased out of the chair and headed upstairs to put the baby down for a nap. As she passed her father's desk, she grabbed the morning paper with her free hand.

Natalie opened her eyes the minute Daria laid her on the crib mattress, but she didn't protest when Daria left the side of the crib and went to sit cross-legged on her own bed, spreading the newspaper out before her.

Daria had secretly pored over the classified ads every day for the past two weeks, growing more frustrated as she realized how under-qualified she was for any job that paid enough to provide for a single woman with an infant. A teaching job would be perfect. If she couldn't be home full time, at least she could have summers with Natalie.

But going back to college seemed an impossibility. She was angry with Nate for allowing her to quit school, even though it had been her own idea to drop out and go to work to help put him through medical school. "I don't even know why I've stayed in school this long," she'd told him back then. "It's just a waste of money. It's not like I'll need a degree in Colombia." But she thought now that he should have insisted that she finish, that she get a degree of some kind.

She was angry with Nate, and she was angry with God for letting him die. It didn't make sense that a loving God would allow someone as caring and giving as Nathan Camfield to die just as he was beginning a life dedicated to serving others. How could God have let them—both of them—sacrifice so much, work so hard toward Nate's goal of becoming a doctor? How could he have called them to the mission field, only to take it all away, leaving her alone and ill prepared to support their daughter? She would never understand it.

Sighing, she forced away the angry feelings and turned again to the classified section of the paper. With a growing feeling of desperation, she folded back the page and began scanning the columns.

An item under the "Help Wanted" section caught her eye: "Receptionist for veterinary clinic in small town. Full-time position with flexible hours, benefits. Will train."

Well, it was far from the teaching field, but "flexible hours" and "will train" sounded promising. And the clinic was nearby in Bristol, where she had attended high school. She scribbled down the address, along with the phone numbers of several other job openings that seemed like possibilities. Then she went to her closet to see if she could find even one outfit she could squeeze into that would be suitable for a job interview.

She glanced down at Natalie, who was still awake but lying quietly on her back. A pair of bright little eyes darted back and forth, seeming to follow Daria as she moved from the closet to the full-length mirror and back, holding various skirts in front of her.

"Oh, Nattie, your mommy doesn't have a thing to wear!" she cooed, as though the baby could understand every word.

She finally decided on a faded but still stylish, straight denim skirt. She could borrow a blouse from her mother to wear with it.

She hated even bringing up the subject of a job with her parents. Margo and Erroll Haydon had fallen in love with their little granddaughter. Natalie was a blessing, and a powerful antidote to everyone's grief. But it was time for them to be on their own—past time. And Daria was ready.

Natalie began to squirm and fuss in the crib. Daria looked at her watch. "Are you hungry *again,* little girl? You must be in a growing spurt."

In reply Natalie puckered her bottom lip and burst into tears. Laughing, Daria scooped the baby into her arms. She sat down in the rocking chair and put her daughter to her breast. The eager little mouth latched on, and soon she was almost choking on the rich flow of milk. They were slowly getting the hang of this breast-feeding thing, and with the rush of milk, Daria felt the familiar sense of well-being spread over her like a warm quilt.

"We're in this together, kiddo," she whispered. "You and me."

The thick, dark hair Natalie had been born with had fallen out within weeks of her birth and was slowly being replaced with silky, white-blond strands that made her look even more startlingly like Nate. Daria smoothed the flyaway hair with the palm of her hand

and wished for the thousandth time that Nathan could have seen his daughter just once.

Daria smiled as the baby's eyelids fluttered, then closed as she fell into a milk-induced stupor. Overcome with love for her daughter, Daria stroked the rounded curve of Natalie's down-soft cheek. A tear rolled down Daria's cheek and soaked into the warm blanket surrounding her daughter.

Set back from the highway, the Bristol Veterinary Clinic was at the edge of town. The unassuming office building in front was dwarfed by a modern, newly built barn that rose behind it.

Daria got out of the car and nervously straightened her skirt and smoothed the wrinkles from her blouse. She went around to the opposite side of the car and opened the back door.

Natalie slept soundly in her car seat. "Please, please, don't wake up, sweetie," she whispered under her breath. Spring had not quite arrived in Kansas and the afternoon breeze was brisk, so Daria threw a light blanket over Natalie, tucking it in around her.

She picked up her daughter, car seat and all, and walked into the waiting room of the clinic's front office.

"Can I help you?" the girl at the desk asked through a wad of chewing gum. Daria guessed that she was a high-school student.

"Yes, I'm here for an interview about the receptionist's position."

"Oh, yeah, sure. Hang on." The girl meandered down a hallway toward the back of the building, reappearing a few seconds later. She handed Daria a clipboard with a job application attached.

Daria put Natalie's carrier on the floor beside her, uncovered the still-sleeping baby, and sat down to fill out the information. When she was finished, she gave the clipboard to the girl, who disappeared through a back doorway with it.

She returned a few minutes later. "Dr. Hunter says to come on back."

Toting the infant carrier, she followed the young woman through the door and down a narrow passageway.

"I'm Jennifer, by the way." The girl offered Daria a shy smile. "Your baby is adorable."

"Thanks," she smiled. "I hope it's okay that I brought her with me. I lost my baby-sitter at the last minute. I called and spoke with someone here about it, and they—"

"Oh, yeah," Jennifer interrupted. "That was me. It's not a problem. Dr. Hunter is crazy about kids."

The place smelled strongly of wet dog fur and disinfectant. Through open doors on each side of the hallway Daria could see rows of cages, several of which held dogs or cats. A high-strung poodle began barking as they passed and Daria winced, fearing the sound would wake Natalie. But the baby didn't stir.

Jennifer showed her into a small office at the end of the hallway. She motioned toward a folding chair in front of a metal desk in the corner, then left, closing the door behind her. A few minutes later, the door opened again and a tall, sandy-haired man in a stained white coat stepped into the room.

He stuck out his hand. "Hello. Daria, is it? I'm Colson Hunter."

Though his hair was beginning to thin and the corners of his eyes were crinkled, his smile made him look like a winsome ten-year-old boy. Daria liked him immediately.

Natalie stirred and stretched her arms.

Hoping the baby's motions weren't a prelude to crying, Daria put out her hand. "Nice to meet you. I-I want to apologize for bringing my daughter with me. I lost my baby-sitter at the last minute. My mom was going to watch her, but my dad's tractor broke down, and he needed her to run to Wichita for parts." She felt like a wayward student in the principal's office. She'd been torn between rescheduling her interview and bringing Natalie with her. Neither made for a very good first impression.

But Dr. Hunter immediately put his hands up as if to ward off her apology. "I grew up on a farm myself," he assured her. "I know how it is." His warm, casual manner instantly put her at ease. "I wonder if I know your parents. Do they farm around here?"

She nodded. "Five miles south of town. Erroll and Margo Haydon?"

He wrinkled his brow. "Hmm, that doesn't ring a bell. I've only been in Bristol a couple of years, but I know most of the farmers around here by now."

"Well, my dad doesn't have livestock, just crops."

"Oh, I see. And does your husband farm too?" he said, looking over her application, as though he might find the answer there.

She swallowed hard. "No. He—I-I'm widowed." *Oh, please, God, don't let me cry.*

He looked up from the papers in his hand. "Oh. I'm so sorry." He looked as if he were going to say more, then, apparently sensing that she was close to tears, he turned the subject back to the interview. "I guess you know from the ad that we're looking for a receptionist—someone to answer the phones, schedule appointments, handle the mail, some of the bookwork, that sort of thing."

He glanced over her application again and asked her to clarify a few of her answers. His relaxed manner calmed her nerves, and she began to enjoy the interview.

"This is a small-time operation," he told her, resting his elbows on the desk and tenting his hands in front of him. "I have a high-school girl who helps out after school—you met Jennifer." He nodded toward the front of the building. "Then there's Travis Carruthers. Dr. Carruthers just graduated from vet school last spring. And our technician is Carla Eldridge. She assists us in surgery and with all the medical procedures. We have a groomer, Doris Kline, who comes in once or twice a week, but that's pretty much the entire staff. You'll find we're a very laid-back bunch. It won't take you long to get the hang of it."

She nodded, trying not to get her hopes up, but she couldn't help feeling optimistic at the implication of his words.

"Your application looks good, Daria," he said, looking directly at her and smiling. "If you're interested, I'd like to offer you the job. I would want you to be here by nine each weekday morning, but as long as you get your hours in, we can be pretty flexible. You'd be free to take a late lunch or leave early if you need to. Jennifer works every weekday after school, so she's here to answer the phone after three o'clock. As far as I'm concerned, you could even take some of the bookwork home with you. All I ask is that you let one of us know what's up." He mentioned a salary figure she thought she could make do with.

The baby began to squirm against the yellow blanket again, and Dr. Hunter, flashing his boyish grin, craned his neck to look over the desk at her. "How old is she?" he asked Daria. With a slight grimace he added quickly, "It is a little girl, isn't it?"

She laughed. "Yes. This is Natalie. She'll be nine weeks old tomorrow."

"Wow. She's so tiny."

"My mother is going to keep her while I work," she explained. "I-I'm living with my parents right now, but I'm planning to start looking for an apartment this weekend. I'm hoping to find something here in town or maybe over in Clayton."

"You know"—he tapped a pencil on his desktop, thinking—"I just talked to someone this week who had an apartment to rent... Now, who was that? Oh, I remember. Kirk and Dorothy Janek. They're an older couple who own a large home over on Maple. They rent out the upstairs. Real nice people. I think you'd like them. I'll give you their number if you'd like."

"Oh, thank you. That'd be great."

He found the number in the phone book on his desk and scratched it down on a notepad that advertised worm medicine. He handed it to her, then rose from his chair. She followed suit.

"If you'd like to think about the job for a few days and get back to me, that'd be fine," he told her.

"No." She didn't want to appear too eager, but she wanted this job. "I'll take it. When would you like me to start?"

"If you want the truth, this very minute." His smile told her he was kidding, but just then Natalie let out a howl.

"She didn't like that idea one bit," he said, laughing. "I guess I'll have to settle for next Monday morning then. Could you start that soon?" he asked, turning serious.

"I'll be here," she told him over Natalie's protests. Daria reached down to take her daughter out of the infant seat. Immediately the baby quieted.

"Mind if I hold her?" Dr. Hunter asked shyly.

Daria was pleased by his request and quickly replied, "Sure."

She started to hand the baby over to him.

"Hang on a sec," he said. "Let me take off this dirty thing first." He slipped off his less-than-white lab coat and draped it over the back of his chair. Then he went around to her side of the desk and reached out to take the baby in his arms as easily as if she were a newborn puppy.

Daria was taken aback by the sight of her daughter in a man's arms. Unbidden, a vision of Nathan holding Natalie—cooing at her the way Dr. Hunter was now—popped into her mind. It was at once comforting and upsetting. Nate would have been such a good father. *Oh, Natalie, how much you will miss not knowing him,* she thought.

The baby began to squirm and fuss and turn her head toward Dr. Hunter's chest as though she wanted to nurse.

Daria was embarrassed, but he spoke easily, "Okay, little one, I get the message. I'm not going to be able to help you out in that department. I better give you back to your mama."

He handed the baby gently over to Daria. Their hands brushed as they made the exchange, and she found his touch strangely intimate. Heat rose to her face, but Dr. Hunter seemed not to notice.

"I'm looking forward to working with you, Daria. I'll see you Monday morning then. If you could come in a few minutes early and fill out all the tax forms, that would be great."

She nodded politely and busied herself with putting Natalie back in the carrier for the ride home.

Through the rest of the day and late into that night, thoughts of Nathan ensnared her. Seeing an attractive man holding Nate's baby, the baby Nate had never seen—hadn't even known about—and feeling the gentle touch of a masculine hand on hers, had brought the memories bolting back. She missed him desperately.

Six

*N*ow I suppose you'd need a place to park your car?" The sprightly, grey-haired woman's mild accent bespoke her German heritage. "I told Kirk you could park your car right up here and use our back door." With one broad motion of her plump arm, Dorothy Janek indicated the end of the driveway, which widened toward the back of the house.

"That would be wonderful," Daria told her. "Actually I don't have a car yet. But I'll be using one of my dad's vehicles for a while—until I've saved a little money—so I'll still need a place to park," she added quickly.

They were standing in front of the apartment Dr. Hunter had told her about. She had arranged to see it today and was immediately taken with the charming, countrylike setting. The main entrance to the upstairs apartment was on the south side of the house; the narrow stairway spilled down to a rather rickety side porch.

"You can use the back entrance," Mrs. Janek said. "We had a bachelor living here before. We didn't know him from Adam, and I certainly didn't want him in and out our door just anytime he pleased. But we can't have you falling down those stairs with that precious bundle in your arms. And come winter, those steps are slicker than a greased pig. No," she said decisively, barely stopping to take a breath, "you'll use our back door."

Daria hid a smile. The Janeks didn't know her from Adam either, but she wasn't going to point that out just now. "That would be wonderful, Mrs. Janek," she said instead.

Huffing energetically, her ample bosom heaving, the old woman led Daria through the back door and up the stairs to the apartment.

Carrying Natalie in her arms, Daria followed her prospective landlady.

Pointing out the large closets and hardwood floors, Dorothy Janek bustled importantly around the little apartment that took up the entire second story of the old farmhouse. Originally a warren of five bedrooms, the space had been recently remodeled to open lovely views of the leafy tops of the ancient elms that stood sentinel around the house. "My grandparents built this house when they came over from Germany in the late 1800s. It was in the country back then, but Bristol just sprang up around them, and before they knew it, they lived in town!" she chuckled.

An oak staircase, which opened onto a large L-shaped living area, split the upstairs hall. Daria could picture a small dining table at the head of the stairs just outside the kitchenette. The pantry had recently been painted, judging by the acrid smell that permeated the room when she opened the door.

Two adjoining rooms at the back—divided by heavy oak pocket doors—would be perfect for her bedroom and Natalie's nursery. And between the kitchen and bedrooms was a small bath that still had an old claw-foot bathtub and freestanding basin.

"We really intended to replace the tub when we remodeled," the landlady apologized, "but we would have had to take out the wall to get that monster out of here, so we just left it be."

Daria loved the quaint coziness of the apartment—and the fact that it was just a few blocks from Dr. Hunter's veterinary clinic. She would still have to make the trip to the farm and back with Natalie each day, but at least she would be able to come home for lunch.

"I'll take it," Daria told the elderly woman when they had circled back to the living room.

"Oh, that's just dandy, honey. We were hoping to get somebody nice and quiet in the place."

Daria laughed nervously. "You might not think we're so quiet when Natalie starts screaming at three o'clock in the morning."

"Ach," Dorothy Janek waved the thought away as though it were a pesky fly. "The sound of a baby crying isn't noise! It'll be music to our ears. Besides, she'll be sleeping through the night before you know it. You just enjoy every minute with this little one. She'll be off to college in the wink of an eye." She reached out and squeezed the baby's toes affectionately.

Before Daria left, she wrote the Janeks a check for the first month's rent plus the small deposit they required. Though the expense depleted the small savings account she had from Nate's insurance, she drove back to her parents' farm with a deep sense of accomplishment and excitement.

"We're going to make it just fine, Nate," she whispered into the silence of the car. "Oh, thank you, Lord, for providing this apartment. It's perfect, just perfect. Thank you, Father, for taking care of us."

She prayed easily during the rest of the drive back to the farm, giving thanks and making her needs known to her heavenly Father. If only it would be so simple to break the news to her earthly father.

Daria's first day on the job was scarcely an hour old when she realized that it was going to be as frenzied as any she'd ever spent in the wilds of Colombia. She had just finished a quick tour of the clinic and was sitting at the desk in the reception room trying to figure out the computer, when a pickup truck raced into the parking lot, kicking up gravel. Through the window, she watched as a man in coveralls jumped out of the passenger seat and ran into the clinic.

"Where's Dr. Hunter?" he demanded, his voice on the edge of panic. "My dogs got hit on the highway. I got 'em out here in the truck. They're hurt pretty bad."

"I'll get Dr. Hunter right away," she said with more confidence than she felt. She started toward the back, but the veterinarian had apparently overheard the ruckus and was already on his way down the hall. He raced past her, motioning for her to follow him outside.

She went, feeling useless standing beside Dr. Hunter while he assessed the dogs' injuries right there in the parking lot.

"This here's Bess," the man told the doctor, rubbing the head of a small English setter.

"Hey, Bess," Dr. Hunter spoke soothing words to the dog, as though she were human. He inspected two deep gashes on her hindquarters and said, "We need to get these cuts sutured right away. This gash on her flank is awfully deep." He rubbed the dog behind the ears, then turned his attention to the larger dog, a male setter that was whining pathetically.

"Feels like we've got a broken bone in this front leg," he said, palpating the leg carefully. "But it'll have to wait until we get Bess sutured. I don't want her to lose any more blood."

Now he turned to Daria. "Travis is out on a call, and Jennifer won't be in until after school. Carla doesn't work on Monday mornings, so you're it, Daria. I'm going to need your help in surgery."

It was an order, not a request, and Daria quickly realized that her job was going to entail much more than answering phones.

Trying not to let Dr. Hunter or the farmer see how badly her hands were shaking, she followed the two men—each carrying a dog—into the surgery room. Dr. Hunter sedated the larger dog and got it settled in a cage, then he prepared to suture the deep wounds the smaller dog had sustained.

"This will be your baptism by fire, Daria," he told her under his breath as he scrubbed his hands in the corner basin of the small examining room. "Ever assisted with surgery before?"

A memory of a day in Colombia flashed through her mind, and she tried to push the gory scene away as she answered, "My husband was a doctor. I helped him sometimes. But I don't know anything about all this." She nodded her head to encompass the room's array of sterile equipment.

"I'll talk you through it. Mostly I just need you to hand me instruments." He showed her how to scrub with special antiseptic soap, giving her a quick review of the procedure he was about to do.

They went to the table where the dog's owner stood attempting to soothe the frightened animal.

"Malcolm, why don't you come around here. Stand on this side and hold her head, talk to her. It'll help calm her." Dr. Hunter gently pulled the edges of the deep wound apart and irrigated it with sterile water from a syringe. The owner turned white, and Dr. Hunter added quickly, "You don't have to look."

Those words brought the memory crashing back again. Daria moved in close to the stainless steel table and gripped its side for support. The memory intruded and, in her mind, she was back in Colombia, standing beside Nate over a crude table where a tiny girl lay screaming. The toddler had fallen on a sharp rock and sliced a deep gash in her forehead. There was blood everywhere, and the child's mother was as hysterical as the wounded girl. Nate had needed Daria's help to restrain the toddler so he could clean and close the wound.

Daria had assisted Nate with minor procedures before, but she found herself lightheaded and shaky at the grisly sight. Nate had taken one look at her eyes and, apparently seeing the fear in them, had shouted harshly at her, "Daria! Get a grip! I need you! Think of something else. You don't have to look, but hold her head tightly. Don't let her move."

Now she took Nate's advice from the past. She took a deep breath and focused on the instruments lined up on the counter beside the table. Dr. Hunter looked her in the eye. "Ready?"

She nodded bravely, and his eyes crinkled in a smile. "Okay. Hand me the swabs."

Daria made it through her first veterinary surgery. Then after making numerous phone calls to reschedule the afternoon's appointments, she readied the room for the second injured dog.

By the time they were finished with the surgeries, they were hours behind schedule, but Carla came in to relieve her.

"Thanks for your help this morning," Dr. Hunter told her when they finally had a chance to sit down for a few minutes in the office behind the reception counter. "I'm really sorry you got roped into this on your first day on the job."

"It's okay," she told him. She added dryly, "I'm just glad it was dogs and not hogs."

He threw his head back and laughed, a warm, contagious whoop that filled the room. "I wish I could promise you that tomorrow won't be as wild," he said, still laughing, "but chances are I'd be lying through my teeth."

"Thanks for the warning. But it might have been more, um, appropriate, to warn me *before* I accepted this job," she joked, chuckling along with him.

Their laughter died down, and he turned serious. "Well, you did a fine job. You really did." He paused a minute as if considering how to phrase something. "You said your husband was a doctor? You were missionaries—South America, was it?"

She nodded. "Colombia."

"I guess I didn't realize he was a physician."

She swallowed hard. "Yes. We went to Colombia just a few months after Nate finished at KU Med Center. There was no clinic in our village, and since there was no airstrip there we had only what little equipment we could take in with us. It was incredibly primitive. But Nate was a good doctor." She paused, clearing her throat. "It was while we were there that he was killed."

He nodded. "I remember seeing the stories in the paper when he...died. I didn't make the connection when I first met you." He hesitated again before speaking. "I heard that he was missing for a while before you learned that he'd died."

"More than two weeks." She realized with a little surprise that this was the first time she'd told her story to a stranger. Her friends and everyone at her church already knew her circumstances. Revisiting that time aloud now, eight months later, she felt herself choking up. She cleared her throat again, struggling for control.

But Dr. Hunter looked into her eyes, unabashed. "What a tragedy. It must have been very difficult for you."

"It *is* very difficult."

"Yes." He shook his head sympathetically, his eyes never wavering from hers. "I'm sorry. I know a little of what it must be like for you. I suppose you've heard that I'm also widowed."

Daria nodded. Dorothy Janek had told her that Dr. Hunter was a widower. She sometimes forgot that she didn't have the corner on grief. "Yes, I know that. I'm sorry. Of course you know what it's like."

"It's been several years—since the accident." He put his head down, then looked back at her with a sad smile. "It gets easier. Don't give up."

"Thank you." It was an awkward moment, yet something tender passed between them.

The phone rang and broke the tension. But later Daria decided that it had felt good to talk about Nate, to affirm his life to someone who hadn't known him. She felt as though she had taken an important step forward, and she was grateful to Dr. Hunter for making it easy—and for causing her to remember that she wasn't the only one who had ever lost a love. She tried to picture the kind of woman to whom Colson Hunter might have been married. No doubt she had been a sweet, patient woman.

The day continued at a frantic pace, and it was midafternoon before Carla finally had a free moment to show Daria how to run some of the office machines and further explain the duties that would be expected of her.

"These need to be sent out on the fifteenth of each month." Carla was reviewing the billing procedure when Dr. Hunter stepped into the office. "And you can work on updating the medical files whenever you have time."

"That is, when you're not assisting in surgery," Dr. Hunter chimed in, winking.

Jennifer Daly came in after school and took over where Carla had left off, teaching Daria how to use the printer and explaining the filing system. In spite of the boyfriend who came to pick her up at closing time, it was apparent that Jennifer had a serious crush on her boss. She flirted demurely with Dr. Hunter and, when he wasn't looking, gazed at him through dreamy, hooded eyes. But she was a sweet, personable girl and a good teacher, and Daria enjoyed the time spent with her.

By the time Daria picked Natalie up from her parents' and fixed herself a sandwich for supper, she was utterly exhausted. She wasn't sure how she was going to do this all over again tomorrow, but she was strangely excited at the prospect.

The following morning found her under Carla Eldridge's tutelage again. Carla, the clinic's lone technician, was a single mom herself, with two boys in elementary school. With her petite figure and her pixie haircut, she would have been perfectly typecast as Peter Pan.

"So your first day wasn't exactly a breeze?" she said to Daria as the two grabbed a quick lunch behind the reception counter.

"Not exactly—I don't mind telling you I was scared to death."

"Cole said you did a great job."

"Cole?"

"Dr. Hunter."

"Oh. Is everybody on a first-name basis here?"

Carla nodded and mumbled over a bite of celery, "Oh, don't even try to call Cole 'Dr. Hunter.' He might let you get by with just plain 'Doc,' but he asks everybody to call him Cole. I'm surprised he hasn't corrected you yet."

"Well, I haven't exactly *called* him anything yet." She smiled. "So…he said I did all right?" she asked coyly, fishing.

"He said you were great."

"Well, surgery sure wasn't in the job description. But to tell you the truth, I did kind of enjoy it, at least when it was all over and I saw that everything came out okay."

"I don't want to scare you off, but you'll be surprised what a receptionist-slash-bookkeeper does around here."

Carla's wry grin worried Daria a little, but she chose not to ask her coworker to elaborate. She supposed she'd find out soon enough.

"You haven't met Travis yet, have you?"

Daria shook her head.

"You'll like him, too. He's very patient, like Cole. They never try to pull the 'we're the big bad doctors and you're the lowly peons who work for us' routine. Even though we *are* the lowly peons who work for them." She laughed.

While Daria finished her sandwich, Carla filled her in on the office politics and small-town gossip. Their lunch was interrupted several times by customers calling to make appointments or coming in to buy supplies.

The day flew by and then the week, and before she knew it, she had settled into a comfortable routine. Because her off-duty hours were taken up with caring for her daughter, the clinic was really Daria's only social life. She and Natalie attended worship services with her parents each Sunday morning, but she'd felt so uncomfortable the one time she'd attended the singles' class there that she'd never gone back. Yet she couldn't have chosen better friends than her coworkers at the clinic. She genuinely liked everyone she worked with, and there was an easy rapport among the staff. Day by day, she was feeling more confident in performing her duties—even when they sometimes included very un-receptionist-like tasks.

Natalie was growing like a Kansas sunflower and seemed to be thriving under her Grandmother Haydon's care. Daria's parents had adjusted to her and Natalie moving out. She even thought they were secretly happy to have their house back to themselves. Her mother helped her sew new curtains for the apartment—no small feat since there were fourteen large windows to cover. Together they also sewed slipcovers and plump pillows for an old sofa her brother had found at a garage sale. Between her family's generosity, flea-market finds, and several castoffs on loan from the Janeks' attic, she managed to assemble a cozy mishmash of furniture and dishes. In no time, the apartment had become a warm haven to come home to each evening.

The ache of loneliness was abating and, though Nate still seemed very real to her in many ways, Bristol was slowly becoming her world, her reality. There were times when it seemed as though her life with Nathan in Colombia had been nothing more than a pleasant dream.

s Daria pulled into the driveway one sweltering June evening after an especially exhausting day at the clinic, she spotted her elderly landlady waving from the garden behind the house.

"Yoo-hoo! Daria!"

Daria cut the engine and removed the keys from the Toyota her father had found for her at auction. Going around to the passenger door, she released Natalie's seat belt. Then scooping the little girl up from the car seat with one arm, she returned Dorothy Janek's greeting.

"Can you smile for Dorothy?" she asked Natalie. "Come on, give us a smile." Smiling was a recently learned social skill, but one that she didn't always perform on demand.

Dorothy brushed the garden dirt from her hands and bustled over to the car. "Why don't you have supper with us tonight, sweetheart? I've made a pot roast that is more than Kirk and I can ever eat ourselves."

Supper had become a frequent invitation and one that Daria usually accepted with deep gratitude and more than a little guilt.

"Are you sure, Dorothy? You just fed us Monday night—"

"Oh, nonsense," Dorothy argued. "You work all day. You don't want to come home and cook every night too, now do you?"

"You've got a point there," Daria told her, smiling. "Thank you, Dorothy. We'd love to. Wouldn't we, Natalie?"

The little girl rewarded them with a wide, toothless grin and a vigorous kicking of her pudgy feet.

Dorothy laughed and clapped her hands together, delighted.

With Kirk and Dorothy Janek living right below her, Daria felt completely safe in her little apartment. The elderly couple had adopted her and Natalie as family, and they were as proud of Natalie's latest accomplishment as any grandparents would be.

"Come down around six and help me set the table," Dorothy's voice brought her out of her reverie.

Daria gave her landlady a quick hug, sandwiching Natalie between them. "Thanks. I don't know what I'd do without you."

"Ah, you'd get along just fine and dandy! But since you do have me, you may as well take advantage of me," the old woman added with a twinkle in her eye.

⌒

"Natalie Joan!"

Daria's shriek brought her daughter to an abrupt halt at the edge of the stairway. Barely six months old, Natalie had recently mastered an odd belly-flop crawl that had her scooting across the apartment's hardwood floors like a little lizard.

Natalie glanced up at her mother, oblivious to the cause of Daria's alarm. Daria dropped the basket of clean laundry she'd been carrying on her hip and flew across the room to rescue her daughter from certain disaster.

Natalie immediately screamed to be let down, furious that her progress had been impeded. The child had a stubborn streak in her that Daria was certain had not come from her side of the family.

She swung Natalie in the air, trying to distract her with her favorite acrobatics routine. "Nattie, Nattie," she cooed. "What is Mommy going to do with you? Now we're just going to have to make a Wal-Mart run and get a gate for those stairs."

Fortunately the staircase balusters were spaced closely enough to prevent her from slipping between them. A simple safety gate would keep her from tumbling down for now, but how she would cope when Natalie started walking—or heaven forbid, climbing—she couldn't imagine.

She sighed. "Come on, sweetie, let's go get your shoes on."

Hearing her favorite word, Natalie bounced happily on Daria's hip. To her, *shoes* meant they were going someplace.

Twenty minutes later, Daria was trying to keep Natalie's hands inside the shopping cart with one hand and attempting to inspect the selection of child safety gates with the other. She stooped to pick up Natalie's stuffed bunny for the third time.

"Natalie Camfield, this is not a fun game for Mommy!" Natalie gave her a toothless grin and tossed the bunny over the side of the cart again.

Daria checked her watch. How would she ever get everything done? She had three loads of laundry waiting for her at the apartment, this gate had to be installed immediately if she didn't want to spend the rest of the week carrying her daughter on her hip, and on top of all that she was behind on the billing at the clinic. She'd brought the laptop home from the office, hoping to get caught up tonight. The chances of that happening were looking slimmer by the minute.

As much as she adored being a mother, sometimes she longed to be relieved of the financial burden of being the sole provider, to be able to stay home with Natalie and have time to run a simple errand without throwing her whole schedule out of whack.

Deciding on a safety gate, she balanced the unwieldy box across the top of her cart. She grabbed a package of disposable diapers and a few other items as she passed the baby department. By the time she got to the parking lot, packages were sliding everywhere. She made sure Natalie was safely strapped into the cart, then, using one hand to steady the bulky box that held the gate, she turned to open the trunk of her car.

She had just managed to get the key into the lock when she felt the box sliding out from under her hand. She whirled around to grab it and came face to face with Cole Hunter.

He held the box securely in his arms, smiling his boyish smile. "Sorry. I didn't mean to scare you, but you looked like you could use some help."

Her heart started to beat faster. "Oh, hi Cole. I could use an extra pair of hands."

He balanced the box between one knee and an elbow and wiggled ten fingers at her. "One extra pair of hands, at your service."

She smiled. "Thank you."

Cole helped her load the packages in the trunk, then went around to the front of the cart where Natalie sat in one of her rare patient moods, enthralled by the activity in the busy parking lot.

"Hey, little girl! What's up?" Cole cooed, leaning down to the baby's eye level. "Is your mommy teaching you how to shop till you drop? Can't get started on that skill soon enough, you know." He glanced up at Daria with a wicked grin.

"Very funny," she said. But she couldn't help smiling back.

"Here," he said, inspecting the straps that secured Natalie's infant carrier to the shopping cart. "If you'll show me how this works, I'll help you get her in the car."

While Natalie jabbered loudly at them, they worked together to get her buckled into the backseat of Daria's car.

"All fingers safely out of the way?" he asked before he carefully shut the door. "I like your new car, by the way," he told Daria.

"Thanks. It's not really new, but hey, it's mine. Well, mine and the bank's."

"Yeah, don't I know how that goes."

After a moment of awkward silence, he said, "I'd better let you go."

"Thanks so much for coming to my rescue, Cole. You didn't have to do that."

"My pleasure." His mock salute turned into a full-fledged wave. "See you tomorrow."

"You too. Thanks again."

As she backed out of the parking space, she caught a glimpse of herself in the rearview mirror and was embarrassed to realize that she was blushing. *Good grief. I'm worse than Jennifer.* She replayed her encounter with Cole over and over in her mind as she drove home.

He was so sweet with Natalie. And so thoughtful to help her with her packages. The sound of his deep, gentle voice warmed her heart at the same time it made her ache for a voice she would never hear again.

Sitting in the quiet of her living room that evening with crickets chirping outside the open windows, Natalie tucked safely in bed in her nursery, and the laptop open in front of her, Daria's life in Colombia with Nate seemed an eternity ago.

That first July anniversary passed quietly. The date of Nathan's death. Sometimes it frightened her that she was forgetting him. She could still close her eyes and conjure up his face, but sometimes she knew that all she was seeing was the photograph on her nightstand. The camera had locked onto a tanned, blond man sporting a handsome cleft in his chin and flashing white, even teeth. But she knew that the camera had failed to capture the split second before the shutter released, when Nate had hammed a goofy grin, or the moment after, when his expression had turned serious, trying to explain to her how to set the shutter speed. She felt panicked sometimes that she couldn't see his face clearly in those daily memories anymore.

And his voice. She was losing that, too. She knew there were some cassette recordings Nate had made in Colombia, documenting his findings about the dialect and customs—things he'd wished Evangeline Magrit, the former missionary to the Timoné, had left for him and Daria. The tapes were stored away with the few belongings she had brought back from Colombia, but she hadn't had the courage to get them out and play them yet.

She desperately needed to do that. Because sometimes, to her dismay, when she sat in the quiet of evening and her thoughts turned to Nathan, the voice that came from his lips in her memories was the voice of another man.

She didn't want to admit it, even to herself, but she knew to whom that voice belonged. Colson Hunter. And knowing made her feel like the worst kind of traitor.

Eight

aria hung up her jacket and went around behind the reception desk to put her purse under the counter. "Good morning," she sang cheerfully to the staff gathered around the coffeepot.

Carla Eldridge and Travis Carruthers returned her greeting, but their response was subdued. Colson Hunter, who stood reading a chart in the doorway between the office and the reception room, ignored them all and started back toward his office. Daria noticed that he had a stubble of beard and heavy circles under his eyes. She wondered if he'd been called out for an emergency during the night. Maybe they'd had to euthanize a family pet. That always tended to sober this usually lively group.

She looked at Carla for an explanation, but couldn't catch the technician's eye. Halfway down the hall, Cole's footsteps halted, and he barked to no one in particular, "I've got to have that vaccine this morning! Has anyone called the supplier? Daria, what time is Avery Knudsen bringing those hogs in?"

She scanned the columns in the appointment book that lay open in front of her. "I have him down for ten," she told him.

"Well, that's not going to happen," he growled. "Call him and reschedule." The back door slammed behind him before she could ask him what time he wanted to reschedule for.

Bewildered, Daria watched out the window as Cole trudged toward the barn, head down, shoulders hunched inside the upturned collar of his jacket. Without comment, Travis followed him out.

Daria turned to Carla, incredulous. "What is wrong with him?" She'd never seen her boss so surly. If it hadn't been so unlike Cole, she would have been angry at his rudeness.

Carla came to stand beside Daria at the window that overlooked the barn and corral. "You've got me," she shrugged, obviously as puzzled as Daria. "He's been going at it since he walked in the door this morning. He doesn't usually get that way unless he's been up all night. But he didn't mention getting called out. And the surgery room is just like I left it yesterday."

Daria shook her head. "Boy, that's a side of him I haven't seen before. I don't think I like it very much."

"Me neither," Carla agreed. "Maybe today is one of those anniversary dates or something."

"What do you mean?"

"You know, maybe it's Bridgette's birthday, or it would have been their anniversary or something like that."

A small knot started in Daria's stomach. "Bridgette? His wife?"

Carla nodded.

"Did you know her?"

Carla shook her head. "She died before Cole came here. Back in Colorado, I think."

"He doesn't talk about it much, does he?"

"No. It must be tough for him. I would guess he probably still has some ghosts to deal with," Carla said thoughtfully as she walked out to the coffeepot and poured herself a cup.

Daria tagged behind her. "What do you mean, 'ghosts'?"

"Well, I have a feeling he blames himself for her death," Carla said over her shoulder.

"Why?" Daria was taken aback by the comment. "Was he driving?"

Carla stopped stirring her coffee and turned to look at Daria as though she'd gone mad. "Driving? What are you talking about?"

Daria shook her head in confusion. "The accident."

"What accident?"

"Cole...said she was killed in an accident. I-I guess I just assumed it was a car accident. It wasn't?"

"You seriously don't know what happened?"

Daria shook her head, wanting desperately to hear the story but feeling guilty that they were talking about Cole behind his back.

Carla walked back to the office and set her stained, chipped coffee mug on the counter in front of them. She cocked her head and studied Daria as if deciding whether she should continue. Finally she shrugged. "It wasn't that kind of car accident."

Daria waited, her brows knit together.

"Cole found her in their car. Carbon monoxide poisoning. They ruled it accidental," Carla said, emphasizing the word *accidental.* "It might just be rumors," she added quickly, "but I've heard she was pretty messed up in the head. It's hard for me to picture Cole with someone like that. But, like I said, this all happened before he came to Bristol."

Daria was stunned. Cole had mentioned his wife's death that first day she'd come to work, but he'd never hinted that it was anything like this. He'd never talked about it since. Now she understood why. No wonder he always seemed so uncomfortable whenever she inched too close to the subject of widowhood.

"But why?" she finally managed to ask Carla. "How could that have happened? Do they really think she, you know…"

Carla shrugged. "Offed herself? Who knows. Like I said, it happened before he moved here. I can't believe you haven't heard this before, Daria."

Daria put her hands to her face. "Oh, Carla, that's just awful! But"—she wrinkled her brow—"I'm sure Cole told me that she was killed in an accident."

"Maybe it's just easier to tell it that way. You have to admit the real story is pretty shocking."

"I can't believe my parents never mentioned it."

"People in town really like Cole, and everyone knows he doesn't like to talk about her."

Daria thought for a moment. "It's more likely that they didn't want to upset *me*. My parents have been pretty protective since I came back from Colombia."

Carla gave her a sympathetic smile and leaned back against the counter. "They probably figure you have enough problems of your own."

Daria opened her mouth to reply, but the slam of the back door stopped her. She heard the distinctive thud of Cole's work boots on the tile floor and felt her face grow warm. She hoped he hadn't overheard them talking about him.

"Carla?" he hollered before he reached the front office.

Carla threw Daria a here-goes-nothing look, jumped up, and met him in the doorway. "Yes?"

He appeared to be in a better mood, and his manner was polite and almost friendly now. "Can you help me out in the barn for a minute? I think I'm looking at a C-section with this mare, and Travis is up to his ears doing blood tests on Meyerses' hogs."

"Sure. Let me get my coat on."

Carla grabbed her lab coat and headed down the hall toward the back door. Cole started to follow, then turned abruptly. Hanging on the doorjamb, he swung around and stuck his head through the doorway of the office, looking contrite and boyish in spite of his day-old beard.

"Good morning, Daria." He gave her a quick smile and greeted her as though he was seeing her for the first time that morning. Just as quickly he was out the back door again.

"Good morning, Cole." She waved to the empty air, baffled by his sudden change of mood.

She sighed heavily, dumped the dregs of her coffee in the sink, and headed back to the kennel to feed the dogs. The conversation she'd just had with Carla gnawed at her. The things Carla had related about the way Bridgette Hunter died didn't fit with the information Cole had given her. She didn't like the way that fact made her feel.

When Daria went to pick Natalie up at her parents' house that night, she asked her mother about the rumor concerning Bridgette Hunter.

"Yes, I did hear that she committed suicide. But you know how people in this town talk, Daria."

"Mom! Why didn't you tell me?"

Margo perched on a high barstool at the kitchen counter where Daria was seated. She gave her daughter a searching look. "Why, would it have mattered, Daria?"

"I don't know. It's just— I don't know, it just seems strange. Cole is so easygoing and happy all the time. It just doesn't fit." She picked up a pencil from the counter and started scribbling on a scrap of paper, retracing her lines over and over until the lead shone against the white page. "You don't know why, do you?"

"Why she killed herself?"

Daria nodded, not looking up.

"Honey, who knows why anyone ever does something like that?" A strange timbre had come into her voice, the tone that told her that her mother understood more than Daria had intended to reveal. "This really has you upset, doesn't it?" Margo said.

"I-I was just surprised, that's all."

"Look at me, Daria."

Daria lifted her head, trying not to look as sheepish as she felt.

"You really like Dr. Hunter, don't you?"

She nodded. "I do, Mom. Is that awful?"

"Honey, why would that be awful?"

"Well, for starters he's my boss. And—" The lump in her throat took her by surprise, and she felt tears well behind her eyelids. "Mom, Nate's only been gone a little more than a year. I-I feel like such a traitor."

Margo put a warm hand over Daria's. "Daria Lynn Haydon, what are you talking about?"

Daria smiled, but her mother seemed not to notice her subconscious use of Daria's maiden name. "You have just been through the worst year of your life. It's about time you had some happiness. I'm thrilled for you!"

"Mom, Mom, slow down. It's not like he's asked me out or anything."

The wind went out of her mother's sails a bit. "I think it would be wonderful if he did. And I don't want to hear any more of this guilt business. You know Nate would have wanted you to go on with your life. Especially for Nattie's sake."

Daria pushed the pencil and paper away and scooted her stool back from the counter. She cleared her throat. "Speaking of Nattie, if I don't wake her up now, I'll never get her down tonight."

She looked at her mother, who seemed deep in thought. Reaching out, she put a hand on Margo's arm. "Thanks, Mom. For everything."

That night she lay in bed and thought about what her mother had said, that it would be wonderful if Cole asked her out. Part of her was relieved to have talked to her mother. A larger part of her was sorry that she'd revealed her secret desire to anyone. Especially since the revelation of his dark past left her unsure of who Colson Hunter really was.

Nine

Cole drove his pickup along the dusty country road toward home.

He'd congratulated himself too quickly for shaking off the depression that the anniversary of Bridgette's death always seemed to bring. A busy day at the clinic, with a harrowing but successful emergency surgery thrown in for good measure, had helped keep his mind off the dark memories that begged his attention. But now, with the day behind him, the dusk taking over the sky, and an empty house to go home to, the blanket of oppression settled over him again.

This was the fifth bleak anniversary he'd marked, and though none had been as bad as the first, he wondered how many years would pass before he could look at this day as any other. Ten years? Fifteen? What was the magic number?

He wondered if Daria Camfield celebrated such an anniversary. *Celebrate* was hardly the right word. But no, he remembered her telling him that she didn't even know for sure when her husband had died. It was a blessing, Cole thought, not to have that number etched on her brain to torment her every time it turned up on the calendar. If she was anything like him, she wouldn't want to be reminded, wouldn't want to talk about the heartache of losing the love of her life. But then her husband's death didn't carry with it the stigma that Bridgette's death always would.

He had come to Kansas, in part, to get away from the entire population of Sierra Lake, Colorado, who thought they knew all the ugly facts of his wife's death. But it seemed Kansas wasn't far enough, and the story had followed him here. He seethed with anger when he thought of the transformation the tale had undergone.

Sometimes he thought it would be better just to come out and tell every detail himself so they would get it right. Trouble was, he wasn't sure he knew the truth himself. Besides, he wouldn't give the gossips the satisfaction. Let them talk. They would anyway. It was part of the "charm" of living in a small town. He'd lived in the big city, and he had to admit that most days the real charm of small-town life— the deep friendships, the community loyalty, the active compassion for the guy who was down-and-out—far outweighed the inconvenience of a little gossip here or a false rumor there.

He sensed that Daria would understand his feelings if only he could get up the courage to share them with her. He knew that a large part of his attraction to her was the shared tragedy in their lives. Not that she wasn't the kind of woman who would have caught his eye anyway. She was sweet and kind—and beautiful, in a natural, down-to-earth way that appealed to him deeply. But it was something more profound that drew him to her, that caused her face to appear in a significant percentage of his dreams, both waking and sleeping. Common sense told him that mutual sorrow was not a good thing on which to base a relationship. Still, that hadn't stopped him from asking her out a thousand times in his mind.

He wasn't sure what was stopping him in real life. He had certainly done his share of flirting with her. *Flirting.* Man, he hated that word. He had never liked all the games men seemed to have to play with women. That was one of the things that had attracted him to Bridgette. He hadn't had to flirt with her to get her attention. She was beautiful, and she didn't know it. She was studious and intelligent. They'd first met at Colorado State in a philosophy class.

He'd liked her seriousness at first. He had just become a Christian, and, though she was a believer herself, she was loath to accept anything on faith alone. She constantly challenged him to defend his faith against her questions, and he was never one to turn down a challenge. Those solve-the-problems-of-the-world conversations had set the tone for their growing relationship. He hadn't seen the dark side of her analytical nature until after they married. The depressions would come on her like a Seattle fog. He didn't know who she was during those grey times, and she couldn't tell him why they came or what he could do to make it better. They'd mostly just waited it out. And eventually time would lift the shroud of fog, and he'd have his wife back. Until that awful summer. Then time had lost its magic and by the time he realized it, it was too late.

Driving down the rutted back roads, buried in memories, Cole had become oblivious to his surroundings. Suddenly his driveway loomed in front of him, and he almost overshot the entrance to the shady lane that led to his old farmhouse.

He pulled up beside the mailbox and, as was his evening ritual, stopped for a moment and peered over the steering wheel, surveying the sixteen acres that spread out before him. Even on this day it heartened him to turn down this lane and realize that he owned a piece of God's green earth. A small piece, to be sure, and one that could use some TLC, but in a couple years it would be his, free and clear, and that never failed to fill him with a quiet joy.

Sighing, he rolled down the window and opened the mailbox. Extracting a bundle of junk mail and a depressing number of bills, he slammed the metal door shut and roared on up the long drive toward the house, leaving a cloud of dust in his wake.

Rufus, his yellow Labrador retriever, met him and ran alongside the pickup for the last hundred yards, barking an enthusiastic greeting.

Cole parked the truck in the unattached garage and walked to the back door, talking to the panting dog as he went, "Hey, boy. How's it goin'? Did you miss me? Huh, did you miss me, boy? How's my big ol' Rufus-boy?" He would have been embarrassed for anyone to overhear the affection in his voice for this dumb, slobbering dog. But Rufus was one of the best friends he had. Nobody listened like Rufus.

On the back porch, Cole pried off his work boots and unlocked the door, letting the dog in ahead of him.

He threw the mail on the kitchen table and went back to the mud room to fill Rufus's dish from the forty-pound bag of dog food that sat in the corner by the back door. The dog nudged his jean-clad leg, panting impatiently, almost knocking him over.

"Hey, fella, give me a break. I'm working on it."

Rufus moved in for the feast, crunching noisily.

Cole went back into the kitchen and searched the refrigerator until he found some bologna that hadn't yet turned green.

He built a thick sandwich and threw it on a plate along with some corn chips. Then, pouring a glass of cold milk, he took his supper into the living room. The large L-shaped room wouldn't win any interior design awards, but it was warm and inviting—and surprisingly clean for a house sans a woman, if he did say so himself.

Cole had remodeled the entire downstairs over the two years he'd lived there, and he was proud of the place. He had painted the walls throughout the house in various shades of tan and beige. The effect was masculine, and rather rustic, though anything but dark and dreary since the new oak-framed windows were left bare to take advantage of the sweeping prairie vistas that surrounded the farmhouse.

He switched on the television and plopped into the leather recliner positioned in front of it. He watched too much TV, especially since there was seldom anything on worth watching. But he liked the noise. It kept him company. And tonight he could use some company.

Ten

*E*veryone else had gone home for the day, the animals had been fed and watered, and the office was unusually quiet for a change. Daria had made arrangements for her mother to keep Natalie for an extra hour so she could catch up on printing out some billing statements.

The last appointment for the day had been cancelled, and she locked the office doors and hung the *closed* sign in the front window. Cole and Travis were in the barn repairing some cattle chutes, but Daria didn't expect either of them back in the office.

She flipped the switch to warm up the printer and began to sort through a list of addresses on her computer screen. She had just sent the first batch of files to the printer when a knock on the back door made her jump.

She got up and cautiously peered down the hallway that led to the rear entryway. Through the small high window in the door, she could see Cole waiting for her to let him in. She hurried down the hallway and turned the lock.

"Sorry, Cole, I thought you were done in here for the night."

"No problem," he said, tipping his Stetson at her but not taking it off. He stamped his feet and rubbed his hands to warm them. "Is the coffeepot still on?"

"It is, but it'll be stale as all get out. I can make another pot…" She stood in front of him, twisting the rings on her fingers, hoping her offer hadn't sounded too—well, too *obvious*.

But he just grinned. "Would you mind? I'd make it myself, but I'd like to be able to actually drink the stuff."

Daria laughed, but she was surprised that he hadn't waved off her offer. She had fully expected him to tell her that he'd just stop by Nellie's Café on the way home, as she knew he often did. "I'll make it," she told him. "It won't take but a minute."

She went to the counter in the reception room, emptied the old coffee grounds into the wastebasket, rinsed out the pot, and filled it with fresh, cold water from the tap.

Cole leaned on a high stool behind the reception counter. She felt his eyes on her.

"What are you doing here so late?" he wondered.

"Oh, I wanted to finish up this billing," she said over her shoulder. "Natalie had a doctor's appointment yesterday, so I took the afternoon off and that put me a little behind."

"I wondered where you were. Is she sick?"

"Natalie? Oh, no. They put off her vaccinations at her last checkup because she was still getting over a bad cold, so she got a whole bunch of shots yesterday. She was none too happy about that."

"I bet. Poor baby."

She wondered why Cole was hanging around the office, yet she felt excited—and nervous—at the chance to be alone with him. As comfortable as they'd become working together, she didn't think she was imagining the undercurrent between them. With the coffee brewing, she went back to her desk and tried to work on the billing. It wasn't easy with him perched up there looking over her shoulder.

Cole got up and wandered through the office, and Daria watched him surreptitiously as he straightened papers on desks and read notices on the bulletin board that she knew he'd posted himself. Something was bothering him.

After a few uncomfortable minutes, he cleared his throat. "I'm glad I caught you here, Daria. I wanted to talk to you about something. A couple of things, actually."

She sent one more file to the printer and wheeled her chair to face him, unable to hide her curiosity.

An odd smile crossed his lips, and she could have sworn that he was feeling nervous too, though it was a side of him she'd certainly never seen before.

She waited.

He laughed softly, lifted his hat, and ran a hand through his hair before putting the Stetson back on his head. "To tell you the truth, I can't decide whether to give you a promotion or fire you."

She swallowed hard and felt her face grow warm. She could hear the printer churning out an invoice behind them, and a dying fluorescent light flickered overhead. "Have I done something wrong, Cole?"

He waved the thought away. "No, no. In fact, Travis and I have been talking. We need to hire another technician. Since he came on staff full time, we've been able to take on more work, and well, shoot, you've practically been doing a tech's job anyway. We wanted to officially offer the position to you before we advertise it…if you're interested?"

She'd known they were understaffed, but she honestly hadn't seen this coming. "Oh, Cole, I'd like that. I'd like it a lot. But, well, wouldn't I have to go to school or something?"

"Not unless you want to get licensed. You could always do that down the road, but for now it would just be on-the-job training. Like I said, you're practically doing a tech's job now. The only drawback I can see is that you wouldn't be able to take your work home as much with this position." He waited for her to respond.

"I think I could handle it now that Natalie's a little older. But—" She swallowed hard. "What did you mean about firing me?"

He grinned and cleared his throat, dipped his head slightly. "I've always made it a point not to date my employees," he started, then grinned sheepishly. Daria's heart started to race. "Actually, I've made it a point not to date *anyone*. But, to tell you the truth, Daria, you've got me rethinking both those points. Would you…" He lifted his Stetson, raked a hand through his hair again, then put the hat back on, suddenly looking like a little boy.

"Are you trying to ask me out, Dr. Hunter?"

"That was the general idea—"

"Yes," she cut him off, then put a hand to her mouth. "I can't believe I just said that."

He burst out laughing—that unfettered, cut-loose laugh of his that she'd grown to love so much.

"We're talking about the date, right?" he said warily, teasing. "Not the promotion?"

"Well both, actually. Yes to both." She grinned impishly. "But the enthusiasm was for the date."

He laughed again, this time with relief, she thought.

"Saturday night? Wichita? Dinner…maybe a movie?"

"Sounds good to me," she said. "What time?"

He stood and took his hat off, revealing an appealingly matted head of sand-colored "hat" hair. He pointed the Stetson at her and winked. "I'll pick you up at seven sharp."

Whistling a lively rendition of "Yankee Doodle," he headed down the hall, then came back abruptly. "Oh," he said, sticking his head back around the corner into the office, "and don't worry about a baby-sitter. I've got it covered."

He was out the door, his truck kicking up gravel in the back drive before Daria could say a word.

Ten minutes later as she gathered up her things to head home, she realized that a fresh pot of coffee—full and untouched—sat on the counter emitting a delicious aroma into the room.

Friday morning, as Daria rushed around trying to get ready for work, the phone rang. She picked it up to find Vera Camfield on the other end.

"Hello, Vera," she said, trying to put more enthusiasm in her voice than she felt.

"Hello, Daria. How are you?"

"Oh, we're fine. But I'm kind of having one of those mornings," she hinted. "Seems like everything that can go wrong has."

"Well, I won't keep you then, but I just wanted to see what you were doing this weekend."

Daria's mind raced, trying to come up with an excuse to the request she knew was coming. She had kept in close contact with Nate's parents, especially right after Natalie's birth, but as the months passed and her job tied her down more, the visits had become fewer and further between. Lately, however, Vera Camfield had become more and more demanding, calling nearly every weekend either wanting her to bring Natalie to Kansas City, or inviting herself and Jack to Bristol. It seemed to Daria that they expected her to reserve every spare moment for them.

"Let me tell you what we were thinking," Vera said, not waiting for Daria's reply. "We thought we'd come and take you and Natalie out to dinner tonight, and then we'd like to bring Natalie back here to spend the weekend. Will that work?"

"To Kansas City? By herself?"

"Well, of course you're always welcome here, Daria. But now that Natalie is weaned, we just thought you might enjoy some time to yourself."

It was a generous offer. So why did she feel resentful? She loved Nathan's parents, and naturally she wanted Natalie to be close to them. She knew that the little girl was as much an antidote to their grief as to her own. Still, Daria wasn't prepared for what they were asking. The thought of having Natalie three hours away in a strange house, a strange city, unsettled her. She'd never been away from her daughter for more than a few hours. The little girl always seemed to enjoy her time with the Camfields, and there was no question that they adored her. It wasn't that she didn't trust them. It was just that Nattie was still a baby. And, at almost eight months, she still wasn't sleeping through the night. What if she woke up in a strange bed and became scared? What if she got sick? Would they know what to do?

Vera's voice broke in on her thoughts. "We'll bring her back Sunday, right after lunch. It shouldn't be past four-thirty, five at the very latest. Please, Daria. We need to spend time with her. She's just growing up so fast. Every time we see her, she's changed so much."

How could she tell them no now, when she was going to be out with Cole all evening Saturday anyway? She couldn't very well tell them that she was denying them their granddaughter so Natalie could spend the time with a baby-sitter. Guilt washed over her, and she debated whether she dared tell Vera that she had a date. This was turning out to be so much more complicated than she'd anticipated.

Cole had arranged for Jennifer Daly to baby-sit Natalie at Daria's apartment. "That way, she can be all tucked in for the night when you get home, and I'll drop Jennifer off on my way home," he told her.

Daria was grateful for his plan. Besides the fact that it was thoughtful of him, it would also eliminate that awkward moment when she would wonder whether she should invite him in for coffee afterward.

Vera's insistent pleas tugged her back to the present. "Please, Daria. If you don't have any plans, I don't really see how you can deny us the privilege of spending some time with our only connection to Nathan." Though Daria knew the emotion that came over the line now was genuine, it rankled her that Vera would use it against her this way. She was glad Vera couldn't see her clenched jaw, couldn't hear her slap her fist on the desk in frustration.

"All right, Vera," she said finally. "I-I guess we can try it this once. But Natalie still wakes up at least once in the night, you know."

Vera's tears turned almost instantly to glee. "Oh, don't worry about that. I haven't been sleeping well myself. We'll just be up together. We'll get along fine."

Vera insisted that she and Jack take Daria and Natalie out to supper as soon as Daria got off work that evening. "We'll probably just leave from the restaurant though," Vera informed her, "so could you have her things packed and ready to go?"

"Okay, sure," she answered, feeling somehow defeated.

Daria hung up and rubbed her forehead with the tips of her fingers, wondering what she had done. She was angry with herself, for she knew her main reason for giving in to Vera was because she did not want to have to confess that she had a date Saturday night.

She dialed the clinic to let Carla know she was running late, then she called Jennifer to tell her that she was off the hook for Saturday night.

She wove her hair into a quick braid, hurriedly brushed her teeth, grabbed Natalie from her playpen, and bundled her up. By the time she arrived at the clinic her head was throbbing.

Dinner with the Camfields that evening went fine until Jack asked innocently, "So, what are you going to do with a weekend all to yourself, Daria?"

She drained an invisible swig from her empty water glass, desperately trying to think of an answer. She decided on honesty but took her time getting there.

"Well, I don't mind telling you I'm looking forward to sleeping a whole night without this little squirt waking me up." She threw a smile Natalie's way. "Then tomorrow morning I'll clean the apartment and then"—she put the empty glass to her lips again—"well, tomorrow evening I'm invited to dinner with Dr. Hunter."

Vera Camfield's coffee cup halted midway to her lips. She set the cup firmly back in its saucer and looked Daria in the eye. "Your boss? Oh, is it a company party or something?"

"No, we're just going out to dinner, maybe a movie."

"Well," Vera said, as if the word summed up the whole situation.

"So you have a date, Daria?" Jack Camfield sounded rather pleased.

"I guess you could call it that. We're friends."

"I guess it's a good thing we'll have Natalie then," Vera said accusingly.

"I have several good baby-sitters, Vera," she said, knowing it came out sounding defensive. "In fact, Cole had already arranged for a sitter. I had to call and cancel."

"Cole?"

"Yes, Dr. Hunter."

"That's awfully…friendly, isn't it?"

"Vera, *everyone* at work calls him Cole. We've always been on a first-name basis." She bit her tongue, struggling to remain civil.

"Vera," Jack Camfield shot his wife a look of warning, then cleared his throat and pushed his chair back from the table. "Well, I suppose we'd better get on the road if we're going to have this little pumpkin in bed before midnight." He pinched Natalie's cheek, and she rewarded him with a wide smile.

When the Camfields pulled out of the parking lot, Daria felt a catch in her throat as she watched her daughter gaze out the window from her car seat. Natalie looked so small and vulnerable in the back of the huge sedan.

Daria drove back to an empty apartment, her apprehension mounting by the minute at the thought of a date with her boss.

She turned on the television for company, but on this night of all nights, Nate kept intruding into her thoughts. She wandered around the apartment and finally went into the bathroom to wash her face and get ready for bed. As she reached to put the toothpaste away in the medicine cabinet, the simple gold band on her finger caught the light and glimmered, reflected in the mirror. She had continued to wear her wedding ring—because of Natalie and the Camfields, she supposed. She wondered what Cole thought about it—or if he'd even noticed. Before she could talk herself out of it, she slipped the ring off and dropped it into a small porcelain dish that sat on the counter in the tiny bathroom. The slim band rolled around the edge and nestled itself among the earrings and other trinkets.

She finally crawled into bed with a book. It was barely nine o'clock. She reached for the lamp, and there was Nate staring at her from the picture frame on her nightstand.

She threw the covers back and jumped out of bed, heading down the hallway, not sure why. She paced through the house with her thoughts in a miserable jumble.

What was she doing, going on a date with another man, when she still said good night to a picture of her husband every night? When she still wore his wedding ring on her finger? What had she been thinking when she said yes to Cole?

She picked up the phone and started to dial the office number.

Was she losing her mind? Cole wouldn't be at the clinic at nine o'clock on a Friday night. Then she'd just call him at home. She quickly pulled Bristol's thin phone book from the drawer and flipped to the *H*s. Then just as quickly she slapped the book shut and put the phone back on the hook.

You're just nervous, she told herself. *Cole is just a friend. It's not like he asked you to marry him.*

She paced some more and finally wrapped herself in an afghan, flopped down on the sofa, and grabbed the remote. She clicked on the television, muted the volume, and sat there in the dark, the flickering lights from the screen casting eerie shadows over the room, reflecting the chaotic direction of her thoughts.

It was 1:00 A.M. before she finally switched off the set and crawled into bed, and another hour before she slipped into a fitful sleep.

~

Daria paced nervously through the rooms of her apartment, stopping to push the curtains aside and watch for Cole's car each time she passed the window that overlooked the driveway.

She'd been having second thoughts all day long. There was no doubt that she was attracted to Colson Hunter, no doubt that a part of her wanted to get to know him better. But maybe it was too soon. And he was her boss. She needed her job. What if things went sour between her and Cole? She couldn't afford to lose this job, especially now that she'd been promoted with a nice raise.

She went into the bathroom and fussed with her hair for the dozenth time, tucking it behind her ear, untucking it, then tucking it again. She picked a nonexistent piece of lint from her sweater and flipped off the lights over the mirror, then went back to the living room to resume her pacing.

The sound of tires on gravel made her heart lurch. "Okay," she whispered under her breath, "this is it."

She grabbed her purse and a light jacket and ran down the stairs to the door. She opened it a moment before the doorbell chimed in the hallway above her.

"That was quick!" Colson Hunter stood in front of her, smiling, hand still raised to the doorbell button. He wore neatly pressed chinos, a cream-colored rag wool sweater, and a light jacket. She caught an appealing whiff of cologne.

She ran her moist palms over her corduroys and attempted a smile. "Hi."

"Hi. How are you?"

"Good, how about you?"

"Great. All ready?"

"Sure." *What in the world would they talk about all night?*

He led her to the passenger door, opened it for her, and waited as she got in. She thought he looked like a teenager as he ran around to the driver's side door and hopped behind the wheel. She suddenly felt fifty years old.

"Do you like Mexican food?"

"Sure."

"There's a new place on the west side I thought we'd try. I haven't eaten there, but I've heard it's pretty good."

"Okay."

He drove to the end of Bristol's main street and down a blacktop road toward the interstate. They rode in silence for several minutes.

"Did you get Natalie off to Kansas City all right?" he ventured.

"Yes. Vera called this morning, and I guess they got along pretty well last night. She only woke up once."

"That's good."

Silence.

She twisted her watch on her wrist and stared straight ahead.

"So…" Cole said. "It sure has been windy lately."

"It sure has," she replied.

Silence.

"The Regier dog seems to be recovering well from the C-section."

"Yes."

"For a while there, I was afraid we'd lose her and the pups both."

"Me, too."

"I think we can probably send her home Monday."

"Okay." Daria looked at her watch again.

Finally, as they neared Wichita he turned to face her, his voice insistent, forcing her to look at him. "Daria?"

She turned toward him.

"Are you all right?"

She was afraid she would cry, but she couldn't answer his probing gaze with anything other than complete honesty. She put a hand to her forehead. "No, Cole. I'm really not all right. We need to talk."

hat's wrong?" His voice was rough, and his brow was etched with worry, but his eyes held a deep tenderness.

"It's just…I…" She bit her lip then put her head in her hands with a sigh of exasperation. "Oh, Cole, I don't know if we should be doing this. I'm not sure I…" She raked her hands through her hair in defeat.

"Do you want me to take you home?" He sounded hurt.

"No, but…can we talk?"

"Uh, I don't know if you noticed," he said wryly, "but I've been *trying* to talk since I rang your doorbell."

She looked at him, saw the glint in his eyes, and couldn't help but grin. The tension eased a little. "I'm sorry. I'm having a thousand reservations about this whole thing."

"This date?"

She nodded.

"Like…?"

"Can I be really honest, Cole?"

"Please."

"Okay. Like should I be dating my boss? I can't afford to lose my job, Cole. What if you hate me after tonight?" She gathered steam, her words tumbling out as she listed her concerns. "Like, has it been long enough since…Nate died? Have I given myself enough time to get over him, and if not, is it fair to you? And what about Natalie? If things were to get serious between us, I don't know how you feel about—"

"Okay, I get the picture," he interrupted. "How about this? Number one"—he held up a finger—"I promise not to fire you for at least a couple of months."

She smiled, but she was frustrated that he seemed to be taking this so lightly. He seemed to read her mind, for he shifted in his seat, and his next words were dead serious.

"Daria, I do understand about Nate. If you'll remember, I've been down that road. I promise we'll take it nice and slow until you're sure you're ready for more than just friendship. And as for Natalie, she's an angel. She doesn't scare me one bit."

Daria smiled, feeling at ease again.

As they drove into Wichita, the sun was sinking behind the city's spare skyline. Cole took the Kellogg exit and turned west, maneuvering through the evening's heavy traffic.

He turned to her suddenly. "How 'bout we do a drive-through instead of the restaurant? I've got an idea."

She nodded, curious, but grateful. She was in no mood to be in public.

He exited on West Street and drove past its mecca of fast-food joints. "Want to stick with Mexican?"

"Um, sure, it sounds good."

He changed lanes and turned into the Taco Bell drive-through, ordered for both of them, then headed north again after they got their food.

He drove to Zoo Boulevard, past the huge empty parking lot of the Sedgwick County Zoo, and turned into another nearby lot that served a nature park and walking paths.

He cut the engine, unbuckled his seat belt, and turned toward her to dole out tacos and chips. He stripped the paper off a straw and stuck it in her Diet Coke, handing it to her. Then he took her left hand in his and bowed his head.

"Lord, please bless this food, bless our time together, and please, Lord, please, help Daria think of *something* to say so I don't have to carry the conversation this entire evening." He peered up at her through half-closed eyes, a mischievous, lopsided grin on his lips.

Head still bowed, she let go of his hand and whopped him

on the arm, grinning madly. "Amen," she said, feeling better by the minute.

"Okay, let's hear it," he said, peeling the wrapper off a taco. "Talk to me."

She took a sip of her drink. "It's a lot of things, Cole."

She looked at him, unsure of how much she should open up.

But he persisted now. "Daria, let's just get it all out in the open. Let's be totally honest with each other and not hold anything back. Then we'll know where we both stand and where to go from there. Okay?"

He sat waiting for her, his taco dripping salsa down his hand.

She handed him a napkin, took another sip of her Coke, and tried to think of how to begin.

"Okay," she said finally. "I think mostly it's… I'm just not sure I'm ready to date again. Every time I'm with you, Cole, I can't help but think about Nathan. It's not that I have you mixed up with him or anything, but the same things that attracted me to Nate are the things I like so much about you."

He raised one eyebrow coyly. "I like the sound of this. So what exactly is it that you like so much about me?"

"You know, for someone who wanted to put everything out on the table, you sure aren't making this easy for me." But now she was glad for a little levity, glad that they were finding the easy manner they'd always had with each other.

"I'm sorry," he said. "You're right. Go on. We'll get back to why you like me in due time."

She smiled, acknowledging his wisecrack, but plunged ahead, wanting to get this over with. "I know Nate is gone, Cole. I'm not in denial. I know he would have wanted me to go on with my life and not grieve too long for him. But it doesn't seem quite right—or fair to you—when I feel as though he's"—she struggled to find the word—"*present*. It's almost like he's here now, between us."

"I don't believe in ghosts, Daria."

"No, of course not. I don't mean it that way. But the feelings I have for you are so close to what I had with Nate. You tease me or say something funny, and I can't help but think of the way Nate used to do that."

He looked at her intently, seeming to drink in every word. "Is that so terrible, Daria? Your husband was a huge part of your life—your other half. From what you've told me, you had a great marriage. It's only natural that you think of him often. That doesn't threaten me. I don't think it should."

She cocked her head. "Really? Do you…do you think of your wife that way?"

He dipped his head, ran a hand through his hair. "It's a little different for me, Daria. For one thing, it's been a lot longer. Bridgette's been gone for over five years now. Time has a way of erasing a lot of things. And we had some rough times at the end. I don't know how much you know…"

She waited, not wanting to tell him what she'd heard, wanting his own version of the story.

"You probably heard that Bridgette killed herself." It wasn't a question.

"Carla said they didn't know for sure."

"Well, that's true enough. *I* don't even know, Daria. I still don't know for sure. I came home from work one night, and the car was running in the garage. She was sitting inside, the radio on. I honestly don't know if it was an accident or not. I-I'd like to think that she was listening to a talk show or something that caught her interest, and she just didn't realize what was happening. It was cold outside, so maybe she let the car run to keep warm."

His voice was trembling now, and his face took on a troubled expression. "I'd like to think that's what happened," he went on. "But Bridgette was very intelligent. And she was always so cautious about things like that. If she caught a whiff of gas from the furnace, she wouldn't rest until the gas company came out and assured her it was safe. Things like that. I think deep down I know that her death wasn't an accident." He said it as though it might be the first time he'd admitted it aloud.

"Oh, Cole," she said.

He looked up, and his eyes found hers. "It's okay, Daria. Like I said, time has healed a lot of the wounds. It was horrible at first. I wasn't sure I was going to survive. People seemed to blame me for not doing enough, for not seeing her pain—rumors can be so vicious. And I *felt* guilty. Bridgette was dealing with—well, a lot of junk." He swallowed hard. "I should have known something was wrong. But you do what you have to do to get through. You, of all people, know how that is. But God has been with me through it all. I have peace about it. I really do, even if the very worst *is* true."

She nodded.

"Daria—" He started to say something else, then shook his head as if to ward off the gloom his words had brought over them. Then he started gathering up the empty wrappers from their dinner. "Do you want to walk for a while?" he asked finally.

"Sure," she said, relieved for the change of subject.

He got out and locked his door behind him, tossed the Taco Bell bags into a nearby trash bin, and went around to open her door. They buttoned up their jackets as they walked across a small playground to catch the trail. They'd only gone a couple hundred yards when the trail disappeared under a canopy of trees. The air grew instantly cooler and smelled of pine needles and damp earth. The path circled a shimmering lake, and Daria felt as though she'd walked out of the plains of Kansas onto a Colorado mountain trail.

"I didn't even know this was here," she told him, enchanted by the surprise.

"Best kept secret."

It was dusk and, except for a few teenagers on in-line skates and a bicyclist now and then, they had the trail to themselves. As they walked companionably, Daria watched Cole. She had admired him for the way he had overcome the deep sorrow of his past, for the strength of his faith. He could have wallowed in the tragedy life handed him, but instead he had allowed God to heal him. And tonight she was seeing yet another side of him and she liked what she saw—the way he'd been so thoughtful of her feelings, so sensitive to her struggles. So selfless. *So much like Nate.*

She must have cringed at the thought because Cole turned to her, concern in his eyes.

"Something wrong?"

She shook her head, not wanting to tell him.

"What is it?"

She hesitated. "Just Nate intruding again."

He stopped walking and reached out to touch her arm. "Daria, don't let it bother you. I'm not offended. Is it so terrible that I remind you of someone you loved deeply?"

The glint in his eyes assuaged her guilt.

"Speaking of which," he ventured with a sly grin, "you were going to tell me all the things you liked about me."

"You just don't give up, do you?"

"Huh-uh, no way."

They followed the trail until it circled back to the car. The sun was sinking fast, the trees above reflecting a blaze of gold and orange. The air had turned chilly, and Daria shivered involuntarily.

"You cold?"

"A little," she admitted.

"Here." He took off the light jacket he wore and put it around her shoulders.

"Do you still want to see a movie?"

"Would you mind if we don't?"

"Not at all. Are you ready to go home?"

She nodded, grateful that he understood. "But I've really enjoyed the evening, Cole."

"Me, too—once we got going."

They were quiet as they drove out of the city, each lost in their separate thoughts. But when they were on the interstate again, they talked all the way back to Bristol. They discussed movies they wanted to see, books they'd read. They talked about Natalie and about the veterinary clinic. And when Cole walked her to the door, she grinned up at him, and her heart filled with emotion. She'd been so lonely. But tonight she'd made a wonderful friend. He was a good man. And she knew they'd turned a corner.

She wasn't head over heels in love with him—yet. But she knew there would be time for them to work out all the questions they had, to explore the possibilities for their relationship.

She went into a silent house and stood over Natalie's empty crib, and her heart ached with longing to hold her baby. She climbed into bed and stared at Nathan's photograph for a long time, engulfed by memories. Then she thought of Cole, and she knew that underneath the ache, her heart was mending, thread by fragile thread.

Twelve

The following Monday morning Cole hung around the clinic's reception room drinking coffee and chatting with the staff, all the while keeping one eye on the parking lot, watching for Daria to drive up. He had thought about her all weekend, and he was anxious to see her again, to gauge how things would be between them now. He wanted to let her know that he thought she was something special and that he had no intention of letting her get away if he could possibly help it.

When he saw her little Toyota pull into the clinic's parking lot, he cut Carla off midsentence with a quick wave and headed outside.

"Good morning," he said, opening Daria's car door for her.

"Good morning yourself," she said, climbing from the front seat. Her smile assured him that her memories of the weekend were as fond as his own.

"Did you get your little girl back?"

"All in one piece. I hate to admit it, but I think she had a great time."

"That's good. Don't be sorry."

"Oh, I'm really not. I sure missed her though."

"And that's good too."

"Where are you headed?"

"Nowhere. I just wanted to see you."

She smiled as though she wasn't sure how to take him.

"I've been thinking a lot about all the things we talked about the other night. I'm glad we could be honest."

"I am too, Cole. I really am."

He cringed inwardly. He hadn't told her anything that wasn't true, but as he realized how much he still had not revealed to her, he felt a twinge of guilt. But there would be time for that. He would make sure of it. "Want to talk some more?"

"Are you asking me out *again?*" she teased, a hint of exasperation in her voice.

He laughed. "And what if I were?"

"Well," she sighed. "I suppose I'd be forced to go out with you, seeing as you're my boss and all."

"Yeah," he played along, "if you want to keep your job, you'd probably better not turn me down. Besides, you never did get all the way through that list of 'Things I Like About Colson Hunter.'"

She slugged him halfheartedly with her purse. "You're not even funny." But her eyes belied her words. How he loved those blue, blue eyes.

He fended off her playful attack and resisted the urge to take her arm possessively and escort her into the office in full view of Carla, Travis, and Doris Kline. Instead he opened the door for her and followed her in. He knew by the way they all suddenly went into a flurry of activity that his staff had been riveted to the front window. He wasn't going to play games with any of them. They might as well get used to it, because if he had his way, he and Daria Camfield were going to be much more than friends.

He was amused to see that Daria was blushing as she hurried past the other employees to hang up her jacket and put her purse away. Cole ignored Carla's raised eyebrows and the conspiratorial smile on Travis's face and walked straight back to his office.

But later that morning, when he and Travis were alone in the barn, he couldn't ignore the young vet's comment. "Daria looked like the proverbial merry widow this morning," he said with a smirk. "That must have been some date this weekend, you old devil you. Guess you made her one happy woman, huh?"

Cole threw down the feed bucket he'd just emptied and glared at his partner.

Travis drew back and threw up his hands in mock surrender, his face a mask of astonishment. "Hey, man, I'm kidding. Don't get all bent out of—"

"Carruthers, don't even talk that way! Don't make this into something cheap."

"Cole, I'm sorry. I didn't mean anything by it. I was only…"

Travis's words trailed off feebly, and Cole sensed true contrition in his voice. Realizing that he'd overreacted, he put a hand on his partner's arm. "I'm sorry, Trav. I was out of line. Just please don't turn this into something crude. You know me better than that."

Travis brushed him off, turning his back on Cole and walking to the other end of the barn. He was obviously taken aback by Cole's harsh reaction. As he walked away, he muttered another apology, leaving Cole feeling guilty for being overly defensive.

The two men finished their work in the barn without speaking.

That afternoon they were forced to work together during an emergency surgery on a Saint Bernard pup that had been mangled in a freak encounter with a grain auger.

As they worked over the sedated puppy, Cole attempted to smooth things over.

"You want to ride with me to the high-school game Friday night?" he asked Travis.

"It's over in Clayton this week, right?"

Cole nodded.

"Yeah, sure. Man, it's shaping up to be quite a season, isn't it? They hammered Hillsdale last week."

"I'll say! If I was a betting man, I'd wager we're headed to the state play-offs."

"You really think so?" Travis sounded doubtful.

"Well, it's probably too soon to tell, but we've got the best defense in the league by a long shot."

They bandied around play-off match-up possibilities and traded stories about their own prowess on the high-school gridiron. By the time they'd finished the surgery, things seemed to be back to normal between them.

But after Travis had gone out to check the large animals in the barn, and Cole was left alone to put the final sutures in the dog's cuts and gashes, his thoughts turned again to his confrontation with Travis that morning. Why had he lashed out at his friend like that?

Inexplicably Bridgette's face flashed before him, and he vividly remembered when he was just beginning to fall in love with her. Bridgette had been the first woman he had ever loved. The only woman. Talking with Daria about her had brought those memories to the foreground. He realized that the speed with which Daria's and his friendship had turned into something obviously romantic echoed his and Bridgette's whirlwind courtship. He struggled futilely against the comparisons.

It hurt him to call his marriage a mistake, but he had begun to face the truth that it probably was. Bridgette had too many emotional issues in her life to be able to give much to a marriage relationship. Looking back he could see that the signs had been there all along if he hadn't been so blinded by love. Now he asked himself, was he blind to Daria's wounds? She'd certainly suffered her share. And yet, Daria seemed whole and at peace. Was he missing something? Something told him to slow down, to back off a bit. And yet his longing for love and companionship, his loneliness, and their undeniable chemistry all shouted, "Grab her before someone else does!"

He wished he'd had the courage to tell Daria the whole story surrounding Bridgette's death. It would have been a relief to get it off his chest, to relieve the burden of the secrets he carried. But it seemed too much to put on her—on any woman—on a first date. He didn't want to scare her off, and yet already they had become so close that he felt like an impostor for not having told her everything.

Until Daria Camfield, he hadn't found anyone he felt was worth the risk of laying himself open. There was something exhilarating and hopeful about finally having met a woman to whom he was willing to reveal his true self. But if things were going to become serious between them, as he so desperately desired, she needed to know the whole truth—before she'd invested her love in him and it was too late to turn back.

He went through the rest of the day like a robot, performing his duties perfunctorily and keeping to himself as much as he could. But as he drove home that evening, his thoughts ran wild. He knew that, though he must give Daria a chance to know the real Colson Hunter before he could expect her to love him, for him it was too late. He had already fallen in love with her. And the joy of that realization caused him to quash the whispered voice of caution he had thought to heed just hours ago.

Thirteen

*O*h, Cole, look at this. Isn't it gorgeous?" Daria knelt on the floor of the gift shop in front of a tiny ceramic village. The window of each little house and store in the display glowed from within, casting yellow patches of light on the sparkling "snow" that surrounded the village. The shop was draped in greenery and lights, smelled of cinnamon and apple cider, and the effect was magical.

But the magic for Cole Hunter was simply in being with this woman. Every morning during the past weeks, as their friendship had deepened and romance had blossomed between them, he awakened feeling as though his life had been returned to him. Daria had brought something back into existence that he hadn't dared to hope for. With a full heart, he put his hands on her shoulders and bent to look at the tiny cottage she was cooing over.

"It's very pretty, Daria."

She looked up at him and then gave the display one last longing glance. "Oh, why does everything have to be so expensive?" she moaned.

He drew his lips into a pout, imitating her. "Poor baby." But then he pulled her up beside him and placed a hand tenderly on her cheek. "Well, save your pennies."

She rolled her eyes. "That's what I like about you, Dr. Hunter. You're so sympathetic."

"Well, correct me if I'm wrong, but I was almost positive that I was told we were shopping for *Natalie* Camfield today."

"Hey, a girl can look, can't she?" She smiled.

She moved on to the next aisle and he followed, her obedient puppy. Their little shopping trip had turned into more of an ordeal than he'd bargained for. When she'd asked him to go with her to Wichita to pick out Natalie's gift, he'd pictured a quick run to Toys "R" Us, maybe a nice lunch together, and back to Bristol by three. It was two o'clock now, and not only had they not found the elusive "perfect" gift for Natalie, neither had they had lunch. And they had yet to set foot in the toy store.

His stomach motivating him now, he spotted a shelf overflowing with stuffed animals. "What about these?" he asked her, steering her to the display. "She really likes teddy bears."

Daria inspected the stuffed animals, but he could tell she was only being polite. Soon they were on to the next store and, by the time she finally found a little dollhouse for Natalie, he was beyond famished. Fortunately one didn't have to wait long for a table at four o'clock on a Saturday afternoon.

They sat across from each other in a cozy booth at the Olive Garden. She sipped her coffee and picked at her salad. He wolfed down his salad and half a basket of breadsticks before he said, "What's taking them so long to bring my lasagna?"

Daria laughed at him. "I guess I should have warned you that shopping with me is *not* a lunch-at-noon kind of event."

"So I've discovered," he mumbled over a hot bite of bread.

Finally, the empty spot in his belly satisfied, he leaned back in his chair, watching her. She looked especially beautiful today, her face flushed with excitement and the effects of the biting autumn air. He didn't deserve to be so blessed. Immediately a shadow fell over his thoughts, reminding him that he had promised himself that today he would tell Daria the rest of the story about Bridgette. He'd waited too long already.

As though she'd read his thoughts, she looked up. "What are you looking so serious about, Cole. Is everything all right?"

"No. Nothing's wrong. I'm just sitting here thinking how beautiful you are." That part, at least, was true. "But—"

"Oh, Cole," she interrupted, blushing at his compliment. "You're so sweet. Thank you." Her pleased smile faded. "I'm sorry. I interrupted you. What were you going to say?"

"Just that there's something I'd like to talk to you about."

She leaned forward and put her elbows on the table, her eyes intent on him. "Okay. I'm listening."

"No, not here," he said, looking around the restaurant.

A troubled look crossed her face, and he felt terrible for having caused it. "It's nothing to worry about, Daria," he told her. "I just don't want to talk here."

Now curiosity sparked in her eyes, and she looked eager, as though she assumed that what he had to tell her was a surprise for her. He was completely blowing this.

Their server appeared at the table with his food just then. He didn't think he'd ever been so happy to be interrupted by a waiter.

Later, when they got out to the parking lot, a fine sleet was coming down. At the first stop sign on Rock Road, he realized that the roads were quickly becoming slick. It was already beginning to get dark, and Cole maneuvered the car carefully through traffic, worrying about what condition the interstate would be in by the time they got there. The highway wasn't quite as bad as he'd feared, but they drove in silence, Daria clutching the dashboard and nervously watching traffic for him.

When they arrived back in Bristol, she had either forgotten that he'd wanted to talk to her or had decided that this was not a good time to try to have a conversation. Either way, he felt he'd been given a reprieve. Once again he pushed the nagging thoughts to the back of his mind. At least he'd tried to talk with her. Maybe his timing hadn't been the best anyway. Why spoil a day of Christmas shopping with something that was ancient history. Yes, Daria needed to know everything about him, but it didn't have to be today.

Daria sifted through the stack of mail strewn across the tiny table in the dining area. She heaved some catalogs and fliers toward the trash can in the kitchen. Preoccupied and smiling to herself, she tried to sort the bills and other mail that needed to be dealt with further.

Oh, she thought, *I've got to remember to call Mom and see if she can baby-sit tomorrow night.* She and Cole had tickets to the symphony, and Jennifer had backed out at the last minute. Her coworker and favorite baby-sitter had started dating the star of the basketball team, and the Bearcats had made it to the playoffs of a big tournament. Daria could hardly blame Jennifer for canceling. *Love should win out over a baby-sitting job any day.*

Her smile grew as she thought of Cole. Their friendship had blossomed into something so deep and so precious that it almost scared her.

She pushed the mail aside and let out a sigh of satisfaction as she picked up the phone to call her mother.

"Mom? Hi, it's me."

She could hear the familiar whir of her mom's old electric mixer in the background. "Hi, honey. What's up?"

"I hate to ask on such short notice, but would you be able to keep Natalie tomorrow night? Cole got tickets to the symphony, and Jennifer backed out on me because of the tournament."

The mixer died, and Daria could hear Margo licking batter from her fingers. "Hang on, let me ask your dad if he has any plans."

She went back to sorting the last bit of mail while waiting for her mom. A small white envelope caught her attention. The address had obviously been typed on an ancient manual typewriter, but there was no return address. It was postmarked Kansas City, Missouri.

Daria slipped her thumb under the flap just as her mother came back on the line.

"Dad says he can't think of anything he'd rather do than keep his favorite little girl. Why don't you just bring her things and she can stay the night."

"Great," Daria said, distracted now by the letter. "Thanks a million, Mom. I'll call you later about the time."

She hung up and pulled a thin sheet of onionskin paper from the envelope. As she unfolded it, her eyes hurried to the wobbly signature at the bottom of the neatly typed page: Evangeline Magrit, the missionary who had first worked with the Timoné in Colombia. Daria hadn't heard from the elderly woman—hadn't even known for sure if she was still living—since her sympathy card had arrived shortly after Nathan's memorial service.

She pushed her chair away from the table and skimmed the letter once. Then, pacing the length of the apartment, she read it again slowly.

Dear Daria,

I've thought of you so often in these last months. My heart has gone out to you in your sorrow. I read in the Gospel Outreach newsletter that your little one arrived safely, and I was quite grateful to hear it. I suppose she is close to walking by now. They grow so quickly. Which brings me to the reason I am compelled to write to you.

Though my physical heart will not allow it, my spiritual heart is still in Colombia with my beloved Timoné. You and your husband were an answer to a lifetime of prayer on my part and on the part of dear Anazu and his little family of believers. I've struggled, as I'm sure you must have as well, to understand why our Lord allowed such a tragedy as befell Nathan. And yet I am so grateful that you were spared. You have been heavily on my mind in these last weeks because I know that you, too, felt the strong call of the Lord to live and minister among my dear people.

I pray the Lord has not revoked his calling on your life, and I know that your daughter must be old

*enough now that she would adapt well to the changes
of life in Colombia.*

    *I write to encourage you, and to tell you that I
am praying that you might return to your ministry as
quickly as you are able. I have been in contact with
the mission board and, while they are as eager as I am
to have you back in Timoné, they "don't make a practice of soliciting" missionaries, as Dr. Bennett so suc-
cinctly put it in his correspondence with me. I,
however, have no such policy, so I am boldly soliciting
you, trusting that you are seeking the Lord as to his
perfect will.*

    *I would cherish hearing from you, and I shall
keep you ever in my prayers.*

    *Please know that the board assures me there are still
funds available for your support, and I would consider it
a blessing to finance your return trip personally.*

In his service,
Evangeline Magrit

Daria slumped into the chair and let the letter fall to the floor.
She felt herself being wrenched back in time. As though it were yesterday, she remembered the sultry heat of an August night almost a
decade ago, sitting with Nate outside his cabin at the youth camp
where they had spent the summer as counselors. She had been a
sophomore in college, still unsure what she wanted to do with her
life. Nate was about to graduate from college and enter medical
school.

The elderly missionary woman from Gospel Outreach had spoken at the rally that last night of camp. Evangeline Magrit was old
and ill, and she believed that God was telling her that her time with
the Timoné people of South America had come to an end. Though
she spoke with passion, the teenage audience had been inattentive

and boisterous, and Daria and Nate had spent most of the evening intercepting spit wads and confiscating firecrackers. And yet, somehow, the woman's message pierced through the commotion straight to Nate's heart.

Afterward Daria and Nate sat in the dark on the steps outside his cabin. Nate sat with his elbows on his knees, his head down, his thoughts seeming a million miles away.

"Hey, you. What are you so deep in thought about?" she asked, putting a hand on his knee.

He ran his hands through his hair, not looking at her. "I'm just thinking about what that missionary woman said tonight. It really hit home with me."

A twinge of foreboding rose in her. "What do you mean?"

He turned to look at her, his gaze capturing hers. "I think maybe God is calling me to the mission field."

"Well, sure, Nate. The medical field is a mission field—"

"No, I'm serious, Daria. I think maybe I'm supposed to go to Colombia."

"South America?" She was incredulous. "You mean go there to live? Like a full-time missionary?"

"Yes. I can't explain it except that I've never felt God's presence so strongly. It's almost as if he spoke out loud."

Daria felt threatened. Was he talking about breaking up? Leaving her for some tribe in South America? This was not the dream they'd shared for their future, the dream they'd been talking about since they realized they were in love.

But then Nate told her, with awe in his voice, "I think God wants us to take Mrs. Magrit's place, Daria."

Us. Of course. The call was for her as well. God had simply chosen to send his message through Nate. By the time she closed her eyes in her own cabin that night, she had begun to embrace the idea that she and Nathan were to take Evangeline Magrit's place among a people who had rejected the gospel message for more than forty years. And as the days passed, her enthusiasm had grown in proportion to Nate's. Through the four long years that Daria worked as a teacher's aide and waitressed evenings to help him finish medical school, they kept their eyes steadily on their call.

Mrs. Magrit had told them about Anazu and his growing faith. The challenge of winning the rest of Anazu's village to Christ seemed to energize Nate. Though Daria had sometimes secretly wished that he could be happy with a ministry closer to home, his enthusiasm had not flagged through all the years of medical school. And by the time they finally stepped on Colombian soil for the first time, Daria had grown to believe with her husband that they would be the ones to lead Timoné to the truth. God had blessed their obedience, and when they were in Colombia, Daria felt that she was where she belonged.

Yet since Nathan's death, she had not given a thought to returning. She stared down at the letter lying on the floor at her feet, and a mantle of guilt settled over her.

She supposed that subconsciously she had used Natalie as an excuse. And surely a tiny baby *was* a valid reason not to go to the mission field. *And I am a widow,* she thought defensively. But immediately she remembered that Mrs. Magrit had gone to Colombia as a newly widowed young woman. Her mind scrambled to come up with a better reason. Conviction nipped at her.

She realized that she had not only abandoned her calling to go to Timoné, but she had also abandoned any responsibility whatsoever for the people God had given her to care for. She had not written to the board of Gospel Outreach to find out whether they had been able to place another missionary there. She hadn't even sent them the tape recordings Nate had made while they were in Colombia. For months, she had scarcely uttered a prayer on behalf of the people of Timoné. The children, little Tommi and Jirelle and the others, were a distant memory, like much-loved characters in a book she had read long ago.

Her life had been taken up with the mundane duties of a single, working mother—and, yes, with the exciting discovery that she was falling in love with Colson Hunter.

But surely, after all she'd been through, she had a right to some happiness. She'd sacrificed a husband to the mission field. Her baby was without a father because of the mission field. Surely she had paid her dues and done her duty where missions were concerned. Besides, Gospel Outreach had *sent* her home.

The heat of anger rising to her face, Daria picked the letter up off the floor and slapped it onto the table, trembling. She read the letter a third time and calmed down a bit as she realized that Evangeline Magrit had in no way meant to cause Daria to feel guilty. It was merely the passionate plea of a woman who had a heart for bringing the lost to Christ, who couldn't imagine anyone not desiring to return to their calling as quickly as possible. No doubt Mrs. Magrit's physical limitations to do what her heart ached to do must have frustrated her grievously.

Why did the gentle words of this saint gnaw at her so? Trouble her to the core of her being? Deep down she knew there could be only one reason. And she did not want to think about it. She wanted to throw the letter away and pretend she had never received it. She wanted to enjoy her baby, to sit beside a handsome man at the symphony tomorrow night and hold his hand and fall hopelessly in love with him.

She fell to her knees as though stricken. "O God," she whispered. "Surely you don't expect me to go back! To take Natalie to Colombia, away from Mom and Dad, away from Nate's parents. She's their only consolation."

She stopped herself. She knew she was making excuses. A verse from the Psalms played through her mind, and Daria caught her breath as the words seared her conscience: *But you desire honesty from the heart, so you can teach me to be wise in my inmost being.*

"O God, I believe you called me to Timoné before, but, Lord, I don't feel that calling now. Before, I-I went because I was Nathan's wife, and because he was going to Colombia, I knew that's where you wanted me, too. Give me wisdom, Lord. I don't want to be out of your will. But you…can't be telling me that I'm to go back there. You *can't*. Please, please, God. Don't ask that of me. I don't think I can do that. Please, God."

She was sobbing now, confused and tangled up in a rope of guilt, not knowing if it was deserved or self-inflicted. She remained on her knees for long minutes, silent before God, yet not really wanting an answer, terrified of what it might be.

Finally Natalie's persistent cries brought her from her knees. She went into the nursery where Natalie was waking from an overlong nap. She picked her daughter up and took her to the rocking chair beside the crib.

Still drowsy and perhaps sensing her mother's melancholy, the little girl lay her head against Daria's breast. They rocked back and forth, the only sound in the room the soft *slurp, slurp* of Natalie's thumb in her mouth.

Daria sought to put Evangeline Magrit's letter from her troubled mind. For now she drew comfort from the warm, compliant body of Nathan's child heavy against her own.

That night, Daria's dreams carried her down the Rio Guaviare, deep into the Colombian rain forest. She saw Anazu and his family, grief-stricken because Nate had left them. They stood at the door of the hut she and Nate had shared—the hut that she had given them, that they might have a place to worship. Anazu and Paita and Casmé cried and wailed, holding on to each other for comfort. But Daria ran toward them. "No!" She shouted to them in perfect Timoné, "Stop crying. Nathan is all right. Look he's right here. See, here he comes." They followed her eyes across the stream where Nate came jogging down the trail from which he'd disappeared.

But in her dream Daria never knew whether Anazu and his

family saw Nate or not. She was too busy running toward him her-self, her arms outstretched, her heart light as air.

She awakened to the sound of her own soft laughter and a feel-ing of happiness and well-being. The vision was so vivid that for a minute she thought it was real. Then she came fully awake and knew that it had only been a dream.

She wept as though she had lost Nate all over again.

Fourteen

*T*he Christmas music that filled the Century II concert hall in downtown Wichita was rapturous, but Daria was distracted, oblivious to its beauty. Her mind was overwhelmed with nagging questions provoked by the missionary's letter.

As Cole helped her with her coat in the lobby afterward, he squeezed her shoulders. "Hey, you. What's wrong?" he whispered.

She looked over her shoulder and gave him a wan smile. "I'm sorry. I haven't been very good company tonight."

He wrapped an arm around her and steered her toward the parking lot. "Are you all right?" There was no beating around the bush with him anymore. He read her too well.

"I'll tell you on the way home, okay?"

He gave her a questioning look, but didn't press her. When they reached his car, he opened the door for her before getting into his seat. Turning the key in the ignition, he eased into the line of vehicles leaving the concert. They were on the interstate a few minutes later. Cole reached across the console and stroked her hair. "So, what's troubling this pretty head?"

She ignored his compliment and plunged in. "Yesterday I got a letter from the missionary woman who inspired Nate and me to go to Colombia. I've been feeling guilty ever since."

"Guilty?" In the dark of the car she sensed more than saw his quizzical expression.

"She assumes that I'm going back to Colombia, Cole."

"Going back? You mean as a full-time missionary?"

She nodded.

"I don't understand. What would make her think that?"

123

"That's what's eating at me, Cole. She thinks that because I felt a calling from God to go there, that I should be making plans to return. She even offered to pay for my travel expenses."

"Wow," he breathed. He was silent for a minute. "*Have* you thought of going back, Daria?" he asked finally.

"Oh, Cole, not once! It's been the furthest thing from my mind. At least it was until I got that stupid letter. Now I wonder if, well, what if I *am* supposed to go back? Do you think when God calls you to something he means it to be forever?"

"No, of course not." Cole's response was immediate and adamant. "God obviously called you to be a mother to Natalie, but someday she'll grow up and your calling to motherhood will be over. Right now I feel called to be a veterinarian, but I suppose someday I'll retire and then God may have another calling for me."

She thought about what he'd said. "But why would God call Nate and me there to take an old woman's place? Why would he begin to work in the lives of the villagers…and then just abandon them?"

Cole thought for a long time. "I don't know, Daria. I'm not sure that's something we will ever understand. Why would God take a good man like Nate? Someone who was serving him so completely? He didn't even get to *be* a doctor for as many years as he studied to become one. None of it makes sense. But surely God would make it clear to you if he expected you to go back, the same way he made it clear to you when he called you there the first time."

"Oh, Cole, I'm terrified. What if that's what this letter is all about? What if he *is* calling me back? What if Mrs. Magrit's letter is God's way of telling me that I'm supposed to go back?"

"But Daria, what about Natalie? You have a responsibility to her now. What kind of life would she have in Colombia?"

"I wish I could use her as an excuse, Cole. But there are many people who take their entire families to the mission field. The truth is, kids adjust better than their parents do most of the time. You only have to leaf through a couple of Gospel Outreach's magazines to know that."

"But Colombia is a dangerous place, Daria! Even more so now with all the cocaine cartels and the guerrilla violence that's going on. It just doesn't seem"—he struggled for the right word—"*responsible* to take an innocent child into one of the most dangerous places on the planet."

She wanted to tell him that if God had truly called her to minister in Colombia, then God was big enough to protect her while she was there. But Nate's death seemed to nullify that argument.

"I wrestled with this all night, Cole. I've even wondered if I was ever truly called to Colombia in the first place. Maybe I was riding on the coattails of Nate's calling all along. I-I loved him so much. Maybe I didn't want to risk losing him, so I just followed him blindly." Her shoulders slumped in frustration. "I don't know. Maybe I'm just looking for an out. Oh, I'm so mixed up. What should I do?"

"I'll be praying for you, Daria. I don't know what else to tell you." His voice sounded strained, and she felt bad that she'd dumped all her confusion on him.

They rode the rest of the way home in silence, but when they pulled into her drive, he cut the engine and turned to her. She thought she read something akin to fear on his face. Cole stared at her across the darkness, and she heard the apprehension in his voice as he asked her, "Daria, are you seriously thinking about going back?"

She put her head in her hands. "Oh, Cole, I don't know. I'm just seriously confused."

"Don't you think Nate's death changed your calling, changed everything?"

Her voice rose an octave. "I don't know. I don't even pretend to understand why he had to die. But don't you see? I didn't die. What if God still wants me to be the one to bring the gospel to the Timoné? What if all this time…" She threw her hands up, exasperated that she couldn't express her own thoughts clearly.

He waited for her to finish, and when she didn't he pounded the palms of his hands on the steering wheel and blurted, "Daria, I can't even imagine that God would ask that of you, that he would ask you to go back, take a baby, by yourself, to such a dangerous place, a place where the greatest tragedy of your life took place. Your life is hard enough *here,* trying to raise a daughter on your own, trying to make a living. Surely there is someone else who can go to Colombia and—" He cut his own sentence off and held up a hand. "I'm sorry. I am not a very good person for you to be seeking advice from."

"No, Cole," she protested. "I trust your advice. That's why I told you about this. I know you see things from a spiritual perspective. I know you understand what it means to have God's calling on your life. I'm *asking* for your advice."

"No, Daria, no." He started shaking his head, agony on his face. "You're wrong. I can't possibly give you advice on this issue. How could I be unbiased when the woman I want to marry is talking about leaving and taking the little girl—the child I love like my own—away with her."

She sat, transfixed at his words. "Oh, Cole," she breathed. It was the first time he had spoken of marriage.

"I'm sorry, Daria. That wasn't fair." His voice shook with emotion.

"Is it true?" she breathed.

"That I want to marry you? That I love Natalie like my own? That since I met you, I've never been so happy in my life? Oh, Daria, of course it's true! Are you blind? I love you. I think I've loved you since the first day I saw you."

"Oh, Cole…"

Then they were in each other's arms, she crying, he apologizing over and over. "I'm sorry, Daria. I'm so sorry. I'm only making this harder for you. My timing stinks. This isn't how I wanted to ask you."

"No." She leaned back and looked at him, put a hand on his cheek. "Maybe you're giving me my answer."

He brushed a tear from her face with his thumb. "I don't want to hurry you, Daria. I admire the way you've been so careful not to rush into anything. I want you to have all the time you need—to get over Nate, to make sure about your calling, whatever it is. To make sure...you feel the same way about me."

He took her face in his hands and kissed her, his touch both tender and urgent.

She responded with more tears. "Oh, Cole, I'm so happy. I didn't know—"

"Hey, shh, shh. Don't cry. It's nothing to cry about, for Pete's sake."

She laughed through her tears, and he pushed her away gently and looked at his watch. "It's almost midnight. Your landlady is going to start flashing the porch light at us."

She giggled.

"Come on. I'll walk you to the door. You've got a lot to think about. Do you want me to pick you up for church in the morning?"

"Sure. Just not the early service, okay?"

"Definitely."

He leaned over to kiss her again. "I love you so much, Daria."

"Oh, Cole, I lo—"

He cut her off with a gentle hand to her lips. Then tenderly, but sternly, he told her, "Don't say it just because I did. Make sure, Daria. I don't want to hear it if you're just going to break my heart someday. I want to hear it—oh, how I want to hear those words from your lips—but please don't say it until you're absolutely sure."

She nodded and, feeling chastened, lowered her gaze.

He put a finger under her chin and lifted it toward his face. "I'll see you in the morning?"

She nodded again. Then he was off the porch and driving away before she could respond.

She climbed the stairs and unlocked the door to her apartment. The letter was still lying on the table in the dining area. Daria walked past it and went to the closet to hang up her coat.

One lovely thought rang through her head: Colson Hunter wanted to marry her.

He loved her. He loved Natalie like his own child. Her mind was suddenly crystal clear. She loved this man. She wasn't a schoolgirl. She knew what love was. She had known a true, abiding love with Nathan Camfield, and what she felt for Cole was every bit as deep and mature and right. She didn't need to ask anyone for advice on this. This she knew more surely than she'd known anything in a very long while.

She went over to the dining table and picked up the letter. She unfolded it slowly and forced her eyes to skim the paragraphs. But she did not try to analyze the words any longer—they had no meaning for her after what Cole had told her.

God had given her her answer. She would be loved again. Her daughter would have a father. She would know true happiness once more. She couldn't have dreamed of a more perfect answer. Soon she would hold Cole's hands and speak the words she'd wanted so badly to say to him tonight—*I love you too, Colson Hunter.*

That night Daria dreamed the same dream she'd had the night before. It seemed so real that she could almost smell the dank floor of the rain forest. She felt that if she opened her eyes she'd find herself in Timoné, that Nate would be standing in front of her and she could reach out and touch him.

Then Nate's face melted into Cole's, and Daria startled, fully awake now. The clock on the nightstand read 9:30 A.M. Beside it, Nate stared at her from the framed photograph. She could feel her heart thumping beneath the thin flannel of her nightgown.

She threw her legs over the side of the bed and sat up, breathing hard.

Disoriented and agitated, she grabbed the frame that contained Nathan's picture and opened the pocket door that led from her room to Natalie's. Her daughter had spent the night with her parents, but the crib still held the faint scent of her.

Daria set the photograph on Natalie's dresser and picked up a rumpled baby quilt. She held it to her nose for a minute, studying Nate's picture, fighting a menacing feeling that she couldn't identify.

Then she dropped the quilt into the crib, walked back through her bedroom, and down the hall to the shower.

Her parents would be bringing Natalie home in twenty minutes, and Cole would come by to pick them up for church shortly after that. She desperately needed to see him. She needed to be with someone who loved her. Someone who was real and alive.

❧

Daria slid the silver ribbon off the box and carefully peeled the tape from the shiny foil wrapping. "A Christmas present already? Cole, are you sure you don't want me to wait?" she asked him for the second time.

"Daria! Would you just open the package," he laughed. "You'll understand when you see what it is."

She folded the paper neatly and set it on the sofa beside her, then she lifted the lid on the shiny white box. "Oh!" she gasped, when she saw what was inside. "Cole! You didn't! You remembered!" She took the little ceramic cottage from the box and held it in the palm of her hand, admiring it.

"Do you like it?"

"You know I do! I love it."

"I couldn't afford the whole village, but it's a start." He knelt down beside her and took out the little brochure that was folded up in the box. He spread it out on her lap, pointing to a photograph of the display she had seen in the gift shop the day they'd gone shopping for Natalie. "There are forty-eight pieces in this collection, Daria. This is the first one." He took her hand and squeezed it tightly. "If God answers my prayers, there will come a Christmas someday when I'll have to choose something else to give you because this whole village will already be twinkling on our mantel."

Her heart quickened and tears stung her eyes as she realized the implication of what he'd said.

"I'm not asking for an answer, Daria," he told her just as he had that first night he'd declared his love. "I'm just telling you what my heart desires."

And in that moment, she knew for certain that—even though the memory of Nathan was still heavy, and maybe always would be—her heart longed for the very same thing.

She set the cottage aside, put her arms around him, and buried her face in his shoulder. Then she pulled away to look at him, to make sure that he could read her words in her eyes as well as hear them from her lips. "I love you, Cole. I love you with all my heart."

Fifteen

*T*he highways were clear, but the ditches and fields as far as the eye could see were covered with snow. The canted afternoon light painted Maxfield Parrish shadows on the canvas of snow, and the beauty of the scene took Daria's breath away. It was one week before Christmas, and she and Cole were headed to Wichita for an evening out.

"Where do you want to eat?" he asked her now.

"I really don't care, Cole. You decide. I chose last time."

"Can you remember that far back?" he said with a sigh.

"I know," she told him. "It does seem like it's been forever since we had a chance to go out together."

He reached over to take her gloved hand. "I'm looking forward to it."

"Mmm. Me, too. Maybe we could—"

The sharp blare of Cole's pager interrupted her. "No!" Daria groaned. How many times she had wanted to toss that interloper out the window. But he was a vet, and she had resigned herself to the fact that it was a part of his life.

Cole checked the message. "It's Bill Wyler."

Cole dialed his cell phone, and Daria listened while he talked to the rancher.

"Bill," Cole said. "Okay…how long has she been that way?" Another pause. "Well, it'll be another half-hour before I can get there. No, it's okay. You did the right thing. Yep. I'll see you."

Cole powered down his cell phone and put it back on the console. He turned to Daria with a hangdog expression on his face. "I'm sorry, Daria."

"I know, I know. I understand. I'm just disappointed, that's all."

"Do you want me to take you home or to your folks'?" Daria's parents were baby-sitting.

"Could I go with you?" she asked, brightening at the thought.

He looked surprised. "Sure. If you want to." He looked at the soft corduroy slacks and sweater she was wearing. "I don't have time to take you home to change though."

"Maybe Bill will let me borrow a pair of coveralls."

He smiled. "I like your attitude, woman."

"I'm learning, I'm learning…"

They spent the next hours in the chilly barn on Wyler's ranch, delivering twin calves and then trying frantically to save the smallest one. They almost lost the little fellow, but after an hour of working with him, the calf responded, struggling to stand on wobbly legs and finally nursing greedily beside his sister. Oblivious to the cold and exhilarated by their success, Daria and Cole cheered and whooped and gave each other high-fives.

Bill had left to feed his cattle, so Daria and Cole were alone in the barn. Cole grabbed her gloved hands across the metal fence of the stall, and his eyes held hers with an urgency that made her heart beat double time.

"Marry me, Daria." His voice was winsomely demanding. "Just marry me and I'll be the happiest man alive."

It was all she'd wanted since the night of the symphony. "Yes, Cole. Oh, yes."

She gave her answer without a second thought. It was an answer to a prayer she hadn't even prayed yet.

Christmas Day dawned cold but clear. The skies of Kansas had cooperated beautifully, unfurling a fresh blanket of snow over the state the night before. The sun sparkled on the fields and on the rooftops of the farm buildings, almost blinding Cole and Daria as they drove up the long lane that led to the Haydon farm. Natalie chattered happily in her car seat behind them.

"Looks like Jason and Brenda beat us here," Daria said, spotting her brother's two boys throwing snowballs in the backyard.

Cole parked the car, but before he cut the engine, he turned to Daria. "You nervous?" he asked.

"A little," she admitted. "But I think they'll all be thrilled with our news."

"Even your dad?"

"Cole," she chided. "You know Dad thinks you hung the moon."

"Yeah, but you're still his little girl. I know how I'm going to feel the day some young whippersnapper wants to take Nattie away from us."

"Quit it! I don't even want to think about that day." She reached over and patted his arm with a gloved hand. "Come on, let's get this over with."

Laden with gifts, two cherry pies, and a tightly wound Natalie, they made their way up the freshly shoveled path to the back door.

Jason met them in the mud room, eyeing the stack of packages Daria balanced in one arm. "Hey, sis. Let me take those off your hands. Is my name on one of these?"

"That depends," she teased her brother. "Were you a good boy this year?"

Margo, wearing a festive apron, appeared from the kitchen. "Merry Christmas! Here, honey, let me get those pies. Jason, did you check on the boys?"

"We just saw them," Cole interjected. "They're fine. They're playing in the snow."

Daria's father came and snatched Natalie from Cole's arms. "Hey, squirt!" he said, tickling the little girl under the chin. "Did Santy Claus visit your house last night?"

Natalie giggled as her grandfather helped her out of her coat and mittens and took her off to see the Christmas tree.

The house was fragrant with the aromas of freshly roasted turkey, pumpkin pie spices, and the massive Scotch pine that Erroll had grown from a seedling and brought in from the pasture just last week.

After dinner, they sat around the table, groaning even as they took a second slice of pie or one more of Margo's famous dinner rolls.

Finally Daria glanced at Cole, and he gave her a look that said, *Now?* She nodded imperceptibly, and Cole cleared his throat.

"Well, everybody…" The entire table turned to look at him while Daria sat beaming at his side. "Daria and I have an announcement to make."

"I knew it!" her brother crowed.

"Jason!" Daria laughed. "You don't even know what Cole's going to say."

"Want to bet?" he challenged with a grin.

"That's one you'd probably win," Cole laughed, while everyone else held their breath. He looked around the table, and Daria thought he was enjoying the moment. "Well," he told them, drawing out the suspense. "If you were betting that I was going to tell you that Daria and I are getting mar—"

Before he could finish, the table erupted in cheers and happy laughter. Even Natalie clapped her pudgy hands together. Margo wept for joy, and Daria thought she even saw a tear in her father's eye.

Jason and Brenda smiled smugly. "I just knew you two would end up getting hitched," Jason said. He reached out to shake his future brother-in-law's hand. "Congratulations, Cole. You take good care of her now, you hear."

Cole put an arm around Daria. "I'll do my best—but sometimes this woman has a mind of her own."

"You don't have to tell me that," Jason countered.

"Hey! Watch it, you two," Daria chided. But it warmed her heart to see how easily Cole fit into her family.

If only it would be so easy to tell Nathan's parents. So far the Camfields had only met Cole once and since then had politely declined every invitation of Daria's that included him. Though they were planning a small family wedding, their engagement would be big news in Bristol. And once word got out, Daria knew the Camfields would eventually hear it. It wouldn't be right for them to find out through the grapevine.

Later that evening, as the family cleaned up their leftovers, Daria pulled Cole aside.

"I'm going to call Jack and Vera," she said, leading him to the extension phone in the guest bedroom. "Do you want to be in on this?"

He stopped in his tracks and held up his palms. "No, thank you."

"Chicken," she teased, more nervous than she let on.

"Are you going to tell them over the phone?"

She shook her head. "No, I'm just going to invite them to dinner. I think I should tell them in person."

He turned more serious now. "Good idea. But really, Daria, I don't think I need to be in on this. To put it mildly, Jack and Vera don't seem very comfortable with me."

She took his arm. "Okay. But stay here. I need your handsome face for moral support." She planted a kiss on his cheek and lifted the receiver.

While she waited for an answer, Cole reached for her hand.

"Vera? Merry Christmas!" she said, forcing cheerfulness into her voice.

"Oh, hello, Daria. Did you have a nice holiday?"

"Very nice. We're still at my folks', actually."

"Well, we certainly got our white Christmas, didn't we?"

"Yes, isn't it beautiful?"

"Jack is out shoveling the rest of the driveway right now. We've had almost six inches, and it's still coming down a little. Now where is my little girl?"

"She's by the Christmas tree—playing with the wrapping paper, I think," Daria chuckled.

"Oh, isn't that the way it always is?" Vera exclaimed. "Well, let me talk to her."

"Of course, but actually...I was calling to invite you—and Jack, of course—to join me for a late Christmas dinner. Would you be able to come next Sunday?" Daria flashed Cole a smile.

"Why, that's very nice of you, Daria. We'd love to come." There was a pause, and then Vera's voice became guarded. "Your friend... Dr. Hunter...isn't going to be there, is he?"

"No, it will just be Natalie and me." Daria rolled her eyes at Cole.

"Well, we'd love to come."

"Wonderful. Let me get Natalie. I know she'll be happy to hear your voice."

She motioned to Cole, and he went to retrieve the toddler so she could stare at the receiver while her grandmother made baby talk from the other end.

Balancing three bowls of Rocky Road ice cream with the grace of a former waitress, Daria emerged from her kitchen. With a free elbow, she pushed Natalie's half-eaten bowl of spaghetti from the edge of the highchair tray as she passed by. Then she set two of the desserts in front of her former parents-in-law and one at her own place.

"After that delicious meal, I don't have room for another bite, Daria," Jack Camfield groaned. "But I guess I'll choke it down if I must." He laughed at his own joke, and Daria joined in nervously.

The clock on their evening together was ticking, and still she had not found an opening to tell the Camfields of her impending marriage.

She couldn't let them leave without knowing. She felt deceitful, having left the diamond Cole had given her—the one she ordinarily wore so proudly—in her jewelry box that morning.

Poking her spoon at her ice cream, she took a deep breath and plunged in. "Vera, Jack. I have something I need—something I *want*—to tell you."

Vera turned toward her, her heavily penciled brows raised in innocent interest. This was going to be harder than Daria thought.

"I— Well, I have an announcement to make. As you know, Cole and I have been dating for a while now."

Natalie perked up at the sound of Cole's name and began banging her chubby fists on the plastic highchair tray. "Da-da-da-da-da," she sang plainly and happily.

The effect on Vera Camfield was devastating.

Daria tried to ignore Natalie's happy chattering. "We… Cole has asked me to marry him, and I said yes." She tried to put a cheerful inflection in the words.

"I had a feeling this was going to happen," the woman spat.

Daria looked at her, shocked, near tears, and uncertain how to respond. "I know this isn't easy for you, Vera—"

"So," Vera cut her off, "you're just going to marry the first man that comes along, is that it?" She twisted a tattered paper dinner napkin in her hands.

Jack Camfield sat silent now.

Daria fought to remain calm. "Vera, I love Cole very much. I haven't made this decision rashly."

"Do you have any idea how this hurts us, Daria? Any idea whatsoever? Did Nathan mean *nothing* to you? How do you think this will look to our friends? Our son is barely cold in his grave and you have just gone on with your life, as though he meant nothing to you."

"Vera!" Daria hadn't meant it to come out so harshly. She took a deep breath and forced her voice down an octave. "Nate has been dead for a year and a half. Oh, Vera, you know I loved Nate—more than I ever thought it was possible to love another human being. But he's gone! He's not coming back, and I have to go on with my life. I don't want to raise Natalie alone. She needs a father. And Cole loves her like his own."

Vera recoiled as though she'd been slapped.

From her chair, Natalie started her happy litany again. "Da-da-da-da."

Daria cringed inwardly at Natalie's chatter, but she reached out and put a hand on Vera's arm. "I'm sorry, Vera. But surely you do want Natalie to have the influence of a good man in her life. Do you want me to be alone for the rest of my life? I love Cole. He's a wonderful man. I'd like for you to get a chance to know him." Daria knew she was whining, hated the way her voice sounded in her own ears.

Vera softened a bit, let out a tremulous sigh. Or maybe it was merely defeat Daria heard in her voice. "All I'm asking is that you not rush into this, Daria. You've only known the man for a few months—"

"I've known him for almost a year, Vera," Daria interrupted. "Yes, we've only been dating for four or five months, but I worked with him before that. In some ways it's better, because I saw him exactly as he is—kind and loving and full of integrity."

Daria knew from Vera's vacant stare and the tight fold of her arms across her breast that she had shut her out.

Daria turned to Nathan's father. "Jack?"

He sighed and put a protective arm around his wife. "We can't tell you what to do, Daria. You have to decide that for yourself. We only want what's best for you, and for Natalie. It does seem that this is a bit hasty. I"—he cleared his throat—"I just hope that this won't change the relationship we have with Natalie. She's all we have left of our son." He fished a handkerchief from his pocket and blew his nose noisily.

"Oh, Jack and Vera," she said, humility tingeing her words. "Of course you'll still see Natalie. I would never keep her from you. I want her to spend time with you. You're her grandparents. She loves you!"

"We appreciate that," Jack said and reached to squeeze Daria's hand. "We care about you."

Daria felt tears well in her eyes and she looked up, trying to hold them back. There was a long, awkward silence, and Natalie started crying.

Vera got up. "Is my baby fussy?" She reached to scoop the little girl from her highchair.

Jack cleared his throat again and said, "I suppose we should get on the road pretty soon."

They played with Natalie for a few minutes, then started to gather their things to leave.

Not wanting to leave anything unsettled, yet not wanting them to think that they had swayed her decision in any way, Daria went to her desk drawer and pulled out one of the wedding invitations she had been addressing. The envelope on top bore the Camfield's name in Daria's flowing script. She carried it into the living room where they sat.

Handing it to Vera, she told them, "We would very much like to have you at the wedding." It was a lie, and she immediately felt guilty. Under the circumstances, having them at the wedding would cause everyone to feel uncomfortable.

Vera started to take the card from the unsealed envelope, then apparently changed her mind. She handed the invitation back to Daria. "Thank you, dear, but I don't think that would be a very good idea."

Daria searched for the right words, hoping they would come out with graciousness rather than the immense relief she felt. "I understand," she said finally.

When the Camfields had gone and Natalie was down for her nap, Daria called her mother and told her about the confrontation.

"Well, of course they're hurt, Daria. But don't let it bother you. They'll get over it and come to realize that this is best for everyone, especially Natalie. Everything will be fine when they see how happy you are, how good Cole is with Nattie. Don't let it ruin things for you. This should be the happiest time of your life."

"Thanks, Mom." She sighed heavily, feeling as confused as a teenager. "Why does everything have to be so complicated?"

"Oh, honey, I think every wedding, every joining of families, has its pitfalls. Just take it in stride. Don't let it get you down," she repeated.

She tried to take her mother's words to heart, but she couldn't help feeling sorry for the Camfields. She tried to imagine her own parents' grief if it had been she who'd died and Nathan who was marrying another woman to become the mother of their grandchild. She could see how it might threaten their relationship with Natalie. She determined then to make an extra effort to allow Nate's parents to have time with their granddaughter.

"Oh, Lord," she prayed, as she hung up the phone, "just be with Jack and Vera. Help them to understand. And God—" She cut short her prayer. She had been ready to pour out her heart to God. A torrent of words was on her tongue, begging release. But something stopped her. A place deep inside her heart recognized that she couldn't come honestly before God because she had ignored his gentle, beckoning voice, a voice that was calling her even now. There was something he asked of her that she wasn't willing to give. It dismayed her, but at the same time it caused her to withdraw further.

Deliberately she turned her mind to other things, allowed her brain to become cluttered with all the tasks, important and mundane, that she needed to accomplish before February fourteenth.

After that, she promised herself, she would deal with the uncertainties that nagged at her, with the doubts that seemed to creep in when they were least welcome. After that—when she and Cole and Natalie were settled in, when they were a family—then she would square things with God.

Daria leafed through the hymnal to find the page number the lector announced. She turned to look at Cole who sat beside her, holding

Natalie proudly in his arms while they stood to sing the worship choruses. Seeing them together warmed Daria. The love that had grown between them couldn't have been deeper had Cole been Natalie's biological father.

Pastor Greene took the pulpit to begin the sermon, and Cole settled Natalie on the padded seat between him and Daria. The toddler quickly grew restless, wanting to practice her newly acquired walking skills. Ordinarily she looked forward to playing with the other children in the nursery, but she had awakened in a rather testy mood that morning. So when she screamed in protest as they tried to leave her in the nursery, Daria gave in and brought her to the worship service with them. Now Natalie fidgeted in the seat, sliding to the floor and then climbing back into the pew. When she stretched out on her back on the cushioned seat and began kicking the pew in front of them with her black patent leather Mary Janes, Daria quickly picked her up and pulled her onto her lap. Immediately Natalie went rigid, stretching her legs to kick the pew again.

"Natalie, no," Daria whispered in her ear. "Don't kick the seat."

Natalie stretched out her chubby leotard-clad leg and kicked again, this time harder. The two elderly women in front of them turned their heads to see what was causing all the commotion. One of them smiled sympathetically, but the other frowned with a look of irritation and shifted in her seat as though the kicking was a personal affront.

Daria rummaged in the diaper bag for something to distract her daughter. She found a Tupperware container of Cheerios, took off the lid, and offered Natalie one.

"No!" Natalie shouted in her best spoiled-brat voice, stretching to kick the pew again. Muffled laughter rippled through the congregation. It was always funnier when it was someone else's child disrupting the service.

She looked over at Cole, who was trying to ignore what was happening. Natalie continued to misbehave, and when Cole finally looked Daria's way, she motioned that she was going to take Natalie out. He nodded and turned in the pew to let her pass to the outside aisle. Daria stood and picked Natalie up in one motion. But the minute Natalie realized that her mother intended to take her back to the nursery, she started bucking in Daria's arms. She weighed a full twenty-five pounds now, and it was all Daria could do to keep her balance.

They made it to the wide double doors at the back of the sanctuary, and Daria set Natalie on the floor and took her hand. But the little girl's hand slipped from her grasp as though it were a wet bar of soap. With a squeal, she toddled down the center aisle, toward the pew where Cole was. By now the pastor had stopped midsermon to crack a joke at her expense. Daria didn't hear him clearly, since her face was on fire and blood was pounding in her ears—something about him wishing all his congregants were so eager to return to services each Sunday.

Natalie wiggled in front of the people in Cole's row and climbed into his arms, but instead of welcoming her, he stood and carried her down the outside aisle. Daria met them at the back doors and followed Cole out of the sanctuary and down the hallway toward the nursery.

He transferred Natalie to Daria's arms. "Do you want to try to put her back in the nursery?"

"Could we just go home?" she pled, utterly humiliated.

Cole smiled, but Daria could tell that he, too, had been embarrassed by Natalie's antics. "Is her coat in the nursery?" he asked.

"No, I hung it up with mine in the foyer."

"Okay. I'll go get them."

Daria was almost in tears on the way home. "I just don't know what to do when she gets like that, Cole" she whined. "It's like I have no control over her whatsoever."

"You just need to keep being firm with her, Daria. Every time you give in, she thinks she's won."

In the seat behind them, Natalie sat in her car seat, sucking her thumb furiously, looking from one to the other as though she knew she was the subject of their conversation—and was rather enjoying that fact.

"Do you think I should have made her stay in the nursery this morning?"

He thought for a minute, then nodded. "I do, Daria. You rewarded her fit by giving her exactly what she wanted."

"But it didn't seem fair to leave the nursery helpers with a screaming brat," she defended herself.

"I have a feeling she would have stopped screaming almost as soon as we were out of sight."

Daria sighed. "You're probably right. But it's so hard."

He reached across the console and patted her arm. "She'll learn."

Daria knew Cole was right. She did let her daughter have her own way whenever she threw a tantrum, while Cole seemed mostly immune to the little girl's whims.

When Cole stopped at the apartment a few minutes later and Daria unbuckled Natalie from her car seat, she couldn't help but long for the soon-coming day when she would go home with Cole and share the mixed blessing of this stubborn little girl who now smiled up at her with the face of an angel.

The supper dishes were done, and Natalie was down for the night. Daria flipped on the television set and wandered through the apartment straightening up. While a mindless sitcom droned in the background, she gathered up toys strewn across the floor, piles of magazines she'd yet to read, and stacks of mail that needed sorting.

On top of a "to keep" stack of magazines lay the newest issue of *Brides*. Daria smiled even while a mild sense of panic came over her as she thought of all there was to do in the next few weeks.

With the toys tucked away in their baskets and the magazines neatly stacked on the floor by the sofa, Daria tackled the dining room table. She tossed junk mail into the trash and gathered up receipts and bills to file. As she sorted through a stack of old mail, a familiar sheet of onionskin paper appeared among the envelopes. Daria was filled with a sense of dread she couldn't quite name.

She started to unfold the thin sheet of paper, but impulsively put it, along with its envelope, on the stack of junk mail. She carried the whole pile into the kitchen and stuffed it into the wastebasket. The letter sat on top of the heaping container, accusing her.

On impulse she went to the closet in her bedroom and rummaged on the top shelf until her hand touched an old shoebox. She pulled it down, slipped off the elastic bands that secured the lid, and gingerly opened it. Inside, along with some Gospel Outreach newsletters and some old newspaper clippings, were a dozen black cassette tapes, each labeled in Nate's sloppy printing. She took the box into the living room and slipped one of the cassettes into the stereo. Pushing the Play button, she sat back on the sofa, trembling.

The tape wound silently for several seconds, and then there was a scratchy sound like static. She sat, staring far beyond the stereo speakers, waiting. The static continued, but suddenly Nate's voice filled the room.

"Uh, it's June fifteenth," he said in his soft, matter-of-fact "taping" voice. "We've been here almost five months now, and we're adjusting well to the climate. It's been raining for almost three days straight, but we're staying pretty dry in the hut…"

At those words, Daria recognized the sound she'd mistaken for static as one of the torrential downpours they'd had that first rainy season in Timoné. Over the rain and Nate's quiet voice, a bird squawked. She closed her eyes, transported.

Nate's voice droned on. "Daria's been making some progress with the kids here, just getting to know them mostly, learning their names, but she has plans to start formal lessons soon. They really seem to have taken a liking to her and follow her all over the village.

I've been calling her the Pied Piper." He chuckled, then cleared his throat and continued, his voice serious again. "I'm working with Anazu, trying to get a feel for the best way to reach the other villagers. I'm still far from fluent in Timoné, but from what I can make out he thinks they—"

Daria jumped up and turned off the stereo. She couldn't stand to hear any more. It hurt too much, hearing Nate's voice so clearly, hearing his laughter and the jungle sounds that had been such a familiar part of their lives together. She had forgotten about him calling her the Pied Piper.

Dry eyed, she opened the tape deck and removed the cassette, dropping it back in the box with the others. She went to the desk, took out a label and sturdy strapping tape, crumpled an old newspaper, and packed it around the cassette tapes. At the last minute, she removed the tape she had just listened to from the box and slipped it into an envelope. She wrote Natalie's name on the front, sealed the flap, and put it in the bottom drawer of the desk. Then she taped the lid securely on the box that held the remaining cassettes, took Evangeline Magrit's letter from the trash, and copied her address onto a mailing label, which she pasted onto the box. She would mail it from the clinic on Monday morning.

She threw the letter back in the wastebasket without reading it again, then grabbed some old magazines and threw them in on top of the letter so she wouldn't have to see the guilt-inducing missive anymore. She shook her head back and forth as though she could cast out the thoughts that were churning in her brain. Then, before she could change her mind, she pulled the white plastic garbage bag out of the basket, tied it tightly, and grabbed a book of matches from the drawer beside the stove. She lugged the trash down the stairs and out to the incinerator behind the house.

Unless it was windy, which it often was in Kansas, Kirk Janek burned the trash every day. Daria had rarely lit it herself, but this time she struck a match and threw it on top. It flared, melted a tiny hole in the plastic, and fizzled out. She lit another match with the same results. Feeling agitated, she tore a hole in the bag and lit a corner of a newspaper that protruded from it. The flame grew and quickly engulfed the contents. Daria closed the door of the incinerator and walked back to the house with a heavy heart.

CRUX:
THE CROSS

The flames were hot…so hot. He ran to the east side of the hut where the doorway should have been, but it was gone. Everywhere he looked, on all four sides, only walls of flame rose around him. He sucked in a breath and immediately choked on the thick smoke that filled the air.

He could hear screaming all around him. He had to find the children. They were too weak to get out by themselves. But the smoke obscured his vision. Stretching his arms in front of him, he connected with the rope of a hammock. It swung heavily under his touch, still occupied. Fumbling blindly, he managed to lift the frail body from the sling. He cradled it in his arms and ducked his head. If he ran into the flames, surely he would run through into fresh air. Then miraculously an opening appeared in front of him, a way out. He raced into the light and placed the child on the damp forest floor, gulping oxygen like a drowning man. He knelt over the limp body, and though his eyes were swollen and watering, he saw that it was little Miguel he had carried out. It was too late. The boy was gone.

The terrible screams had stopped now, but he ran back into the burning hut, groping desperately for another heavy hammock. A loud crack split the air, and a wall of the hut fell outward, admitting fresh air, exposing the rows of smoldering cots and mats, but also fanning the flames higher. He had to get the rest of them out! He lifted a body from a mat. Then everything went black.

Nathan Camfield opened his eyes and sat up on one elbow. His heart was beating violently in his chest. He had dreamed the dream again. And as they had so many times before, the tears came. For the dream was real. It had happened. And no matter how he tried, he couldn't escape the horrifying visions being replayed over and over and over again. Day after day, night after night. Every time he closed his eyes the fire raged anew.

He shaded his eyes and looked up. The sun burned brightly through the narrow gap in the roof of his tiny hut. He knew that the light would soon move on, and he would be left in the grey-green shadows that had colored his existence for what seemed an eternity.

But for now, the sunshine was blinding—and he welcomed it. He struggled to pull himself to a sitting position. He knew from experience that the ropes of vine that bound his feet were loosely tied, affording him reasonable movement, but he also knew—again from experience—that the ropes that lashed the door of the cagelike hut were expertly knotted and closely guarded.

He sucked in a breath of the heavy jungle air, scarcely aware of the searing pain in his lungs, pain that had been with him now for as long as he could remember—since the fire, since his nightmare had begun.

Too quickly, the sun crawled lower, leaving him in the shadows once again. He felt his spirits sink with it, and he forced himself to think of hopeful things. *Sing the songs, recite the lists, say the prayers.* He'd played the games for so long that they came almost automatically.

"*A* is for *air.*" He would never again take even one breath for granted.

"*B* is for *bananas. C* is for *coffee.*" The two staples had sustained him day after day.

"*D* is for *Daria.*" *Oh, Daria. Are you safe? You must be sick with worry. Why haven't you been able to get help? Has something happened to you, too? Surely the men from this village hadn't followed Tados and Quimico to Timoné. No! Stop it. Stop it!* he silently chided himself.

"Go on now," he said aloud.

"*E* is for *elms.*" Thoughts of his childhood tree house in an ancient elm cooled him on sticky tropical afternoons.

"*F* is for *family.*" Oh, Daria… *No!* "Go on… *G* is for *God:* 'I will never leave you nor forsake you.' " He continued, picking up *I* through *Q.* Then, "*R* is for *rice.*" Another life-sustaining gift. He went the rest of the way through the alphabet, forcing himself to visualize each blessing as he counted it, not just to recite it by rote.

The Scriptures were next: " 'The Lord is my shepherd, I shall not want…' "

Then the bones in the body: "Mandible, scapula, ulna, radius, tibia, fibula…"

And, finally, the books of the Bible: "Genesis, Exodus, Leviticus, Numbers…"

The afternoon rains had come and gone when he finished these litanies of sanity. Though he wasn't sure why, it helped give some purpose to his days to have those tasks before him.

The days and nights melded into one another, and he could not guess if he had been here for weeks or months or years. He remembered picking up little Miguel from the fire, discovering that he was already dead. He remembered going back into the flames, then the wall of the hut falling outward. He remembered moving toward the opening as though in slow motion. Everything was a blank after that. Until he woke up here in this hut, in agonizing pain, burns searing his legs and arms, his lungs on fire. He wondered now if perhaps he had also contracted the illness he'd come to cure, for he had been delirious, drifting in and out of consciousness for days—or perhaps it was weeks. If that were true, it was a blessing, for when he'd begun to regain consciousness for short periods of time, the pain from the burns was excruciating. He was ashamed to remember that he had prayed to die—he had screamed in agony for death to come. In his anguish, he'd cared nothing for Daria's grief, for the safety of Tados and Quimico, for the Timoné people he'd been called to serve. He'd wanted only to be released from the unbearable, torturous pain.

Though he had no memories of being cared for during the time immediately after the fire, at some point food had begun to appear at the door of his hut and eventually a drink that he suspected contained something that eased the pain and caused him to sleep deeply. As time went on, his delirium ceased and his wounds began to scar over. His were second-degree burns, and he knew if he could stave off infection, they would heal completely. Then he would find a way to get home.

But where were Tados and Quimico? Since the fire, he had not seen them. When they'd first arrived in Chicoro, his guides were careful to keep a wide berth of the sick hut he'd set up, lest they, too, contract the deadly fever. For that reason, he felt certain they hadn't perished in the fire with the others. He assumed they had gone back to Timoné for help. Surely they'd had time to get there and back by now.

When he had begun to remain conscious for longer periods, he had tried to mark the passage of time by scratching marks in the dirt floor of the hut. But he'd soon become confused. There were too many marks. He must have forgotten and tallied more than one mark for each day. Finally he had given up, certain that any day now the Timoné would come for him and the marks would not matter any more.

The first day he had felt strong enough to leave the hut, he walked several hundred yards, into the village, looking for the chief. The children saw him first and ran away into their homes, obviously frightened of him. Alerted, the village leaders met him near the center of the compound and began to motion wildly for him to leave. He tried to speak with them, but they made it clear that they would not allow him to remain inside the village. At first he guessed that they were still afraid they would contract the disease from him. But as the days went by and he lived in exile in his hut outside the village, he noticed that some of the older Chicoro boys sneaked away and came to peer at him. They kept their distance, but from what little of their dialect he had picked up, he was horrified to realize that their superstitious beliefs had made him into some kind of a god or good luck charm in their eyes. The Chicoro were a very superstitious people, and they apparently held him in awe because he had escaped not only the deadly illness to which he had been exposed again and again, but he had also walked through fire. He had defied the flames of a deadly inferno that had killed twenty-eight people in the sick hut. Of course, he himself believed his escape from the fire to be miraculous. But it was certainly no miracle of his own doing.

A million times he had gone back in his memory to the day of the fire, wishing he could have had a chance to do things differently. When he and Tados and Quimico had first come to Chicoro, the fever continued to devastate the village, taking ten more lives in the first two days he was there. Nate could not positively diagnose the illness, but he believed it to be a strain of influenza to which these people were highly susceptible. The only way to stop the spread of the disease was to isolate the ill downriver from the stream that supplied their drinking water. And there had been indications that the measure was working. At the time of the fire, it had been three full days since they'd had to isolate anyone new. But when the chief's young son died on the fourth day, the village leaders had begun to lose faith in Nate.

Tados and Quimico sensed that the good will of the chief had soured, and they implored Nate to slip away quietly in the night. But he insisted that they remain for a few more days. He should have trusted the judgment of his two guides. They knew the culture, and they understood the malice of the chief toward Nate. But he had not wanted to leave until he knew he had the outbreak under control.

He knew in his heart that his motives hadn't been totally altruistic. In his mind, he had written a glowing report for the board of Gospel Outreach, telling of his success in putting down a major epidemic. His pride had gotten in the way of his good judgment.

So he had been forced back to the hut outside the village. Night after night he watched the fires from afar and listened to the chatter of the children playing before bedtime. Loneliness overwhelmed him, and he began to make desperate plans to return to Timoné. In his weakened physical state, without a guide, without provisions, he knew it would be suicide to attempt such a journey alone. But every attempt to secure a guide to take him down the river was met with a firm refusal. Finally desperation and the torture of his isolation caused him to toss prudence to the wind.

Early one morning, he had set out along the Rio Guaviare, planning to follow the river to the next village where he hoped to find a more sympathetic response.

He hadn't been walking more than an hour when he heard the sound of a boat's motor in the distance. He had almost shouted with joy, but remembering the warnings of the mission in Bogotá about drug traffickers and the paramilitary factions that controlled some parts of the country, he stepped back into the trees to wait and watch.

As the sound grew nearer, Nate peered through the palm leaves. He didn't recognize the lone occupant of the boat, but he was a bronze-skinned man wearing the traditional garb of the Chicoro. He racked his brain to think of something of value with which he could bribe the boat's pilot. His gold watch had been lost in the fire—or perhaps stolen from him while he was unconscious. Never had he regretted its loss as much as he did now.

Without anything to offer the man in exchange for passage on his boat, Nate took his chances and showed himself on the riverbank.

"Hollio!" he shouted. "Hello? Can you help me?"

The man cut the motor and shaded his eyes, trying to locate where the shout had come from. Nate called out again. *"Hollio!* Over here."

The man seemed surprised to see him. He hesitated a moment before sculling slowly toward the bank.

When the boat touched shore, Nate reached out to hold it steady while the man got out. *"Hollio,"* Nate said, putting up a hand in greeting. "Could I come with you?" he asked in broken Chicoro, motioning toward the boat.

"*Seshu!* Silence!" the man barked. Though he spoke in the Chicoro dialect, his inflection was less nasal, more refined, perhaps that of the Castilian Spanish spoken widely in the country.

The man circled Nate, looking him up and down. Nate pled with him again—in Spanish this time. "*Por favor,* can you help me?"

"*Silencio!*" the man roared. To Nate's horror, he took a pistol from the waist of his loose-fitting trousers and turned it on Nate.

Nate held up his hands in surrender, and the man motioned for him to get into the boat.

Nate did so, and within twenty minutes he was back on the bank of the Chicoro village, not a hundred yards from the hut he had left an hour ago. His captor led him up the trail toward the village at gunpoint. As they rounded a sharp curve in the trail, they came face to face with Vidalé, one of the young men who often brought Nate's meals. He was carrying gourds of rice and fruit, presumably not realizing yet that Nate had tried to leave.

Vidalé appeared surprised to see Nate coming toward the village, but when he saw the man behind Nate, his eyes grew wide and he stopped short. "Juan Mocoa!" he whispered, obviously recognizing the stranger.

Mocoa spoke to Vidalé, gesturing toward Nate.

Nate could not understand all of their exchange, but the man seemed to wield an unexplained power over Vidalé. The young man answered him, speaking rapidly, his eyes darting nervously, his dialogue peppered with the word *Americano.*

Juan Mocoa motioned for Vidalé to continue on the trail, and, still holding his gun on Nate, he followed the young native back to Nathan's hut. Shoving Nathan inside, he motioned for Vidalé to give Nate the food, then he took a length of vine rope from the pouch he wore on a string around his waist. Vidalé set the food on the floor and went outside with Mocoa. Nate could hear them tying the door securely with the rope. When he was finished, Mocoa spoke harshly to Vidalé as the door jiggled from the outside—no doubt being tested by Mocoa for security.

Nate watched them through a narrow crack in the bamboo wall of the hut. Vidalé cowered, but suddenly, Mocoa gave the knot a final tug, smiled, and put a friendly arm around the young man's shoulders. He took something shiny from his pouch and put it in Vidalé's hand. He lowered his voice, and Nate could no longer hear their exchange.

Vidalé remained to stand guard at the door to the hut. Nate couldn't imagine what kind of threat he posed to Juan Mocoa, but since that time, his hut had been closely guarded at all times.

Twice each day, food and drink were brought to him, and twice each day his hands were tied in front of him and he was led to the river to relieve himself or to bathe. He had tried to communicate with the young men who had been assigned the duty of escorting him, but though the walls of this prison and the strong vine ropes with which they tied him rendered him harmless, his captors seemed to fear him and refused to speak with him.

He prayed continually. Though he didn't understand why God had allowed him to live this nightmare, he knew he was not alone. He had felt God's touch many times, had often been filled with a quiet peace that only the presence of God could explain. On two separate occasions he had felt an actual physical presence—a benevolent entity that he believed to be an angel—inside the hut with him. He grasped tightly to the memories of those incidents, and they strengthened him when his faith faltered.

Yesterday morning, Nate had awakened to the sound of the engine of Juan Mocoa's boat. The sound was music to Nate's ears as it faded into silence downriver. But his beliefs that the man's departure would end his confinement proved unfounded. If anything, his guards seemed to take their duty more seriously than ever now that Juan Mocoa was gone.

As another sun melted into the jungle, Nathan lay back on the hard-packed earth and let his mind drift, waiting for the blessing of nightfall when he would lie awake, as he did every night, fixing his eyes on the split in the roof. The foliage that grew above his hut was thick, but sometimes when the wind parted the palm fronds and the night sky was blackest, he would catch a glimpse of a single star. It was a split-second twinkle of light, but he told himself that it was Spica, the bright star of Virgo that was his and Daria's. When that happened, hope would swell in his breast again. He would remember his last night with Daria, and he would dream that miles down the river, she was looking at the same star, sending her love to him on a whispered prayer.

olson Hunter rose at five o'clock on Valentine's Day to find the countryside buried in a thick blanket of snow.

He dialed the Haydon's number, where Daria was staying, while he measured coffee into the coffeemaker.

Daria answered with an uninterpretable mumble.

"Hey, sleepyhead. Do you know what day this is?"

"Valentine's Day," she said archly, that impish grin of hers coming through the line as clearly as if she'd been in the room.

"So what do you want for Valentine's Day?" he played along.

But she turned serious. "I just want you. Oh, Cole, I just want you. I can't wait."

"Me neither. But, um, have you by any chance looked outside?"

"Why?" He heard her stumbling out of bed and raising the blinds at her window. He waited for her response, fully expecting her to moan in dismay. But she surprised him.

"Cole! It's gorgeous! What a beautiful day for a wedding."

"Yeah, if anyone can get there. The roads are pretty bad, Dar."

"As long as you and the minister show up, I really don't care if anyone else makes it."

"Are you nervous?"

"No, just excited. I just want it to be tomorrow!"

He laughed his pleasure at her comment. "Well, my love, you just snuggle under those warm blankets for a few more hours. I, on the other hand, have to get out in this white stuff and plow my way through to the clinic. The animals don't really give two hoots that it's my wedding day."

"But Cole, can't Travis do it?"

"I don't mind. I'm too nervous to sleep anyway."

"Are you? Nervous, I mean."

"A little," he admitted. "Now go back to sleep. The next time I see you, you'll be just minutes away from being Mrs. Colson Hunter."

"Mmm," she sighed. "I like the sound of that."

"I love you."

"Not as much as I love you." It was her standard response, but he never tired of hearing it.

Still smiling, he hung up the phone and poured himself a cup of coffee. He was almost afraid to think about how happy he was. Since Bridgette's death he hadn't dared to hope for this kind of happiness again. And now he'd been blessed not only with the most wonderful woman in the world to love and who'd loved him in return, but with a little girl who called him *Daddy.* He thought of God's promise to "restore what the locust hath eaten," and he was humbled to realize how amazingly that had been borne out in his own life.

At one time he had lost everything that was precious to him. No one, not even Daria, knew just how much he had lost. But he had decided long ago not to dwell on the past. Nothing could ever change the fact that things had happened as they had. It had all been forgiven and mostly forgotten. And now here he sat on a beautiful winter morning about to have the blessing of love restored to him. He felt unworthy. Deep gratitude welled up inside him, and he bowed his head and gave thanks—though it seemed there were no adequate words.

He drained his coffee cup and went to the mud room to pull on his coveralls and boots. He stepped off the back porch into almost a foot of snow. Crunching around to the front of the house, he saw that the snowplow had yet to make it down the dirt road. He would have to clear the driveway and the short stretch of road to the highway himself. He trudged down the lane that led to the barn and went in to hook the snow blade to his little farm tractor.

Two hours later the road was clear, the clinic chores were done, and he was back home to shower and eat a quick breakfast.

He pulled on blue jeans and a sweater, grabbed the black pin-striped suit—the one he hadn't removed from the cleaner's bag since he'd worn it in his cousin's wedding three years before—and headed for the church.

The country church where Cole and Daria were to be married looked like something out of a fairy tale. The county road grader had already been down the side roads to the highway. Most of the family members who lived nearby would be able to get there, but Cole doubted if anyone would come from a distance on such a day.

Inside the church, Cole stamped the snow off his boots and peeked into the sanctuary. The snow gave it a hushed atmosphere. The organist was quietly running through the songs one last time, and Daria's mother and her friend Beth were fussing with the garlands of ivy and the hurricane lamps that decorated the altar and the ends of the oak pews.

Margo Haydon looked up, distracted. "Oh, hi Cole."

"Hi, Mom," he said. He'd begun calling her that teasingly when he and Daria announced their engagement. She smiled at him. It was nice to have someone to call *Mom* and *Dad* again.

"Is Daria here yet?" he asked, even though the two women had already gone back to an intent discussion about the satin ribbon twined among the ivy.

Margo looked at her friend with mock disgust. "Just listen to that, Beth. 'Is Daria here yet?' " She turned to Cole, wagging a finger. "You've got a lot to learn, buddy. Daria has been here for an hour. She's doing her hair in the nursery. We women are not so lucky as to simply hop in the shower, jump into a suit, and show up at the altar. And don't you dare go in there. You do know that the groom is not allowed to see the bride until she comes down the aisle?"

"So I've heard." He laughed and held up the bag from the cleaners. "Well, I'm going to go jump into a suit."

The two women laughed loudly. Rolling his eyes, he headed down the darkened hallway that led to the Sunday-school classrooms and the rest rooms. The door marked *Nursery* popped open, and Daria stepped into the hallway wearing a simple, ivory-colored satin sheath gown. In spite of the fact that she was barefoot and had two bright red hair curlers sprouting from the top of her head, she looked stunningly beautiful.

She let out a little scream when she saw him. "Cole!"

"Are you superstitious?"

"I guess not." She gave him that smile that melted his heart.

"Then come here."

He took her into his arms, amazed all over again that after today she would belong to him. "You look gorgeous," he whispered.

"Thank you, sir. But don't wrinkle me," she teased.

He held her at arm's length and pretended to smooth the creases from the shoulders of her dress. "I think we're going to have an even smaller wedding than we originally planned. The roads are still pretty bad."

"I know," she sighed. "But you know what? I don't care."

"So you said. Me neither," he said, unable to resist kissing her.

She returned his kiss, then reached up and wiped a smudge of her lipstick from his mouth. "You better go get ready, Dr. Hunter."

He saluted her. "Yes ma'am." He turned on his heel and then remembered something. "Hey," he called after her.

She turned, looking up at him expectantly.

"Happy Valentine's Day, sweetheart."

Barely two hours later the cake had been cut and the wedding toasts made. Hand in hand, Cole and Daria mingled with the few friends and family members who still lingered at the reception. Natalie, enjoying birthday-girl status, toddled stocking-footed among the guests, modeling her miniature pink satin dress, the soles of her white tights sticky with punch and cake crumbs.

Finally Cole grew impatient. He leaned down and whispered in his bride's ear, "Let's blow this pop stand."

She giggled and planted a kiss on his cheek. "Patience, my love, patience."

A few minutes later, Margo saved the day. She sauntered over to the newlyweds and in a husky stage whisper told them, "Why don't you two get out of here so these people will go home?"

They didn't have to be asked twice. They ran down the hallway to change into warm clothes, and a few minutes later—among heart-felt good wishes, repeated goodbye waves to Natalie, and much teasing about their secret honeymoon location—they piled into Cole's four-wheel-drive pickup and plowed through the snow back to Cole's house. No, *their* house.

They pulled into the lane that led to the farmhouse, and Cole parked the truck and went around to open Daria's door for her. She jumped into his arms and he held her, laughing.

The night stretched out ahead of them full of promise. They would build a fire in the hearth and share supper on the sofa. Snow had begun to fall anew, and Cole relished the fact that it would barricade them from the world. They had so much love to share that a lifetime didn't seem enough, let alone these next few precious days.

As Cole carried his wife through the doorway, he knew that he would always look back on this moment—this instant when the woman he loved more than life itself crossed the threshold to share his home and his life—as one of the happiest he would ever know.

Eighteen

aria came awake slowly and smiled when she saw Cole beside her in the big bed. She rolled toward him and snuggled in the crook of his arm, moved at how his embrace tightened possessively around her even as he slept. She lay her head on his shoulder and listened to his deep, even breathing, marveling again that he was her husband. It was the fifth morning of their life together as husband and wife. How wonderful it was to share her bed again, to have the warmth and strength of a man on the pillow beside her.

Theirs had been an idyllic honeymoon. The weather had locked them inside the house—or, more accurately, had locked the world out. They'd romped in the snow like children, camped in front of the fire in the cozy den for hours on end, talking, making love, feeding each other crackers and cheese, sipping warm mugs of hot chocolate. Daria wished it would never end.

She was grateful to be feeling this way now because their first night together had been an emotional roller coaster for her. Cole had been so gentle, so tender, and yet his lovemaking had brought memories of Nathan crashing back. Of course, she didn't want to tell Cole how she was feeling. But she knew that he was probably struggling with old memories himself. Afterward she had lain in his arms in the dark and tried desperately to hide her tears, for she honestly couldn't have told Cole whether they were tears of joy because she'd found him or tears of sorrow because she'd lost Nate.

Now, in the grey light of this new morning, she realized that her tears had probably been a poignant mingling of the two. She determined to concentrate on the present and on the future that hung before them like ripening fruit.

She shook him gently. "Hey, lazybones."

He growled playfully and covered his head with the pillow.

"Cole, let's go get Nattie and bring her back here. She'll love the sled."

At that he perked up. Daria had supposed she would be the one to struggle with being separated from her daughter for five days, especially when the little girl was staying so close by with Daria's parents. The third afternoon of their honeymoon, he approached her with a glum expression on his face. "Don't you think we ought to go check on Natalie?" he'd asked her.

"You big sap! We haven't even been away from her for three days yet. I think that little girl has you on a short leash." She laughed.

"I know, I know." He grinned sheepishly. "I miss her."

"And I love you for it." She leaned across the narrow island in the kitchen where they were fixing fajitas, and kissed him.

"I don't know, Daria," Cole said. "There's just something about hearing that little blond angel call me *Daddy*." He turned away to stir the peppers and onions that were frying on the stove, but Daria didn't miss the catch in his voice, and she was moved all over again by Cole's unconditional love for her daughter.

She had managed to dissuade him then, but now, two days later, she was as anxious as he to see Nattie again. Daria could hardly wait to share this perfect winter day and the coziness of their new home with her. Mostly she couldn't wait to share her new daddy with her.

Cole threw back the covers and started toward the shower. "Better call your mom and warn her we're coming."

"I don't think she'll be too surprised," she said, pulling on her jeans.

They shoveled down bowls of granola and climbed into Cole's truck.

As they drove over snow-packed roads, talking all the way about the plans and dreams they had for their future together, Daria could hardly contain the emotion that welled up in her. These precious days with Cole had been so fleeting, but instead of feeling that her honeymoon had just ended, she felt as though her life was beginning all over again. And she intended to savor every single moment.

Winter seemed to hang on forever, but in spite of the endless parade of grey, frigid days, Daria longed to slow time down. She continued to work at the clinic several hours each morning, but Cole had suggested that she stay home with Natalie in the afternoons. Daria was grateful for the time at home with her daughter. Natalie had adjusted to life in the country as though she'd been born to it, and she was growing so fast that they had trouble keeping her in clothes.

When spring finally came, Daria was delighted at the riot of daffodils and tulips that had sprung up almost overnight along the lane that led to the farmhouse. The brilliant yellow and red blossoms and the flowering crab apple trees that framed the house seemed to transform their humble farmhouse into a charming fairy-tale cottage. Natalie seemed to love spring as much as her mother, and every evening while Daria put dinner on the table, the little girl rode her daddy's broad shoulders down the lane where they plucked a bright bouquet for the supper table. Daria would watch them, Natalie clutching the bouquet tightly in her sweaty palm, Rufus romping and slobbering beside them, Cole looking so happy it almost made her own heart ache with joy. It was such a contrast to the sorrow they'd both known. She wasn't sure life could possibly get any sweeter than this.

In her spare time Daria worked on the house. Cole and Travis had torn down the old garage, which sat fifty yards from the farmhouse. Now, when the weather permitted, they worked on erecting a new one—this one attached to the house. Cole had spent most of his weekends working on the garage, and when she could talk him into it, helping Daria hang wallpaper and new curtains in the house.

One Saturday night late in May, they worked together hanging paper in the large master bedroom upstairs. They had been working since sunrise and were both exhausted. Though still strewn with the paraphernalia of the job, the room itself was finished, and Cole was measuring a length of paper for the walk-in closet.

"Honey, I was thinking of using the other pattern in the closet," she suggested carefully. "Don't you think it would look better?"

Cole threw up his hands, and the heavy roll of wallpaper fell to the floor with a thud. "Do you want my help or not?" he snapped.

"Cole," she said in a voice meant to appease, "I just thought the stripes might be hard to match with those sloped ceilings. I wasn't trying to tell you what to do."

"Well, it sure sounded that way!"

She'd known he was tired and a bit testy, but she was shocked at the anger in his voice now. "I'm sorry, honey. I didn't mean to—" She was on the edge of tears. "Let's finish this tomorrow," she suggested. "We can work on it after church while Nattie takes her nap—"

"No," he spat, "I want to get it over with. I don't want to spend the whole weekend on this stupid project."

Her calm reasoning wasn't having its desired effect. "Are you mad at me about something?" Now she was angry, but she tried to make her voice convey hurt instead.

"Daria, I'm not going to stand here at nine o'clock at night and argue about wallpaper. Bring me that other roll."

"No, if you think this looks better, that's fine with me."

"Well, that's a new one." This sounded suspiciously like long pent-up steam hissing out.

"What's that supposed to mean?" she asked cautiously.

He turned to glare at her. "You haven't exactly asked my opinion on the rest of the house."

"Cole…honey, why didn't you say something? I thought you *wanted* me to redecorate—"

"There was nothing wrong with the way the house was when you moved in."

She was stunned. In all the weeks they'd been redecorating, he had never once hinted that he disapproved of her desire to change the wallcoverings and add a few feminine touches.

He brushed past her and crossed the room to retrieve a roll of the floral-patterned paper. Then he turned his back on her and began measuring again.

Fuming at the unfairness of his accusation, she went for the vacuum and started to clean up the mess in the bedroom. While she put the furniture back in place and tucked fresh sheets on the bed, Cole finished papering.

It was almost midnight when he emerged from the closet and stood in front of the door, waiting to catch her eye. Bowing deeply he gave her a sly grin. "There, your majesty. Come and see if this meets your approval."

Sensing his overtures at reconciliation, she approached cautiously and looked inside. "It's beautiful." The entire room had been transformed from an austere bachelor's den to a cozy lovers' nest.

"Honey, I'm…so sorry if you think I've just moved in and taken over. That wasn't my inten—"

But he interrupted her with a finger to her lips. "Shh. I'm the one who's sorry. Forget everything I said. I was just tired and crabby."

"But those things you said didn't just come from nowhere—"

"The house looks great, Daria. I like what you've done. Really. It's just that I'm set in my ways. It's not easy to teach an old dog new tricks. But hey, I'm adjusting, okay?"

She looked at him, trying to read his true thoughts.

But he reached for her hand, and all the harsh words that had passed between them began to fade. "I would hang froufrou, flowery wallpaper every weekend for the rest of my life if that's what it takes to have you in bed beside me every night."

She cocked her head coyly. "Oh, so now it's all about sex?"

"That's not what I meant, and you know it. Although you do have a point there."

She laughed and whacked him with the roll of leftover wallpaper.

"Besides," he continued, ducking out of her reach, "you know what they say about wallpapering, don't you?"

"What?"

"They say if a marriage can survive hanging wallpaper together, it can survive anything."

Her smile held skepticism. "*Did* we survive?"

Pulling her into his arms, he kissed her deeply, then held her at arm's length and looked her square in the eye. "I think we did. Let's just not test it again too soon, okay?" Tenderly, he brushed back a wisp of hair that had come loose from her ponytail. Laughing with relief, she put her head on his chest and tightened her arms around his waist.

The following days reminded her that there were many other adjustments they would have to make. The first time Cole spanked Natalie, Daria had to bite her tongue to keep from protesting. Cole told the obstinate little girl at least four times to leave the stereo alone. But her fascination with the shiny knobs and dials was too strong. When she reached out again, her watchful eye on Cole proving that she knew better, he hoisted her into the air without warning and turning her over his arm, gave her well-padded bottom three sharp smacks.

Natalie let out a scream that Daria knew was more anger and shock than pain, but nevertheless, when she saw Natalie's eyes pleading with her for rescue, everything in her wanted to spring to her daughter's defense. Trembling, she forced herself to go into the kitchen and stand at the counter, as Cole held Natalie and gently explained why he'd had to spank her.

"Listen to me, Nattie," Cole explained patiently. "Daddy told you four times not to bother the stereo, didn't he?"

Daria stepped into the doorway—where she could see but not be seen by Natalie—in time to see the little blond head nod miserably.

"When Daddy says *no*, he means it. Do you understand that, Nattie?"

Again that pitiful nod.

"Daddy loves you very, very much, but I expect you to obey me and Mommy. Now give me a hug, and you can go find a book for me to read to you."

She wrapped her arms around his neck, and Daria marveled at her quick forgiveness. She knew that her willful daughter needed Cole's firm hand, but oh, it was hard to stand by and keep silent.

One Friday at the end of August, Cole appeared in the reception room of the clinic as Daria was getting ready to head out the door to pick up Natalie at her parents' house. Natalie was scheduled to spend the weekend with the Camfields, and Daria planned to meet Jack and Vera at the café in Bristol for the exchange.

But now there he stood, minus his lab coat, his car keys in hand. "Ready?" he asked, as if his going had been part of the routine all along.

"Y-You're going with me?" she stuttered, gathering her purse and sweater.

He nodded. "Yes, I am." He looked around the office, and, apparently satisfied that they were alone, continued, "These little rendezvous in the café every month are ridiculous, Daria. Whether they like it or not, I am Natalie's father now. The least they can do is acknowledge my presence."

"Cole, maybe we should at least call and warn—"

He held up a hand, silencing her. "Don't, Daria. I know you'd like to keep the peace. I promise I'll be a gentleman, but I'm not going to be the mysterious stepfather anymore. Natalie's getting old enough now that she can sense their feelings toward me. I hate to think what they might fill her head with when she's alone with them."

As though that ended the discussion, he opened the door and held it for Daria. She shrugged and ducked under his arm. In silence, she slid into the passenger seat of their car. Cole started the ignition and backed out of the parking lot, his jaw set. They rode in silence to the Haydons'.

While Cole waited in the car, Daria ran inside to get Natalie. Margo had her dressed and waiting. Daria gave her mother a subdued greeting as Natalie stood sleepily between them, thumb in mouth, eyes darting from one to the other.

When Margo knelt to tie the drawstring on Natalie's sweatshirt, she glanced out the open door to the driveway. "Is Cole out there?"

Daria merely nodded.

"He's going with you for the big exchange? It's about time. Cole has been very patient with the Camfields. I'm glad to see he's taking charge of the situation."

"Mom, please," Daria started, eyeing Natalie deliberately.

"Oh, for heaven's sake, she doesn't understand what we're saying!"

"I think she understands more than we realize. I don't want her to get stuck in the middle of all this, Mom. She loves Jack and Vera, and I'd like to keep it that way."

Margo sighed and rolled her eyes, but she kept quiet as she gave Natalie her ritual goodbye kisses.

As they reached the car, Natalie seemed to realize immediately that it was unusual for Cole to be along. "Daddy!" she cried, delighted when she spotted him. She squirmed to get down from Daria's arms, and the minute she was released she flew to the driver's side where Cole was waiting with open arms.

"Hey, squirt! How's my girl?"

"I go see Dwama-Dwampa," she announced.

"I know," Cole said, pulling her up onto his lap and nuzzling her neck with his chin. "Won't you have fun! Now you'd better climb over the seat and let Mommy buckle you in."

"I dwive!" she told him, turning toward the steering wheel and putting her pudgy hands at ten and two o'clock on the wheel as Cole had recently taught her, much to Daria's chagrin.

"Not today, peachy. We're in a hurry. Grandma and Grandpa will be waiting for us."

"No! I dwive!" she repeated firmly, avoiding his eye and gripping the steering wheel tighter.

Cole made his voice firm. "Nattie, get in your car seat right now."

She pretended not to hear him and shook the wheel vigorously, making little *vroom-vroom* noises under her breath.

"Natalie Joan!"

That got her attention, but she hesitated a split second too long, giving the wheel one more deliberate spin.

With jaw clenched, Cole pried her hands from the wheel and lifted her over the front seat, plopping her into her car seat in the back. She immediately began to wail as though she'd been stung by a bee.

Trying to remain calm, Daria buckled the screeching, bucking child into the car seat.

"Natalie!" Cole shouted, putting his right arm on the back of the seat and turning back to glare at her. "Stop that screaming right now."

Her voice rose another octave, and Cole reached to put a hand gently but firmly over her mouth.

Daria touched Cole's arm and pleaded with him. "Honey, please…"

"She has got to learn that she can't get her way every time she throws a fit, Daria."

She held up a hand, frantic to keep the situation from escalating. "I know. You're right, honey. But you're the one who taught her to love driving the car so much in the first place. Can't we just let it go this time? You're going to have her so worked up she'll be a mess when we get to the café."

His face grew red, and he shouted above the wailing child. "And that's exactly the point! She knows if she screams loud enough you'll give in and then she's won! She is playing you like a violin, Daria, and you don't even see it."

He turned away from Daria and spoke firmly to Natalie again, "Natalie, you stop screaming this instant or you will not get to go to Grandma and Grandpa's house. Do you understand me?"

Daria was horrified. She knew her daughter well enough to know that Cole's threat probably wouldn't faze her. And she knew her husband well enough to know that he would follow through on his promise if necessary.

Sure enough, Natalie took a deep breath and screamed even louder. A look of determination crossed Cole's face, and he turned in his seat and started the ignition. Daria closed the back door and climbed into the passenger seat, fastening her seat belt in silence. Cole headed out of the driveway and toward town.

Natalie began to grow quiet as they drove, and they were entering Bristol's city limits when Daria finally mustered the courage to test Cole's intentions.

"I hope I remembered to pack her dressy shoes," she ventured, trying to keep her tone casual.

Cole stared at the road ahead as he answered tersely, "She's not going to need her dressy shoes, Daria, because she isn't going anywhere."

"What do you mean?"

"She has got to learn that when we say something we mean it. She is not going with the Camfields this weekend."

"Cole! They're waiting for us right now!"

"They'll just have to understand. It is going to take something serious to get through to this stubborn little girl, and today is as good a time as any to start."

"Cole, that's not fair to Jack and Vera," she pleaded. "They've driven three hours to get here, and you're asking them to just turn around and go back without her?"

"I'm sorry, Daria. I'll explain the situation to them, and I'll apologize for their wasted trip. Maybe we can offer to bring Nattie to Kansas City next weekend. But I feel very strongly about this. She has got to start understanding that we mean business, and in order for that to happen, we have to start *meaning* business."

Her mind reeling, she clenched her jaw and tried to steel herself for the encounter with the Camfields.

Nineteen

*T*he Camfields were waiting in their sedan when Cole and Daria drove in to the parking lot of the café. Vera's lipsticked smile evaporated the instant she saw Cole emerge from the driver's seat. She turned away from them and busied herself with something invisible on the dashboard. Jack got out of the car and took Cole's outstretched hand politely, but his downcast eyes refused to meet Cole's gaze.

While Daria released a suddenly cheerful Natalie from the car seat, she waited to see how Cole would explain his decision to Natalie's grandparents.

"Jack, I'm afraid we're going to have to disappoint you today," he started, dipping his head in a show of deference. "We're going to disappoint you *and* Natalie," Cole continued.

Jack cocked his head, obviously curious. Daria saw Vera's car window glide down slowly—she knew that the woman hadn't missed a word.

"What's this all about?" Jack asked.

"I sincerely apologize that you drove all this way for nothing, but Natalie isn't going to be able to go home with you tonight. We've been working very hard to help her learn that she can't get her way by throwing a tantrum, but I'm afraid it's going to take something drastic to get the message through to her. We had to tell her that she won't be able to go home with you this time."

Natalie stiffened in Daria's arms, and her wide-eyed stare told Daria that she understood perfectly the gist of what Cole was saying.

Cole went on to explain what had happened at Daria's mother's, concluding with, "I'm really sorry."

Daria thought she saw a glint of something akin to admiration in Jack's eyes, but when Vera let out a wail of dismay, Jack took his cue from her. "I understand what you're trying to do, but don't you think this is a little severe?"

"Like I said, Jack, I'm terribly sorry that our discipline of Natalie had to inconvenience and disappoint you. But I think it is very important that we not back down on this. We would be glad to bring her up to your place next weekend or whenever it's convenient for you. And I'd like to buy you supper before you head back home."

"That won't be necessary," Jack said tersely.

"Daria, please," Vera implored desperately from her roost inside the car.

Jack joined the appeal. "Daria? Please reconsider."

She opened her mouth to speak, but before she could say one word, Cole answered for her, "No, I'm sorry, but we've already decided. We can't give in to her."

How dare he speak for her! How dare he let them believe that she was in agreement with him when he knew exactly the opposite to be true!

"Cole, I think this is Daria's decision to make. Natalie is her daughter," Jack said firmly, as though he sensed the division between them.

"Daria and I are raising Natalie together, Jack, and we will decide how to discipline her and when." Cole spoke deliberately, and Daria knew he was measuring his words very carefully. "We'll be happy to drive her up to visit you next week, but she is not going anywhere this weekend," he repeated.

At this Natalie started to cry, and Vera leapt from the car, red-faced and trembling. "This is ridiculous!" she seethed, slamming the door behind her. She stormed past her husband and Cole and went to where Daria stood holding Natalie in her arms. "Daria, talk some sense into him! We came to see our granddaughter, and I'm not leaving here without her!"

Again Cole spoke before Daria could think of one thing to say.

"Mrs. Camfield," he said calmly, "I understand that you are disappointed, but surely you can see how important it is that we not let Natalie get away with the tantrum she threw only a few minutes ago. If we give in now, we'll never win her obedience."

"That is preposterous," the older woman sputtered. "Of all the cruel things I've heard, this takes the cake." She was almost growling now. "This child is the only thing we have left of our son, and you are *not* going to take that away from us!"

"Vera!" Jack chided sharply. "Settle down now. There's obviously nothing we can say that is going to make a difference here. We'll just have to arrange another time. Let's go."

Vera ignored him and reached for Natalie. "Come here, Nattie. Come and see Grandma," she coaxed in a voice that was suddenly silver.

Natalie saw her opportunity and began to cry even harder, leaning toward her grandmother's outstretched arms. Cole stepped between Vera and his wife and daughter, taking the kicking, screaming child from Daria. He opened the back car door and began restraining Natalie in the car seat again.

Speechless and struggling to rein in her own rising temper, Daria mouthed an apology toward Jack and Vera. She managed to climb into the passenger seat of the car before collapsing in tears.

Cole walked around to the driver's side as Daria watched Jack and Vera get into their own car and drive away, stricken expressions pasted on their faces.

Cole put the car in gear and pulled out of the café's parking lot, turning in the opposite direction from what the Camfields had taken, even though the shortest route home was the same way.

Daria would have lashed out at Cole right then if she'd thought he could hear her over Natalie's screams. Instead she fumed in silence, wondering what she had ever seen in this stubborn, brash man. What had she ever loved about him?

Natalie screamed the entire way home, and when Cole had

parked the car in the garage, he told Daria in a stern voice, "I'll deal with her."

That was where she drew the line. "No! You leave her alone," she shouted, furious, jumping out of the car before he could beat her to it. Cole got out and came around to where Natalie was kicking wildly at Daria, her little face mottled and purple with rage.

"Daria, I understand you're angry with me, but this is between Natalie and me. Please let me handle it."

She ignored him and went on trying to hold down her daughter's flailing limbs and to undo the restraining harnesses at the same time.

Cole put his arms firmly on Daria's shoulders. "Daria, come on. You're as mad as she is. Please, let me take her."

"Get your hands off of me!" she hissed. The venom in her voice terrified even herself. *What's happening to us?* Defeated, she ducked her head and got out, then sagged against the side of the car in tears.

Cole leaned inside the backseat and calmly muscled Natalie out of her restraints. Without looking back at Daria, he cradled Natalie in his arms and carried her into the house. The door slammed behind them.

Daria waited several minutes, standing motionless beside the car. Finally an urgency to know what was happening drove her inside. Natalie's fresh screams met her in the hallway. Cole had apparently put her in her crib, and he was heading down the hallway.

"What are you doing? She's not tired, Cole. You're just going to dump her in bed and walk away?" she accused.

"She can't be reasoned with right now, Daria. She has herself so worked up she just needs to cool off. She's safe in her crib. It won't hurt her to cry it out."

The fact that he had stayed so calm and rational throughout Natalie's entire tantrum infuriated Daria. He seemed completely cold to her daughter's feelings, to the emotional state she'd worked herself into because of his rash discipline. Didn't he have feelings?

"I'm going to go get her and try to calm her down," she said, brushing past him in the hallway, being careful that their skin didn't touch.

"Daria, please don't. You'll just set her off again."

"Set her off! In case you hadn't noticed she's still going strong, Cole. She doesn't understand one thing that's going on. All she knows is that you denied her what she's been looking forward to all day, and now you've thrown her in bed and left her all alone!"

"I didn't *throw* her in bed, Daria." Still that calm, unperturbed manner. "I explained exactly why she was being put to bed, I gave her a hug and a kiss, and I told her I loved her."

Daria snorted. "And that's supposed to make me feel better?"

She saw the first glimpse of anger manifest itself in the flare of his nostrils. "Daria, I'm sorry, but this isn't about making you feel better. This is about getting control of our daughter. She has to learn that when we say something we mean it. She has to learn to accept our discipline, or we are going to have a completely out-of-control little brat on our hands. I will not be part of that, Daria. I know you think I'm being cruel, and I know you don't like to hear your daughter cry. I don't either. But sometimes that's what it takes."

"What makes you such an expert, *Dr.* Hunter?"

He reeled visibly at the contempt in her voice. "I don't claim to be an expert, Daria, but I do know that what we've been doing isn't working." He turned away from her and started back down the hallway.

"Don't walk out on me, Cole!"

He kept going.

She stormed past him, out the kitchen door, and slumped onto the bottom step in the garage. For several minutes, she sat there with her head in her hands, not knowing what to do. It was stifling, and the acrid odor of the car's exhaust lingered in the air. She sniffed away the stinging sensation it left in her nostrils.

Her mind swirled with an alarming muddle of emotions. Rage

at Cole that he had ripped this decision from her without even listening to her input. Horror that she had felt such deep hatred for a
man she loved. Dismay that Cole had allowed this sickening spec-
tacle to play out in front of Jack and Vera Camfield. And under it all,
contempt for herself that she had allowed Natalie to become so out
of control.

She lifted her head and listened for Natalie's wails. She couldn't
hear the sound of crying any longer, and she wondered how long she
would have to sit there before Cole would come after her. He owed
her an apology, but she wasn't sure she could ever forgive him.

She wiped the sweat from her brow with the back of her hand,
then stood up and brushed off the seat of her jeans before quietly
opening the door to the kitchen. The house was grey in the late
evening shadows—and still, as though no one was home.

She flipped on the light over the kitchen sink and washed her
hands, just to make some noise. There was still no sound from either
Cole or Natalie. Curious now, she tiptoed down the hallway and
peeked through the open door of Natalie's room. It was dark in there
as well, but she could hear her daughter's deep breathing. Breaths of
slumber, with the occasional shuddering of one who had cried herself to sleep.

As her eyes adjusted to the darkness, she saw that Cole was sitting in the rocking chair, cradling Natalie against his chest. His back
was to Daria, and he rocked slowly, deliberately, and stroked Natalie's
tiny back in a soothing rhythm, never stopping. His right cheek
rested atop the little girl's head, and Daria could smell the salty mingling of sweat and tears and sleep.

The scene wrenched Daria's heart. Natalie had forgiven her
daddy. The thought caught her up short. Her daddy. What Cole had
told Jack Camfield was right—he was Natalie's father in every sense
of the word. Why had she suddenly become so possessive of their
daughter? Why had his strict discipline angered her so intensely?

The rocking chair creaked as Cole rose carefully, trying, she knew, to get Natalie into bed without waking her. As he turned toward the crib, he saw her leaning against the doorjamb, and he looked at her with an expression she couldn't quite read in the semi-darkness.

He kept his hand on Natalie's back until her breathing grew steady again, and then he motioned for Daria to follow him from the room.

In the hallway, he reached for her tentatively, and when she didn't push him away, he took her face in his hands—gently, but with an urgency she understood fully—and brought his own face close to hers. "Daria, I'm sorry. That got ugly, and I put you in the middle of it. Please forgive me," he whispered.

She wanted to hang on to the anger she'd felt. She wanted to hear him say that the whole fiasco was his fault, yet she knew that wasn't entirely true, so she said nothing.

"Will you forgive me?" he repeated, brushing a strand of hair back from her temple.

"We need to talk, Cole." In spite of her desire to nurse her grudge, she felt its hard edge softening.

He took her hand and led her to the living room, pulling her down on the sofa beside him. "Okay, let's talk."

While he listened, she poured out all her anger, all her doubts, and especially her chagrin at the fact that the blowup had occurred in front of the Camfields. "You couldn't have handpicked anyone worse to humiliate me in front of, Cole," she moaned.

At that he bristled. "I could say exactly the same thing to you, Daria. From day one those people have made me feel unworthy to be Natalie's father. I can understand why it might be hard for them to see me with their granddaughter, but I don't deserve their resentment. There is nothing I want more than to be a good dad to Natalie. And I don't think I'm being unreasonable in hoping that Nate's parents might even feel grateful that under the circumstances I've made Natalie's and your life a little happier, a little more secure.

I admit that I took my frustration out on Jack and Vera. That wasn't fair after they drove all this way. But I truly felt it was important that we not give in to Natalie."

Daria sat silently, refusing to look at him, mulling his words over in her mind.

After a few minutes he spoke again, "I am sorry, Daria. I was wrong. And I'll call Jack and Vera and apologize to them." He paused a beat, then muttered, "Much as it will pain me."

She gave him a tiny smile.

"Oh, Cole," she said finally. "I'm sorry. I've been so focused on myself that I didn't even think about how this affects you. You *are* Natalie's father. And you're a wonderful father. But—" She hesitated, not wanting to start another argument.

"Say it," he urged.

"Well, it wasn't fair for you to just make the decision yourself. You should have talked to me about it before you came down with your verdict."

"I'll give you that," he said with a meek, sideways grin. "But can we agree right now that we will start being more consistent with her? She's a little toughie—I have a feeling we have one of those textbook strong-willed children on our hands—and she's going to play us against each other every chance she gets if she sees that we're divided on this."

"I'll try, Cole. It won't be easy, but I'll try. And I'm so sorry this turned into such a huge fight. I said some horrible things—and thought some even more horrible things. Things I didn't even mean. I need to ask your forgiveness too."

"You know you have it." He took her hand, and they both sat in silence for several minutes. Finally he turned to her. "So what horrible things were you thinking?"

She shook her head firmly. "You don't want to know."

"Then don't tell me," he said, leaning over to kiss her gently. He drew away and then laughed softly. "Man," he said, shaking his head in feigned bewilderment, "I thought we were going to see steam coming from Vera's ears."

Daria giggled at the vision of the prim and proper Vera literally letting off steam, and for now their shared laughter drew her into the circle of her husband's arms.

Twenty

*E*arly in October, autumn finally made a reluctant appearance in Kansas. Daria bent to retrieve another damp pair of Cole's work jeans from her laundry basket. She snapped them briskly and pinned them to the clothesline. A hint of crispness was in the evening air, and though it was a welcome respite from the heat, she thought with regret that it wouldn't be long before she'd have to go back to using the dryer. She clipped the rest of the clothes to the line in a neat row and straightened to flex her aching muscles. Doing a veterinarian's laundry was no small feat. She sometimes had to run Cole's grimy coveralls through the washing machine three times to get them clean. For him she would have made lye soap and scrubbed his jeans on a washboard. She smiled to herself, realizing that she had never expected she would gain such deep satisfaction from a tidy row of clean laundry flapping in the wind.

But it was the view beyond the clothesline—the stretch of backyard that ambled to the creek—that took her breath away. The trees on their land were beginning to turn, a glorious kaleidoscope of gold and scarlet against the rolling green pastureland. When she'd first returned to the States, especially that first winter, she had sometimes longed for the predictable, balmy tropics of Timoné, but after a year of living on this sweep of Kansas prairie, she realized how much she cherished the beauty of the changing seasons, and especially how much she loved the winter snows.

She heard voices and knew that Cole and Natalie were coming up the lane from their nightly stroll to retrieve the mail. She went to the corner of the house where she could watch them without being noticed. Nattie was chattering away about some little object she held in her hand, and Cole was listening intently, as though what she was telling him was the most important thing in the world. Daria couldn't make out their words, but Nattie's voice was like the song of a little bird, her twittering peppered with an inflection of adoration wrapped around two repeated syllables: "Dad-dy, Dad-dy, Dad-dy."

Natalie said something Daria didn't catch, and Cole laughed uproariously and scooped the little girl up and threw her over one broad shoulder like an unwieldy sack of potatoes. She squealed with delight until he finally swung her back to the ground with a tender pat on the head.

Watching them together, hearing their dear voices, Daria was overcome with gratitude for the life she'd been given. Like the tears that pooled behind her eyelids, a prayer of gratitude welled up in her, and she poured out the words without thinking. "O Lord, I'm so blessed. Thank you, Father," she whispered. Her words wafted away on the evening breeze, and she was suddenly overcome with the realization of how rare communion with her heavenly Father had become lately. She felt so unworthy of the blessings he had heaped on her. Her heart was filled with a piercing mixture of gratitude, and of sorrow that she had kept God at such a distance. A brief glimpse of understanding flashed through her mind, and she realized the origin of that distance. It had begun when she'd fallen in love with Cole. She wasn't quite sure why, but she hadn't sought God about her decision to marry again. Anyone with eyes could see now how very right that decision had been. Still, it had been wrong of her to shut God out as she had. A feather of remorse tickled her conscience, but she brushed it away.

"I am sorry, Lord," she whispered, meaning it, but knowing there was more she needed to say—much more. She hadn't confronted the whole truth, and deep in her heart she knew it.

Cole and Nattie were on their way into the house and were calling for her, but she promised herself that she would make things right with her Creator. Soon, she would seek out a time to get alone before him, to fall to her knees and set things right. She would find her way back to the precious relationship she had once shared with the God of the universe.

Cole's pickup bounced along the dusty country road that led out to Bill Wyler's farm. He'd been called to check on some sick cattle, and he was grateful for the time away from the clinic. He needed to sort out some things.

Immediately a picture of Natalie formed in his mind, causing him to smile. He loved that little girl with a love he'd never experienced before in his life. He loved his wife deeply. Daria had brought him a happiness and a wholeness he'd feared he might never know again. But the love he felt for Nattie had come as a staggering, amazing surprise.

He wanted to adopt her. In every sense of the word, he was Nattie's father, and he didn't want there to be any doubt in anyone's eyes, especially hers. He wanted her to have his name.

Late one night after Natalie had gone to bed and he and Daria were sitting on the porch in the dark, Cole had found the courage to broach the subject. "I want her to have my name, Daria," he said, after he'd pled his case.

"Cole, I just don't know if that would be right to the Camfields. Or to Nate," she said quietly.

"I'm not suggesting that we take away the Camfield name, Daria. She could still use it. A lot of kids go by two last names these days—or hyphenated ones," he told her. "Maybe I'm being too sensitive, but I still remember what it was like to grow up the only Hunter in a house full of Bradshaws.

"But that's not the most important thing, Daria. You know that—" A lump rose in his throat, catching him by surprise. He swallowed hard and went on. "You know if, God forbid, anything ever happened to you, Jack and Vera would swoop down to get custody of Natalie so fast I wouldn't know what hit me." The thought almost paralyzed him. He had never been close to his stepfather and had lost contact with the man after his mother's death. It broke his heart to think of the same thing happening between him and Natalie.

"Oh, Cole, that would never happen. Besides," she assured him, taking his hand in hers, "nothing is going to happen to me."

But he couldn't be so sure. He'd lost too many people who were dear to him. It would kill him to lose Natalie along with Daria. Her vulnerability and, perhaps most of all, her adoration of him caused him to love her with an emotion that was almost painful. He and God alone knew the source of the pain. It ate at him like a cancer.

Though Daria seemed to understand his feelings, she still had deep reservations about what the Camfields' reaction would be. He thought she might be softening though. Just last night when he'd brought up the subject again, she'd said thoughtfully, "I know it would save her a lot of explaining. I don't want her to have to tell the whole story every time someone discovers that her name is Camfield and ours is Hunter. And that will be even more of an issue when she has brothers and sisters."

A twinge of anxiety came over him, just thinking about Daria's words. As much as he wanted to persuade her on the adoption, he'd been noncommittal on the subject of having their own children. The subject was one he could scarcely bring himself to think about, let alone discuss with Daria. During their engagement, he had humored her with all her talk about having three or four more children. Nattie had been such a handful that having another child seemed to be the furthest thing from Daria's mind. But he knew he couldn't put her off forever. The thought filled him with dread.

Sometimes, when he and Daria were feeling especially close, when the sense of being a family filled him with gratitude, he could almost put the fears of the past aside, could almost allow himself to dream that they might have a child together someday. But then a glimpse of his secret would bring him up short, and he would be afraid to examine it more closely.

He came so close to pouring out the truth to Daria during those times. But something always stopped him. When things were good he didn't want to spoil them, and when things were strained between them, he wasn't sure Daria could forgive the truth. It was a thing he should have gotten out in the open before he ever asked Daria to marry him. It had certainly not been his intention to hide anything from her. In fact, he'd tried to tell her several times when they'd first begun dating, but something always seemed to stop him before it was out. And when he finally knew that he needed to share this ugly, secret part of his past with her, he loved her too much to risk losing her. He'd justified keeping it from Daria, convincing himself that it had nothing to do with her. But if that were true, why did it hold him in such a tight grip now? Why was it such a huge weight on his heart?

He realized that it was part of the reason he was pushing Daria so hard to agree to the adoption. Maybe if he was bound by law as Natalie's father, Daria would have no choice but to forgive him—not only for the failings of his past, but for keeping them secret from her as well. And he did fear now that keeping the secret was more unforgivable than the secret itself.

Again he reminded himself that God had forgiven him everything. Long ago the sins of his past had been wiped away "as far as the east is from the west." But it felt wrong to have secrets from Daria, and he knew that this skeleton in his closet had come between them in ways he probably didn't even realize.

The Wyler ranch appeared over the crest of a hill, and he pushed the disturbing thoughts out of his mind. He pulled into the drive and parked the pickup near the barn. In his rearview mirror, he saw Mary Wyler emerge from the farmhouse, her silver-white hair mostly covered by a bright red bandanna. He managed to find a genuine smile to greet one of his favorite clients.

But he knew from experience that, like a lump of yeast dough, he'd only temporarily punched his anxieties down. They would bubble and ferment and rise again in his consciousness.

Eventually he would have to deal with them before they destroyed something precious.

She had left the windows open upstairs, and now it was chilly in their bedroom. Daria was grateful that the bedding in her arms was still warm from the dryer. She unfurled the sheets and smoothed them over the mattress, finishing with neat hospital corners.

When the bed was made, she surveyed the room with satisfaction. She loved its coziness. The sconces beside their bed cast a warm glow over the walls, and she smiled to herself as she remembered the night they had hung the wallpaper. They'd had their share of arguments and adjustments since then, but they'd come a long way and things were good.

She was about to switch off the lights and go downstairs when she heard Rufus barking beneath the open window. She crossed the room and leaned out to see what he was barking at. Her eyes followed the noise and traveled beyond the ripening field of milo to the hedgerow that bordered the property behind their house.

There she could see Cole and Natalie in silhouette against the deepening sky, ignoring Rufus as he bounded in a circle around them, yipping joyfully. Cole knelt in front of the little girl, pointing to the heavens and gesturing widely. Her tiny form was dwarfed by the endless prairie behind them. The night air carried their voices— Cole's deep and serious, Natalie's silvery and full of wonderment— but Daria couldn't quite make out their words. A white sliver of moon had already appeared above the horizon. She guessed from his gestures that Cole was explaining the mysteries of the galaxy.

The happy scene brought a lump to her throat. She had been so blessed. God had restored all she had lost and had given her a life full of small pleasures and deep joy. And yet sometimes when she gazed into a sky like tonight's, alight with myriad stars, and sometimes when she looked into the depths of Natalie's eyes, which were really Nathan Camfield's eyes, memories of Nate would overwhelm her. There was still a knot of sadness inside her because of Nate.

Though they rarely spoke of it, she knew that Cole also harbored some ghosts from the sadness of his life before he had met her. Daria had never wished to "undo" the life she'd had with Nate, especially the child he had given her. But Cole had told her once that he wished he had met her before he'd met Bridgette. He seldom spoke of his marriage to Bridgette, but she knew that there must have been some deep unhappiness and unresolved issues in his first marriage for Cole to have such thoughts. She suspected that he still carried some misplaced guilt for Bridgette's death, or at least for her inability to find joy as his wife.

She shook off the melancholy thoughts and put her hand on her stomach. Perhaps the secret she cradled there would be the medicine that would finally heal both of their pasts. They hadn't planned to have a baby so soon. Dealing with Natalie took every ounce of energy she had, and Cole was still getting on his feet with the clinic financially, but she was happy about the baby. It was a blessing. She wasn't quite sure why she had waited so long to give Cole the good news, but when she did, she wanted it to be a special celebration.

She raised the window a few inches and shouted for Natalie to come in for her bath, then she started plotting how she would reveal her happy news to Cole.

aria dug in the kitchen drawer for some matches, then
went into the dining room to light the five slender
candles that graced the center of the table. The white linen cloth was
set with their good china, and a bouquet of the last zinnias from her
garden provided a rainbow of vivid colors. The aroma of roast beef
filled the house, and a perfect raspberry cheesecake—one she'd spent
half the afternoon baking—sat beside the flowers as part of the center-
piece. Daria was lighting the last taper when she heard Cole's truck
coming down the lane.

She suddenly felt as nervous as she had before their first date.
Wiping her sweaty palms on a dishtowel, she ran to the bathroom
and checked her hair one last time.

The back door slammed, and she heard the familiar sounds of
her husband's work boots dropping in the mud room, Rufus's bowl
being filled with dog chow, and Cole's ritual evening announcement,
"Hey, babe, I'm home."

She heard his stocking feet pad across the hardwood floors.
"Mmm, something smells good. Daria? Anybody home?"

"I'm in here," she hollered from the dining room, trying to sound
casual.

She waited by the table, hands clasped in front of her, with what
she knew must be a silly grin on her face.

He peered into the room and did a double take—first at the ele-
gantly set table, and then at his equally elegant wife. "Whoa! What
on earth?"

"Hi!" she said coyly, smoothing the skirt of his favorite dress. She
smiled at the befuddled expression he wore.

"What is going on?" Suddenly a look of panic crossed his face. "This isn't our anniversary, is it?"

She burst out laughing and pulled him toward her by the collar of his flannel shirt, kissing the tip of his nose. "No, you goose. We got married on Valentine's Day, remember? I did that on purpose so you wouldn't have so many holidays to remember."

"Then what's all this about?"

"You'll see," she said mysteriously. "Now why don't you go jump in the shower and change into something"—she looked his filthy work clothes up and down—"I'll settle for something *clean*," she laughed.

He started down the hallway, shaking his head in puzzlement, then turned back to her. "Hey, where's Nattie?"

"She's with my mom. Just go get in the shower."

He mumbled, questioning, under his breath, but he headed back to the bathroom.

Ten minutes later, they were enjoying roast beef and mashed potatoes, sweet corn, and tangy three-bean salad—all Cole's favorites. He ate the last bite of his buttered crescent roll, leaned across the corner of the table, and put a finger under Daria's chin. "Now would you please tell me what this is all about?"

"Not until you've had your dessert." She had managed to keep her secret all through dinner and was thoroughly enjoying the buildup.

"Daria, come on! I am dying of curiosity!"

"You really want to know?"

"Even more than I want raspberry cheesecake."

"That much, huh?"

He nodded, waiting.

She took his hands in hers. "This, my dearest darling," she said, deliberately drawing out the suspense, "is to celebrate the fact that by this time next year there will be another little set of feet pitter-pattering on these floors."

He looked at her mutely, apparently uncomprehending.

She laughed at the dumbstruck expression pasted on his face. "We are going to have a baby, silly!"

"What?"

She waited for him to whoop and holler, but he obviously was not catching on. "Cole, do I have to draw you a picture? I'm pregnant, honey!"

"Daria? No! You're not…"

Whatever she had expected to see in his eyes, it wasn't this gleam of fear, this bizarre, grim reaction to the wonderful news she'd just given him.

"Cole? Aren't you happy? I thought you'd be happy. Honey?"

He pushed his chair back from the table and got up, pacing, rubbing his forehead as though her news had given him an excruciating headache.

She rose and went to him, frantic now to know why he seemed so adverse to the wonderful news. She put a hand on his back and was alarmed to find that he was trembling. "Cole! What's wrong?"

"Sit down, Daria. We need to talk."

Her heart began to bang in her chest. What was going on? What was wrong with him?

Like a robot, he returned to the table and sat down, his face an expressionless mask. He put his head in his hands and scrubbed his face, sighing again and again as though he was trying to catch his breath.

"Cole? Please, what is it?"

"There's something I have to tell you, Daria. I-I haven't told you everything—"

"What are you talking about, Cole? Please, you're scaring me."

"Daria, you…you don't know everything…about Bridgette …about how she died." He sighed again and then turned to look her full in the face.

"Bridgette had—we had a baby together, Daria." He swallowed

hard. "We lost him—a little boy. He was stillborn, the cord got wrapped around his neck."

Daria was stunned, and tears sprang to her eyes. "Oh, Cole. How terrible!"

"We named him Carson. We held him in our arms, and then we buried him two days later. I don't even have a picture of him." He recited the information as though he were reading it from a newspaper, as though it had nothing to do with him.

"Why didn't you tell me this, Cole?" In spite of the deep sorrow she felt at his obvious grief, she was shocked and angry that he had kept it from her. Cole had been a father! He'd had a little boy! How could she not have known this about him? How could he have failed to tell her something of this magnitude before? What other secrets had he kept from her? And yet her heart was broken, for she knew how deeply he must have felt this sorrow, how great the pain he endured must have been.

"I *should* have told you, Daria. God knows I should have."

"Then why didn't you?" Her voice sounded cold and unsympathetic, but she felt betrayed, not sure if she even knew this man anymore.

"I was afraid. I was afraid it would be more than you could accept. It was a terrible time in our lives. Bridgette had been so happy, so looking forward to the birth. She took the baby's death really hard—understandably. But she couldn't seem to get over it, Daria. Months went by, and she still couldn't even function. She just checked out. She started hating the doctors, hating God… After a while I think she started hating me, *blaming* me. And maybe she was right to blame me."

He paused, and Daria could see that he was trying to gain control over his emotions. She waited in silence for him to go on, her mind racing.

Finally he told her, "When Bridgette went into labor, she wanted to stay home as long as possible. Her pregnancy had been an easy one and, after all, I was the great Dr. Hunter." He spat out a mirthless laugh. "I thought I knew so much, but I didn't even see the signs. Surely they were there. I should have gotten her to the hospital. They said if we'd come in sooner and gotten her on a monitor they might have discovered that he was…that he was strangling, before it was too late."

A part of Daria longed to go to him, to put her arms around him and give him her understanding and comfort. But she couldn't seem to get around the wall of his duplicity, a wall he'd built with his own lies. Why had he kept this from her? This deepest sorrow of his life. And one that had everything to do with Bridgette's suicide.

She asked him again, "Why, Cole? Why didn't you tell me?"

He shook his head. "I don't know, Daria. I meant to tell you. I tried several times, I truly did. But something always interrupted. And then I convinced myself that the time wasn't right. I loved you so much I couldn't face losing you. It's not an excuse, Daria, but it's the only true thing I can tell you."

What he had told her—that he'd had an infant son, that he'd lost not only his wife, but a child as well—completely changed the picture she had carried of him.

"Cole, I'm so sorry. But *why?* Couldn't you trust me?"

"I don't know what else to say, Daria."

"Then neither do I." She felt dead inside. This evening that should have been the happiest in their lives had taken a macabre turn, had become a nightmare. Suddenly she lashed out, not willing to accept the silence between them now. "Did you think I wouldn't understand? Did you think I couldn't empathize with you? What?"

Now he glared at her, returning anger for anger. "If I had been half a husband, Bridgette would be alive today, Daria! Do you understand that? Can't you see that? Her doctor said she was probably suffering from serious postpartum depression, said that was why she couldn't seem to get over it. They gave her some medication, but she wouldn't take it. And I didn't force her. I hated her weakness. I hated that she couldn't handle this, that she shut me out. But I should have seen what was happening. I should have realized that my wife needed more help than I was giving her."

My wife. The words cut into Daria like a knife, but she didn't have time to dwell on the ache because Cole's next words brought her to her senses.

"It wasn't enough that I killed my own son! Bridgette died because I *let* her die! A blind man should have been able to see that she wasn't getting any better. But I just kept waiting and waiting, thinking surely tomorrow she would be a little better. And then one day there weren't any tomorrows left. I think I know in my heart that her death was no accident. And it's my fault, Daria! Would you have married me knowing that? Would you have trusted me with Natalie? Do you trust me now to help you through this pregnancy?" His voice broke, and his shoulders heaved silently.

"Cole." She pushed away from the table and went to him, kneeling in front of his chair. "Oh, Cole. It wasn't your fault. You couldn't have stopped her. And how could you have known about the baby? It wasn't your fault! None of it! Oh, honey, I'm sorry. I'm so sorry."

He fell into her arms and wept, and she felt the anger drain from her heart. "Cole, there's nothing you could tell me that would keep me from loving you. Nothing! We have to be honest with each other. We have to trust each other."

He sat upright and took her hands in his. "How *can* you trust me after what I've just told you?"

"Cole, you shouldn't have kept it from me. That was wrong. But it's in the past now. I think you're taking blame where it doesn't belong—"

"Daria, I placed this all before the Lord a long time ago. I know he's forgiven me, but I'm not sure I can ever forgive myself. No, I didn't willfully murder my family, but are they any less dead because my mistakes were unintentional? I didn't deserve to find you. I certainly didn't deserve Nattie, but when God put you both in my life,

I felt as though it was his way of telling me that I truly *was* forgiven. But I-I must not have believed it completely, because I was afraid. I was flat out terrified to tell you the truth about myself. I should have known you'd understand. But I couldn't, I just couldn't face losing someone I loved again." He spoke as though he were realizing it himself for the first time.

Daria grasped his hands tighter. "Cole, we're going to have a baby. This should be the happiest time of our lives."

"Daria, I'm too afraid to be happy about this. What if something goes wrong? I can't face losing you, losing another baby. And if that happens, I'll lose Nattie, too."

She stroked his head the way she would have comforted a frightened little boy. "No Cole, that's not going to happen. You would never lose Nattie. Nothing is going to happen. I'm fine." She took his hand and placed it over her belly, covering it with her own. "This baby will be fine. Everything will turn out fine, you'll see."

He took her face in his hands, and his voice was fierce when he told her, "I love you, Daria. What would I do without you?"

"It doesn't matter," she whispered. "You'll never have to find that out. Never."

*H*is eyes were open, but he thought he must surely be dreaming. The voices he heard were speaking English—crisp, unaccented American English. After all this time, it was a sound so strange it almost sounded like a foreign tongue to his ears.

There were at least two of them—deep, masculine voices—and they were shouting.

"Show us where it is now, or I'll blow your head off!"

Nate winced as the man let out a string of profanities. These were not the first words of his native language he'd hoped to hear. He threw off the dirty, coarse cloth that had covered him and sat up on the hard dirt floor of the hut. Peering through the thin slivers of space between the bamboo and grasses that made up his prison, he cocked his head to one side, straining to hear the rest of the exchange.

The thick leaves of a palm tree blocked Nate's view of the Americans, but he could clearly see the face of the man called Juan Mocoa. He was on his knees before the Americans, and, judging by the tension in his jaw and the raw fear in his eyes, his life was at stake.

"Please, no. I tell you where it is, Captain," Mocoa squealed. "I give it back. I give it all back, Captain."

Nate was stunned to hear Mocoa plead for his life in fluent English. He had always been suspicious of Juan Mocoa, for the man seemed to have a vested interest in Nate's continued imprisonment—though why, Nate could only guess. Now, hearing him speak English, his suspicions were heightened.

If these men were enemies of Mocoa, perhaps, Nate thought, they could help him escape. Then, taking a chance, he shouted at the top of his lungs in English, "Hey! Help me out here! Hey!" His heart was beating so hard in his chest that it frightened him, yet he felt stronger than he had in weeks.

Still peeking through the wall of his hut, he watched one of the Americans step into view and walk toward the sound of his voice, eyes darting to and fro.

"Who said that?" the American shouted. "Where are you, man?"

Even from his inferior vantage point, Nate could see Juan Mocoa's mind working, plotting to use this interruption to his advantage. But the other American, the one Mocoa called Captain, moved in to stand over him, gun ready, while his partner walked cautiously toward the sound of Nate's voice.

"Show yourself!" the American bellowed.

Nate struggled to his feet and rattled the door of the hut, afraid to let himself realize how close he might be to freedom. "Here! I'm over here!"

The American turned his rifle on the young native guard who had shrunk down outside Nate's door as soon as he heard the commotion.

"Open the door," the American ordered, gesturing roughly with his gun. The youth looked to Juan Mocoa, as if seeking permission. Then, realizing that Mocoa was in no position to give orders, he looked back to the gun and complied, struggling briefly with the vine ropes that served as a lock.

Within seconds Nate was standing before a red-bearded, blue-eyed American.

"Who are you?" the man demanded.

Nate almost couldn't speak over the lump in his throat. "Nathan Camfield. Dr. Nathan Camfield. I'm a missionary to the Timoné village two days downriver." Now the words poured out in a rush. "I've been held captive here for... What's the date?"

The man looked at the bulky watch he was wearing. "It's the sixth."

"No, what month?"

The American scratched his beard. "How long have you been here, man?"

"I don't know. I-I've lost track. It was late July when I came."

"July? Are you sure? It's April."

Had he been here less than a year? It seemed much longer, a lifetime. "My wife...I left her at Timoné. Can you take me there?"

"Briggs!" he shouted at the man guarding Juan Mocoa. "We've got a problem!"

The two men conferred quietly while Nate stood outside his prison hut. Excitement rose in him as he thought of the possibility that these men might be his way out. He guessed—by their coarse language and the fact that they had business with the likes of Juan Mocoa—that they were involved in the lucrative drug trafficking that thrived in the area, but surely their sense of decency would persuade them to help a fellow American.

From their coded conversation Nate surmised that Juan Mocoa had been employed as a courier for their business. Mocoa's greed had done him in. He had apparently tried to get a piece of the action for himself, and now, in spite of giving up the location of his secret cache, it seemed they didn't forgive easily.

Nate watched them carefully, knowing that Juan Mocoa's fate might determine his own. Red Beard started for the river and motioned for Nate to follow him. But before he had taken ten steps, Nate heard the sickening sound of a gunshot fired at close range.

Three hours later, Nate sat in a small flat boat, the *putt-putt-putt* of the outboard motor the sweetest music his ears had ever heard. He leaned against the filthy canvas tarp at the back of the boat, trying not to think about the heavy bundles the tarp concealed. He might be dreaming, yet never had his dreams conjectured fleeing Chicoro on a boat loaded with cocaine and piloted by drug traffickers. If this was real—and he prayed it was—God did indeed work in mysterious ways.

Juan Mocoa had paid a traitor's price and now lay rotting on the floor of the rain forest. But the fact that Nate was now on-board this boat seemed to indicate that the Americans had no intention of harming him. Still he understood that his passage with them depended on his silence.

He remembered the way Mocoa had kept his guards well supplied with cigarettes and rum, and he speculated on Juan Mocoa's motivation to keep him captive in Chicoro. Perhaps because Nate was an American, Mocoa worried that he was sympathetic to the cartel Mocoa had defrauded, the one that now provided Nate passage on this boat. Or perhaps Mocoa simply feared that if Nathan were released, he would report him to the national authorities and ruin his successful little private enterprise.

His mind reeled with all that had happened, and confusion spun a web around his brain. Perhaps he would never know exactly why he had been held here. And yet, as this place of his captivity faded into the distance, one fact gave him peace, one truth made sense of the senseless. He had remained faithful. And he had shared the object of that faith with every villager who had come near his humble prison. Every guard, every youth who delivered a gourd of water or a rice-filled leaf to his hut had heard the name of Jesus. In spite of the language barrier, he had made every effort to point them to the one, true God Almighty. Perhaps that had been God's purpose in this all along.

As the boat entered the wide part of the river and picked up speed, Nathan began to tremble. A spate of adrenaline and renewed hope coursed through his veins, but he was weak from the extended lack of exercise and proper nutrition and from the ongoing effects of the injuries he had suffered in the fire. As a doctor, he recognized that his health was in a gravely compromised state. He felt panic rising within him at the thought of Daria in captivity. Could she have survived the type of imprisonment he had endured? His mind simply could not sort through all the possibilities.

In the front of the boat, the two Americans shouted back and forth over the drone of the outboard motor, discussing the weather conditions and planning their route. The man called Captain filled out some sort of log, stating the date and the year aloud.

Nathan leaned forward. Surely he hadn't heard the man correctly. "What did you say today's date was?" Nathan asked, his heart pounding.

"April sixth."

"No—I mean, the year."

Captain repeated the date.

He had heard correctly.

Red Beard looked at his map again and turned to shout back to Nathan. "Looks like Timoné is the wrong direction, Camfield, but if you're not in a big hurry, we can get you to Bogotá."

Nathan almost laughed at the absurdity of it. "No rush," he told them, still wrestling to grasp the man's matter-of-fact mention of the year—and the stunning realization that he had been in captivity for more than two and a half years.

ARA:
THE ALTAR

*D*aria loaded the last of the lunch dishes in the dishwasher and, still drying her hands on a towel, wandered into the living room where Cole was roughhousing with Natalie.

"Colson Hunter!" she playfully reprimanded. "How do you expect me to ever get her down for her nap when you have her wound up like a top?"

"Hey, I'm just trying to wear her out for you," he panted, galloping across the carpet on all fours, hot on the heels of a squealing Natalie.

"Tickle monster! Tickle monster!" Natalie's delighted screams pierced the air.

The tickle monster overtook her and nuzzled her neck with his scratchy Saturday beard until she begged for mercy.

Natalie managed to escape the monster's clutches, and while she scurried to hide under a sofa cushion, Cole sneaked around behind the sofa and popped up in front of her.

Daria laughed.

As he knelt in front of the sofa, the tempting target of the tickle monster's backside presented itself to Daria and, unable to resist, she snapped him with her dishtowel. The damp corner hit its mark with a loud crack and surprising accuracy. The enraged monster let out a howl and turned on Daria, scuttling after his new victim on hands and knees.

While Natalie looked on, her eyes wide, Daria ran for her life. Adrenaline sped through her veins, and she ran squealing across the living room with Cole right behind.

Breathless, she raced down the hallway and back and finally

sought asylum on the couch with Natalie. Cole attacked them both, roaring and nuzzling until he reduced them both to helpless giggles.

Ignoring Natalie temporarily, Cole concentrated on Daria, and she began to understand what Natalie saw in this game. He planted a kiss on her stomach, patting her rounded belly over her baggy sweatshirt—the belly that held a child he now looked forward to with joy.

Cole lay his head on her belly, and then with a playful gleam in his eye, nuzzled a trail up to her neck. Quickly the nuzzling turned to kisses, and then something more than adrenaline surged through her blood.

"Hey, do we get to take a nap too?" Cole whispered conspiratorially.

"Mmm, if you're a good boy," she breathed against his neck, suddenly wanting him fiercely.

"Cross my heart," he promised. "I'll even help you get this one packed off to bed." He tipped his head in Natalie's direction.

Daria laughed as he scooped Natalie up and headed toward her bedroom with an urgency that she knew had nothing to do with the child's need for a nap.

He wasn't halfway down the hall when the doorbell pierced the silence. Natalie came tearing back out to the living room. "I get it! I get it!" she squealed.

Cole shrugged at Daria over the little girl's head, and Daria went with her to answer the door.

A U.S. Postal Service truck idled in the driveway, and a middle-aged man with a post office insignia on his shirt stood on the porch.

He took off his cap and dipped his head toward her. "Good afternoon, Mrs. Hunter. American Telegram sent this. It went to your old address in town, but we knew you'd moved out here, and we're supposed to deliver these in person. Sorry to bother you on a Saturday. Hope it's not bad news."

Daria couldn't remember ever receiving a telegram in her life. She hadn't even known it was still possible to send a telegram.

She thanked the man and coaxed Natalie back inside as she unsealed the envelope.

Cole came down the hallway with Natalie's quilt over his arm. "Come on, Nattie. It's time for your nap." He turned to Daria. "Who was that?"

"It's a telegram, addressed to me."

"Really? Probably some sales gimmick."

"The post office delivered it."

"On a Saturday? Pretty expensive sales gimmick. Come on, Nattie, hurry up. Get your Pooh bear and follow me."

Daria pulled the yellow sheet of paper from the envelope, unfolded it, and began to read. *Was this some kind of sick joke?*

NATHAN CAMFIELD FOUND ALIVE. FLYING INTO K.C.
INT'L. VIA BOGOTA 12 APRIL. CALL AMERICAN EMBASSY
IMMEDIATELY FOR FLIGHT CONFIRMATION.

This can't be real. But even as the thought went through her mind, she somehow knew the telegram's words were true.

She felt the strength ebb from her body, and she leaned against the wall of the hallway. Though her vision blurred, she read the glorious, damning words again.

Flashes of memory came at her, repeating themselves as though she were seeing them from a carousel spun out of control. There was Nate in Colombia, his long legs jumping across the narrow stream to their hut, smiling in anticipation of seeing her after a day away from the village. She blinked and there was Cole in his office at the clinic the first time they'd met, holding Natalie in his arms and looking down on the baby as though he knew even then that he would someday be her father. Then Nate's face appeared again, the way he had looked the night he first told her he loved her. The carousel continued to spin, and she saw Cole and Natalie walking hand in hand down the lane to their farm, singing. But the song was drowned out by an odd cacophony that roared in her head—the voices of the people she loved, the hushed song of the Rio Guaviare, the nasal dialect of the Timoné, the relentless howling of the Kansas wind.

Daria put her head in her hands and tried to drown out the din, afraid she would be sick. She had a vague sense of Cole standing behind her.

"Be quiet so Mommy can read her letter," he shushed Natalie. He moved in front of Daria.

"Is it from Dwama? Is it from Dwama?" Natalie jumped up and down.

"What is it, Dar?" Cole was watching her face closely, and there was deep concern in his voice.

"Oh, dear God." It was a prayer of utter anguish, but she didn't recognize the low, wretched, tremulous groan of her own voice.

"Daria! What's wrong?"

She shoved the paper toward him and slumped to her knees.

Natalie started to cry. She came to her mother's side and leaned her tiny head on Daria's shoulder, whimpering with confusion.

Cole read the telegram in stunned silence. "No. This can't be right! This isn't…" He turned the paper over and over again in his hands as though he would find an explanation in the small print.

"Daria?" Cole knelt beside her, but before he could pull her into his arms, Natalie transferred from her unresponsive mother into the waiting circle of Cole's arms.

Daria was aware that her daughter was frightened and confused. A rational part of her longed to comfort Natalie, to draw comfort *from* her, but she couldn't seem to make her muscles respond to her brain's command.

Almost involuntarily, she began to rock back and forth on her knees, her arms wrapped tightly around her own shoulders. "Oh, Nathan… What are we going to do, Nate?" she moaned.

Cole stepped back as though he'd been slapped. The echo of her own words reverberated through her mind, and she realized that she had called Cole by Nathan's name.

She reached out for him, disconsolate that she had hurt him, now of all times, desperately needing to feel his arms around her. "Cole. I-I don't know what to do. I don't know what this means," she repeated over and over.

Cole pulled her into his embrace, and Natalie quieted between them, putting a tiny hand on each of their shoulders, her bright eyes darting from one to the other, innocently oblivious to the drama that was being played out in her family.

Daria felt Cole's chest heave in mute sobs and, as she contemplated the reason for his sorrow at this news that should have been rejoiced over, the reality of the situation rolled over her like a tsunami.

Nate was alive! Her first love, the love of her life—the man to whom she had joyfully given the gift of her virginity, the gift of her firstborn—had risen from the dead. The hopeful, desperate wish she had dared to entertain as a grieving widow more than two years ago had come true. But the realization of that dream had spawned a nightmare more horrible than any sleep had ever conjured.

Cole gave her one last hug and stood, pulling her to her feet with him. She saw that look of determination in his eyes that she knew so well, and she felt consoled that he would take care of this, that he would make everything right again.

"Let's get Natalie in bed," he told her, businesslike. He picked the little girl up and started toward her bedroom. "Come on, sweetie. Let's go find that Pooh bear and put him down for his nap."

Daria heard Natalie's giggles as they disappeared into her room. Paralyzed, she stood in the living room, the telegram at her feet. Finally she forced herself to walk down the hallway. She tiptoed into the nursery and stood there, her back against the wall for support, her mind reeling.

Cole was kneeling beside Natalie's bed, brushing her hair from her forehead in smooth, featherlight strokes meant to lull her to sleep. Her eyes were closed, but she was still sucking her thumb furiously, so Daria knew she wasn't asleep yet.

The sight of Cole's tenderness with Nattie, the sudden realization of what this news might mean for the two of them, panicked her. She couldn't stay there another second. She turned and fled the room. Cole must have sensed her fear, for he followed her out of the room. Then, after shutting the nursery door quietly, Cole put his arm tightly around Daria's shoulders as they went silently back to the living room.

The telegram lay crumpled on the floor where they'd left it. Cole picked it up and read it one more time. "We need to find out where this came from," he said. "Maybe it's a mistake."

He went to the desk in the kitchen and picked up the thick Wichita phone book. Turning to the business pages, he found the local number for the company that had sent the message. But before he could dial the number, the phone rang.

Daria started, her heart pounding as if it had been a gunshot. Cole picked up the receiver. "Hello...yes, she's here. May I ask who's calling?"

She couldn't possibly speak to anyone, yet Cole was handing her the telephone. "It's Jack Camfield," he said, his face stark with fear.

She took the handset, trembling. "Hello, Jack."

The man's voice quavered. "Daria, w-we've had some news here. Nate is—" Now his voice broke, and Daria knew that they had received the same telegram.

"Yes, I know, Jack. We just got the telegram."

"We called the embassy, Daria. We've spoken to Nate! He's weak and somewhat confused, but he's alive. Our son is alive!" Now Nate's father broke down and sobbed, and Daria wept with him. Cole put a supportive hand on her back. When Daria glanced up at him, she saw that his eyes were closed and his lips were moving in fervent prayer.

Jack Camfield's voice in her ear drew her attention back to the telephone. "They are flying Nathan back to Kansas City, Daria. His plane comes in tomorrow morning, but they want to take him immediately to the hospital for tests."

She was trying to write down the information he was giving her, but her hands were shaking and useless.

"What happened, Jack?" Her voice rose a pitch. "Where has he been all this time? I don't understand what happened."

"We don't know everything yet, but according to the embassy in Bogotá, Nate was being held prisoner in the village near Timoné where he went to help."

"But I don't understand," she repeated. "How could we have thought he was dead? Tados and Quimico told me they saw him die in the fire!"

"I don't know, Daria. Perhaps they lied to you. The man we spoke with at the embassy said Nate has some burns and severe scarring, so maybe he was in the fire. Nathan is in a Bogotá hospital. We're not really sure of his condition. He spoke to me and told me he was fine, but as I said, he seemed confused about some things. We weren't able to speak but a few minutes."

There was a long pause and then Jack Camfield said, "He asked about you, Daria. His first concern was for you. You will be there to meet his flight, won't you, Daria?"

"Oh, Jack. I-I don't think I can! I don't know what I'm going to do. I-I can't even think clearly right now."

"Daria, Nathan needs to see his daughter. He needs to know that he has everything to live for, that he has a life to come back to here."

"Did you tell him about Natalie?"

"Yes, I did, Daria. I'm sorry if you wanted to tell him yourself, but he needed some good news. He needed to know that he had something to come back to," he repeated.

There was accusation in his voice. And why wouldn't there be? She felt truly sorry that Jack Camfield had had the odious task of telling his son that Daria had remarried. She wanted to ask him how Nate had taken the news, but she wasn't sure she could bear to hear the answer. Her thoughts were spinning out of control. What must Nate think of her. She couldn't imagine how she would feel if the tables had been turned and it was she who returned to find that Nate had left her for dead and gone merrily about his life. She thought then of the baby, Cole's baby. Had Jack told him about that, too? *Oh, dear Lord, please help Nate to understand!*

"Daria, please. I need to know. Will you be there to meet his plane?" Jack was pressing her for an answer.

"No, Jack! I-I can't make a decision like that yet. Please, I'm so confused. I can't." Fearing she might faint, she whispered into the phone, "Would you please speak with my husband?"

She handed the phone over to Cole, scarcely realizing the irony of the words she had just spoken: *my husband.* Who *was* her husband?

She was vaguely aware that Cole was jotting down addresses and numbers on a notepad, speaking with Jack in terse sentences. Finally he hung up the phone and slumped into a kitchen chair beside Daria. He put his head in his hands and moaned.

They sat in silence for several minutes. When Cole finally looked up, he placed his hands on Daria's shoulders. "You need to decide what you're going to do."

"Cole, I—"

"Daria, the man you were married to first is alive." His voice had lost all expression. His eyes were glazed as he continued. "Nathan is on his way home, and he is going to need to see h-his wife and"—his voice caught, and he choked out the final words—"his daughter."

With a loud scraping sound that echoed through the house, Cole pushed his chair back from the table and walked out the back door.

Twenty-Four

ole opened the door and stepped into the kitchen. The house was quiet. He walked through the dining room and saw Daria lying on the sofa. She appeared to be asleep, but her face was swollen and red from crying. Natalie was curled in the curve of Daria's body, sleeping soundly. Everything in him wanted to go to them, to lie down beside them and take them in his arms and never let go. Everything he loved in this world was lying on that sofa—his wife, the precious little girl who called him *Daddy*, and the baby God had created of his and Daria's love. And he was going to lose them all.

He longed to awaken Daria, to wrap her in his arms and tell her how sorry he was for running out on her the way he had an hour ago. But he had lost the right to do that. Daria belonged to someone else.

With leaden feet, he climbed the stairs to their bedroom and lay down on top of the quilt fully dressed. He stared at the ceiling, wishing that Daria would come to him, wishing he knew where he stood with her. He drifted off to sleep, and when he next opened his eyes, he heard Daria and Natalie downstairs.

He went to the bathroom to wash his face. When he went down to the kitchen, Daria was standing there in her jacket, her purse over her shoulder, writing something on the notepad by the telephone.

"Oh," she said when she saw him. "I-I didn't want to wake you." She seemed so awkward, so stiff, as if they were strangers.

"Where are you going?"

"I'm going to take Natalie to my folks. I think it'd be best if she was with them for a few days while we…decide what we're going to do."

He nodded, but he thought bitterly that it wouldn't be "we" who made a decision. This was completely out of his hands. It was a decision Daria would have to make alone.

He heard Natalie pad down the hallway. When she saw him, she ran to his side. "Daddy, I goin' to Grammy's house!" she chirped.

He gulped back tears, and his voice cracked when he told her, "I know, sweetie. Mommy told me. You be good for them, okay, Nattie?"

She put her tiny hands on her hips and declared, "Daddy! I *always* good."

Daria corralled Natalie to put her jacket on her, and then they were gone.

He went to the window and watched the car until it turned onto the main road. Walking back to the kitchen, he noticed the notepad lying on the counter. He picked it up.

> *Cole,*
> *Nattie and I are going to my folks for a while. I'll talk to*
> *you tomorrow. I do love*

She had stopped writing when he had come in. He wished he had come half a minute later.

❧

The next morning in the dead silence of the house, Daria's words—*I do love*—still echoed in his ears, but it seemed as though they'd been written a thousand years ago. He went to the kitchen and picked up the telephone. Rummaging through a stack of papers, he extricated a worn slip of paper, and dialed the long-distance number neatly printed on it.

The phone continued to ring as his thoughts roiled. Finally an impatient voice answered.

"Dennis?"

"Yeah, this is Dennis. Who's calling, please?"

"It's Cole, Dennis. I'm sorry to bother you on a Sunday, but I need your help."

Dennis Chastain was an old friend, a college buddy turned lawyer who had opened a practice in Kansas City. From time to time, he helped Cole with some of the legal intricacies of running a veterinary practice.

"Hey, Cole! Great to hear from you! Whatsa matter, you land yourself in jail?" he said jokingly.

"No, Dennis." He sighed deeply. "I'm not even sure where to begin."

"This sounds serious," Dennis said, immediately contrite.

"It *is* serious, Dennis. You know that Daria was widowed before we married," he said without preamble. "She was told that her husband was killed while they were missionaries in Colombia."

"Yes…" Chastain waited patiently on the other end, understandable curiosity in his voice.

"Well, we received a telegram yesterday telling us that he has been found alive."

"Whoa! That sounds like some kind of hoax to me, Cole—"

"I wish it were. We spoke to his parents yesterday. They received an identical telegram, and they've spoken to their son. He's in a hospital in Bogotá. Everything checks out, Dennis. It's no hoax. Nathan Camfield is alive and flying into Kansas City today."

"You—You're positive?"

"As sure as we can be until we've actually seen him."

"That's unbelievable!"

"Yes. I-I need to know what this means for us legally, Dennis. Is my wife still legally married to this man? What does this do to my marriage? I don't even know where to begin…" He let his voice trail off as the magnitude of the situation rolled over him again.

"Oh, man, Cole! I've never run up against anything remotely like this. I know there were some similar situations after World War II and, for that matter, probably after Vietnam, too. But what the legal ramifications were, I'm honestly not sure. I'm going to have to do some checking on this one. Let's see, how long have you and Daria been married?"

"A little over a year."

"And how long had her first husband been dead—or I should say missing?"

"It's been…" Cole did some quick calculations in his head. "Well, it's got to be close to three years now. Daria is pregnant with our child, Dennis. I can't lose her!" He knew the desperation he was feeling had crept into his voice.

"I'll do everything I can to help you, Cole," Dennis said in a calming voice. "I'll have to look up the actual wording of the laws, but unless there's been deceit on your wife's part, or something like that, my guess is that the law would uphold your marriage since her husband was believed dead. But since you've been married less than seven years, that may complicate things. I'll have to check into this," he added hastily. "Your marriage is probably completely secure. Like I said, I've never come across this situation before, but I'll find out. I promise you that. I'll do whatever I can to help."

When Cole was silent on his end, Dennis asked gently, "Cole, is it clear that Daria wishes to…remain with you?"

Cole hadn't dared to ask his wife that question yet, and neither had she volunteered an answer. "I don't know, Dennis. We're still in shock over the whole thing."

"I can't even imagine," the lawyer said sympathetically. "Give me your number, and I'll get back to you the minute I can find some answers."

Cole recited the number woodenly. Then, thanking his friend, he dropped the receiver in its cradle. *O Father, please help me. I don't understand why you're doing this to us. What do you want me to do, God? Please show me. Please, Father. I need you.*

He put his head in his hands and wept like a child.

When Daria returned from her parents' house, Cole was sitting at the telephone in the dark, his back to her.

She went to him and put her hands on his shoulders. Cole's muscles tensed under her touch, and she took a step back.

"I called Dennis Chastain," he said to her evenly, not turning around.

"Oh... What did he say?"

"He couldn't really tell me anything definite."

She took a deep breath. "Cole, Dad thinks I need to go to Kansas City to talk to Nate in person. Find out how badly he's injured..." She let her voice trail off, hoping for some indication of how he was receiving this idea.

But he sat there in silence, still refusing to look at her.

"Cole," she said, attempting to keep her voice steady, "Nate will want to see Natalie. He'll have to see her—"

He whirled to face her now. "I know that, Daria," he said tersely. "He'll have to see you, too. Do you think I don't know that?"

She was shocked at the venom in his voice, but it gave her a surge of strength. "Cole, stop it!" she said firmly. "I can't do this if you lash out at me! This is the hardest thing I've ever faced. I need your help. I need you to be there for me!"

"You need me to be there for you?" he repeated, finally looking at her. "For what? What exactly are we talking about here, Daria? Are you going back with Nathan?"

She felt as though she'd been slapped. She had barely come to terms with the fact that Nathan was alive, much less the thought of which man was her true husband.

She longed for Cole to take her in his arms, to reassure her that they would work everything out, that this would all soon be over. And yet, a tender place in her heart, a place she thought had died, had been awakened by the amazing miracle of Nate's return. He was her first love. They had such a deep history together. They had practically grown up together. And then she had abandoned him in the wilds! It terrified her to think what he might have endured during that time. Guilt pierced her soul. Perhaps Nate could never forgive her. Perhaps he wouldn't want her back even if she were free.

But then there was Natalie. Nate had given her their precious daughter, and even Cole could not deny that Nathan Camfield deserved to know his child. *Oh, what a tangled mess! God, how could you do this to us?*

The answer poured over her like a flood of icy water. She began to see the truth as if it were projected on the wall in front of her. The dreams she'd had—Nate alive and walking toward her, smiling. The letter from Evangeline Magrit, and the eerie, gnawing feeling it had caused to rise up in her. The strange intuition that had haunted her until she had all but shut God out of her life.

She could not blame God for this dilemma, for she suddenly realized that he had given her warnings, shown her signs. She simply hadn't listened! Instead she had turned a deaf ear to the warnings, to what she now knew were divine nudgings. And finally, she had silenced them.

Cole looked at her, hurt written plainly on his handsome face. He was still waiting for her answer, her verdict on their future together. "I can't even think straight about this yet, Cole. I don't know what Nate will want. I don't know how he is physically, emotionally. I just don't know what is going to happen."

"Well I *do* know what will happen, Daria. You'll go to him, as you must. And you'll stay with him—you and Natalie. You can't do anything less. All I ask is that you don't keep Natalie from me. And that I get to be a part of my own child's life."

"Cole! What are you talking about? You sound as if it's all over between us. Please don't do this! I truly don't know what will happen. But I need your help. I can't do this alone. Please, Cole..." She was sobbing now, begging, but her cries seemed to have no effect on him. He had turned aloof and uncaring before her eyes.

He pushed his chair back from the desk, turned away from her, and went down the hall toward their bedroom. She followed him, still weeping. "Please, Cole."

He whirled to face her in the hallway in front of their room. "Daria, what do you want me to do? *What do you want me to do?*" he shouted again, his face ruddy with rage. He softened a little when he looked into her eyes. "I'm sorry, Daria, but this isn't exactly a decision I can make for you!"

"Cole, I'm not asking you to make any decision. I just—" What *did* she want from him? She wanted him to make everything go back the way it had been before this ordeal began. But no! That wasn't true. Nate was alive, and she couldn't possibly wish him dead again.

She slumped to the floor and leaned her back against the cool surface of the wall. The blood pounded at her temples while she watched, helpless, as Cole went into their room, dragged a large suitcase down from the shelf in their walk-in closet and started dumping his dresser drawers into it. He was leaving, and there wasn't one word she could say to stop him.

Through tears, she watched him finish packing. When he brushed past her without so much as a glance in her direction, the anger finally rose in her. She followed him out to the kitchen and then to the back porch.

"Colson Hunter, don't you dare leave like this! Please! We can't get through this if we can't talk about it!"

He set the suitcase down on the floor of the mud room and turned to face her. "I love you, Cole," she squeaked. Then, abruptly he wrapped his arms around her, as though he were committing the sensation to memory. Finally he held her away from himself and looked into her eyes.

When he spoke, his voice was steady and serene. "Daria, I love you with everything that is in me. The life we've had together has been the greatest blessing of my life. I will never, never stop loving you—or Natalie. I wish to God that everything could go on exactly as it was yesterday, before this…nightmare began. But that isn't going to happen. You have a decision to make that I can't even imagine making myself. But I can't be the one to help you make it. The only thing I can do to help now is to get out of the way so you can decide what you want to do."

She began to cry, but though he appeared to be moved by her emotion, he stepped away from her. "Daria," he said, his voice wavering, "I will be praying for you every minute. I don't know that I can pray without bias, but that will be my goal. I do know I can't stay here. Surely you can see that."

He leaned forward again as if he meant to kiss her, but instead he turned on his heel, picked up his bag, and went out into the night.

Twenty-Five

*I*t was the darkest night Daria could remember—blacker even than that night in Timoné when she'd first accepted that Nathan was dead. How strange that his being alive was now the reason for a night of even deeper anguish. She lay in their bed upstairs, Cole's absence from the bed feeling like a huge lump that threatened and crowded her instead of the vacant space it was in reality. Her mind reeled with questions. How would she ever know what was the right thing to do? How could they ever disentangle themselves from this knot of family ties that had a stranglehold on them all? She tried to imagine where they would be a year from now, and no picture would form.

More immediately, how would she explain to her daughter why Cole was gone? She and Cole had just begun giving Nattie little hints of her story, referring to her "other" daddy and telling her that Grandma and Grandpa Camfield were the parents of her "Daddy-Nate," who had died before she was born. When they had thought Nathan dead, they had struggled with just how to present the particulars to her, but now those details that had once seemed so fraught with confusion seemed simple by comparison. This new truth was so bizarre that Daria couldn't imagine how it would ever unravel itself, let alone how they would explain it to a child—or to *anyone,* for that matter. She took in a sharp breath as it dawned on her that there was no "they" anymore. She was alone in this labyrinth of impossible choices. Hers would be a solitary decision. *Where did she belong now?*

She tossed restlessly for hours, perspiring in spite of the frigid night air that poured in the open window. Finally she got up and went down to the kitchen. She poured a glass of cold milk and took it to the table. Forcing herself to think through the options, she got up and retrieved a pen and pad of paper from the desk in the kitchen and went back to the table, determined to make some sense of the whole mess.

She had to go see Nathan. That was her first priority. And Nathan would have to see Natalie. She would have to offer some kind of explanation to her daughter. She wasn't sure Nattie's two-year-old mind could understand the concept of two fathers, but it wouldn't be fair to Nathan for his daughter not to have been told that he *was* her father when she met him. Coming face to face with Nathan would be like meeting a ghost, and yet Daria thrilled to think of it. It startled her a little to realize that she still loved him. Yet why wouldn't she? She hadn't willingly given him up.

She wondered how he would be after all this time. They still didn't know how the trauma of being in captivity for so long had affected him. Surely there were psychological repercussions and possibly physical ones. She remembered Jack saying he'd been badly burned. She couldn't imagine how the incident might have changed him. But then, her "widowhood" and single motherhood had drastically changed her, too. Neither of them would be the same people they had been when they'd loved each other before.

She shuddered to think how he must feel about her, leaving him there for dead as she had. She began to understand a little how Cole must have felt about his responsibility in Bridgette's death, and in his son's death.

She looked down at the pad of paper in front of her. On it she had written two names: *Nathan. Natalie.* She couldn't even remember writing the words down, and yet they stared back at her in handwriting that belonged to her in spite of the tension in its loops and curls. But it was the absence of a name that jumped off the page at Daria. *Cole.* Where *was* Cole in all this? When she pictured a reunion with Nathan, she pictured him taking Natalie in his arms, that thousand-watt smile lighting his face, and her beside them both—the happy family she had envisioned since the day she and Nate had fallen in love.

As if in protest, the baby within her womb somersaulted, asserting its presence. *Cole's child.* The infant that was to have bound her and Cole and Natalie together as a family. And she could envision that happy family, too. In many ways, *this* was the family that felt real to her, the one that was familiar, the one she was longing for right now. Though Cole had only been gone from her for a few hours, her yearning for him was a deep ache within her.

But her heart broke for Nathan. How could she desert him again after what he'd been through? And how could she even dream of taking Natalie away from him after all he'd already lost? She couldn't. No matter what she decided, he would have to be able to see his daughter.

A terrifying thought crossed her mind. What if she had no decision to make? What if neither of the men she loved wished to remain with her now? What if neither of them could face the specter of the other man that would always hang over their relationship? Certainly their dilemma would tear one of her children from a father's arms. It couldn't help but sever the precious love of siblings, divide their loyalties toward one another. Would this shatter *both* of her families into a million pieces?

A flood of anxiety and confusion washed over her. What could she possibly do to redeem this mess? "O God!" she cried, her voice a hoarse squeak in the silence of the kitchen. "Show me what to do! I don't know what to do."

The reply came as his answers had come to her long ago, before the rift—a still, small whisper in the dark. *Give it to me.*

"But how can I, when—"

Give it to me.

Daria startled, as if the words had been spoken aloud. But when she looked around the kitchen, only the hushed ticking of the clock over the desk broke the silence.

223

Finally beyond tears, she wrung her hands in her lap and put her head on the table. "I don't know how, God. Help me. I want to give it to you, but I don't know where to start."

Just let go.

Again the words seemed almost audible. She slid from her seat and fell to her knees, bowing over the chair. She unclasped her hands, straightened her spine, and turned her palms up in submission, as if going through the physical motions would help her let go spiritually. It seemed fruitless, and yet it was all she knew to do.

"O Father, I *do* give it to you. I can't do this myself. I'm…I'm lost…so lost…"

Almost immediately, a sense of peace washed over her, and she felt sheltered in a haven of security she didn't understand—or need to. A phrase came to her mind: *the next thing*. But what *was* the next thing? And the question seemed to answer itself. *Go see Nathan.*

"Thank you, Lord." Oh, that she could learn to always trust him to guide her each minute, each tiny step of the way, no matter how rocky or treacherous.

She struggled to her feet and went to the sink to rinse out her milk glass. Then she checked on Natalie. She was so thankful she had decided to bring Nattie home from her parents' that afternoon. To be completely alone tonight would have been unbearable. The little girl was sleeping on her stomach with her tiny rump in the air. Deep maternal love welled up in Daria, and she turned away from Nattie, not wanting to think about what the future might hold for her daughter.

She climbed the stairs to their room—*her* room—and crawled wearily into bed. She wasn't any closer to an answer than she had been at the beginning of this night, but she had received something far more precious. She had been given a fragile peace. And for now, she had her assignment. She would do the next thing, and the next and the next. And she would try with everything in her to trust that God would lead her to the place he wanted her to be.

Colson Hunter squinted and rubbed his eyes against the bright sunlight that had awakened him. He reached for Daria, but found her place in the bed beside him empty. He smelled the strong aroma of coffee brewing and wondered why she was up so early this morning. He finally managed to open his eyes, but instead of the sunlight playing on the softly patterned wallpaper in their bedroom, it glanced off of stark white walls through a curtainless window.

Sitting upright, the remembrance of where he was washed over him with cold grief. After driving unseeing down nameless dirt roads, he had found himself at Kirk and Dorothy Janek's apartment where Travis Carruthers lived now. Travis had taken Cole in without question, unwittingly putting him in the bedroom that had been Daria's when she had lived here. Though the room was empty, its blank walls testifying to the status of a bachelor pad, Cole imagined Daria's sweet scent still lingering there. He fell back against the lumpy pillow and let the waves of grief roll over him. He willed himself to sleep, to recreate the dream that he was home, that the woman he loved was brewing coffee in the kitchen, that his precious daughter slept in the cozy nursery below him.

But the dream had been shattered and, try as he might, he could not find that place of refuge again.

Swinging his legs over the side of the high mattress, he planted his bare feet on the cold wood floor. He felt as though he'd run a marathon, his muscles ached so, and yet he knew that his utter fatigue was emotional, not physical.

He pulled on a rumpled flannel shirt and the jeans he'd worn the day before and went into the small kitchen, seeking Travis. A note beside the coffee maker told him that his colleague had gone to the clinic and that he would cover for him this morning. Cole looked around the kitchen for a clock and was startled to see that it was after ten o'clock. He wondered where Daria was right now.

Pouring himself a cup of coffee, his thoughts a million miles away, he barely noticed when the hot liquid burned his tongue and throat. Carrying the steaming mug into the living room, he sank down onto the shabby sofa. In spite of the bare-bones furnishings of the apartment, it was hard not to think of Daria in this place. The curtains she and her mother had made still hung in the lower halves of the windows, and the view of the bare treetops from the sofa was one they'd shared many an evening when they were dating. He shook off the thought and went back to the bedroom to get his shoes.

When he stepped outside, Dorothy Janek was just backing her ancient Ford Fairlane out of the garage. He waved and forced a smile, hoping she wouldn't stop to talk to him. But she maneuvered the old car around the curve in the driveway and stopped right beside him.

She rolled the window down and poked out her cheery grey head. "Well, hello, Cole. I thought that was your truck in the drive. Figured maybe Travis had borrowed it."

"Hi, Dorothy. No, it's me."

Her raised eyebrow asked the obvious question, and he didn't have the heart to leave her wondering. "We've had some trouble, Dorothy. Daria and I. You'll probably be hearing—"

"Cole, no!" she gasped.

He grasped her car door where the window had just disappeared and leaned in to look at her. "It's not what you think. It's…" He ducked his head. *How in heaven's name did one explain a situation like this?* He tried again, "We got word yesterday that Daria's first husband—Natalie's father—has been found alive in Colombia."

Dorothy Janek's hand flew to her mouth. "Alive? Oh, Cole. What will you do?"

He shook his head. "I wish I knew, Dorothy. I— For now I'll be staying with Travis. I hope that's okay with you and Kirk."

She waved him off, obviously still stunned at the news. "Don't even ask. You know you're more than welcome anytime. But, Cole …I'm so sorry. I—" She put a hand to her breast, and he saw that there were tears in her eyes. "I just don't even know what to say, Cole. Is Daria—? Well, she's still at your place, or you wouldn't be sleeping here. Will she go back with him, Cole?" she asked gently.

"I don't know." He knew the woman's questions were asked out of sympathy, but he was painfully aware that they were the questions everyone would be asking of him. He had no inkling how to answer them. "I don't know," he repeated.

She reached out to pat his hand. "Well, you just let us know if there's anything we can do, anything at all. And if Daria needs us, please let her know we're here for her, too."

"I know that, Dorothy. And I appreciate it. Right now I guess we're just taking one day at a time."

Dorothy patted his hand again, and he covered her small, plump hand with his. "I need to get to the clinic," he told her.

"Of course. I'm so sorry, Cole."

He only nodded, his lips set in a grim line.

She revved the engine and backed away, and he went to his truck, debating whether he could face going to work. He drove toward the clinic, but when the driveway appeared, he kept going. The truck seemed to have a mind of its own, and he found himself headed out to their house. He needed to see Daria, needed to know how she was taking this, what she was thinking. They had left things unfinished. They'd both needed time alone to think, but he loved her, and this was *their* problem—they needed to work it out together.

A part of him felt guilty for leaving her alone last night, but he hadn't had a choice. He couldn't very well sleep in the same bed with another man's wife. For that's what she was, what she had been all their marriage. He wondered fleetingly if it was a sin to take another man's wife if he thought the man was dead. But it didn't help to ask those kinds of questions. There were no answers.

He parked in front of the garage and went in through the side door that led to the kitchen. Inside the house, it struck him that maybe he should have knocked. Now he shouted for her.

"Daria?"

Silence.

He called her name again and began walking through the house, looking for her. It could have been an ordinary day—he fresh home from work, anxious to see her, ready to roughhouse with Natalie. He walked down the hallway to Natalie's room. It was empty, but he went in, stooping unconsciously to pick up several stray toys from the floor. He tossed them into the large wicker basket that served as a toy box and headed up the stairs to the room he and Daria shared—*had* shared. Would everything be in the past tense from this moment in his life? It was too much to comprehend.

He went into their room. The bed was neatly made, a row of pillows lined up on the headboard. He had always teased her about that. Who needed three pillows? He sat on the edge of Daria's side of the bed and put his head in his hands. He was still sitting there twenty minutes later when he heard her car in the driveway. He forced himself to get up and go down to meet her.

As he came down the stairs, he called her name.

"Cole?" came her reply.

"I'm here." He walked into the kitchen where she stood. He couldn't stop himself from going to her and taking her in his arms. She burst into tears, clinging to him as though she would drown if she let go.

He wanted to stay like that forever, but after a while he pushed her gently away from him, took her hands, and looked into her eyes. Her lovely face was etched with misery. "You look like you had a night like I did."

She gave him a sad smile.

"Where's Natalie?"

"I took her back to my folks'. We're going to stay there for a while. I can't face this house. You can stay here, Cole. I just came to get some of our things."

"No, Daria. I can't face it any more than you can. Travis is going to put me up." He looked down and scuffed the toe of his shoe on the floor. "We need to talk, okay?"

She nodded.

"I talked to Dennis Chastain again, and he's pretty sure that our marriage is still valid. He's still checking into the details, but he didn't think that by law you are still married to Nate, too. Something about the law presuming a second marriage to be the valid one in a case like this."

She let out a joyless laugh. "I can't believe this has ever happened to anyone else."

"I guess it happened some in wartime."

"Oh."

He hadn't planned what he would say, but suddenly the words were pouring out of him. "Daria, I know you have to go see Nate. I know Natalie will have to see him. But you have to know that no matter what you decide, I can't give her up. I love her as much as any father ever loved a daughter, and whatever happens I want to be able to see her. I know Nate probably has all the legal rights to his child, but I'm her father too, and I don't intend to quit now just because this has happened."

"Cole—" Daria started, but he cut her off.

"Maybe I'm being selfish, but I think it's right for Natalie, too. She's *used* to me. I'm the only one she's ever called Daddy."

"I know that, Cole," Daria said. "I want you to see her. Always." He didn't recognize the strangled voice that came from her throat.

Always. The word seemed ripe with implications, and he suddenly felt uncomfortable with her. He let go of her hands and dropped his own hands to his side. "So you'll take her to see him?"

She nodded, but said, "I want to go alone first…to see how he is. I don't want this to frighten Nattie. But yes, then I'll take her to see him."

She sounded so strong. He didn't like it. He wanted her to be weak, to need him the way he needed her.

Lying in the guest bed at Travis's apartment that night he realized how much she had left unspoken, how much there was between the lines. *I want you to see her. Always.* He was sure then that Daria had made up her mind. She was going back to Nate. She was going to take Natalie and go back to the man she had loved first, the man who had given her Natalie.

And for the first time in his life, Colson Hunter began to understand the despair that had driven Bridgette to take her own life.

Twenty-Six

*I*t rained on her all the way to Kansas City. She was glad for it. The rain was fitting. The reason for this trip was excruciatingly difficult, and it would have been obscene under a bright spring sun.

Her parents had offered to come with her, but she was thankful now that she had declined their offer. This was something she had to do alone. And it comforted her to know that Natalie was safe and happy with her grandparents.

The hours on the road were a time of deep introspection. In a span of three and a half hours, she virtually relived her life. She thought of what Cole had said about Natalie. *I can't give her up,* he'd said. *What about me though?* she thought. He hadn't said he couldn't give *her* up. For the hundredth time, she wondered if she would lose both of the men she loved.

Her exit loomed ahead, and the blue *H* sign confirmed that she was headed in the right direction. The Medical Center was a short distance, and she found a parking space near the entrance.

She went inside and inquired at the desk. The receptionist gave her Nate's room number and pointed her down a long hallway. Daria walked slowly down the corridor, feeling confused and disoriented. Soon she would be face to face with the man she'd long thought dead. The man she'd longed for in her dreams. A dozen emotions fought for supremacy within her. Grief for the pain and anguish Nathan had suffered at the hands of the very people he had tried to help. Sorrow for all they had lost together. Joy for the precious, healing news he had been given about Natalie. And love for the man who had been her husband.

Yes, love remained. The closer she came to his presence, the more her longing grew. She ached to see Nathan's face—to see for herself that he truly was alive. It all seemed so impossible after all this time.

She quickened her steps, suddenly anxious for the reunion.

Her eyes scanned the signs on the doors, darting nervously from one number to the next. She was only steps away from him, and her stomach turned somersaults inside her. She worried a little for the baby. Surely all this anxiety couldn't be good for the child developing within her. Instinctively she put her hand over the small round of her stomach. In her seventh month, her pregnancy was obvious now to anyone who was looking, but she had purposely worn a bulky sweater in an attempt to conceal her condition. Nathan might not know she was carrying Cole's child, and she didn't want to upset him more than the news of her marriage had surely already upset him.

The door to room 227 was slightly ajar, and Daria raised a hand and knocked softly. No response. She pushed the door open and stepped into the room.

She heard his breathing before she saw his face. He was clean-shaven and his hair, which he'd always worn rather long, was cropped close. Under the thin sheets, his chest rose and fell in labored, wheezing breaths. One arm lay on top of the sheets and the drawn, mottled scars she saw there shocked her. For the first time, she comprehended the extent of the physical toll his ordeal had taken on him. The head of the narrow hospital bed was raised slightly, and she could see his face. The familiarity of his pose—one arm behind his head, his eyes closed, mouth slightly agape—took her breath away.

Joy flooded her being, and she hurried to his bedside.

"Nate! Nathan? Wake up."

He started and opened his eyes. Daria smiled when she saw the recognition dawn there.

"Oh, dear Lord! Daria? Is it really you?"

"It's me, sweetheart!" the endearment fell from her lips like a teardrop, unbidden.

He reached his arms out to her, struggling to sit up in the bed. "Oh, Daria."

She sat down on the side of his bed and fell into his embrace as though she'd never left. He pulled her close, stroking her hair, both of them weeping like children.

She had expected their reunion to seem surreal, but now that she was in his arms, he had never been more real to her. He was thin and the scarring on his forearms was severe, but the strength of his embrace had not been diminished. Being in his arms felt so familiar to her that it was as though the years of their separation had been a mere blink.

He pushed her gently from him and reached up to touch her face, as though to prove to himself that she was actually sitting here in front of him.

"Oh, Daria. I can't believe you're really here." Then he looked heavenward, "Thank you, Lord. Daria, I—" Fresh tears choked out the rest of his words. His voice was raspy, whether the result of his injuries or from emotion, she couldn't tell.

Hot rivulets ran down Daria's cheeks as well, yet she couldn't stop smiling. She felt as though they had entered another world, strangely transported back to their beloved rain forest where they were the only two people in their world.

"How are you?" she asked him now, wanting to hear from his own lips.

"I'm okay." He held out his arms for inspection, and she traced the scars lovingly. "I've got some pretty good scars to show for it, but I'm okay. Now." He reached for her again, and she went into his embrace. He wept unashamedly for several minutes until finally he looked up at her. "Daria! We—Dad said we have a little girl?" The quiet joy on his face pierced her heart.

"Yes, Nate! A beautiful little girl. Her name is Natalie, after you. And, oh, she looks so much like you!"

Seeing Nate in front of her now, she was startled to realize how true it was. Strange how Natalie had always reminded her of Nathan, but now looking at Nathan the opposite was true. His eyes were Natalie's. Even his demeanor was uncannily like his daughter's.

He pointed to the nightstand beside his bed where framed photos of Natalie rested. "Mom brought some pictures."

Daria picked them up and smiled at her daughter's face. "She's so like you, Nate."

His eyes damp, his Adam's apple bobbing in his throat, Nate reached up and cradled her head in his hand and drew her face toward his.

An instant before his lips brushed her forehead, she realized that he meant to kiss her. Suddenly reality came crashing back. She shook herself to her senses and pushed away from him.

"Nate, I—"

He tried to draw her possessively, tenderly to himself again, but she leapt up and backed away from his bed, rubbing her arms frantically, as though she could brush away the intimacy of his touch.

"Nate, no! We have to talk."

"Daria? What is it? What's wrong? Is something wrong with the baby?"

She sank to the wide, low window sill across from his bed and put her head in her hands. *O dear God! He doesn't know. How could I be so foolish? Jack and Vera didn't tell him that I'm remarried!*

"No, Natalie's fine, she's fine. Oh, Nathan," she sobbed. "Your parents didn't tell you?"

"Tell me what? What is it, Daria?"

Why hadn't they told her that they were leaving it up to her to break the news to Nate?

"I don't know how…how to tell you."

She forced herself to calm down and took a deep breath, looking into his fathomless hazel eyes. "Nathan, you must understand. I-I thought you were dead. Quimico and Tados—they told us about the fire. They said you had died! How could I have known? Please don't blame me." Again she put her head in her hands, unable to continue.

"Daria, it's all right. I understand what happened. I know you didn't realize I'd survived. I know you would have come for me if you'd known."

She shook her hands in frustration in front of her. "No, Nate, that's not all. That's not what I mean."

"What's wrong, Daria? What are you trying to tell me?"

Though she didn't look up, she heard the fear in his questions.

"Oh, God! This is too hard! I can't do this to you, Nathan! I can't do it. Oh, God, forgive me..."

Now he struggled to take a breath, and anger tinged his voice. "It's the scars, isn't it? I know I must look awful."

"No! Nathan, no. Of course it's not that. You don't understand."

"Daria! Tell me what this is about!" He sat upright, his jaw tense.

"I'm married, Nate." Her voice came out like the growl of an injured beast. "We can't be together. I'm married to someone else now," she sobbed.

"What?" His face registered shock and utter disbelief. "No! What are you talking about, Daria? You are married to me!"

"No! It's true, Nate. I-I thought you were dead. We all did."

"No! There has to be a mistake! It can't be true, Daria. You're my wife! Why didn't someone tell me?" He was shouting now, and his voice came out in terrible, breathless rasps. "We have a child, a daughter to raise. You are my wife!" he choked out. He fought against the linens and the IV lines that shackled him to the bed, and Daria feared he would tear the needles from his arms.

"Stop it, Nate! Stop! You'll hurt yourself."

She went to his side and tried to physically restrain him, but somehow she found herself in his embrace again, both of them sobbing bitterly.

After a long moment, she extricated herself from his arms and stood beside the bed, spent.

His head dropped into his hands, and he scrubbed his face as if to wash away the terrible truth. He must have seen in her tortured eyes that it was all true, everything she had said.

A ragged sob came from his throat, and he started to beat on the mattress with scarred fists.

"Nate, please."

But he only punched harder and then began swinging his arms wildly, fighting the tubes and needles. He began to wheeze, struggling for air. Coughing racked his body, and he gasped for breath.

Daria ran from the room, shouting for help.

A nurse appeared seemingly from nowhere and ran toward Daria. Another nurse came close behind her.

While the women restrained Nate and administered oxygen, a third nurse came in with a syringe.

"Mr. Camfield," she shouted over the commotion, "I'm going to give you something to calm you down."

The injection took effect almost immediately, and he stopped thrashing. Though his eyes remained open, his breathing calmed and he relaxed visibly.

Daria stood in the doorway, trembling violently, watching what seemed to be a scene from a horror movie.

"He'll be okay now," the older of the nurses told her. "The sedative will make him very drowsy. He'll probably sleep for a long time. It would be best if you'd come back tomorrow."

Daria nodded numbly.

Totally drained of energy, she slipped from the room and went back down the corridor. She drew in a tremulous breath. Her mind could hardly grasp all that had just transpired.

Guilt poured over her—a horrible sense that she was betraying Cole—as she realized that she wanted nothing more right then than to run back into Nate's arms, to comfort him, to hold him tightly to her and rejoice that he was safe, that they had been reunited. To rejoice over the little daughter their love had created.

She wanted to bury her face in her husband's chest and cry for the years they had lost. Her husband? No! Nate wasn't her husband anymore. He couldn't be. Could he? But he was! She had never divorced him.

She thought of Cole, pictured the utter devastation on his face when they had learned the news that Nate was alive. It was the same expression she had seen on Nate's face moments ago. Nathan's face became all tangled up with Cole's in her mind, and she felt as if she were being physically ripped in two.

Dear God, she loved them both! Why wouldn't she? Who could expect anything else of her? The blood rushed to her temples, and she could hear her own heart pounding in her ears.

She had to make some sense of the nightmare she was living. She had to find someplace where she could think and pray. She was afraid she would faint, but she kept walking, faster and faster until she was almost running.

Breaking out through the front doors of the hospital, she gulped in the fresh air. She waited for her heart to steady its pace, waited for her head to clear, but instead confusion multiplied with every labored breath she took.

She slid into her car. Gripping the wheel, she crept through the parking lot like an automaton, and pulled onto the highway.

Twenty-Seven

S he drove in the rain without any sense of direction, simply
following the cars in front of her, stopping where they
stopped, turning where the road turned. When Daria recognized
the exit for the residential area where Jack and Vera Camfield lived,
she decided to go see them. But it struck her now that they had more
than likely been at the hospital all this time. Unsure what else to do,
she entered their subdivision and wound her way through the maze
of tree-lined streets until she came to their stately home. She'd only
been there once since returning to the States, to drop Natalie off for
one of her weekend visits with her grandparents. It still surprised her
sometimes to consider that Nathan had grown up with such wealth.
He had been so different from his parents. No, she corrected herself,
he *is* so different from his parents. She had spent the first few months
after Nathan's "death" correcting herself when she thought of him in
the present tense, and now she was doing the same thing with thinking of him in the past tense.

She pulled onto the wide drive and, wiping her perspiring hands
on her slacks, got out of the car. The rain was still falling lightly as
she walked up the front steps. She rang the doorbell and was rather
surprised when Jack Camfield opened the door.

"I've just come from the hospital," she sputtered. "How could
you, Jack? How could you not tell him?" She was only vaguely aware
of Vera materializing behind him.

"Hello, Daria! Jack, what are you thinking? Invite her in," Vera
scolded, her face bright with the joy of her son's return. "Come in,
please, Daria. We were just about to leave for the hospital. You've
seen Nate then?"

Daria remained on the porch, turning her accusations on Vera now. "Yes, Vera. I've seen him. Why didn't you tell him about Cole?"

"Oh, honey, we just thought it best not to go into all that yet. Nathan has been through so much. Once you all get settled and he's gotten to know Natalie a little, then we can explain everything to him."

"Get settled?"

"Jack and I thought you could all stay here until Nathan gets back on his feet," Vera said.

"What are you talking about, Vera? I'm married to Cole!"

"Well, yes, technically. But Jack has consulted with his colleagues, and it sounds like the divorce will be a simple matter. Unless Cole would contest it, of course."

Daria stood with her mouth agape. "I can't believe what I'm hearing! How dare you think you could make this decision for me!"

"Now, Daria, surely you can't be considering anything but going back to the father of your child!" Vera's tone had been condescending, but now her words held a threat. "After all you've put Nathan through, you owe it to him. And besides, Nate will fight to his dying breath for custody of his daughter. You know the courts would crucify you if you tried to fight him on this."

Jack stepped in with his futile mantra: "Now, Vera." He turned to Daria. "Please, honey, we'll iron all this out eventually, but for now, please don't tell Nathan about Cole. The doctors say that he needs to remain as calm as possible. It's going to take some time for him to acclimate to all the changes, to recover from everything he's been through. He needs—"

"Jack," she shouted, "I've already told him! I had no idea you had kept it from him! I thought he knew!"

Vera paled. "You didn't tell him about the baby, did you?"

Daria was incredulous. "No, Vera. I didn't. It was hard enough telling him that I'm married to someone else."

"How could you, Daria?" This from Vera.

Anger took over, and Daria began to tremble. "How could I? He wanted to kiss me, Vera! He was…treating me like any husband would treat a long-lost wife. I *had* to tell him. I had no choice!"

Daria held her hands in front of her, palms out, a shield against her own fury. "I'm sorry. But I can't believe you didn't tell him! At least you should have told me that he didn't know."

"How did he take it?" Vera asked, appearing somewhat chastened.

"He took it very hard—understandably. They had to give him a sedative to calm him down."

Vera gasped. "Jack, we've got to get to the hospital! Our son needs us." She disappeared into the house, and Jack followed, telling Daria over his shoulder, "We'll work this out, Daria. Don't worry. We'll see you there?"

Without waiting for an answer, he closed the front door in her face. She stood there in shock.

She thought about what Jack had said about divorcing Cole. She wondered, *Who is my husband in God's eyes?* What about the Scripture that said, "What God hath joined together, let no man put asunder"? She certainly believed that God had blessed—even ordained—her marriage to Nathan. Yet, if she were to go back to him, she would have to divorce Cole, and the Scriptures were clear on that topic, too. And didn't she believe God had equally blessed her marriage to Cole? He had been an answer to prayer during the most difficult time in her life.

Where *was* God in all this? He had known all along that Nathan was alive. Why had he allowed her to fall in love with Cole? Why had he allowed their marriage plans to proceed, knowing it would end this way? *Dear God, how did this all get so complicated?*

And then it hit her like a punch in the stomach, leaving her breathless.

She hadn't asked for God's direction when she married Cole. She hadn't prayed for guidance. She had *assumed* that Cole was the answer to her sorrows, to her unspoken prayers for a father for Natalie, her prayers for someone to love. But she knew now that she had been wrong. Tragically wrong.

Now broken, she stood under the portico of the Camfields' house as the signposts of the past paraded through her mind. The letter from Evangeline Magrit that had convicted her so deeply. The trepidation she'd felt about dating Cole from the beginning. Even the dreams she'd had—dreams in which Nathan was alive and real. How many times had she ignored God's portents? Finally she had simply turned her back on him and gone her own way, pretending all the while that the things that seemed good in her life were from God.

She had become so wrapped up in her relationship with Cole, had been so relieved to find happiness with him, that she had not wanted to face the possibility that Cole might not be in God's plan for her.

And until now, it had worked. She and Cole had been happy. Cole was a wonderful man and a loving father to Natalie. And she did love him with a true, unselfish love. But theirs was a marriage God had not intended. She knew that now—now that it was too late.

Now where did all this leave Natalie? Would this put her daughter in the middle of a huge custody battle? And what about the baby in her womb? It still galled her to think of the Camfields' assumption that she would leave Cole as easily as she might toss out a pair of too-tight shoes. The Camfields knew that she was carrying Cole's child. Why did they think that she would choose the father of one of her children over another?

In anguish Daria realized how many people she had dragged into this devastating maelstrom by refusing to heed God's gentle leading so many months ago. Would any of them survive the turbulence now?

The garage door opened, and the Camfields' car rolled down the drive and into the street, Jack and Vera's eyes straight ahead. Daria forced herself to get in her own car. But she couldn't follow them. She couldn't face Nate just yet. Instead she sat numbly, bowed over the steering wheel. "Father, this is all my fault."

Those five simple words opened a floodgate, and Daria stood face to face with the truth of her own guilt. Sick at heart, she slumped in the seat and put her face in her hands. "Oh, Father," she groaned, "what have I done? I've caused such sorrow for all the people I love the most. I didn't mean to, Lord. But I-I should have listened to you. I went my own way and now— I'm so sorry. Please don't let Nattie suffer for my stubbornness. Please, God, don't let this cause any bitterness to grow in Cole's heart or in Nate's."

The tears came then. Great racking sobs that shook her body and drained her spirit. Finally she choked out the words, speaking them aloud in confession, "Forgive me, Father. And please show me where I belong now."

She poured her heart out to God and found solace in the release of tears. It was such a comfort to finally have the freedom to be honest before God. She felt cradled in his arms, wrapped in his mysterious peace, and enveloped in a love that was eager to forgive. Her task now was to put the past behind her and to simply follow God's leading, day by day.

She sat in the driveway crying out to God, mourning Nate, mourning Cole, as though she had lost them both to death. Finally she lay across the front seat of the car, spent, prostrate in her grief. When the murky haze of rain lifted and the afternoon sun peeked out only to sink quickly to the horizon, she sat up, straightened her clothes, and craned her neck to check her reflection in the rearview mirror. Her eyes were red and swollen, and she tried in vain to blot away the dark circles that ringed them. Then she fastened her seat belt and turned the key in the ignition. The engine came to life, and Daria carefully maneuvered the car onto the street and turned toward the hospital.

Nathan stirred at the sound of his parents' voices. His head felt swollen and heavy, and he struggled to open his eyes against the bright light that came from above him.

"Nathan? Wake up, son."

"Dad?"

"It's me, Nate. Your mom's here too."

"Hi, honey," Vera said.

"Mom? Where's Daria?" Daria had been here earlier today, he was sure of it. Or was it days ago? The drugs had dulled his senses. But a heavy sorrow lingered, and it took him a minute to remember why he felt so sad. And then it all came back to him.

"Where is Daria?" he demanded.

"She'll be here later, Nate." His mother's face came into focus.

"Is she okay? Have you seen her?"

"She's fine. Everything is fine, Nate. Daria was at our house just awhile ago. She's probably on her way to the hospital right now. And she's going to bring Natalie to see you in a day or two, and you can get acquainted. The doctor says you can come home soon, maybe as early as tomorrow. Are you hungry?" Vera looked at him as she spoke.

Nate shook his head. As much as he loved his mother, her voice grated on him now. He just wanted her to be quiet. If he wasn't so lightheaded, and if he wasn't tethered to the bed by all these poles and tubes, he'd get up and walk down the hall, get some fresh air. He wondered if he was sicker than he realized. Why did they have him on an IV and hooked up to this catheter? He would ask the doctor, first chance he got. He would ask them to get rid of all this unnecessary equipment and to stop sedating him. After all, he was a physician himself. He ought to have some say in his own treatment.

In a remote part of his mind, he knew that he was fretting about these things to block out the news Daria had delivered. He could not face it yet. It was all he could do to grasp the fact that he had truly been rescued from the prison he'd been locked in for over two and a half years, that he had come home to discover he had a daughter. In all the fantasizing he'd done from his bamboo cell, he had never imagined that.

But neither had he dreamed that Daria would find someone else.

It was too much to fathom. Yet against his own will, he found himself wondering. How long had she been married? Did she love this man? Was he a good father? Jealousy threatened to consume him, but he forced himself to remember that Daria had believed him to be dead for years. Why wouldn't she go on with her life? Especially when she had a baby to provide for.

"Dad, I need to talk to Daria. Can you find her for me? Please? She told me that she's…remarried. She was very upset—"

"You are the one who should have been upset," Vera interjected.

"Mom, please—"

"I'm sorry, Nathan, but this is so unfair." She dissolved in tears.

Nate turned to his father again. "Will you find her, Dad?"

Jack glanced at his watch. "She was planning to follow us when we left the house about an hour ago. She should be here by now. Maybe she's out in the hall."

He left, and Nate leaned back against the stiff pillow and closed his eyes. His mother's manicured nails dug painfully into the tender, scarred flesh of his forearm. He didn't have the heart to tell her she was hurting him.

Daria entered the hospital for the second time that day. She knew she had to face Nate. She wasn't sure if he was ready to confront the truth, to discuss the decisions that needed to be made, but she knew they had to talk.

Starting down the corridor, her heart stopped when she saw a crowd gathered in the hallway and realized that the commotion was right outside Nathan's room. Had something happened to him? She ran toward his room, her heart in her throat.

The attention seemed to be focused on what was happening inside Nate's room. Several nurses were shouting at the crowd, impotently waving their hands. Then a carefully coifed brunette in a tailored navy suit rushed to meet Daria.

"Are you Daria Camfield?"

"I-I'm Daria Hunter," Daria began uncertainly. "How do you know my name? What's happening? Is Nathan all right?"

The knot of people all turned toward her, and only then did she see the cameras and microphones they wielded.

"Mrs. Hunter, Mrs. Hunter," they all shouted at once.

She was confused at their presence and still wondering if something terrible had happened to Nathan. "Let me through! Please," she pleaded.

"Mrs. Hunter, can you tell us what you plan to do now that your husband has been found alive?"

"Will you go back to your first husband, Mrs. Hunter?"

"Where is Mr. Hunter? Has he met Dr. Camfield?"

They lobbed questions at her one after another, and suddenly she understood. The media had somehow gotten wind of their story and, if these people had their way, her face would be seen on every television in the state.

Ignoring them, she ducked her head and plowed through the gauntlet of reporters and photographers and somehow got inside Nathan's room.

Twenty-Eight

*C*ole rubbed the stubble of his unshaven cheeks with trembling hands. The two-day growth of whiskers made his own face feel foreign to him. He raked his hands through a head of grimy, disheveled hair and carried a bowl of corn flakes and a cup of coffee into the living room of Travis's apartment.

He plopped down at the cluttered desk that overlooked the driveway. In the distance a field of tender young wheat rippled in the April sun. The elm trees that lined the drive burgeoned with pale leaf buds, and the lawn was turning green with the recent rains.

He wondered what Daria was doing at this moment. It was Monday, barely three days since their world had been turned upside down.

Daria had left for Kansas City yesterday to see Nathan. Natalie was at the Haydons', although yesterday Daria had offered to bring her to Travis's to stay the night with Cole. He had declined, telling her that he'd just have to take her back to the Haydons when he went to work. It was an excuse. In truth, he didn't know if he could bear seeing the little girl again if he was just going to lose her in the end. He had told Daria that he would never give Natalie up and yet, in reality, he was already withdrawing from her. He knew subconsciously that he was preparing himself for the possibility that he might lose her altogether.

He daydreamed of going to the Haydons', getting Natalie, and just taking her off somewhere. He would never actually go through with it. He wouldn't harm Natalie for the world, and he would never do anything to hurt Daria. Still it frightened him that his imagination had actually allowed him to entertain the thought of kidnapping.

It was too hard to think about losing her. He massaged his temples and picked up the newspaper, trying to force his thoughts elsewhere. Instead he found himself wondering again what Daria was doing. She had probably seen Nathan by now. Was there still a spark between them? He wondered if a person could still be in love with someone they'd already buried and mourned. If Bridgette were to suddenly appear in his life again, he didn't think he could suddenly stop loving Daria and conjure up the love he'd once had for his first wife, no matter how deep it had been. But then theirs had been a difficult love. And he didn't have a child with Bridgette—at least not a living child—that bound them together the way Natalie bound Nate and Daria.

He folded back the last page of the front section of the *Kansas City Star* and realized that he couldn't remember one word he'd read. Absent-mindedly, he opened the local news section, and a headline jumped off the page at him: KANSAS WOMAN TORN BETWEEN TWO LOVERS. He broke into a cold sweat as he read the subheading— FIRST HUSBAND THOUGHT DEAD, RETURNS FROM CAPTIVITY IN COLOMBIA—and realized that the crass headline referred to their story.

His stomach churning, Cole scanned the story. They had obviously not interviewed anyone directly involved. The article quoted "sources at the hospital" and stated that "the families refused to comment." He shook his head in disgust. As if things weren't difficult enough without this becoming a media circus. He wondered if any reporters had tried to reach him at the clinic. He hadn't gone in to work Monday, but he thought surely Carla or Travis would have called him if someone from the *Star* had been looking for him.

Grabbing the rolled-up copy of the *Wichita Eagle* from the floor by the stairway where Travis had dropped it, he stripped off the elastic band. Spreading it out on the kitchen table, he hurriedly paged through, searching desperately to see if the injurious headline had made that paper as well. He didn't find anything. Picking the *Star* up, he skimmed the story again. It didn't have a UPI or AP tag, so it was most likely a local story. But it did mention "Bristol, a small town in south-central Kansas." That alone would probably ensure that the *Eagle* would be all over it within hours. Then everyone would know.

The phone's sharp burr split the silence, making his heart leap. He pushed back his chair and went to the phone in the kitchen. Caller ID indicated that the number was unavailable. He started to walk away when he heard Daria's voice leaving a message on the answering machine.

"Travis, it's Daria. I'm trying to reach Cole. Carla said he wasn't in the office yesterday, and I need to talk to him right away. If you happen to come home for lunch could you—"

Cole grabbed the handset. "Daria?"

"Cole, thank God you're there." She started to cry. "Somehow the *Kansas City Star* got hold of our story, and it's plastered all over this morning's paper. I haven't seen the *Eagle,* but I'm afraid it will be in there, too."

"I saw it, Dar. But it's not in the *Eagle.* Not today's anyway."

"Oh, Cole, what are we going to do?"

"I don't think there's anything we can do, Daria. Word is traveling pretty fast here, so it won't be news to anybody in Bristol anyway. If the *Eagle* prints it, they print it. Have Nate or his parents seen the *Star?*"

"I haven't talked to them this morning, but I'm sure they have. Reporters were crawling all over the hospital yesterday, so we were all expecting something."

He cleared his throat. "So did you see him?"

"Yes...I saw him." She spoke so softly that he had to strain to hear her.

"And?"

"It was terrible. Jack and Vera hadn't told him that I remarried!"

"You're kidding—"

"They just assume that Natalie and I are going to move in with them—and Nathan."

Did her words mean that she thought the Camfields' assumption to be unlikely? A spark of hope ignited in him. "Did you tell him, Daria? That we're married?"

"Yes. He was going to—" Cole could sense that she'd been about to say something but changed her mind. "When I realized that he didn't know, of course I told him."

"About the baby, too?"

"No, Cole. I didn't tell him that. He was so upset about the other news that the nurses had to sedate him."

There was silence on the line between them. Then she said abruptly, "Oh, Jack said pretty much the same thing Dennis told you."

"Which was—"

"That my marriage to you is the legal one."

He wished he could see her face. Her voice was expressionless. He wished she would say, "Cole, honey, we're safe. Everything is okay. Thank God, nothing's changed. I'm still your wife." But she didn't.

"Do you want me to call your parents and warn them about the news story?" he asked, eager to change the subject.

"I already called them. I know Nattie isn't big enough to understand, but I didn't want them to freak out when they read it and end up scaring her."

"Yeah," he agreed, not knowing what else to say.

More silence. Finally he asked, "When are you taking Natalie? To the hospital, I mean."

"Well, Nate is supposed to be discharged today or tomorrow, so I'll wait and bring her to Jack and Vera's later this week. It'll be easier for her there—on familiar territory."

"Will you go back to the hospital today?" he risked.

"I'm afraid to, Cole. I just know there will be reporters everywhere. No, I'm going to start home in just a little bit."

"Daria," he asked, closing his eyes, willing her to give him the answer he wanted to hear, "where *is* home?"

"Don't ask me that, Cole. Not now. I don't know." She started to cry.

"I'm sorry, Dar, I'm sorry. Please don't cry."

He could hear her soft weeping on the other end, and he felt like a jerk for causing it.

"I'm sorry, Dar," he whispered again. "Are you okay? Is everything all right with the baby?"

She whispered a yes and sniffled. "I'd better get going."

"Be careful on the road," he said softly.

He hung up without waiting for a reply.

Twenty-Nine

N ate gazed out the passenger window of his father's car as the Kansas City skyline receded, giving way to flourishing residential neighborhoods west of the city. He marveled again that he was actually back in the United States. The events leading up to his escape and the long journey to Bogotá remained a blur. It seemed they had happened a lifetime ago.

But he remembered clearly the moment Daria had walked into his hospital room. The elation he'd felt at finally seeing her beautiful face again, and at hearing from her own lips that she had borne him a precious daughter.

And today he would meet little Natalie, hold her in his arms. It had thrilled him when Daria told him that Natalie looked like him. He tried to envision a two-year-old female version of himself, but the only pictures that came to his mind were the tiny brown-skinned Timoné children. And he was also strangely frightened by the prospect of meeting her. *What if she's afraid of me? What if my scars repulse her?*

He looked over at his father, who was concentrating on the heavy, noon-hour traffic.

"Dad, what time did you say Daria was planning to get here?"

Jack checked his watch. "I think she said one o'clock. She should be at the house by the time we get there. I'm sure Mom and Betsy will keep her and Natalie entertained. You nervous?" Jack asked, keeping his eyes on the road.

"A little."

Nathan pulled down the visor on the passenger side and looked into the undersized mirror. After nearly three years without seeing more than his reflection in a river stream, it still startled him whenever he caught a glimpse of his own face. His eyes were more crinkled at the corners than he remembered, and his cheeks were even thinner than they had been, but other than that, his face was unmarred by his ordeal. His hands and arms were another story. The long-sleeved shirt and jacket his mother had brought to the hospital for him covered the ugliest burn scars, but striations of scar tissue marred his hands as well. He had been deeply relieved to discover that he could still maneuver a pen, could still handle a razor without nicking himself, could still hold a woman in his arms.

He shook the thought off. He wouldn't dwell on that now. What was important was that he could still practice medicine, could still provide for his family. In every way that mattered, he was whole.

His father turned onto a side street, and suddenly everything was familiar to him again. He was going home to the house he'd grown up in. A lump formed in his throat, but he was hard-pressed to identify the emotion it signified.

He swallowed hard. "Do the Milbrandts still live there?" he asked, pointing to a stately Georgian revival, attempting small talk.

"John Jr. moved in a couple of years ago. Berta died, you know, and they put John in a home."

He didn't know, but it didn't really matter. They were just blocks away from the Camfield house, just a minute away from Daria and Natalie.

Jack reached for a remote control Velcroed to the dash. By the time they pulled into the driveway, the garage door had opened to allow them entry. The huge door slid closed slowly behind them, leaving them in the dim light of the garage.

The door that led to the large laundry room off the kitchen opened, and Vera appeared, her arms outstretched, her face crumpled by emotion. "Oh, sweetheart, you're finally home. I can hardly believe it."

His sister, Betsy, stood beside their mother, beaming. "Welcome home, bro."

He reached out to return Betsy's warm embrace and rumple her hair in a way that at one time would have made her furious, but now only made her cry with joy.

"Hurry, Nathan, come in. Natalie is waiting," Vera urged, ushering them through the kitchen.

His heart started pounding, and his palms began to perspire. He followed his mother through the formal dining room and into the living room. Daria sat on the edge of a sofa across the room, as though she might spring up at any moment. But she remained seated, smiling sadly at him. "Hello, Nate. Welcome home."

At her feet sat the most beautiful child he had ever seen. Her cherubic face was framed in wisps of white-blond hair, and she gazed at him with curious, hazel eyes. He saw Daria in the high cheekbones and the tiny, slightly pug nose, but they were undeniably—as Daria had told him—his own eyes that peered at him from beneath pale lashes.

Daria stood now, picked up the child, and walked toward him. He stepped forward to meet them.

Though her eyes were dry, Daria's voice quavered, and Nate knew that she was struggling to maintain her composure. "Nattie, this is your Daddy Nate. This is Dwama-Dwampa's son." She spoke it like a line rehearsed for an important business meeting.

He smiled. "Dwama-Dwampa?"

Daria laughed and opened her mouth, but Vera jumped in with an explanation before Daria could respond. "It's what she called us when she first started talking. We liked it so much we made it official. I'm Dwama," she said unnecessarily.

Daria put Natalie on the floor and sat down again. Nate knelt in front of the little girl, put out his hand and touched her arm. "Well, hi there, Nattie. I'm glad to meet you." It was all he could do not to take her into his arms and squeeze her tightly to himself.

But Natalie turned suddenly shy and scrambled up onto Daria's lap, burying her face against her mother's shoulder. "Can you say hello?" Daria coaxed.

Natalie burrowed deeper into the sleeve of Daria's corduroy shirt.

"I'm sorry," Daria offered.

Nate held up a hand. "It's okay. Give her time. How are *you?*" he asked, taking a seat in a wingback chair near the sofa.

"I'm doing all right."

An uncomfortable moment passed. Finally Vera got up. "Why don't I fix us some tea?" she asked brightly. "Nate, would you rather have coffee?"

"No, Mom. Tea is fine."

"How about you, Daria?"

Before she could reply, Natalie announced suddenly, "I want sugar in my tea, Dwama." They all laughed.

Vera rose and headed for the kitchen.

"I'll help you, Mom," Betsy said, going after her.

Jack took his cue and followed them. "I'll be sure Dwama puts plenty of sugar in your tea, Nattie," he said, laughing nervously.

"Well, she knows what *she* wants." Nate grinned, then cringed inwardly, afraid Daria might infer another meaning from the inflection of his words.

But Daria smiled back and, in a stage whisper over Nattie's head, told him, "She does have a mind of her own. She's sometimes more than we can handle." Daria cleared her throat, obviously embarrassed by her innocent reference to Cole.

He tried to think of something to say that would put her at ease, but before the words came, Natalie pointed at his hands. "My daddy doesn't have that on his hands," she stated matter-of-factly.

Her mention of "my daddy" hurt far more than the fact that she had drawn attention to his scars.

"Natalie!" Daria's voice came out in a horrified whimper. "Oh,

Nate, I'm so sorry. I-I didn't think to warn—to tell her that you'd been burned."

He waved her apology away and turned to the child. "These are scars I got from a very bad burn," he explained patiently.

"Does it hurt?"

"Not so much anymore. It hurt very, very badly when it first happened."

"Was it in the trash?"

He looked to Daria for an interpretation.

"We live in the country and burn our own trash," she explained.

"Oh. No, Natalie, it wasn't the trash. A hut—a building—caught on fire while I was inside."

"My daddy says never, never go by a fire, and don't never, never, never play wif matches." She shook a finger in his face.

"He's right," Nate agreed, charmed by her sweet seriousness, in spite of the pain the exchange caused him.

He glanced up at Daria and saw that she was crying. He leaned back in his chair. "This isn't easy, is it?"

She only shook her head.

Afraid that Natalie would notice her mother's tears, Nate attempted to distract her. "Natalie, shall we go see if Gram—I mean, Dwama—has that tea ready yet?" He stood and held out a hand to her. She reached up and intertwined her tiny fingers trustingly into his scarred, rough fingers. She smiled up at him, and he wasn't sure he could hold back his own tears as Natalie pulled him to the kitchen.

Daria sat on the sofa and sobbed, scarcely able to control herself. Her stomach churned and she felt achy, as though she were coming down with the flu. But when she heard Natalie calling her from the kitchen, she pulled herself together, wiped her eyes, and went toward her daughter's voice.

From the doorway, Daria watched Nate. He had never been so thin, and it was hard to get used to his hair being cut so short. His voice still sounded a bit hoarse, and the scars were disturbing to her. But being up and around and nicely dressed, he seemed much improved from that first day she'd seen him in the hospital.

Natalie was sitting at the counter beside Nate, who was blowing on her little plastic cup of tea in an effort to cool it enough that it wouldn't burn her tongue. Natalie had always warmed to people easily, but she was watching Nate with such unreserved adoration that Daria wondered for a moment if she instinctively sensed who Nate was.

Nate poured a little more milk in Natalie's cup and stirred it, then put the spoon to his lips. "There," he declared. "That's just right. Hang on. I'll carry it to the table for you."

He scooped her from the counter and set her on a high stool at the table in the breakfast room just off the kitchen, where Jack was already settled with a cup of coffee. Then he went back for her tea, delivering it with a gentle warning, "Sip it slowly now. It's still pretty warm."

Vera noticed Daria. "Oh, Daria, there you are. Do you want milk for your tea, dear?"

"No, thank you." She really didn't want tea at all. She pulled her loose corduroy shirt tighter around her, suddenly feeling chilled. Her stomach still felt queasy, and she'd begun to feel cramps in her lower abdomen. "Maybe a little honey if you have it," she told Vera. "Can I help?"

"No, no, I'm just about finished. You have a seat," Vera told her.

Daria went to sit between Betsy and Natalie at the table, and Nate brought his steaming mug of tea and took a seat across the table from them.

Vera joined them, and for a long moment, the quiet sipping of tea and the clock on the wall counting off the seconds were the only sounds.

"Your plants sure look healthy, Mom," Betsy said finally, reaching over to pluck one yellowed leaf from an English ivy that trailed over the edge of a shelf in the bay window.

"They *are* beautiful, Vera. You have such a green thumb," Daria offered.

Vera waved off their compliments. "Oh, it's just this window. They get light from three directions. They can't help but flourish."

Silence.

From her perch, Natalie reached for Daria's spoon.

"Wait, sweetie. Let me get it before you fall off your stool," Daria said. "Do you need to stir your tea?"

"*I* stir it," Natalie insisted when she saw that her mother intended to help her.

"All right, but you be very careful."

The little girl looked in Nate's direction as though to be sure she had his attention, then she put the spoon in her half-empty cup and stirred slowly as she had seen him do earlier. She dipped a spoonful of tea and slurped it loudly.

"No, Natalie. It's time to put the spoon down now," Daria said gently, grateful that her daughter obeyed without debate.

"Is that pretty good stuff, Natalie?" Nate asked her.

"Uh-huh," she nodded, gazing at him over the rim of her cup.

"I have more," she said, holding her cup out to Nate.

"What do you say, Nattie?" Daria prompted.

"Peese?"

Nate smiled and pushed back his chair.

"I can get it, Nate," Daria said.

"No, please. I'm already up. Would you like another cup, Daria?"

"No. Thank you." She was grateful not to have to get up. She was still experiencing some mild cramping, and her head had started to throb.

Nate took Natalie's cup to the counter and began to prepare the tea. Daria watched him stir in a generous amount of milk, testing to be sure the liquid wasn't too hot. His simple gestures warmed her heart.

He brought the tea back to the table and set it down in front of Natalie.

Again Daria reminded her daughter of her manners. "Nattie?"

"Tank you," she told him shyly.

"You're very welcome."

They sat in silence again.

Jack cleared his throat. "Hasn't this weather been something?"

They murmured their agreement and fell into silence once again.

After a while, Jack pushed his chair back from the table and took his dishes over to the sink. "Vera," he said, "I need to run to Wal-Mart for a minute. Why don't you and Betsy come, and she can help us find that new plant food she was telling you about."

Vera started to protest, then apparently realized his brazen pretense. "Let me get my jacket," she said. It was generous of them, and Daria smiled her appreciation, especially knowing how desperately Nate's mother longed to remain with them to keep an eye on the way things were progressing.

Natalie noticed them putting their jackets on, preparing to leave. She slid down from her stool. "Me too! I wanna go to Wal-Mart too!"

"No, honey," Vera coaxed. "You stay here and spend some time with your daddy."

Natalie screwed up her face and put her hands on her hips. "My daddy's not here, Dwama," she said, as though Vera were the dumbest woman on the earth.

"Nattie! You don't talk that way to your grandmother," Daria chided.

"Well, he's not!" Natalie huffed.

Vera knelt down beside her. "I meant your Daddy Nate, honey. Dwampa and I will bring you back something from Wal-Mart, okay?"

That seemed to appease Natalie, but when they'd gone, leaving Daria and Natalie alone with Nathan, Daria felt awkward. There was so much they needed to talk about. Nate seemed strong and in control now, but she didn't want to upset him again as she had in the hospital. She pulled her shirt around her and folded her arms over her stomach. She carried her babies "inside," as her mother always said, so it wasn't hard to conceal her pregnancy. And yet she wondered why Nate hadn't noticed the change. He was a doctor, after all.

She and Nate went back to the table in the breakfast room while Natalie sat on the carpet, leafing through the picture books Vera kept on a shelf especially for her. Twice she and Nate both started to speak at once and ended up laughing together over the absurdity of it.

Nate rubbed his arms briskly. "This cool weather is hard to get used to after Timoné. Was it like that for you, when you first came back?"

"Well, it was summer when I came back."

"Oh. Of course."

There was a long pause.

"Nate, I-I want to talk to you about what happened in Timoné. About why I left—"

He held up a hand. "Daria, Dad told me. I know you thought I was dead. We don't have to go there. It sounds like the mission did everything they could. I don't blame anyone for what happened."

But she rushed on. "Quimico and Tados told me—they told everyone—that you'd died in the fire. Tados said no one survived. I don't know why he would have lied to me. He brought me your gold watch, Nate. I was sure then that you were dead!"

"Tados was a good man, Daria. I don't think he lied. I think he probably thought I *had* died in that fire. I still don't know where he and Quimico were that day. They…"

A faraway look came to Nate's eyes, and he narrated his memories in a voice that was scarcely a whisper. "I know they were starting to distrust Peetro—the leader of the Chicoro. They tried to talk me into leaving before things got out of hand, but I was making progress, Daria. There hadn't been a new case of fever for several days. I was close to getting it under control, and I was determined to stay until I did."

How many times had she heard that tone of ardent persuasion in his voice? It startled her to realize that it was exactly the tone Natalie used when someone tried to thwart her plans. She reached out and touched the sleeve of his shirt. "Your daughter has that same determined streak, Nate." She said it proudly, with a smile, but he didn't return it.

"My stubbornness nearly got me killed, Daria. It's not something I want her to be proud of—her stubbornness."

"I know," she said, chastened.

"We have to direct that streak in a godly way, Dar. Maybe if we catch it while she's little she won't have to struggle with it like I have."

"Nathan—"

He looked at her and started, as though he'd just realized the implication of his words. "I'm sorry. I'm…assuming things I have no right to assume." His eyes held the pain of a wounded animal.

"Are you happy, Daria? Do you love him?" he asked suddenly.

"Of course I love him, Nathan. But, I-I love you, too."

"But you can't. You can't love both of us."

"Tell my heart that," she said, her voice breaking.

"I want to watch my daughter grow up, Daria. Every single night I lay on that hard dirt floor and begged God to get me out of there. I begged him to bring me back to you so we could finish the work God called us to do, so we could raise children together. In a way I'm glad I didn't know about Natalie then. It would have killed me to know she was growing up without me. I don't understand why things happened the way they did, but I have to believe that God allowed me to live, allowed me to escape, and brought me back here for a reason. I have to believe Natalie is part of that reason."

"Cole loves her too, Nate. H-He's been good to Nattie, and he loves her like his own." She regretted the words as soon as they were out of her mouth. Not just because of the fresh pain they brought to Nathan's eyes, but because they reminded her of the secret she still kept from him, the secret that churned within her even as she spoke the words.

"Well, she's *not* his own!" Nate barked.

"I didn't mean—"

He scraped his chair back from the table and went to the window, looking out over the muddy garden.

"Nathan, I'm sorry. Of course Natalie is your child. But please don't blame Cole. He had no idea—neither of us knew that you were alive!"

"I said I don't blame you, Daria. That's not the issue here."

"What is the issue?"

"I think you know very well what it is." He looked down at Natalie and continued softly, "Natalie is my child, and I want to be part of her life, Daria. I want us to be a family, the family God meant us to be."

"Oh, Nate, I wish it was that simple." She had to tell him the truth. They couldn't have this discussion when she was withholding the fact of her pregnancy. Her stomach was in a knot and her head pounded, but she knew she *must* tell him.

She opened her mouth, not sure how to begin. "Nathan, there's something I have to tell—"

At that moment, a sharp pain sliced through her back, and it was all she could do to keep from crying out. She excused herself and started down the hall to the bathroom. By the time she reached the door, the cramping was excruciating. She had thought she was feeling ill because of the emotional distress of this day, but now she knew something else was terribly wrong. The cramps felt too much like labor contractions. She locked the door behind her and was horrified to realize that she was bleeding. She began to tremble, terrified that she was losing the baby. "Dear God, help me, please," she prayed.

What an awful way for Nathan to find out the truth. She reached for the door and started back to the kitchen, leaning on the wall at intervals for support.

"Nathan," she croaked, as another contraction swelled. "Nathan!"

He met her in three long strides, took one look at her face and put a supporting arm around her. "Daria, what is it?"

"Oh, Nate, something's wrong. I'm bleeding! Something's wrong with…the baby."

Thirty

aria blurted the cruel words out on a sob. "I'm pregnant, Nate."

"You're...you're pregnant?" The words hung stagnant in the air between them, and Nate's mind spun out of control at the ramifications.

She was trembling and completely unaware, he was certain, of how her announcement had affected him. How it had taken away his hope in one moment.

He looked at her now and wondered how he had missed the fact that she was pregnant. The thick corduroy shirt, which she wore unbuttoned over a long-sleeved T-shirt, concealed the fullness of her figure, but still, it should have been obvious to a physician.

"It's too early, Nate! I'm only seven months along," she breathed. "Something's wrong. Oh, dear God, I'm so scared. What should I do?"

A thousand thoughts went through his mind, but when they'd all sifted through his subconscious—long after his physician's instincts should have kicked in—one thought remained principal. And it horrified him.

He held a terrible power in his hands. The child Daria was carrying was the one thing that tied her to Colson Hunter. This unborn child had the potential to keep him from Daria and from his own precious daughter—the daughter he already loved with a father's heart, the daughter who stood wide-eyed now watching them.

He knew he should call an ambulance. Daria was continuing to have contractions and seemed on the verge of hysteria. If she didn't get to the hospital quickly, she would almost certainly give birth prematurely. And if she was no further along than she said, the baby's chances were not very good. But if they could stop the contractions, they might very well be able to stave off labor long enough that the infant would have a chance. Medically these things sometimes happened for a reason—because the developing fetus was malformed or blighted or because the womb could not adequately support the pregnancy. Couldn't it be for the best to simply let nature take its course? Perhaps this was God's solution.

He stood there, looking into Daria's eyes, seeing the depths of fear in them, seeing in her gaze that she trusted him to help her. And he felt as though he existed in another dimension, as though all time waited while he made his choice. He was aware of standing on that mental precipice between prudence and justification. The rationalizations to do nothing were coming at him hard and fast, and he knew he was but a half-step from plummeting into an abyss where wisdom would not be found.

It took every ounce of will to back away from the desires of his basest self. *Help me do the right thing, God,* his spirit cried out. Then, as though a curtain had suddenly parted to reveal the truth, he *knew* what was right, and he allowed the panic in Daria's eyes to compel him to compassion. Gratefully aware that she had no idea of the profound struggle that had taken place in his mind, he helped her to a chair and picked up the telephone. While they waited for the ambulance, he timed her contractions and tried to determine how heavily she was actually bleeding. Within minutes they heard sirens.

Now that he had made his decision, he embraced it fully. He ran to the door and directed the paramedics to the breakfast room where Daria was. With Nate's help, they lifted Daria onto the stretcher and loaded her into the ambulance. In the corner of the breakfast room, Natalie stood, sucking her thumb, a bewildered look on her tiny face. Daria reached out to comfort the little girl, reassuring her with soft words as she passed. Watching them, an ancient love for Daria welled up in Nathan's chest.

"You stay with Nate, honey. Mommy needs to go to the hospital for a checkup." Her smile was pitiful.

"Do you want me to ride with you, Daria?" he asked. It was a struggle to keep his voice steady.

"What about Nattie?"

The driver of the ambulance tilted his head toward Natalie. "I'm sorry, but she can't ride with us."

"Stay with her, Nate, please." Daria raised her head and looked at Natalie, as though memorizing her face. "Mommy will be okay," she told her, but Nate wasn't sure her weak smile hid her desperation, even from a two-year-old.

He reached down and scooped his daughter into his arms. "It's all right, Natalie," he reassured her. She wrapped her arms around his neck and clung tightly to him. "They're just going to take your mommy to the doctor so they can check her over and make sure everything is okay. She'll be back before you know it."

The paramedics closed the door of the ambulance, and the driver went around to take the wheel. As the ambulance backed down the driveway and headed up the street, Natalie put a thumb in her mouth. Her gaze grew vacant, but she didn't cry or even whimper. Again Nathan felt the overwhelming desire to enfold her tightly to himself. Even with Daria, he'd never known a love so fierce and protective, and he was astonished that it had blossomed so quickly inside him. She was *his,* and his heart grasped that truth.

But in spite of the love that remained for Daria, the awful knowledge of her pregnancy made her seem a stranger to him. Her pregnancy was a vivid reminder that she had another whole life that didn't include him. He could scarcely fathom that Daria had a home and a family apart from him, that her life had gone on—and quite happily, it seemed. He shuddered involuntarily. He didn't like the feelings and emotions that were welling up in him. He had never been a jealous man. Daria had never given him reason to be, even when they were in college and she'd had plenty of opportunities. But to know now that she carried another man's child—and the intimate history that fact entailed—called up primitive emotions over which he seemed to have no control.

He stood in the driveway, staring down the street until the ambulance was out of sight. But his gaze was trained far beyond the place where the street dissolved into the horizon. His eyes were fixed on some great gulf in time. And he could not begin to see to the other side. Tightening his hold on Natalie, he went into his parents' house to call ahead and give the hospital his trained appraisal of Daria's condition.

Colson Hunter was en route to a meeting in Wichita when Carla Eldridge reached him on his cell phone. Cole knew from the quaver in her voice that the news wasn't good.

"Cole, I think you'd better come back. A hospital in Kansas City just called to say that Daria's been admitted there."

"What? What's going on, Carla?"

"They wouldn't tell me. They said she was in stable condition, but they need you to call them right away."

"Did you get the number?"

Carla repeated the number twice while he scribbled it on the palm of his hand, trying to stay in his lane on the interstate. He jabbed at the handset until he had a dial tone again, then tried twice before he could get the phone's minuscule buttons to register the numbers his fingers punched in.

An eternity later, his call was transferred to a nurse who gave him the information he needed.

"Your wife is fine, Dr. Hunter, but she is having contractions and we need to get them stopped. The doctor has her on full bed rest, and we're doing everything possible to save the baby, but I think you should know that it's very tentative at this point."

"What do you mean by that?"

"We've managed to get the bleeding stopped, but she's still having contractions. Dr. Hammond has started her on a different medication, but we won't know for a while if it's going to do the trick."

The nurse launched into a string of medical jargon, but he had all the information he needed. Daria was losing his baby, just as Bridgette had.

"I'm at least three hours from Kansas City now," he told the woman, "but I'll get there as quickly as I can. Please tell her I'm on my way."

Cole got directions to the hospital, ended the call, and kicked the cruise control up several notches. He turned around at the first exchange on I-35. He was halfway to Topeka when he thought to wonder where Natalie was. With a sinking feeling, he realized that he already knew in his heart exactly where she was. She was with her father. He was ashamed of the petty jealousies and fear that rose up in him. Shaking off the self-centered feelings, he thought of how frightened and alone Natalie must feel, and his heart broke for her. He longed to see her, to comfort her and assure her that her mommy would be all right. He inched the cruise control up again and prayed that God would get him there safely.

It was almost dark when he pulled into the parking lot of the Medical Center—the same hospital where Nate had stayed.

Five minutes later he was standing in front of the door to Daria's hospital room. He paused, wondering what he could say. Without knowing what had transpired between Nate and Daria, he didn't know how he should act with her.

Finally he took a deep breath and pushed the door open. Daria was lying in the bed, her head barely elevated. If she heard him come in, she gave no indication. She stared blindly out the window at the darkening sky.

"Daria."

She took in a short breath as though she'd been awakened suddenly. "Cole? Oh, Cole, the baby—" She started to cry.

He rushed to her side. "Did you lose… Is everything all…?" He couldn't make his words come out right.

"No, no…the baby is fine, Cole. His heartbeat is strong. See?" She pointed to a monitor that sat ominously on a table beside her bed. He hadn't noticed before that she was hooked up to the monitor and an IV.

"It's just that it's too early. They're trying to get the contractions stopped. Oh, Cole. I'm so sorry! I know this was what you were afraid of all along, Cole. I'm so sorry it happened. But it doesn't have to be like Carson. Even if they can't stop my labor, the baby might still be okay. We've just got to keep praying."

"I prayed all the way here, Daria."

"I know."

She sounded stronger, confident almost. He wasn't sure he liked hearing this resolve in her voice. What did it signal? Something had changed since he spoke with her last. He was afraid to know what it was.

"Where's Natalie?" he asked abruptly.

"She's at Jack and Vera's. She's fine."

"What can I do, Daria? I want to help, but I don't know what you want me to do."

She bowed her head for a moment. When she looked up, it was to gaze directly into his eyes. "Just keep praying, Cole. For the baby and…for everything…"

"Do you want me to stay with you, or do you want me to go?"

She didn't have a chance to answer before the door to the hallway inched open and a tall, thin man with pale, close-cropped hair poked his head in. Thinking it was a nurse or an orderly, Cole stepped away from Daria's bed and waited, expecting the man to ask him to leave while he took her blood pressure or something. But then the door was wrenched from the man's hands and flung wide open as Natalie burst into the room crying excitedly, "Mommy! Mommy!"

The little girl stopped short when she saw Cole standing there. Instantly her cries turned to squeals of joy. "Daddy! It's my Daddy!" she said, turning to the man in the doorway. She galloped across the room.

"Hi, punkin." He knelt to embrace her, and she wrapped her arms around his neck and nuzzled his face with her own like a puppy beside itself with happiness. He stood with Natalie in his arms, and a sob rose in his throat, taking him completely by surprise. Over Natalie's shoulder, he looked into Daria's eyes. She was looking at the other man, her face veiled in anguish. He now noticed the scars on the man's arms and hands and realized that this man he'd thought to be a stranger was indeed Natalie's father. Cole squeezed her tightly to himself, amazed at how featherlight she was in his arms, how sweet her silky fine hair smelled.

Natalie let loose of his neck long enough to lean down and touch Daria's toe through the sheet. The little girl smiled shyly at her mother and wrinkled her nose. "You look funny, Mommy."

Daria's lovely features had been transformed into a mask of utter misery. This couldn't be good for the baby. What must this stress be doing to her?

"Daria," he started.

Nate apparently saw the same thing in her face, for he strode to her bedside and bent to read the monitors. "Are you all right?" he asked. But it seemed to Cole to be the loving, possessive husband, not the physician, who was asking the question.

Daria nodded. Smiling wanly, she looked from one man to the other. "Nate," she said softly, her voice quavering. "This is Cole. Cole, Nathan."

Thirty-One

*N*athan stared at Colson Hunter, his emotions running the
gamut from fury to compassion and back again. Hunter
reached out tentatively to shake his hand, and Nate took it, truly
uncertain if it was anger or possessiveness or sheer terror that moti-
vated the fierceness of his own grasp. Without speaking, they
released their hold on each other. Nathan turned away quickly,
ostensibly to adjust the dials on the fetal monitor that displayed the
baby's heartbeat.

Struggling to put aside the unsettling feelings that meeting this
man had incited, he tried to remember from his obstetrical training
what the safe parameters were for the baby's heartbeat. The machine
emitted a steady *whoosh, whoosh,* but the pace seemed quite rapid
to him.

"Did they tell you what this number should be?" he asked Daria,
trying to keep his voice even, painfully aware of Hunter's presence
behind him.

"It's been staying between 115 and 140, I think," she told him,
her voice forced and artificial. "I heard a nurse say they didn't want
it to go much above 150."

"Okay," he said. "Good."

He continued to busy himself with the medical equipment in the
room. It had been half a decade since he'd worked with such tech-
nology, but some things were beginning to come back to him. He
took his time, acutely aware that he would have to look Colson
Hunter in the eye again at some point. Right now he wasn't sure he
trusted what his own response might be. He felt as though Hunter's
eyes were boring into his back. And the fact that his daughter was

happily ensconced in this man's arms caused his own heart to beat too quickly and a bitter taste to rise in his throat.

He checked the monitor one more time and straightened. "You're sure you feel okay, Daria?"

She nodded wanly.

"I'm going to go check on something at the nurse's station. I'll be right back."

As a paltry atonement for his cowardice, he met Hunter's gaze and nodded as he left the room. He spoke with the head nurse. After he was satisfied that the reading on the fetal monitor was within reason and that they were watching Daria closely, he walked away from her room. He simply couldn't go back in there with the man who had taken over his life while he suffered alone in the jungle. *Is this how God rewards his servants? Stop it,* he chided himself. But his emotions did not submit. As he walked down the hallway the disturbing scenes continued to play over and over like a film on a continuous loop. In his mind's eye, he watched his daughter run into Colson Hunter's arms again and again. Daria's quiet introduction pounded in his head, a haunting soundtrack to the film. *Nate, this is Cole,* she'd said. He wondered if she had rehearsed her words, if there was significance to the order of the introduction. He seemed to remember that the rules of etiquette gave special importance to the person who was introduced first? Did Daria know that? Or was it merely happenstance that had put her words in that particular order?

The hallway ended in a small waiting room comfortably furnished with overstuffed chairs and a small television set that droned a continuous weather report. The room was empty, and Nate sank into the nearest chair and put his head in his hands.

What in heaven's name are we going to do? How are we ever going to make sense of this whole mixed-up disaster? And how deep will the wounds be for all of us when everything is finally settled?

Above him, the perky weather girl was predicting severe thunderstorms in the Kansas City area. *How appropriate,* Nate thought.

Cole watched Nathan Camfield leave the room. In spite of the threat the man was to his own happiness, he couldn't help but put himself in Nate's shoes. How must it have felt for him to watch the daughter of his own flesh run into another man's arms? Instinctively he tightened his grip on Natalie. He looked down at her and saw that her eyes were heavy. She had her thumb firmly in her mouth, but she kept one hooded eye on her mother.

Cole went to the chair beside Daria's bed and sat down, arranging Natalie's spindly legs across his lap, turning her head so she could still see Daria, until he could sense she was comfortable.

"Daria?"

She gazed up at him, the sadness in her eyes spilling over in tears.

"Hey…it'll be all right." He wished he could believe his own words.

"Oh, Cole…how can it possibly be all right?"

"Shh," he whispered, knowing that she was talking about much more than the baby, but choosing to pretend otherwise. "You just need to stay calm until this baby is safe. That's all you need to think about for now."

She nodded, closed her eyes, and burrowed back into the firm pillows.

He resisted the urge to caress her face, to take her into his arms and reassure her, as he would have before Nate had come back into the picture. Even taking her hand seemed too fraught with implications.

On his lap, Natalie relaxed. Within minutes her thumb fell from her mouth and her deep, even breaths told him she was asleep. He sent up a prayer of gratitude for one more precious opportunity to hold her in his arms. He couldn't allow himself to think that this might be the last time he would hold her.

Daria opened her eyes again and looked from Natalie to Cole. "Do you think she understands?" she asked.

"I don't know. Probably not everything."

"Cole, if"—her voice broke, but she went on—"if I lose the baby, please promise me you won't blame God."

He shook his head and swallowed hard. "I won't, Daria. But you're not going to lose the baby. The doctor said if you can just go another week or two there's every chance that he'll be fine."

Daria nodded and turned to gaze out the window. Tears brimmed in her eyes and shone brightly, but she didn't weep.

He tried not to think how final her words had sounded, as though it was her last request of him. He watched her closely, longing to find some hint of her decision in her voice, in her eyes. Of course he wouldn't speak to her of such things now. He'd always been sensitive to her every thought and emotion. Only now did he realize what a gift it had been.

The whir of the fetal monitor, the antiseptic odors of the hospital, even the hushed sound of the nurses' footsteps on the tiled floor in the hallway brought back memories of the time Bridgette had spent in the hospital when Carson was born. If that happened—God forbid that it happen again—he knew he would lose Daria forever. *God, don't let this baby die! Don't let this be Carson all over again. Please, God. Don't do that to me again.* His prayer was selfish, but he prayed fervently nevertheless.

He shifted Natalie on his lap and rubbed his face with a work-roughened hand, forcing his thoughts back to the present. Daria needed him. And for now he would sit beside her. He would hold the child he loved as much as life itself on his lap, and he would wait for as many days as God granted them.

Thirty-Two

N ate paced the length of his boyhood bedroom and rubbed the stubble of beard on his chin. If he had to remain under his parents' roof another day—if he had to live under this cloud of oppression, not knowing what the future held for him—he would go mad. The impending birth of Daria and Cole's child had put everything on hold, and while he knew Daria had never planned for events to unfold the way they had, still the waiting was excruciating.

She had to make a decision. He knew it wasn't fair under the circumstances to rush her, but he had to know what she wanted to do. He had made his intentions very clear: She was his wife, and he still loved her. He wanted to raise their daughter together, wanted to make up together for the lost years of his life—of *their* life.

Still he struggled with feelings of anger—toward Daria for leaving him behind in Colombia, toward the Chicoro for refusing to help him, toward Juan Mocoa for ensuring his captivity, and finally, toward God for allowing any of this to happen in the first place. And yet he knew that on Daria's part, it had all been a tragic mistake.

He bowed his head and prayed the prayer that had become his watchword over the last days: "Father, forgive them. And help me to forgive them. Help me to forgive Daria. She couldn't have known."

He thought again of the child to whom Daria would soon give birth. Cole's child, if it lived, would complicate matters immensely, but Nate was completely willing to take it in, to raise it as his own. His father assured him that any court would quickly grant Daria custody of the child with reasonable visitation rights for Cole Hunter. Nate was even prepared to allow Natalie to have visitation with Hunter. After all, the man was the only father she'd known until now. It was obvious that he loved her—and that she loved him as well. Hunter seemed like a decent man, a reasonable man.

A twinge of guilt rose in him, and it made him furious. Why should he feel guilty for wanting to be reunited with the woman he loved and the daughter he'd never had a chance to know? He felt deep sympathy for Colson Hunter. He knew it would be a huge grief to give up Daria—and yes, Natalie, too. Of course he knew that! Hadn't he been forced to do that very thing? He had no doubt that Hunter loved Daria and Natalie both deeply. But right was right. A man belonged with his wife and child.

He wished he could have some time to talk to Daria, find out what she was feeling. He'd learned from his mother that Hunter had stayed in Kansas City, that he was visiting Daria every day in the hospital. That fact scared him to death. He could only imagine the kind of bond that waiting for this child had formed between them.

His heartbeat quickened, and he felt the bile rise in his throat. It was wrong to let himself become so angry. He knew the only right thing was to leave this in God's hands. He held his scarred hands in front of him and despised the fact that they were trembling. He longed for the sense of peace that he'd been granted so many times before. How strange that in the danger and squalor of a jungle prison he had known that peace, yet in the affluent luxury of this house, in the safety of this free country, it eluded him.

He crossed the room and picked up the Bible that lay open on his dresser. Leafing aimlessly through the thin pages, his eyes were drawn to the twelfth chapter of the book of John. He read the words, whispered them aloud, seeking comfort in the very pronunciation of the syllables.

> The truth is, a kernel of wheat must be planted in the
> soil. Unless it dies it will be alone—a single seed. But
> its death will produce many new kernels—a plentiful
> harvest of new lives. Those who love their life in this

world will lose it. Those who despise their life in this
world will keep it for eternal life. All those who want
to be my disciples must come and follow me, because
my servants must be where I am. And if they follow
me, the Father will honor them.

At first the words were meaningless, but as he continued on, they
seeped slowly into his heart, the words of Jesus echoing the cry of his
heart.

Now my soul is deeply troubled. Should I pray,
"Father, save me from what lies ahead"? But that is
the very reason why I came! Father, bring glory to
your name.

He wasn't sure exactly what the words meant for him, but
nonetheless he sensed that they *were* for him. He knew the context
in which they had been spoken. They were Jesus' words before he
went to his death on the cross. Suddenly he felt that precious peace
begin to flow over him, to fill him up.

He flipped the pages, anxious to be comforted, anxious to discover just what the words meant for Nathan Camfield. He read on:

In his kindness God called you to his eternal glory by
means of Jesus Christ. After you have suffered a little
while, he will restore, support, and strengthen you,
and he will place you on a firm foundation. All
power is his forever and ever. Amen.

He had surely suffered for more than a little while. Was this
God's promise that his suffering would soon come to an end? Was
this confirmation that Daria would choose to make her life with
him? Was that the restoration God meant for him?

He turned the passages over and over in his mind, knowing the
answer was there, but not quite getting a grasp on the true meaning

of it. And yet, there was no anxiety, no fear connected to this unknown. Only peace.

He lay down on top of the quilt on his bed, arms behind his head, staring at the ceiling, but seeing far beyond it.

Scenes of Colombia materialized before him, and he felt a longing, a physical homesickness like he hadn't experienced since he'd gone to camp the summer he was eight. He missed his Timoné family. They still thought him dead, and he longed to see them, to tell them of God's goodness to him even while he had been imprisoned. He feared they had felt deserted by Daria and him—and perhaps by God. He prayed that Anazu had not grown weary of seeking God's truth. He prayed that the man's wife and daughter continued to walk in faith toward God.

After a long while, he rose to shave and dress.

Thirty-Three

C ole was beside Daria when Nicole René Hunter came screaming into the world at six o'clock on a brisk April morning, eleven days after Daria had been admitted to the hospital.

The baby was a tiny four pounds, five ounces, but her lungs were strong and healthy, and the doctors were optimistic that she would be fine. Daria had always pictured this baby as a little boy. Perhaps she thought a son would heal the wounds little Carson's death had inflicted on Cole. They had planned to name him Colson, after Cole. But they had also chosen a name for a little girl—Nicole, also after her father. Daria wondered now if it had been wise to give both her daughters their fathers' names.

Forty-eight hours after the delivery, she walked down the hallway toward the Neonatal Intensive Care Unit, still sore and aching from the birth. The nurses in the outer room greeted her with the same mix of compassion and pity that had been the hallmark of her stay in the hospital. Their situation was no secret to any of the employees here since the press had tried continually to breach hospital security to get pictures to go with their stories. The Associated Press had picked up the story, and they'd heard reports that it had run in one form or another all over the nation. Daria knew they could not escape the press's insatiable curiosity about this story forever.

Daria scrubbed and put a sterile gown over her robe before she went into the room where a sea of Isolettes, radiant warmers, and plastic bassinets stretched. Each vessel cradled the tiniest, most precious cargo imaginable, and the rhythmic *beeps* and *whooshes* of the various monitors and respirators reverberated through the room like waves against a rocky shore. Over the two days since Nicole's birth,

Daria had learned many of the other babies' names and had shared a bond with the other parents who visited this room daily. It had torn her apart to come in the first morning after Nicole's birth to find that one baby hadn't made it through his first night. She hadn't thought she had the energy to grieve anymore, but she had cried bitterly for the young single mother, a girl she'd never even met.

Now Daria made her way to Nicole's Isolette and reached in to stroke her tiny back. The baby was lying on her side, naked save for a diaper that dwarfed her in spite of its miniature size. At Daria's touch, the infant stretched slowly and her eyelids fluttered ever so slightly. Love for this child welled up within her, but sorrow welled up alongside it. The doctors were optimistic that she would grow and develop normally, but what would life hold for Nicole Hunter? Would she know the blessing of a mother and a father who loved each other and tucked her into bed together each night? Or would hers be a life of being shuttled from one home to the other, with secrets about her circumstances whispered everywhere she went? And what about Natalie? Oh, how Daria ached for her firstborn.

Natalie had not even met her baby sister yet. Daria's parents had come to Kansas City to get Natalie when they heard that Daria had been admitted to the hospital. However, they hadn't gone back to Bristol before hearing Vera Camfield's protests. Though she felt mildly guilty about it, Daria had finally resorted to using her tenuous condition to persuade Vera to give up the fight and quietly allow Natalie to go back home. She was certain that Vera was afraid that Cole would have ready "access" to her granddaughter. With some reassuring from Jack and Nate, Vera had conceded that in the interest of Daria's health and the baby's, Daria's wishes should be granted where Natalie was concerned.

As it turned out, Vera needn't have worried about Cole—not regarding Natalie anyway—for even before Nicole's birth, he had been staying in Kansas City with his college friend and lawyer, Dennis Chastain. He'd visited Daria every day until the baby's birth, and now he went to the Neonatal ICU nursery with her several times each day, holding Nicole every chance he got. The tender mixture of joy and sadness Daria saw on his face every time he picked up his tiny daughter broke her heart.

Nathan hadn't been to see Daria in the hospital since Nicole's birth. Daria wondered if the pain of seeing her with another man's child was too strong, too searing for him to ever forgive. Vera, however, had called to check on her several times. She never asked about the baby, but only inquired about Natalie and tried to find out when Daria would be released. She always made it a point to tell Daria what Nate was up to, going on and on about how well he was recovering and how anxious he was to "get settled."

Her doctor had informed her early that morning that he would be discharging her the following day, but Nicole would need to remain in the Neonatal ICU at least an additional week. Of course Daria would remain in Kansas City until Nicole was discharged, but even if she'd desired to do so, her insurance wouldn't allow her to remain a patient. Vera had offered her a place in their home. But even though she would only be there to sleep, she felt funny about staying at the Camfields' with Nathan there. It didn't seem fair to him, and it certainly didn't seem fair to Cole. Finally she'd decided to get a room in a hotel near the hospital. She could walk the short distance to the hospital to nurse the baby several times a day.

To complicate matters, Daria's father had fallen off a ladder and broken his collarbone, which meant that her mother had her hands full caring for him and Natalie. Margo would not be able to make the planned trip to Kansas City to be with Daria.

Daria still did not know what was going to happen with Nate and Cole. She had been too wrapped up in Nicole's birth and her own rather tentative condition to think about the decisions that still loomed. Now she wanted to put the decision off as long as possible.

She reached into the radiant warmer bassinet and picked Nicole up, carrying her gingerly over to the large overstuffed chair that sat ready nearby. Already the baby felt sweetly familiar in her arms. And though Nicole was still featherlight, Daria imagined that she could feel the weight of a few added ounces. Barring any unforeseen complications, she would bring her daughter home from the hospital this time next week.

Home.

But where was home? And more important, *who* was home?

⟋⟍

Cole and Daria sat side by side on a comfy sofa in the Neonatal ICU nursery. Little Nikki—as Cole had taken to calling her—lay on her mother's lap, her wide eyes staring at the bright lights overhead.

"Look, Cole! She smiled! Did you see that?"

He turned to meet her gaze and smiled. "I think the nurses would tell you that's just gas."

"Well, they can say what they want, they'll never convince me. Why wouldn't a baby smile? Really now?"

"It looked like a real smile to me," he said. In spite of the dark circles under her eyes, Daria looked beautiful. He resisted the urge to reach out and brush her hair away from her face.

Daria sighed. "Oh, Cole, I'm so anxious for Natalie to meet her. She's going to be so excited. I miss that little scamp."

Cole saw tears gather in the corners of her eyes, and in them he saw an opening for an idea that had been brewing. "Daria, I'm heading back to Bristol tonight to help Travis with some calves. It'll probably take us most of the morning tomorrow, but when I come back I could bring Nattie with me."

"Oh, Cole, that would be wonderful!"

"Daria, it will be a gift for me to have the time with her."

"Of course it would," she said softly.

He opened his mouth to ask—he wasn't sure what. Daria had stayed in a nearby hotel since the day she was discharged from the hospital. Of course, she needed to be near the hospital since she was nursing the baby, but they could have transferred Nikki to Wichita, and then Daria could have stayed at home in Bristol. Cole couldn't help but wonder how much her decision had to do with being near Nathan. He had given up hoping that things could ever go back to the way they'd been before. He just wanted some reassurance that no matter what happened he could remain part of little Nikki's life—and part of Natalie's life.

Now, before he could say anything, he saw a nurse making her way toward them through the rows of Isolettes and bassinets. She waved to get their attention. "Daria, you have visitors," she said, pointing toward the nursery's anteroom.

"Oh?"

"Mr. Camfield—and Mrs. Camfield," the nurse said.

Daria looked at Cole.

"Do you want me to leave?" he asked.

"No, of course not," she told him. "I'll go talk to them in the waiting room. I wonder what they want?"

The nurse waited while Daria juggled Nikki into Cole's arms.

"I'll be back in a little bit."

Cole watched Daria walk away, then looked down into his daughter's bright eyes and wondered how many more times he would get to hold her like this.

In the hallway Daria was surprised to see Nate and his mother. She had expected Jack and Vera.

"Hello," she said, a question in her voice.

"Hi, Daria. How is everything going?" Nate asked.

"Good. I think they're going to let the baby come home in a couple of days. At least that's what the doctor said this morning."

"That's great, great. Listen, Mom had an idea we wanted to float by you. I know Natalie hasn't met the baby yet. And since you can't leave the hospital long enough to get her, we thought we could drive to Bristol and pick Natalie up at your folks' and bring her back here.

Then she could just stay with us for a couple of days until the baby is ready to go—to be discharged."

Vera had stood uncharacteristically silent behind Nate, but now she jumped in, "We can keep Natalie while you're at the hospital. It sounds like it would only be for a few days anyway."

Daria hesitated. "Oh, Vera, Nate, that's so thoughtful of you, but, well, Cole has already offered to bring Natalie. In fact he's here right now, but he has to go back to the clinic in Bristol tonight. He's planning to bring her back with him late tomorrow afternoon—"

"Oh, heavens no. That won't be necessary. We'll go," Vera interrupted. "We can leave first thing in the morning and have her back in time for lunch. We could even go today," she said brightly.

"Well, I appreciate the offer, really, I do, but like I said, we've already made other plans."

"Why don't you just tell, uh, Cole that you've found another ride for Natalie. We really would like to have the time with her."

"I understand that, Vera," she said, measuring her words carefully. *The woman can scarcely bring herself to speak Cole's name.* She took a deep breath, trying to keep the anger she was feeling from creeping into her voice. "It's just that Cole would like some time with her too. And Natalie needs to see him. They haven't had a chance to be together for a long time."

Vera sniffed. "Daria, I don't think this is wise at all. It will only make it harder on Natalie in the end."

"Mom! Stop!" Nate stepped forward, shaking his head in apology. "I'm sorry, Daria. It sounds like you have everything worked out. We'll—"

Vera spun toward her son. "Nathan, are you just going to let this go? There is no reason in the world why you shouldn't be able to go get your daughter in Bristol if you want to! This tiptoeing around has gone on long enough. It's time we got some things out in the open, and if you won't do it, then I will."

"Mom—" Suddenly Nate looked beyond Daria, and his face

registered surprise. Daria turned to see that their raised voices had drawn Cole from the nursery.

"Hello, Cole," Nate said.

Cole nodded a greeting. "I heard my name," he said carefully.

Nate looked at the floor. "Yes."

Cole cleared his throat. "Is there a problem?"

Vera glared at him. "We just came to let Daria know that we would be picking Natalie up in Bristol tomorrow."

Nate scolded, "Mom, stop. That's enough!"

"Nate?" Vera said, her voice wounded.

Now Nathan took charge. He took his mother's arm firmly and turned her toward the hallway. Like a repentant child, Vera went to the outer hallway, her sobs muffled by a wad of tissue she'd dug from her purse.

"I'm sorry to interfere," Nate said quietly when his mother was out of earshot. "I didn't realize you'd made other plans."

Daria looked back and forth between the two men she loved. She could sense the disparate emotions warring within each of them. But now Cole's expression softened, and he looked Nathan in the eye. "It's just that I have to make the trip back to Bristol anyway," he explained. "I have some things to take care of at the clinic. But if other arrangements might work better…" Cole's voice trailed off, leaving the ball in Nathan's court.

"We would like to spend some time with Natalie while she's here," he said, his expression unreadable. "If you could let us know when it's convenient?"

Daria nodded. "Of course."

Nate tipped his head toward the hallway. "I'd better get Mom home. I'm sorry about all this." He dipped his head in farewell, then turned quickly and disappeared through the wide doorway into the hall beyond.

Thirty-Four

*I*t was almost six o'clock when Cole arrived at the hospital the next evening with Natalie in tow. They had called Daria on the cell phone to let her know they were running late, and she was already in the Neonatal ICU nursery when they arrived. She had nursed Nicole, changed her diaper, and carried her over to a cozy seating area when she heard Natalie's voice in the anteroom. Through the large window, she could see the excitement on Cole's face as he ushered the little girl in and showed her how to wash her hands at the sink. One of the Neonatal ICU nurses gave her a tiny sterile gown to don over her clothes. When she was properly attired, she and Cole hurried to the vinyl-covered settee where Daria sat holding the baby.

"Now remember what we talked about, Nattie," Cole said quietly. "You have to be very quiet because some of the other babies are sleeping. And we don't want to scare our baby either."

"Our *Nikki*," she corrected him.

"That's right. Our Nikki."

"Come on, Mommy's waiting."

Natalie spotted Daria across the room and ran full speed toward her. When she got close enough to see the baby lying on Daria's lap, she skidded to a stop and tiptoed with exaggerated steps over to their side.

"Ooh! She's teeny!" Natalie exclaimed, holding out one finger to touch the baby on the head.

Daria fought back tears and put her free arm around Natalie. "Oh, Nattie! Honey, you've grown a foot! What has Grammy been feeding you?"

"Just some food, Mommy," she said, hands on hips.

Cole and Daria laughed, and Cole sat down beside her, pulling Natalie up to sit between them.

Natalie leaned heavily on her mother and touched the baby's feet through the thin blanket she was wrapped in.

"Do you want to see her toes?" Cole asked.

Natalie grinned and nodded, and Cole reached over to Daria's lap and carefully disentangled the baby's feet from the blanket.

Immediately Natalie touched a tiny toe and began a singsong recitation. "Dis liddle piggy went to market…dis liddle piggy stayed home…"

Daria looked over Natalie's head to smile at Cole. But instead of the return smile she expected, she saw that he was crying. Tears coursed down his cheeks, and he made no attempt to wipe them away.

Nate maneuvered his father's car into a narrow space in the hospital's parking garage and checked the car clock before he turned off the ignition. Even though he was still getting used to driving a car again, it hadn't taken him quite as long to get here as he'd thought it would.

He locked the car and entered the building that housed the Neonatal ICU. He was eager to see Natalie again. And Daria. He knew her most important task right now was taking care of herself and her newborn daughter, but he was growing anxious to get their situation straightened out. The three of them—he and Daria and Cole—needed to sit down and decide what they were going to do. He didn't think Cole Hunter or Daria wished to solve their dilemma in court any more than he did. But in spite of the many nights he'd lain awake turning the endless possibilities over in his mind, in spite of the hours he had spent reading the Bible, seeking answers, he didn't have a clue how this would all work itself out. The passages of Scripture that had spoken so strongly to him that night in his room continued to sustain him, though he wasn't sure exactly why. He was only grateful for the remarkable peace that continued to hold him up.

He neared the Neonatal ICU and deliberately slowed his pace. He was a little nervous about seeing Daria, never knowing quite how to act with her. Wiping moist palms on his khakis, he pulled his sleeves down over his scarred forearms and ran a hand through his close-cropped hair, checking his reflection in the window that separated the waiting area from the Neonatal ICU.

Looking past his reflected image in the glass, he spotted Daria's pale head across the room. He started walking into the outer room, knowing he was not allowed into the nursery without washing and gowning. He looked around for a nurse who could let Daria know he was here, but finding no one, he looked through the window hoping to get Daria's attention.

He craned his neck to see across the room full of Isolettes and medical equipment. There they were. And Colson Hunter was with them. He hadn't counted on that. He moved into the shadows where he wouldn't be seen, but where he could still watch them.

He couldn't actually see the baby from his vantage point, but Daria had a flannel bundle on her lap that was squirming, apparently much to Natalie's delight. Cole sat close to Daria and, though Nate couldn't hear their voices, he could see that Natalie and Cole were in deep conversation, apparently about the baby. Now Natalie leaned over to kiss the bundle, then stood to say something that made Daria and Cole laugh.

A sick feeling started in the pit of Nate's stomach. It was as though he was being shown a snapshot of a happy little family. One that had nothing to do with him. Yes, it was his daughter—his flesh and blood—at the center of the tight knot, but he could see with his eyes, and feel in his heart, that Natalie was where she belonged. Her joy was obvious. Her love for Colson Hunter—and his for her—was clear.

The Scripture passages began to churn in his mind. *The man who loves his life will lose it, while the man who hates his life in this world will keep it for eternal life.*

What was God trying to show him? He was terrified that deep

in his heart he knew the answer. *God, would you ask that of me? Would you really expect me to make such a sacrifice?*

Another fragment of Scripture came to him. *Nevertheless, not my will but thine.*

No. I can't do it, Lord. It's too much!

He leaned heavily against the doorjamb, still watching the happy family scene being played out behind the glass. His return, while a deliverance from captivity and an answer to prayer for him, had wreaked havoc in Daria's life and his daughter's. Daria could not have known all those months that he was alive, that he would return. Certainly after so much time had gone by, she had a right to seek a new life, even to seek someone who could be a father for her daughter, his child.

As if to confirm his thoughts, through the window he saw Natalie climb up onto Cole Hunter's lap and wrap her arms around his neck. Hunter had innocently loved his wife and daughter and provided them with a Christian home. And now this new child had truly bound them together as a family. Already Natalie was smitten with her sister. He thought of his own sister, Betsy, and the deep affection they shared. Would he deny his daughter that relationship with little Nicole? Certainly not intentionally, but if he were to claim even a fraction of Natalie's time, that time would wrench her from the only family she'd ever known.

There was a simple solution to the dilemma they'd all found themselves in, and as he began to see quite clearly what that solution was, he felt his knees buckle under him. He put his hand on the wall beside the door and steadied himself. He knew what God wanted him to do. Though it would break his heart, though it hurt so deeply he could scarcely bear it. Yet he knew without a shred of doubt that it was the right thing to do.

He closed his eyes. *Help me, Lord. Give me your strength.*

He pushed the door open and knocked gently on the doorjamb, trying to get their attention.

Natalie saw him first.

"Nate! Daddy Nate! Come see our new baby!"

Daria looked up, and an expression of utter sadness crossed her face. But she bent to tell Natalie something, and the little girl navigated the labyrinth of bassinets and came to stand beside Nate in the doorway. He looked back to Daria, who transferred the baby to Cole's arms and came to stand near him by the door.

Nate squatted down beside his daughter. "Hi, honey."

"Are you gonna come see our baby, Nikki?" she asked again.

He swallowed hard and ran a hand over his face before he spoke. "I don't think so, Natalie. Not tonight. Grandma and Grandpa Camfield are waiting for us at home." He scooped her into his arms and stood up, whispering in her ear. "I think Grandma is making us macaroni and cheese for dinner tonight."

That information was met with a loud whoop, totally inappropriate for the halls of a hospital.

"Nattie!" Daria laughed uneasily.

"Is it okay if I take her now?" he asked Daria.

"Sure," she said nodding gently. "I'm going to stay for Nikki's last feeding tonight. Would you let your mom know I won't be there to pick up Nattie till late?"

Nate nodded and cleared his throat. "There's something I'd like to talk to you about. Could we talk when you come tonight?"

"Okay," she said simply, but her eyes asked a thousand questions.

He couldn't offer any more right then. He had to think this through. He needed some time.

"I'll see you later," he told her.

"All right, Nate. I'll try not to be too late."

Daria went for Natalie's bag, and when she'd kissed her daughter goodbye, Nate picked Natalie up and carried her to the parking garage, committing the feel of her light frame in his arms to memory.

It was after ten when Nate heard Daria's car on the drive. He'd been in the kitchen listening for her car for an hour, when he'd finally convinced his parents to go to bed. He knew how devastated they would be by the decision he'd made, and he didn't want to deal with their reaction until after he had talked to Daria.

He went through the garage and out to the drive to meet her, turning on the outside light as he went. He opened her car door for her.

"Hi, Nate," she said. "I'm sorry it's so late."

"The baby's okay?"

"She's doing fine. They might even let her come home tomorrow."

"That's good."

"Natalie's asleep?"

He nodded. "Do you want to go sit on the terrace? It's pretty warm out tonight."

"Sure." Again those aching questions in her blue eyes.

She followed him around the house and through the side gate, and Nate pulled a chair up to the table for her beside his.

The moon was only a sliver in the sky, but a nearby street lamp cast a warm glow over them. He looked into her face and wasn't sure he could do what he meant to do. His love for her was as strong as it had been that day he'd said goodbye to her in Colombia and followed Tados and Quimico into the rain forest. The urge to take her hand was strong, but he kept his hands in his lap.

She sat waiting, gazing across the lawn.

"Daria," he began, "I've made a decision that I need to tell you about. It might affect the decisions you will be making soon and"— he took a deep breath—"I need to ask you, Daria, do you love Cole?"

"Yes, Nate. I do," she said quietly. "But, oh, Nate, I love you, too! I love you both. I know you might not think that's possible, but it's true! I love both of you."

He held up a hand to silence her. He hadn't meant to make Daria defend her love for either of them. He only wanted to hear from her own lips that what he had seen pass between her and Colson Hunter in the nursery was truly love, the kind of deep, committed love he and Daria had had for each other in their brief marriage. "I believe you, Daria. I can see that you are happy with him, that he is a good man. I—Well, as you can imagine, that's not easy for me to acknowledge. But the Lord has been speaking to me over the last few days, and I think I know what I'm supposed to do."

She waited, looking intently at him.

"I'm going back to Colombia, Daria."

"Oh, Nate," she gasped, cupping her hands to her mouth.

But he continued. "I know my work there isn't finished. And I think it's best for you—and especially for Natalie—if I go. I'm not sure what has to happen legally before I go, but I want you to know that I won't stand in the way of your happiness—"

"No, Nate! You were never in the way of my happiness. You *were* my happiness." She started to cry.

"I can't tell you what to do, how to live your life, but I want you to know that I give you my blessing to stay with Cole. He's made Natalie happy. He's made you happy, and my presence here can't do that anymore. I'm only an obstacle."

"No, Nate, please. You mustn't think that."

"Daria, I didn't mean that to sound so martyrlike. It's just the way things are."

She started to speak, but he cut her off. "Please, Daria. Let me finish. I know I'm doing the right thing. I won't sit here and tell you it's easy. But the right thing isn't always the easy thing."

He stood up and walked to the edge of the terrace. He looked into the sky and, at the smudged edge of the street lamp's glow, he found a cluster of stars. A lump rose in his throat, and he wondered if she remembered their last night together in Colombia. Did a starry sky make her think of him the way it would forever make him think of her? He turned to look at her and saw that she, too, was gazing at the dark southern corner of the sky. Neither of them spoke of it, and yet he felt certain that at that moment, their thoughts were one.

"I'm going to begin making arrangements to return to Timoné as soon as possible, Daria. I'll stay long enough to do whatever needs to be done to make this all legal. Cole should have a father's say where Natalie is concerned since I'll be so far away. I—" He swallowed hard. He didn't want this to become maudlin. "I want to be a part of Natalie's life as much as I can from afar. I'd like to write to her, and see her whenever I come home. And please, I want my parents and Betsy to be allowed plenty of time with her. This won't be easy for them, especially for Mom."

Daria was weeping openly now, but she nodded her agreement.

"I'll talk to Dad about the legal end of things. I—"

"Oh, Nate," she sobbed, "I'm so sorry. I do love Cole, Nate. But my decision to marry him was—rash. I wasn't seeking God's direction, and now look at the heartache it's brought us. Oh, Nate, if you only knew how wrong I was. If only I'd sought God the way you have—"

"Don't, Daria. Don't make me out to be a saint. You don't know the things I had to beg forgiveness for before God brought me to this decision. I'm human, Daria. I've had my struggles."

"It doesn't matter, Nate. You obeyed. You did what was right. I'd give anything to be able to go back and do the same. I'm so sorry, Nate." It came out in a sob.

He sat down at the table with her, and this time he took both of her hands in his. He bowed his head as she did the same. "O Lord, this has been so hard...so hard. But we know that you can make even this into something good. Please do that now, Father. We've both confessed our mistakes. We are sorry, God, for what's happened, for our part in it. But we know that you are a God of grace. We ask for your grace to us now. Direct us and guide us in the days to come. Help us to make wise decisions. Above all, Father, let us seek your direction as we sort this out. God—" He struggled again for control. "God, please don't let the tragic things that have happened over the last few weeks leave scars on Natalie or on little Nicole. Heal those wounds by your blood, Father. Let these children grow up strong and whole. Let their hearts always be soft toward you." He squeezed Daria's hands, feeling stronger for having prayed.

She looked up at him with tears in her eyes and whispered two words, but for him those two words held a lifetime of meaning— "Thank you."

Thirty–Five

*N*ate couldn't help but compare the entourage that left the courtroom to a funeral cortege—the mood was somber, the people were gathered in silent little groupings as they made their way down the hallway that led outside. The judge had ordered that security keep the media outside, so the hallway was quiet. But when the doors that led to the wide courthouse steps opened, a maelstrom of microphones, the nagging shouts of reporters, and the blinding flash of a dozen cameras assaulted the small group.

"Dr. Camfield! Dr. Hunter!" they shouted. "Daria!"

The media overtook them when they were halfway down the wide stairs. Daria leaned heavily on her father; Cole Hunter walked on the other side of her, beside Dennis Chastain. Nate's own father strode beside him with the confidence of a seasoned lawyer.

Nate ducked his head and, in an irony of solidarity, he and Colson Hunter and Daria, with their loved ones, trudged through the gauntlet together.

"Dr. Camfield!" one reporter shouted above the din. "Is it true that you have decided to give up your rights to your daughter?"

Nate winced at the ugliness of the question. It made him sound uncaring, irresponsible even. Anger rose in him, but he pushed it down, praying desperately that God would give him wisdom in handling this mob, that he would not forget the absolute certainty he had felt about his decision only a few hours earlier.

Suddenly the words he had read again that morning seemed to be printed in the air before him like a divine teleprompter. *Unless a kernel of wheat falls to the ground and dies, it remains only a single seed. But if it dies, it produces many seeds. The man who loves his life will lose it, while the man who hates his life in this world will keep it for eternal life.*

Nate turned and stopped in his tracks. He held up his hand, indicating that he wished to make a statement. "Please," he said simply.

The clamor of the crowd died to a hushed murmur. Cole and Daria turned as one to the sound of his voice, and Nate saw the cautious expectancy on their faces.

His father put a hand on his arm, whether to warn him or bolster him, he wasn't sure, but he went on. He looked full into the camera in front of him. *O Lord, let my words be a witness for you.*

He cleared his throat. "As you can imagine, this has been a nightmare for all of us."

He paused and let his gaze encompass Cole and Daria. It still hurt to look at her. But now—by a strength he knew was far beyond his own—he was being lifted above the hurt, above the sorrow.

In spite of the slight rasp the fire had left in his vocal chords, his voice was strong, and even he could hear that it held more confidence than he felt. "This is not a decision any of us ever dreamed of being faced with," he told the crowd, "but it was one we were forced to confront nevertheless. Through it all, as we have tried to sort out the questions, as we have sought answers to our dilemma, we have— all three of us—been guided by our deep, shared faith in God and, most of all, by our desire to do what is right, what is best, especially for the children involved."

The crowd was utterly silent now, entranced by his words. He prayed he wasn't overstepping the bounds of privacy for the others, but he felt compelled to continue. He stepped closer to the bouquet of microphones being offered him. "Over the past weeks since my return to the States, I have come to know Dr. Colson Hunter. I have seen with my own eyes that he has been a wonderful father to my daughter at a time when I did not even know I had a daughter. I *love* my daughter with all my—" *O God,* he pleaded silently, *let me get through this without breaking down.*

He took a deep breath, swallowed hard, and looked again at the crowd in front of him. "I love my daughter deeply. But I believe that it is in her best interest to remain with the only man she has ever known as her father. My decision reflects my deep love for her."

Nate took another labored breath and continued. But now he felt lifted up by unseen hands, and the words began to flow from his mouth as though someone else were speaking for him. "We are human—all of us," he told the crowd, "and as you can imagine, we have each had our moments of anguish, of guilt—of anger. But the world won't understand how our situation has been resolved without hate, without lashing out at one another, without lawsuits aimed at destroying each other. Listen carefully because I'm going to tell you exactly why."

He paused and, when the silence reached deafening proportions, he told them in an unwavering voice, "It is because we have placed our faith in the Lord Jesus Christ. It is because of our belief that our treasures are stored up in heaven, not here in this fleeting life on earth. That is the reason we are able to see beyond our own selfish desires."

He looked at Cole and then at Daria, who were each nodding in agreement, looking at him with tears streaming down their faces and with a glow that Nate knew came from the same source that allowed him to speak his next words. He opened his mouth and preached the gospel unashamedly.

"If you can see the peace written on our faces in the midst of this horrible situation, don't think that it comes from within ourselves. Never. It is peace that only comes from God Almighty through his son, Jesus Christ, a peace that I can testify passes all understanding. It is a peace that comes from a sure knowledge that we have given our wills, our very lives over to Christ. We have put our faith and trust in him alone. And we are filled with the assurance that he can take even tragedy and turn it into something beautiful."

Nate saw that Cole and Daria were nodding again in agreement, and he suddenly felt drained and empty. Some of the reporters were looking at him as though he'd lost his mind, as though they were recording the ravings of a madman. But among the people gathered on the courthouse steps, Nate saw that many were crying, and a few had even bowed their heads.

When he had finished, he bent his head and started down the stairs.

Colson Hunter cleared his throat and raised his hand in the same way Nate had. Hunter did not speak with the poise and confidence of a preacher, and his voice quavered with emotion, but his words were powerful and meaningful—and a gift that Nate would always treasure.

"Soon enough," he started, "the news will leak out about what took place in this courthouse today. Although this is an intensely private, personal matter, I think all of us realize that regardless of our wishes, this story *will* be written about and talked about. I think we could all agree that we want the story to come from us, to be told exactly as it is, without any conjecture on the part of the media."

He looked to Nate and Daria for consent. When they both nodded, he continued. "We are grateful that Judge Garcia was sympathetic to our wishes to avoid what seemed inevitable in this case—the dissolution of one marriage. We were—we *are* all in agreement that divorce is wrong, that it is against everything we believe about the God-given institution of marriage." His voice broke, and he put his head down, struggling for control. "These are circumstances that, frankly, none of us understand. But we are grateful that the laws of this state have allowed us to avoid the necessity for dissolving that marriage through divorce."

A buzz began among the crowd, and reporters began jockeying for position again, launching questions. "Will Dr. Hunter get legal custody of the children?" a young reporter shouted above the growing din. "Will you tell Natalie who her birth father is?" another queried.

Nate winced, wondering how to respond to the delicate questions. Beside him, his father tightened his grip on his arm. "May I?" the older man whispered.

Nate nodded, and Jack Camfield stepped in front of him toward the phalanx of microphones. With the sonorous voice of a lawyer, he reiterated the judge's decision. "Because of the way Kansas law reads, Daria's marriage to Colson Hunter was recognized as valid by the law even after my son was found alive. In this state the presumption of validity of a subsequent marriage is stronger than and overcomes the presumption of a previous marriage. And as Dr. Hunter said, the judge today affirmed that the first marriage is dissolved under the law without necessity of divorce. The decisions that have been made—and that will be made in the future—are understandably very private and extremely sensitive, and we respectfully request that you honor the privacy of all involved. But we do want to note for the record that there is mutual agreement and deep mutual respect among all parties involved. Obviously there are no easy answers in a case such as this, but it is our desire—and we feel assured—that every decision will first and foremost take the children's well-being into account."

Reporters were scribbling furiously, dialing cell phones, tinkering with tape recorders. Jack Camfield held up a hand, and for the first time, his confident demeanor cracked. "I believe that is all we have to say." As Nate had, he looked to Cole and Daria for affirmation. They both nodded, gratitude in their eyes.

Inexplicably undisturbed by the press, they all continued down the stairs to the parking lot.

Using the keyless entry on his key chain, Jack Camfield unlocked the door to his black Intrepid while they were still several hundred feet from the car. Nate hurried ahead of his father and climbed into the passenger side. The car was an oven, and the strength he had felt moments earlier as he gave his statement to the press—as he testified to God's hand in unraveling their dilemma—drained from him. He felt as though his bones had turned to liquid. Trembling and overcome with a sadness too deep to be expressed, he put his head in his hands and moaned.

His father climbed into the driver's seat beside him. Jack Camfield put the keys in the ignition and then dropped his head and began to weep. Nate put a scarred hand on his father's shoulder. The older man looked up at him with such love in his eyes. And it occurred to Nate that, perhaps for the first time, his earthly father had begun to understand the father-heart of a God who watched his only son suffer an anguish that only the hope of heaven could assuage.

The July sun was blistering, but the Camfields' yard offered a cool haven with its ancient shade trees and striped canvas awnings. Daria sat on a formal wrought-iron bench, Nicole napping in the infant carrier at her feet, and watched Natalie romp in the sunshine on the grounds' lush acres of grass.

The back door opened, and Nate came out carrying a tray of drinks. He handed Daria a frosty glass of iced tea and took one himself. Natalie came running when she heard the ice tinkling in their glasses.

"Mommy, I'm thirsty," she hinted, eyeing the juice box that remained on the tray.

"I brought you some apple juice," Nate told her, holding out the container. "Does that sound good?"

"Yeah!" she crowed, then cocked her head. "Do I hafta stay here with it?"

Daria looked to Nate.

"Would you like to take it into the garden?" he asked her.

She nodded vigorously and scampered across the lawn, disappearing behind the gate to Vera Camfield's rose garden.

"Just bring the empty box back," Daria called after her. "And don't pick any of Grandma's flowers!"

"She's all right," Nate reassured her. He watched Natalie run across the lawn. "She's beautiful, Daria. So beautiful."

Her throat tightened. She didn't know how to respond, so she said nothing.

They sat sipping iced tea, not looking at each other, an uncomfortable silence between them.

"What time does your flight leave?" she asked gently.

He glanced at his watch. "It's a four-thirty flight. Mom and Dad will be back to pick me up about three."

"Oh." They had such a very few minutes left.

Jack and Vera had gone to pick up Nate's sister, Betsy, who would fly with him to Bogotá. Betsy planned to stay there until Nate arranged passage to Timoné. He was going back. It was where he belonged. She tried not to think about him going alone. She was grateful that Betsy would go with him as far as Bogotá.

They sat in silence for several minutes, and then each spoke the other's name at the same time.

Nate laughed. "You go first."

"I just want you to know how sorry I am, Nate. For everything. I'm so grateful to you for all you've done."

He waved her words away. "Don't, Daria." He rose and went to stand at the edge of the terrace. "That's all behind us now," he said firmly.

She stood up and went to stand beside him. "Is it, Nate? Can you ever forgive me? Can you ever forgive me for leaving you there? For going on without you?" She started to cry.

He reached out and touched her arm. "Daria, there was no way you could have known what was happening to me. I know that now. Nothing you could have done would have brought me home a minute sooner."

"Maybe not, Nate," she sniffed, "but if I'd only listened to God, if I hadn't run ahead of him, it would have saved us all this heartache."

He only nodded.

At the front of the house they heard the blast of a car horn.

"They're home," he said.

Time was running out. As difficult as it was, she didn't want them to part with anything unsettled between them. She couldn't let him leave without making sure he knew. "I'm so very sorry. I hurt you so much, so much." She struggled for control. "Can you forgive me, Nate?"

He turned to look at her and nodded slowly.

She kissed the tips of her fingers and touched them to his cheek. He reached up and put his hand over hers.

"I *have* forgiven you, Daria. And I'll always—" He stopped abruptly and closed his eyes. When he opened them again, he took her hand and gently pushed it away, letting his arm drop to his side. "I want to tell Natalie goodbye," he said finally.

Her heart started to pound. *O dear God...this hurts too much!* Over the lump in her throat, she called out, "Nattie!"

Natalie came running through the garden gate.

"Nate has to leave now, Nattie. Can you"—she put her fist to her mouth, willed herself not to break down, forced a false cheerfulness into her voice—"can you tell him goodbye?"

Natalie wrapped her arms around Nate's legs. "Bye," she said matter-of-factly.

Nate stooped to pick her up. He kissed her cheek tenderly. "Bye, sweetie. I love you."

"I love you too. Can we come see you in Lumpia?"

Through tears, Nate and Daria laughed at Natalie's childish pronunciation of Colombia. "I don't know, Nattie. It's a long way away. Maybe...maybe when you're older. But I'll see you next time I come back here," he promised.

He gave her one last squeeze and set her down. Then he reached out and put a warm hand on Daria's cheek. "Goodbye, Daria. God be with you."

Then he turned and walked away.

Through a curtain of tears, Daria watched him disappear around the side of the house. As Natalie ran back to the garden to play, Daria collapsed on the bench, sobbing as though her heart would break, yet overwhelmed with gratitude for the gift Nathan Camfield had given her.

Only one other gift in her life could compare to what this man had done for her and for Natalie. Only one sacrifice in all time and eternity had surpassed the sacrifice Nate had made for them. And as with that heavenly sacrifice, she could never—however many years she had left on earth—be worthy of Nate's sacrifice.

But she would love him for it forever.

aria checked the biscuits in the oven one last time and went to the refrigerator to get ice for the glasses. Nicole was in one corner of the kitchen, playing contentedly with a set of wooden building blocks. Across the room, Natalie sat in a toddler-sized chair, using the kitchen window seat as a makeshift drawing board. Daria smiled as her elder daughter labored over a colorful drawing, her little tongue echoing each tracing of the crayon. She was becoming quite an artist.

"Natalie, go out and tell Daddy it's time for supper."

"Not now, Mommy. I hafta finish coloring the horsey's tail."

"Natalie, you don't talk to Mommy that way," Daria said firmly. "You can finish your picture after supper. But right now I need you to go get Daddy. And please hurry. The soup is getting cold."

Natalie harrumphed and threw her crayon down, but she scooted her chair away from the window seat and headed toward the mud room.

A few seconds later, Daria heard her gasp from the back porch, "Mommy! Ooh, come look! Hurry!"

Daria recognized the fresh childlike wonder they so often heard in this little girl's voice. She dried her hands on an already damp dish-towel and started for the porch. But before she reached the door she heard Cole's voice.

"Hey, punkin! What's all the yelling about?"

"Look, Daddy! Look at dat sky!"

"I know. I saw it. Isn't it pretty?"

Daria smiled to herself. The awe in Cole's voice was equally childlike. She leaned to look out the kitchen window and saw that the sunset was indeed stunning. Iridescent strokes of purple and orange were burnished against a velvety blue-grey sky. She went to the doorway and stood in the shadows, watching her husband and daughter. Such love there was between them.

Cole knelt beside the little girl and pointed to the western horizon. "God painted the sky just for you, Nattie," he told her, planting a kiss on the curve of her cheek.

Without a word, Natalie broke from Cole's embrace, zipped by Daria, and tore through the kitchen to the front door. Cole stepped into the mud room looking to Daria for an explanation.

"You've got me," she shrugged.

They heard the front door open, and Natalie's silvery voice floated in from the east porch. "He didn't paint dis side yet!" she shouted.

Cole looked at Daria and at the same instant they burst out laughing. He held his arms open to her and she walked into them, achingly aware that in this simple everyday moment of shared laughter they had turned a corner somehow.

The past weeks had not been easy, and yet she treasured each day. Like thorns on a rosebush, the pain of all they'd been through was still sharp and real. She ached for Nate, and she missed the easy way things had been between her and Cole before. In an unguarded moment, she would find herself crying and not know for sure which thing she was grieving. Sometimes, when she thought about all that had happened, it seemed impossible that it had actually happened to *them*. Yet, like the imperceptible unfolding of the rosebud above the thorns, she was taken by surprise to find so much joy mixed in with the sorrow.

Sometimes she found herself arranging each little moment in her mental scrapbook. Like tiny bits of colored glass in a kaleidoscope, each piece sparkled with its own beauty, but together—reflected again and again—the memories were beautiful beyond words. She turned the pages and enumerated some of the recent moments:

Nikki learning to sound out a new word; one single branch on the Bradford pear tree Cole had planted in front of the farmhouse wearing leaves of the most brilliant scarlet and bronze; an overheard exchange between Natalie and Nicole that reminded her of the wonderful bond that sisters share; sitting on the front porch steps with Cole on a day so cool that they were glad to be sipping hot tea from mugs. Even the mugs were special—chunky blue pottery that Kirk and Dorothy Janek had brought back for them from a long-awaited trip to England. All the little details of life seemed so wonderfully significant now, each one to be savored and treasured. She pondered whether it was possible that grief somehow sharpened the senses. Or was it only that she'd begun to realize that life was truly so short, so precious, that one dared not waste a single moment? And yet she was more inclined than ever to spend a day doing almost nothing, simply enjoying the quiet of the house, playing silly games with the girls. Whatever it was, she considered it a gift and was delighted that in the midst of heartache so deep it was a physical pain, she was finding a deeper joy and contentment in life than she'd ever known.

And at night, in the darkness of their room—with their daughters asleep in the room below theirs—she and Cole held each other with a fresh tenderness after they made love. It was a tenderness that testified not only to their deep love for each other, but of the naked, aching realization of that love's vulnerability—and of the piercing sacrifice that had allowed it fruition. Yet somehow that knowledge caused them not to look to the past, but toward a future ripe with the completion of redemption. Theirs had been a tangle of circumstances so knotted and gnarled it had seemed too impossible to ever right itself. And yet, through Nate's love and wisdom—and his terrible sacrifice—God had redeemed their lives.

Natalie had received a simple letter from Colombia that Daria knew was meant to ease her own mind as much as it was meant to express Nate's love for his daughter. Still in Cole's embrace, she looked over his shoulder to the kitchen desk where the letter was tucked in a basket. She didn't need to open the thin, crisp airmail envelope to remember what it said. The words were etched on her heart, as she knew they would someday be etched upon her daughter's:

> *Dearest Natalie,*
>
> *I am back with my Timoné people now, and I am happy to be here. I know I am where God wants me to be. Someday your mommy can tell you about these people and this village where your life began.*
>
> *I hope you will always know how much I love you and how precious you are to me. I pray for you every day, as I know your mommy and daddy there in Kansas do, too. God has blessed you with a wonderful home in which to grow up, Natalie. I hope you will never forget how greatly God has blessed you. You are a special girl with so many people who love you, and I know God has great things in store for you. I will write again soon, but for now, remember that I love you with all my heart.*
>
> > *Keeping you in my prayers,*
> > *Your Daddy Nate*

Daria sighed in Cole's arms and reached up to caress his face. Life on this earth was so hard sometimes. But if they had learned nothing else, they had learned that after the darkest night, after the most impossible trial, joy comes in the morning. Always.

The old boat sliced through the turbid brown water—as it had for nearly three days now—advancing along the river to the slow rhythms of the Colombian rain forest and the lulling *putt-putt* of its own outboard motor.

The sun was just dipping below the trees on the western horizon when the coffee-skinned pilot steered into a shallow inlet and maneuvered his craft as close to shore as the tangled undergrowth would allow.

His passengers, two fair-haired American women—mother and daughter—stepped wearily from the boat and followed the lead of the Colombian, slogging through the murky water to shore. In silence, the small party followed a well-worn trail until they came to a village secluded in the dense tropical forest. All around them, the natives began to emerge from their huts into the clearing, chattering quietly among themselves in their nasal dialect, pointing and gesturing excitedly.

As they came nearer, the younger woman smiled and greeted several of the native women.

"*Hollio,* Miss Natalie," they returned her greetings. They did not approach her, but stood at a distance, watching.

Daria Camfield Hunter marveled at her daughter's easy way with the villagers. She looked about her, trembling, then set her eyes on a point to the north. As though led by an unseen guide, she walked across the clearing and climbed a slight rise to a stand of palms that stood behind a hut set apart from the others.

Approaching the largest tree, she reached out to touch its rough bark. Her long fingers found the scars of an old carving. Two and a half decades of sun and rain had not erased the deep furrows, and she traced them now as though touching the face of a loved one.

Natalie Camfield stood respectfully behind her mother, still silent. After a few minutes she put her hand on Daria's bowed shoulder and spoke softly, nodding toward the head of a trail that led into the forest hills. "I'll show you where he is buried."

Giving the carved epitaph on the tree a final caress, Daria straightened, pushed a strand of faded blond hair from her forehead, and followed. The two climbed the trail for several hundred yards where it turned off into a small clearing. It was obvious that this small plot of the forest was a singular grave site. The mound of earth at the center was overgrown with vines and decorated with the lush flora of the Colombian rain forest, but the freshly turned soil underneath left no doubt that the vegetation covered a fairly recent grave. A cross fashioned of cane and vines had been planted at the head of the mound, and a smooth, flat rock served as a tombstone. On the stone, beneath a name carved out in crisp English letters, other cryptic marks had been chiseled into the surface with a crude instrument.

"What does it say?" Daria asked.

Her daughter translated, reverence in her lilting voice.

"He would like that." Daria nodded, approving. Smiling sadly, she reached out to touch the smooth, sun-browned hand of her daughter. "Let me stay for a while, just a few minutes and then I'll be down."

"I understand." Natalie turned and started back down the trail.

Daria watched as her daughter made her way back down the forest trail, navigating the path as gracefully as a gazelle. Pride welled in her breast. Natalie was a beautiful young woman, her hair as pale as Daria's had been at that age, bleached white by the Colombian sun; her skin was almost as brown as that of the Timoné people she lived among. But Natalie's beauty went far deeper than her smooth skin and her flashing hazel-green eyes. She had inherited her giving, energetic, joyful spirit from the two men she called Daddy. No, three men she called Daddy. Daddy Nate. Daddy. Abba, Father.

This child who belonged to so many had struggled mightily to find her niche in the world. She had borne the pain of having her heart wrenched from one continent to another. She had finally made peace with her story when she realized that both of her earthly fathers loved her deeply, but neither could give her the love her heavenly Father offered. It was then that she had made the decision that broke Cole and Daria's heart, yet at the same time healed all their hearts.

In her third year of college, they lost Natalie to Colombia. She came home that Christmas and announced that she had quit school and was going to work with Nathan. They knew this strong-willed child well enough to know that their feeble arguments would fall on deaf ears. And, too, they trusted that she had been called of God to go. So they had sent her with their blessing. And in losing her, they had found her again. Two years working in Timoné beside Nathan had erased the angst of her teenage years. She had returned to her father the precious relationship he had sacrificed, and for all of them her gift had redeemed the hurt of that dark time in a way they could never have guessed.

Nathan's sudden death of an apparent heart attack three months ago had shaken the foundations of Natalie's faith, but in the end, her resolve to remain in Colombia had only been strengthened.

Natalie disappeared into the forest and, when Daria could no longer hear her soft footsteps on the trail, she sank to the cool, damp earth beside Nate's grave and closed her eyes.

All around her, myriad birds and insects chirped and whirred among the fern fronds and palm leaves. A warm tropical zephyr came in soft gusts as the trees allowed it passage. And in the distance, the river and its trilling streams accompanied in perfect cadence. The song of the rain forest lifted her and carried her back to a time when its clarion notes had been as familiar to her as her own breath.

A light rain began to fall—a rain she knew visited almost every afternoon. And over the musical staccato of raindrops, she heard a voice from the past, equally familiar, calling her name. She gave herself to the memories one last time, and eternity seemed to be suspended as the rain and her tears became one.

Minutes passed and the shower ceased as quickly as it had come. When it was over, Daria raked her hand across the damp and pungent earth that covered Nathan's grave. She scooped up a handful of the rich Colombian soil and let it sift through her fingers. She thought of the carving in the tree near the hut she had shared with a young Nate and realized that this was the second grave where she had mourned him.

She reached out and traced a finger over the crude inscription on the stone that marked the grave. The Timoné had the beginnings of a written language now. God's Word was coming to life for them day by day because of Natalie Camfield's tireless work side by side with her father, Dr. Nate. The little hut that Daria and Nate had shared was now a church. It had been enlarged not once, but twice, and still its walls often bulged with Timoné men and women and children who came to learn more about the one true God. Seeds of faith were sprouting—seeds that Evangeline Magrit had planted, and that she and Nate had cultivated. And Natalie's joy in nurturing those nascent buds was another precious gift of redemption for all the sorrow that had gone before.

Natalie had told her mother the meaning of the cryptic writing on her father's gravestone. Now Daria moved her lips, stumbling over the familiar syllables, smiling to herself as she remembered how Nate had always teased her, mimicking her attempts at the language.

In heart-wrenching circumstances, Nathan Camfield had exemplified the words from the gospel of John that now marked his burial place: *Greater love hath no man than this, that he lay down his life for his friends.*

She brushed the damp earth from her hands and rose to her feet to gaze one last time at the final resting place of the man who had relinquished everything he cherished for her sake. Her throat tightened as she realized anew the magnitude of the sacrifice Nate had made for her and for Natalie and, yes, for Cole and Nikki as well.

She turned her face to the sky as Timoné's sun appeared again to warm her skin.

"Thank you," she whispered to One who had made a far greater sacrifice. That sacrifice had for all time granted forgiveness for her mistakes, her disobedience—her *humanness*. That sacrifice had stretched across two millennia and offered redemption, not only for eternity, but for every tragic consequence they would bear in this life as a result of their humanity.

Nothing in this earthly life could ever completely erase this aching sorrow, but as an artist smudges the sharp line of a charcoal drawing, God's thumb had blurred the hard edges of their trial and had given even this black gash of sadness a poignant and haunting beauty.

She turned away, keenly aware that she was closing the cover forever on another chapter of her life. Yet the pages that lay ahead, still to be written, held sweet promise.

Eager now to look back upon the years when this place had been her home, she started down the forest trail, impatient for Natalie to reintroduce her to the Timoné people she had once loved as her own.

Tonight she would walk alone into the forest behind the hut that had once been their home. She would gaze at the starry heavens, hoping for a glimpse of the star Nathan had declared theirs on a long-ago night. And one last time, she would say goodbye.

Three days hence she would begin the journey back to Bogotá. Cole—her sweet, dearest Cole—was waiting for her there. And he would be anxious.

Acknowledgments

I would like to thank the following people for their roles in helping inspire, research, and write this novel:

Miss Linda Buller, whose many years as a missionary in Colombia were an inspiration to me.

Karen Baehler and Missie Wyatt for sharing their knowledge in the field of veterinary medicine.

Chad Jenkins and his dad, Jerry B. Jenkins, for allowing me to put some of Chad's childhood wit in Natalie Camfield's mouth.

Cyndi Kempke for invaluable input on life in South America.

Tim Larson for generous assistance in researching Kansas state law.

The many others who helped with research, including Anthea Burson, R.N., Cathy Hay, R.N., Laurel Hunsinger, Ryan Layton, Dan Miller, and Kristin Sanders, D.A., R.N.

I would also like to thank the many others who read my manuscript in its early stages and offered suggestions and encouragement: Debbie Allen, Kim Hlad, Ramie Schulteis, Terry Stucky, and Bev Sullivan, along with my parents, Max and Winifred Teeter; my sister, Vicky Miller; my daughter, Tobi Raney; and Lorie Battershill, wordsmith extraordinaire, encourager, and friend.

My talented editors at WaterBrook Press, Lisa Tawn Bergren and Traci DePree, for sharing the vision I had for this story, and for making my writing so much better than it really is; along with production editor, Laura K. Wright.

Tarl Raney, my firstborn, as well as my Webmaster and computer guru.

And as always, my sweet and talented husband, Ken, who loves me even when I'm on deadline, and who makes our home (and my writing "studio") my favorite place to be this side of heaven.

Finally, a note to my readers: Although Timoné and Chicoro are based on actual settlements in remote regions of South America's vast rain forests, the villages, people, and native languages portrayed in my story are products of my imagination.

I'm always delighted to hear from my readers. For more information, or to write me, please visit my Web site at: http://www.deborahraney.com.

⌒

Other books by Deborah Raney:

After the Rains

A Scarlet Cord

A Vow to Cherish